ALL THE CHAOS OF CONSTELLATIONS

HILLARY RAYMER

MAGIC, FAE, AND MORALLY GREY

For the ones who are always dazzled
by the night sky

TRIGGER WARNINGS

* Adult language

* Mild Violence

* Loss of a family member

* Mention of off page suicide

* Sexual themes/explicit scenes

* Anxiety

* Mention of physical abuse

Check out this post on the Pages & Playlist website to learn more about your book box!

All the Chaos of Our Constellations Curated Playlist

Listen for free on Spotify by opening the app, clicking the camera icon next to the search bar, and scanning the above code.

1. Wrecking Ball – Midnite String Quartet
2. Kiss Me – Sixpence None The Richer
3. Black Balloon – The Goo Goo Dolls
4. Ain't No Crying – Derivakat
*5. This Town – Niall Horan
6. Shadow – Livingston
*7. Can't Help Falling in Love – Kacey Musgraves
*8. Let Me Down Slowly – Alec Benjamin
*9. Rewrite The Stars – Zac Efron & Zendaya
*10. Still Falling For You – Ellie Goulding
11. The Night We Met – Lord Huron
*12. Glimpse of Us – Joji
13. Some Devil – Noah Guthrie
14. Dancing On My Own – Calum Scott
15. Poison & Wine – The Civil Wars
16. Before You Go – Lewis Capaldi
*17. Say Something – A Great Big World
18. The Sun Is Rising – Britt Nicole
19. Always Been You – Shawn Mendes
*20. The Joker And The Queen – Ed Sheeran
*21. Yellow – Coldplay
*22. Skyfall – Adele   *author pick
*23. All of Me – John Legend
*24. I Get to Love You – Ruelle
*25. A Thousand Years – VioDance

Pages & Playlist

All the Chaos of Constellations
Hillary Raymer

★★★★★ score your read 🕊🕊🕊🕊🕊

Book Club Guide & Book Journal Prompts

♥ From Novalise and Asher's first fated kiss through the very last page, there were many ups and downs to their love story. Do you have a favorite moment from their romance? Or was there one that brought out any big feelings? (That forest scene had us **IN IT**.)

♥ Despite rejecting the bond between them, Asher encouraged Novalise. Saying things like "defy the stars" and urging her to reach her full star-studded potential. How do you think his support impacted their journey?

♥ Do you think Novalise and Asher would have always found their way back to each other despite their objections? Given what we learned about this world, do you think it was even possible to have changed their fate?

♥ We're dying to know: are you more drawn toward the bookish and broody fire lord or the villainous shadow wielder? The good news is there's no need to choose between these two babes, since book 2, All the Sacrifice of Shadows (releasing 11/13/24) focuses on shadow daddy, Drake!

Pages & Playlist

CHAPTER ONE

The stars never lied.

At least that's what Novalise Starstorm told herself as she gazed up at the blanketed night sky. A veil of clouds shrouded the glow of the moon, and snow fell around her like scraps of lace, making it nearly impossible to see the constellations.

The breath of winter had settled across the kingdom, coating the mountains in a thin layer of frost and encasing the limbs of every tree in glimmering ice. Wind billowed down from the north, carrying with it the scent of ripened berries, snow-topped evergreens, and something that reminded her of the warm toffee cider found throughout Aeramere during the coldest season. Another gust of wintry air swept across the balcony, bitter against her cheeks and skin as it cut through the heavy layers of her velvet gown.

Novalise shook off the chill crawling up her spine.

She'd stopped shivering long ago.

Because tonight was the Winter Solstice, an evening built upon promises whispered by the stars and making wishes. It was a season of blessings and magic, when anything seemed

1

possible. A dream could become truth if the fates were so inclined. According to legend, if one gazed up at the sky during the midnight hours of the solstice, the stars would reveal a secret—anything from a darkest desire, to the most cunning of ambitions, to even the name of their soulmate.

Of course, that was only a myth.

For as long as Novalise could remember, the skies were never clear on the Winter Solstice.

She was a Starstorm fae, born in House Celestine under the sign of Estrela, the goddess of the moon and stars. She was expected to be compassionate, obliging, and unable to stand for anything less than perfection. While she was usually sensible, every so often she found herself entranced by the wonders of the world. She shouldn't be dazzled by the idea of fairy tale love stories or swooning at the prospect of meeting her soulmate on a night full of wintertide celebrations.

Yet there she was, on the highest balcony of her family's house, waiting for the clouds to clear. Just to see if she could catch a glimpse of...something.

Novalise reached out, imagining she could catch a falling star in her hand. Her pale skin glowed in the faint swath of hazy moonlight, but the stars revealed nothing.

She sighed, her breath misting in front of her like ribbons of silver smoke.

"Novalise." A masculine voice sounded from behind her, one she would recognize anywhere, one that always came across slightly disappointed.

She turned to face her brother, Ariesian Starstorm, Lord of House Celestine. Clad in their house's colors of sapphire and silver, he looked every inch the noble title his birthright afforded him. Their house crest, a star with eight points flanked by two crescent moons, was stitched in pale thread along the lapel of his trim coat. Silver hair was swept to the side, and smoothed back, highlighting the strong planes of his face. With his head cocked to the side, his dark brows pinched together.

Ariesian crossed his arms over his broad chest, towering over her. "You'll catch your death without your cloak."

"There's no need to be ridiculous," Novalise murmured. She turned away from him, knowing if she continued to stargaze, he would chide her for abandoning her duties. It was time to return to the ballroom, where she was expected to play the role of gracious hostess. She would smile and nod and placate the attention of would-be suitors. Smoothing her long, lavender tresses to make sure not a hair was out of place, Novalise headed toward the double glass doors. "You know as well as I do that fae don't fall ill simply because it's cold outside."

Ariesian flicked away a snowflake from the collar of his coat. "What are you doing out here, anyway?"

Avoiding the speculative gazes and rumors surrounding the fact that, come Midsummer, if she didn't already have a mate, the stars would choose one for her. Taking a moment to breathe and desperately wishing that fabled myths were more than just stories made up by dreamers.

All valid reasons she kept to herself. She didn't need to trouble Ariesian with her own inconsequential worries.

"I needed some fresh air." Novalise waved her hand dismissively as Ariesian held open the door for her. "You know how overcrowded and stuffy the Yuletide Ball can be with everyone…breathing."

It was a pathetic excuse, at best.

To her surprise, Ariesian chuckled. "I've never known you to have such an aversion to the norms of social engagements."

"On the contrary, I don't mind the engagements at all." She rounded the corner of the hallway toward the grand staircase that would deposit her into the decadent ballroom below. "I've just never enjoyed being the topic of conversation."

Something she could hardly avoid.

She paused at the top of the staircase, taking in the scene before her. The ballroom of House Celestine was stunning, decorated to impress the nobles from all five houses of Aeramere by making everyone in attendance think they'd walked into a winter wonderland. Vases in every corner spilled with gold-tipped poinsettias, waterfalls of frosted blue winterblooms cascaded down from the encircling balcony, and sporadic sprigs of sparkling mistletoe tied with red ribbon hung from discreet entrances. The mistletoe was no doubt the work of Novalise's younger sister, Caelian, who swore anyone who shared a kiss beneath the enchanted mistletoe was bound to fall in love.

Overhead, snowflakes swirled through the air, giving the effect of being caught in a delightful snow globe. Twinkling lights of faerie fire were strung across the dark wooden ceiling in a series of constellations, casting the entire space in a warm, welcoming glow. Banquet tables overflowed with platters of roasted meat and vegetables, bowls of pastries and freshly baked rolls, and tiers of varying desserts like cream-filled puffs and chocolate-glazed berries.

Music and laughter soared all around her and the air seemed charged with a kind of electric energy. It simmered along her skin, overwhelming her inner peace with a sense of disquiet. There was a shift taking place, an unnatural urgency that left her anxious, as though something life-changing was about to happen. It caused her stomach to flutter, her heart to pound.

"Sister."

Novalise glanced up at her brother, then down at his proffered arm.

"Shall we?" He gestured before them. Each step was a rich hue of deep blue flecked with silver glitter, so it looked like thousands of tiny stars inlaid in the floor.

"Of course." She tucked her hand into the crook of his elbow, hefting the hem of her gown with the other, and together they descended the curving staircase to the party below.

Novalise didn't need to look to know that every pair of eyes was focused on them. For one, she was on the arm of Ariesian Starstorm Celestine, Keeper of the Stars, Lord to the First House of Aeramere, and High Councilor to Queen Elowyn Willowblade.

Ariesian also happened to be the most eligible bachelor in Aeramere, next to the queen's son.

How quickly those curious gazes slid from him to her. Their scrutiny was understandable—while her brother may be the Keeper of Stars, Novalise was the one who could read them. It was a gift she did not take for granted. Though it seemed like she held fate in the palm of her hands, such magic came with a limit.

Her own destiny was beyond her control.

Star readings were an indispensable form of magic in House Celestine. Readings were used to determine the fate of any fae in Aeramere, and they were also utilized to assist Queen Elowyn in manners of court politics. Since the queen's magic was tied to the earth, she relied on the stars for guidance. It was Novalise's mother, Trysta Starstorm, who offered such council. She was the current Reader of Stars and foretold Novalise's destiny on the night she was born. Though Novalise might have hoped for something more substantial than the promise of a good marriage, she had readily accepted the fact that in the coming months, she would be the one to take her mother's place as the next Reader of Stars.

Novalise skimmed the ballroom looking for someone, anyone, to distract her from the probing glances and the softly spoken whispers that were loud enough for her to hear.

"I wouldn't want the stars to choose my mate for me."

"Could you imagine? Being forced to marry someone you don't know?"

"Sounds dreadful."

She tuned them out, as she always did, relegating their criticisms to nothing more than uninformed opinions. No one in the ballroom knew her on a truly personal level. They only saw what she projected—a lady from one of the most powerful houses in Aeramere with quintessential taste and superb manners. Her upbringing had been exemplary, and her reputation was held in high regard. She would marry whomever the stars chose for her and she would not object, because she'd known from the day she was born that her fate was out of her hands.

That, and she hadn't yet been able to snag a male on her own.

But no one else needed to know about such a trivial detail.

Just as Novalise was about to release her brother's arm to go in search of a refreshment to take the edge off, an unfortunately familiar face came into view.

"Oh no." She tightened her hold on Ariesian's arm.

"What is it?" He glanced down at her sharply. "What's wrong?"

She gave the barest incline of her head toward the male who approached them. "It's Lord Marintide."

Amusement highlighted the lines of her brother's usually somber face, so the curve of his mouth was *almost* a smile. "Didn't he court you some time last year?"

Novalise scoffed. "I'd hardly call trying to lure me into his bed a form of courtship."

Ariesian's silver eyes widened, the sapphire flecks in them brightening. A rush of color bled into his high cheekbones. "Nova..."

"What?" She angled herself so her back was facing the incoming threat. "Don't act like you didn't know."

Because he did.

Ariesian was well-informed of the exploits and accomplishments of his siblings. All seven of them. He knew every detail about every aspect of their lives, so much so that Novalise wouldn't be at all surprised if her brother had spies who reported back to him. As the eldest male, he'd been groomed to become Lord Starstorm, a role he assumed after the death of their father almost a year prior. And he took his responsibilities, as well as the wellbeing of his seven siblings, very seriously.

"That's not the point." He ground the words out through a clenched jaw.

"Then what is?" Novalise's feigned smile caused her cheeks to ache.

Ariesian's brows knitted together once more as he studied her. "I would've thought you well suited with the Lord of House Azurvend."

She thought so too, once.

The fae of House Azurvend were a bit more wild and free-spirited, something she imagined had everything to do with the fact that their magic connected them to the sea. House Azurvend ruled anything from the ocean to the rivers of Aeramere. It was the home of water nymphs and selkies, and some of the less inhibited fae. Reif was no exception. He was spontaneous, something she admired, and as unpredictable as the waves. When he carried her out into the surf last summer, kissing her until her body was pulsing with need, she thought for sure she could spend the rest of her days with someone as reckless and carefree as Reif Marintide. But the stars had other plans. When Novalise caught him with his tongue miles deep between the legs of another female, she'd been furious and humiliated.

She wanted a male whose head wouldn't turn the moment someone prettier walked past.

"You have to save me." Novalise usually considered herself above begging, but desperate times called for desperate measures. The last thing she wanted was to fall victim to Reif's charms again. Because if he was anything, it was convincing.

Ariesian stared at her, unblinking. "You're serious?"

"Of course I'm serious." She clutched the fabric of his coat between her fingers, clinging to him. "Tell him I've caught my death out in the cold and have lost my voice."

"I thought you said that was impossible," Ariesian countered, a nearly invisible smile tugging up the corner of his mouth.

She rolled her eyes to where the crystalline snowflakes continued to swirl above them. "What difference does that make? Please, Ariesian."

"Absolutely not. I have my own demanding admirers to deal with, many of whom have rather ambitious mothers." He patted her hand, then disentangled himself from her hold. "You're fully capable of taking care of yourself. That being said, if he lays a single unwelcome hand on you, say the word."

With that, her brother dipped his head and strode off toward the other side of the ballroom. She was helpless to do anything but watch as the gathering crowd parted for him, then just as swiftly swallowed him whole.

Novalise cast a hasty glance over her shoulder and was met with Reif's wide, charming smile. His golden skin was kissed by the sun and his sandy blond hair was tied in a knot at the back of his head. Wisps of those shimmering strands framed his angular face, managing to make it look like he was standing on a windswept beach instead of inside the confines of a suffocating ballroom. Turquoise hoops pierced up one side of his pointed ears and when those eyes, as green as the Chantara Sea, washed over her, Novalise knew she was in trouble.

"Lady Novalise." He bowed, then held out his hand.

She hesitated before giving in and he captured her fingers, placing a kiss upon each knuckle. Forcing a polite smile, she pulled her hand back and was rewarded with another devastating grin. Except this time, his teeth skimmed along his bottom lip, and she tracked the movement.

Oh yes, he knew *exactly* the effect he had on her.

Reif clicked his tongue. "You look absolutely ravishing."

"Thank you, my lord." She schooled a neutral expression into place, refusing to give him the reaction he sought.

He shoved his hands into the pockets of his pants and moved closer. "I was hoping I'd get to see you tonight."

Novalise dug her heels in place, willing herself to stand her ground against his alluring confidence. She clasped her hands before her, tilting her head in consideration. "I can't imagine why."

"Considering the last time we saw each other—"

"You had your head between the thighs of someone else?" she prompted, grateful when he had the decency to look away.

The shame was short-lived.

"It was only one time." He took another step so only a few breaths of air stood between them. His presence was overwhelming, the scent of him a mixture of sandalwood and the sea and entirely too tempting. "And she didn't taste nearly as good as you."

Fates divine, she had to get away from him. She knew his words were all sugar-coated fabrications intended to weaken her knees, but why did he have to be so ridiculously good at it?

A servant passed by carrying a tray filled with flutes of starberry sparkling wine. Novalise grabbed two and when Reif reached out to take one from her, she downed them both. The bright taste of ripe berries played across her tongue and mingled with the fizzing bubbles, easing some of her frustration.

His grin only widened. "Thirsty?"

"If you only knew," she mumbled.

"What was that?"

"I said, not for you." Novalise silently cursed Ariesian for discovering her on the balcony and forcing her to come back inside. She would always play the part required of her, but right now, she needed an escape. A moment's peace. Anywhere that wasn't near Reif Marintide and his gorgeously persuasive smile.

"Is that…" she gasped, feigning shock. She quickly set down the two empty flutes on the ledge behind her, then rose up on her toes. "No, it can't be."

Reif stole a glance behind them. "Who?"

"Prince Aspen." The lie tasted sour, but she swallowed it down. "I knew Ariesian invited him tonight, but I didn't think he'd actually show up."

Novalise pointed to the far side of the ballroom where a cluster of fae were talking excitedly, their faces likely animated by some absurd story that had nothing to do with the prince of Aeramere.

Instantly, Reif whipped away from her. He was forever trying to earn himself a position within the prince's exclusive circle. The moment he left her side, Novalise seized her opportunity.

She hoisted her skirts and darted toward a curtain of winterblooms, ducking swiftly behind the icy blue flowers to conceal herself in one of the ballroom's many alcoves. She would only stay hidden away for a few minutes, just until she could find a way to leave the ball for good without being noticed, and her plan would have worked except she wasn't alone.

Novalise swallowed a yelp.

Crammed into the alcove with her was none other than Asher Firebane, Lord of House Emberspire. He was quite possibly the most presumptuous male in all of Aeramere and apparently had a fierce temper. At least, that's what everyone told her. She'd been blessed to avoid any interactions with him and whenever they were in the same place, he was almost always preoccupied with a book. A pity, really, considering he was rather handsome.

His hair was the color of night with a streak of silver

slashing through it, and the front pieces were cut longer than the rest, so they fell in a wave, concealing half of his face. His jawline was strong and smooth-shaven, and his eyes reminded her of still-lit coals beneath a brooding brow. He wore a trim black coat with fine stitching and the silk shirt beneath it was the color of stormy skies. To make matters worse, he had the fullest lips she'd ever seen. Oddly enough, she couldn't stop staring at them.

"Fancy meeting you here."

Novalise's lashes fluttered back in shock. She hadn't expected his voice to be so...deep.

"I live here." She straightened, her spine snapping into place. A mistake that sent the fullness of her breasts right up against his obscenely hard chest. Shrinking back, she pressed herself into the cool stone of the alcove. "What are *you* doing here?"

"Same thing as you, I imagine." His gaze flicked to the wall of winterblooms. "Hiding."

"From?"

"This entire shit show of a holiday."

Novalise reared back, affronted, and her head knocked into a protruding chunk of stone. She hissed, wincing against the pain.

Concern etched its way across Asher's brows. "Are you alright?"

"Never better." She rubbed the sore spot on the back of her head. "My family's Yuletide Ball is *not* a shit show. Not only is it tradition, but it's an event loved by even the most haughty of fae."

"Beg your pardon. Of course it isn't." He leaned his broad frame against the wall opposite her and she looked away, mortified that she'd noted the way his muscular arms strained against the confines of his midnight coat. "Yet here you are."

Vexation fired through her. She had no idea a lord of

Aeramere could be so irritating. "I'm not hiding. I simply needed a reprieve."

From Reif Marintide and his exceptionally dashing smile.

The corner of Asher's mouth ticked upward. "Is that all?"

"Yes, that's all."

"Then your time is up, because I was here first."

Novalise's mouth fell open. "You can't kick me out, this is *my* house. Do you even know who I am?"

"Oh, yes." He shoved off the wall, closing the distance between them until she was squished up against him once more. Cold stone pressed into her back, but the heat from his body overwhelmed her, causing tiny beads of sweat to slink down her spine. "You're Lady Novalise Starstorm Celestine, spoiled darling of Aeramere who thinks herself worthy of reading the stars. In other words, you're an obnoxiously pretty fae who enjoys attending parties despite adding no real worth to them."

Novalise might've been flattered by the compliment of her looks had it not been for the fact that he'd insulted her at the same time.

Lord Firebane had left her with no choice.

Novalise reached back, aiming to slap that smirk off his beautiful face.

CHAPTER TWO

*A*sher snagged Novalise Starstorm's wrist right before her hand met the side of his face.

"I wouldn't do that if I were you," he warned.

She wrenched her arm free, and he released her. "First you try to kick me out of this alcove and now you're telling me what to do?"

He shrugged, falling back against the other side of the stone wall. "Not that I'd expect you to listen."

"I'll have you know, I'm an exceptional listener." She shimmied a little, crossing her arms over her chest, and it took every shred of Asher's willpower not to steal a glance at her ample cleavage. "To those I respect."

An impatient sigh escaped him.

He'd been perfectly content in this alcove, ignoring the ball and hiding from his sister, who saw fit to throw him at the mercy of every single female within earshot. Cyra had practically forced him to abandon the solitude of his study, then dragged him here to partake in forced conversations and uncomfortable silence. She didn't understand why he preferred the company of his books to social gatherings, and he supposed she never would. It wasn't every day a fae of Aeramere, especially one as powerful as himself, wanted nothing more than to be left alone. He didn't like parties or celebrations, he despised crowds, and he certainly didn't enjoy the petty small talk that usually accompanied such events.

Glimmers of light peeked in through the petals of the winterblooms, dancing around Novalise and illuminating her like she was a fae of Emberspire and not Celestine. But there was no mistaking her birthright, not with those silver eyes that sparkled like pools of stardust. She looked away from him then, pretending to smooth the deep blue velvet skirt of her gown. The thin straps were dusted with diamonds and the bodice cut low, nearly to her navel, drawing even the most honorable of gazes. Fine silver threading entwined her waist, exploding down around the fabric like bursting stars. She wore her pale lavender hair twisted away from her face. It fell down her shoulders to the middle of her back, and moonstone charms were scattered throughout the tresses like constellations.

She was regal. Exquisite. Perfection in every sense of the word. And he wanted nothing to do with her.

Asher stole a glance through the slivers of space between the flowers and caught sight of Reif Marintide. The damned fae looked like he was on the hunt for a bounty, likely one that would make for a fine tumble. "Lord Marintide looks like he could use a companion."

Novalise actually groaned. "I'd rather not. When I take a lover, I prefer not to share him."

"I see." His gaze betrayed him and slid to the necklace she wore. Dangling from the chain of gold was the Faerie Star with an outward facing crescent moon on either side. He flashed a cunning smile. "And how often do you take lovers, my lady?"

Her skin flushed, and the corners of her mouth pinched tight. She looked downright furious.

"That, my lord," Novalise spoke with an air of authority, "is none of your concern."

"Pity."

She rolled her eyes and bent low, peering out between the waterfall of florals, while offering Asher a rather splendid view of her backside.

Gods, of all the alcoves in this entire house, why did she have to hide in the one he'd chosen? Granted, he'd never had any sort of interaction with Novalise. He knew she was beautiful, but he also knew she was obliging, polite, and the epitome of a lady. She was exactly the type of female he avoided. Not that those attributes were intimidating by any means, but more so because they oftentimes brought a whirlwind of chaos into his quiet, orderly life. He enjoyed catching the sunrise during the stillness of dawn before the rest of the world awoke. He liked to stroll through the forests of Emberspire when autumn snatched away the last breath of summer and painted the leaves in shades of ruby, gold, and topaz. Novalise, however, was quite the opposite.

She attended every social event, from the seafaring games of House Azurvend, to the Festival of the Skies of House Galefell, to even the all-night dances deep within the forests of House Terensel. Everyone adored her. She seemed to thrive in the boisterous celebrations of Aeramere, the pinnacle of all the things he loathed.

If Asher had been smart, he would've brought a book with him to the Yuletide Ball. At least then he could have been too preoccupied with the studies of magical creatures to pay attention to anything or anyone else. Most notably, a pretty female with remarkable eyes whose lips looked entirely too kissable.

He shook the ridiculous thought from his mind. He had no business assessing the kissability of her mouth.

Novalise huffed out a breath, sinking back further into the

alcove. She faced him, wrapping her arms around herself. "He's still out there."

Asher blinked, her words drawing his attention back to her lips that happened to be painted a glossy, rose color. "Who?"

"Lord Marintide." Her gaze drifted back to the waterfall of flowers hiding them. "I wish he'd set his sights on someone else for the evening."

"You mean he's looking for you?"

"Yes, he's looking for me. That's why I'm in here with you."

She loosed a breath, and a few fallen strands of her lavender hair fluttered around her face. Her nose crinkled. "I imagine he intends to pick up where we left off."

A strange sensation seized Asher's gut and his jaw clenched.

"Fine." He bit the word out. "You can stay."

Though it sounded more like a gruff command than a kind offer.

"Thank you," she said dryly, and cut him down with a look. "How thoughtful."

Asher couldn't help it when the corner of his mouth lifted into a smirk.

The air above them shimmered and filled with a faint tinkling sound, stirring the darkness ensconcing them. A plant slowly unfurled from the stone ceiling, its slender green leaves sprouting as round, white berries decorated the stem.

"Mistletoe." Asher reached up and flicked one of the leaves.

"The work of my sister." Novalise glared up at the flowering plant as though it had somehow personally offended her. "She placed them all over the house, apparently even the alcoves."

Asher chuckled. "Do you suppose it's too late to pretend we haven't seen it?"

It was barely imperceptible in the dim light, but he didn't miss the way a wave of tension stilled her entire body. She recovered quickly, lifting one shoulder, then letting it fall dismissively.

"I mean, it *is* tradition." Novalise reached up and lightly touched the sprig of greenery. "Not that I think Caelian's theory is accurate. It's practically impossible for two people to fall in love just because they share a kiss beneath enchanted mistletoe."

"So," he drawled, leaning in a bit closer, catching the faintest scent of roses and dark berries mixed with tempting vanilla. "You don't believe in such fancies? Fairy tale endings and happily ever afters?"

"I..." Novalise's starlit eyes dipped to his mouth, stirring desire to life inside of him. "Maybe. Sometimes."

"And you don't think we should test your sister's theory?" They were so close now, he could almost hear her heartbeat. "Just to prove her wrong?"

He didn't know why he was suddenly intrigued by Novalise Starstorm or why he was attempting to seduce her. Maybe it was the captivating melody thrumming beyond the alcove and knowing they were hidden away while the rest of the world carried on without them. Maybe it was the enchanted mistletoe dangling overhead, luring them to tempt the fates. Or maybe it was simply the fact that Novalise's lips were slightly parted while her chest rapidly rose and fell, and she was looking at him like he was the only air she needed to breathe.

"It could be fun," she whispered, her voice soft and lusty, "to prove her wrong."

Asher bent his head toward her, oddly pleased when she rose up on her toes, placing both of her hands lightly against his chest. "For the sake of tradition."

She nodded. "Tradition."

Her eyes closed, her long lashes casting tiny shadows across the highest points of her cheeks. He meant for it to be swift, a brief and fleeting kiss, nothing more.

But the moment his lips pressed against hers, his entire world tilted on its axis. He planted one hand on the wall behind her head to steady himself, and without thinking, his tongue started tracing the seam of her lips. She opened for him willingly, grabbing his coat, her fingers twisting into the fine fabric. When their tongues meshed, the explosion of power between them nearly stole his breath. What should've been an innocent kiss morphed into dizzying passion. His skin hummed, his blood burned. Her arms wrapped around his neck, her fingers tangled in his hair. Angling her to deepen the kiss, he snared her by the waist, dragging her flush against him as they gave into the need to touch, to feel, to taste.

Novalise's hips tilted forward, urging him closer, and he wanted nothing more than to diminish every last shred of space between them. His magic raced toward hers, a fiery blend of black and silver flames wrapped in a moonless night of shooting stars. She nipped his bottom lip as their magic collided. Power throbbed between them, an incandescent pulsing of midnight fire and celestial starbursts.

It was too much. She was too much.

He wasn't supposed to want her. He wasn't supposed to want anyone.

Again, she arched toward him, grinding herself against the hardened length of his shaft. His nails bit into the stone where he still gripped the wall of the alcove. If he let go now, he'd lose himself to her completely.

Threads of magic illuminated between them, pulling and twisting, entwining together to form a never-ending strand of power. It snared them both, wrapping around their wrists and fingers, securing them to one another. Gods, she was intoxicating. Addicting. He couldn't get enough of her. Their magic moved together in a dance of frenzied longing. He tried to fight it, to break free from the curse, but Novalise's soft mouth was fused to his own, and he simply could not release her.

A thousand sensations Asher had never known rose before him like an angry tide during a storm out at sea. Wave after wave crashed into him, drowning him. Novalise's heartbeat became his heartbeat, her breathing an even match to his own. The heightened awareness only amplified as he attuned to every last one of her emotions, as her scent caused his knees to damn near buckle. In the back of his mind, he could hear her thoughts if he listened closely enough, a torrent of dreams, fears, and hopes.

Her stars kindled his flames, devouring one another, sealing the bond.

Fuck.

Asher jerked back, breaking their kiss.

Novalise stared up at him, lips swollen and cheeks flushed. But the hollowing out of his heart was the look in her eyes. The understanding. The realization. The *knowing* of what just happened between them.

"Lord Firebane." Her voice sounded distant, like she was calling to him from the mountains but all he could hear was the echo of his name.

He shook his head violently. "Don't say it."

"But you felt it," she sputtered, confusion clouding her once lust-filled gaze. She blinked and her eyes cleared. "Surely you felt it."

"I didn't feel anything." The lie gutted him, but it was better than facing the truth of the matter. The truth he refused to acknowledge or believe.

Novalise's lips pressed together, and he didn't know if she was trying to keep herself from crying or screaming. He hoped to the gods it was the latter.

"You and I both know that was more than a simple kiss." The soft lines of her face hardened into chiseled anger. "The stars never lie, and what happened between us was fate. It was—"

"Mistletoe," he fired back. "It's a damn enchanted flower and nothing else. This isn't the stars giving you a sneak peek into your future. It's nothing more than a childish fantasy, a myth based around the charm of the Winter Solstice. Do you want to know what makes me so certain? Because I know for a fact I could never make you happy. And I sure as hell don't want you."

Novalise reared back like he'd struck her.

Her bottom lip quivered and her eyes filled.

Perhaps he would've been better off if someone had ripped his soul from inside him instead.

She sank her teeth into her bottom lip, likely to hold back the tears threatening to slide down her cheeks at any moment. Then she pointed to the waterfall of winterblooms. "Get. Out."

Asher wasn't sure he heard her correctly. He tugged on the collar of his shirt, his brow furrowing. "What?"

"Get out of my house. Now." Fury radiated from her, causing her to tremble. "And do not *ever* show your face here again."

He inclined his head and bowed stiffly. "Gladly, my lady."

Without looking back, Asher stormed out of the alcove, ignoring the shouts and disgruntled muttering of anyone who stood in his way. He had to get away from here. Away from *her*.

He told himself she'd get over it. It was only a matter of time until she found someone else worthy of her, someone who would undoubtedly worship the ground she walked upon. It was a good thing she was furious with him. It would make it all the easier once she realized this was a mistake. A lapse in judgment. A fallacy.

Leaving House Celestine, he strode out into the bitter night. Frigid wind slashed through him, punishing him for his foolishness. The towering mountains seemed to mock him, he could almost hear their whispers echoing from the tallest peaks.

Asher probably should've hailed a carriage to take him home, but he was already stalking through the glittering city streets of Celestine, and he wasn't about to turn back. He didn't care if his lungs froze solid before he reached Emberspire or if every muscle screamed, then snapped, from the miles-long trek it would take to reach the doors of his home. The more distance between himself and House Celestine, the better. It was bad enough a mating bond had inadvertently fused him to Novalise Starstorm, but the crime he committed afterwards was far more heinous.

Asher turned himself away from her. Abandoned her. Rejected her, and in turn, rejected their bond.

But it was better this way.

Because Asher had sworn to never fall in love, and that was a vow not even a bond could break.

CHAPTER THREE

inter thawed to spring. Spring bloomed into summer. All the while, Asher Firebane had done exactly as Novalise demanded of him.

He stayed far, far away.

Yet every second of every day it seemed the mating bond connecting them continued to strengthen. She'd tried, oh goddess, how she had *tried* to forget him.

But Lord Firebane was always there, in the early waking hours and the late sleepless nights. He occupied every spare moment of her mind. If she let her guard down, she could hear his thoughts, his voice as clear as though he were whispering the words right past her ear. It was a constant pull, a tether. His heart had been tied to hers, so she was always conscious of him, always knew where to find him. More often than not, his emotions got the best of her. Frustration. Anger. Loneliness.

That last one nearly broke her.

For no matter how badly she wanted to see his body impaled and his head skewered on a stake for rejecting her, a tiny, insignificant part of her wanted him to change his mind. If he would accept the bond, he wouldn't be so lonely all the time, and then perhaps her heart would cease its constant aching.

But her pity only extended so far.

Right now, she had more important things to deal with, like preparing for her star reading. It would be the one that would seal her destiny. She'd yet to secure a mate on her own, no thanks to the ill-tempered fae lord who refused to acknowledge her existence, so now the stars would choose for her.

Which was fine.

She'd reached the age where marriage was no longer met with childish fantasies but was now a looming necessity. As the eldest daughter of House Celestine, it was expected of her, a dutiful obligation. Queen Elowyn deemed the end of Midsummer as the perfect opportunity for her wedding to take place, and Novalise was in no position to refuse her queen.

Tonight, the star reading would confirm all that was predicted on the night of her birth. Novalise would take her mother's place, becoming the next Reader of Stars. She would foresee the fates of all those who came to her for assistance, and she would carry the weight of Aeramere's future upon her shoulders, becoming a member of Queen Elowyn's prestigious council. She would wed the one the stars chose for her, who was decidedly *not* Lord Asher Firebane, produce heirs to House Celestine, and live out the remainder of her days as one of the most prominent and celebrated fae in Aeramere.

Songs would be written in her honor.

Legends would be woven from the fibers of her life.

All wonderful things, and yet she still felt as though something was amiss. It prodded at the back of her mind, startling her in the middle of the night so she woke up with her heart racing as she gasped for air.

Novalise flopped down onto her bed, sending a flurry of plush pillows to the floor. She stared up at her ceiling to the glamoured night sky glittering before her, where an array of stars displayed her favorite constellation—Estrela's crown. Estrela, the goddess of the moon and stars, used her Wheel of Stars to determine the fate of every soul. It was said she once lived in a palace in the clouds, hidden away by the Mother Goddess who claimed if Estrela ever left, only heartache would follow in her wake. One day she was discovered by the sun god Sol, who instantly fell in love with her beauty, though many said it was her power that lured him instead. Sol promised Estrela an eternity of happiness, vowing to make her his wife, until he attempted to steal her Wheel of Stars and use it for himself to alter the fate of the world. Upon learning of Sol's betrayal, Estrela cast her Wheel of Stars up into the heavens, ascending to the stars herself, never to be forsaken again.

It was Estrela's Wheel of Stars that was the source of Novalise's magic, through generations of star readers.

A gentle tapping sounded outside her bedroom door.

"Come in," she sighed.

The door to her room swung open and two feminine voices sang her name like a song. "Novalise!"

She propped herself up on her elbows and glanced over to where Caelian and Creslyn stood in matching gowns of amethyst satin studded with black diamonds in the shape of falling stars. As the youngest children of eight siblings—with both of them recently having entered their twentieth year— they were the only set of twins to have ever been born in the Starstorm lineage. They were identical, vibrant and full of ambition. Their straight, silver hair hung to their waists, and was threaded with shades of lavender, frosted pink, and icy blue. Both possessed eyes of the darkest sapphire, framed with impossibly long lashes. Together, they could light up any room like a star-filled sky with their infectious laughter and brilliant smiles. It was nearly impossible to tell them apart, the only significant difference being Creslyn had a light smattering of freckles dusting her cheeks. Though, oddly enough, they looked more like constellations.

Creslyn swept into the room, joining Novalise on the bed. "Are you almost ready?"

Novalise wasn't sure she would ever be ready. "Not entirely. I haven't even decided what to wear."

"What about the dress Mother had made for you?" Caelian asked, idly toying with the diamond beading trimming her bodice.

The gown in question was not at all what Novalise would have chosen for herself. Though it was made of luxurious satin, it was a murky grayish-purple color. The bodice was painfully snug, so much so that it made it difficult to breathe. Covered in heavy beading, the skirt flared at the waist, accentuating the width of her hips. When Novalise tried it on for the first time, her breasts had been squished up to her chin.

"I'm not sure it's the best option." Novalise hated to disappoint anyone—it was her lot in life to please all those around her. She'd done so without fail since drawing her first breath. If there was one thing she couldn't do, it was tell someone *no* outright.

The thought of it caused her palms to dampen.

"It's not the worst option either." Caelian gave Novalise's hair a gentle tug. "Remember last year when she forced you into that turquoise gown that was covered in feathers?"

How could she forget? She'd felt like an overstuffed peacock.

Creslyn shoved up from the bed and glided across the room. She flung open the other door to the wardrobe, scouring the contents. "I'm sure we can find you something else. You have more dresses than Caelian and me combined."

"I should've gone into Celestine and ordered a new gown when I had the chance," Novalise murmured, wishing she'd made the trip. Instead, she'd stayed home, feigning a headache while secretly agonizing over the slim chance she might run into Lord Firebane. She wasn't necessarily afraid of seeing him, but if she could avoid the possibility, she would. At all costs.

In her absence, her mother had selected a gown for her. Though Novalise imagined Trysta Starstorm would have decided on the muddy purple dress anyway, whether or not Novalise was there.

"What about this one?" Creslyn asked, tossing a gown of violet tulle and pearls onto the bed, then reaching in to find another.

Caelian's nose crinkled in distaste. "That will never do. Nova wore that less than a fortnight ago. Everyone will recognize it."

Creslyn continued to shuffle through the overflowing wardrobe, picking through the explosion of fabrics. "But this... this is lovely."

She pulled out a flowing skirt that mimicked the rise of twilight and a cropped bodice heavily decorated with magenta beads. She deposited the skirt and top onto the bed.

"I've always loved the color." Novalise ran her fingers across the delicate material. "But I fear it's too informal for the occasion."

"Novalise, you're running out of time." Caelian grabbed two more dresses and a pair of heels. "You must be quick or else you'll be late. Mother is preparing for your star reading as we speak, and Queen Elowyn will lift the Veil shortly after."

"I know." Novalise sat up, worried if she continued to lie down any longer, she'd be buried beneath a pile of satin, tulle, and silk. "It's impossible to forget."

Not only was tonight her star reading, but it was also the start of the Season. Every year during Midsummer, Queen Elowyn lifted the Veil of Aeramere. The Veil was rooted in the queen's earth magic and served as an invisible shield to protect their land. But for only a fortnight, fae, magical beings from other realms, and mortals of the human kingdoms were invited to take part in the revelry of the summer season. The longest days were celebrated in fashion, with parties and festivals filled with music, splendor, and the chance at finding love. Anyone was welcome to attend, and anyone who found their match was guaranteed to receive Queen Elowyn's blessing. It was a season of romance and love, one Novalise had always looked forward to, at least until that damning kiss she'd shared with Asher Firebane.

How would she find love if she was bonded to someone who rejected her?

Caelian spun around in a circle in front of the floor-to-ceiling mirror inlaid with gold dust and opals, admiring her own reflection. "Perhaps a mortal will catch your eye."

Novalise offered one of her practiced, insincere smiles. "I think Mother would lock me in a tower before she ever let a mortal ask for my hand."

What little excitement she clung to for the evening was already waning, succumbing to the rise of acidic dread twisting in her stomach. Anxiety pinched her lungs, and she sucked in a shallow breath. She was quite skilled at pretending. She'd long ago mastered the art of being compliant and obedient, even though every time she was put on display her skin crawled with unease and her stomach wrenched, leaving her empty.

The door to her bedroom opened again and Sarelle stepped in, a swirl of iridescent silk cocooning her lithe body. Younger than Novalise but older than the twins, Sarelle was born fourth in the Starstorm line. Her eyes were the deepest blue, like the twins', and her midnight hair glimmered like it had been coated in stardust. Clasping her hands together, her dark brows pulled into a frown. "Fates divine, what happened in here?"

Sarelle's gaze stole over the pile of dresses on the bed, then widened when she realized Novalise was still wrapped in a black satin robe. "Why aren't you dressed?"

Novalise glanced over at Caelian and Creslyn, who were

perusing through her drawers of jewelry. "The twins were helping me."

Creslyn held up a necklace clustered with diamonds and shooting stars, admiring it in the mirror. "Novalise doesn't want to wear the dress Mother chose for her."

"I think she's nervous," Caelian tossed over her shoulder, holding an intricate silver ring up to the light.

"Mm." Sarelle took inventory of the mess, then focused on the twins. She offered a kind smile then pointed to the door. "Alright you two, out. I'll take it from here."

There was a collective groan of displeasure but just as quickly, Caelian and Creslyn were out the door, whispering and laughing, Novalise's troubles all but forgotten.

"You don't have to stay." Novalise gestured around the mess of her bedroom. "I'm sure I can find something."

"Nonsense." Sarelle fisted her hands on her hips, surveying the disaster of dresses once more. "I'm not leaving until my sister returns."

Novalise blinked up at her. "I'm right here."

"Are you though?" Sarelle scooped up a pile of silk and tulle, depositing the layers of gowns onto the tufted chair in front of the vanity, and joined her sister on the bed. "You've been present, yes, but your mind is always elsewhere."

Another truth Novalise wasn't quite ready to face.

Sarelle reached out and took Novalise's hand, covering it with her own. Dark eyes roved over her face, noting every detail. "This doesn't have anything to do with Lord Asher Firebane, does it?"

Novalise looked away, suddenly more interested in the indigo tiles decorating her floor than the conversation.

"Nova…" Sarelle prodded gently.

"He'll be here tonight." A sigh of annoyance escaped her. She knew she couldn't avoid him forever, but she could at least try.

"And? So will everyone else."

"That doesn't exactly make me feel any better."

"I doubt you'll even see him. He'll just be another blurry face in the crowd." Sarelle squeezed Novalise's hand in affirmation. "Tonight is all about you. It's your star reading. Your destiny. You'll be the center of attention, at least until Queen Elowyn lifts the Veil. But even if you do see him, you are Lady Novalise Starstorm Celestine, and you won't even spare him a glance."

If only it were so easy.

Novalise had confided in Sarelle about the fortuitous kiss with Lord Firebane, but she withheld everything that happened afterward. The bond they shared was a secret to only her heart. She couldn't tell anyone about it, especially not after he dismissed her. The humiliation alone would ruin her.

"He's not worth a second of your thoughts." Sarelle attempted to reassure Novalise, but it did nothing to ease the compounding apprehension building up inside her. "It was only a kiss."

"A rather passionate kiss." One Novalise replayed in her mind over and over. For the briefest of moments, she'd felt desired. Savored. Treasured. She'd felt like someone truly cared about *her*, not her title, namesake, or worse, the magic she controlled.

"A passionate kiss beneath enchanted mistletoe, Nova. You know how talented Caelian is, and if you ask me, she puts entirely too much effort into their success. A lover of happily ever afters, that one." Sarelle stood and pulled Novalise up with her. "Tonight, your true soulmate will be made known to you and you will have all that you were promised. I'm sure of it. Besides, the stars never lie. I see no reason they would fail you now."

Sarelle embraced her then, hugging her fiercely.

"Thank you." Novalise held on a little longer, grateful for the boost of confidence, no matter how slight.

"Now, let's get you dressed." Sarelle held her out at arm's

length. "You know as well as I do that if you show up in any other gown besides the one mother had made for you, she'll bemoan the fact for days. Besides, it could always be worse."

Novalise shifted on her feet, uneasy. "How so?"

"She could be the one choosing your mate."

Novalise laughed, even though it pained her heart. "Well, we wouldn't want that. Knowing mother, she'll pair me off with some arrogant fae lord who thinks everyone should kiss the ground he walks upon."

"Exactly," Sarelle agreed, helping her into the gown that crushed the fullness of Novalise's figure. "At least she's not forcing you to marry Prince Aspen."

Novalise met her sister's gaze in the gilded mirror, a wedge of panic nestling its way into her spine. "Prince Aspen?"

"I hear he's looking for a wife." Sarelle wove Novalise's hair into a thick plait so it fell over one shoulder, then sprinkled it with stardust. "Just be grateful it isn't you."

Novalise pitied the female who would be wedded to the Prince of Aeramere. On most occasions, he was cold-hearted and insufferable, his devastating good looks belied the cruelty of his nature.

"There." Sarelle painted Novalise's lips a deep berry, blended rouge onto her cheeks, and lined her silver eyes with kohl. She leaned back, cocking her hip to one side. "You look positively ethereal."

Novalise opened her mouth to reply when another knock sounded on her door.

This time it was Solarius, their second oldest brother, next in line after Ariesian. His black coat was trim and sharp, the lines clean. Silver hair with jet-black tips fell to just above his shoulders, and his tall, broad outline took up nearly the entire doorframe. The crest of House Celestine was faintly embroidered onto the pocket of his coat and power radiated from him, causing the silver of his eyes to glow.

"Well." He tucked his hands into his pockets, his solemn demeanor instantly replaced by boyish charm. "Don't the two of you paint a pretty picture?"

Sarelle's smile was cutting. "Remember that the next time I'm covered in stardust and you tell me I look like I've rolled around in a pile of glitter."

Laughter erupted from Solarius, echoing through the bedroom. Then he offered his arm. "Novalise. Ariesian is waiting."

Of course.

Ariesian would escort her to the observatory, where their mother would conduct her star reading in front of all the lords and ladies of Aeramere.

Novalise swallowed the rise of panic building in the back of her throat.

But then Sarelle was there, squeezing her hand once more. "No other star in the sky will shine as bright as you tonight."

Novalise nodded and accepted Solarius's arm.

But she couldn't rid herself of the fear threatening to swallow her whole. A tiny voice whispered in the back of her mind. The words were indistinguishable, but the underlying sense of warning was ever-present. Trepidation settled across her shoulders like a weight, dragging her down as each drudging step she took brought her closer to some unknown demise. No matter how desperately she tried, she couldn't shake the sensation that she was walking upon a glass ceiling. At any moment, it would crack, then shatter.

Novalise swallowed down the burn of terror in the back of her throat, and though her knees trembled, she assured herself of one thing.

The stars never lied.

CHAPTER FOUR

*A*sher could think of a million other places he'd rather be than the observatory of House Celestine—his study, in a library reading up on the wild magic of Aeramere, lost in the woods of Emberspire, facing imminent death. But alas, he couldn't refuse his sister. Especially not when she claimed she was going to the lifting of the Veil in the hopes of finding a suitable match.

He scoffed.

No one would ever be worthy of Cyra Firebane.

Now, however, he was stuck in the observatory waiting for every fae in the room to throw themselves at Novalise's feet. Members from all five houses of Aeramere were present. The Marintide fae of House Azurvend, the Skyhelm fae of House Galefell, and the Everland fae of House Terensel were all in attendance, along with other lords and ladies from their prominent houses. All of them were mingling together, laughing, and making a general mockery of one another with snide glances and backhanded compliments.

Though, he supposed there were *worse* places to waste time. The observatory of House Celestine was magnificent.

Gilded pillars rose to form ornate arches all around the wide, circular expanse of the room. Three archways were open and led to a balcony overlooking most of Aeramere. The remaining arches were all walled in and painted a dark blue, with gold constellations glinting in the light. Lapis lazuli stone steps led up to a dais near the balcony's entrance at the far end of the room, though to Asher it looked more like a stage. Stars crafted from iridescent glass floated throughout the room, suspended by magic. Glittering opals were inlaid on the floor and scattered like stardust. Teal candles danced around the outer edges of the space, flickering and casting tiny shadows along the furthest of walls. Bronze moons and stars were melded together, forming individual trifectas before stretching up over the glass dome of the observatory. Ancient runes depicted every season, every holiday, and the constellations of every star sign.

If one believed in such nonsense.

Which Asher absolutely did not.

Cyra looped her arm through his, and her gown of flame red and black billowed around them. She looked up at him with eyes that reminded him of molten gold. "I'm so glad you decided to come with me."

He made a derisive noise but gave her hand a gentle pat. "Pretty sure I didn't have much choice in the matter."

"Still, I'm glad you're here." Cyra moved toward the dais for a better view. Up close, he realized the dais was composed of crushed glass, a mosaic of celestial wonders. "Besides, once Lady Novalise has her *star reading*, then the real party starts."

There was something about the way Cyra said "star reading," as though she held an air of contempt about the whole process. Like she thought the entire ordeal was an absurd waste of time. How interesting, considering his sister was usually rather fond of the ostentatious celebrations hosted by other houses. He could've sworn he was the only one who thought the stars were bullshit.

"The real party," Asher repeated dully, and Cyra flashed him a look of warning.

"The Season." She stared up at him, her golden gaze darkening as she tried to discern whether or not he was being serious. "Don't tell me you've forgotten about the Season."

"Alright." The corner of his mouth lifted. "I won't."

Cyra's lips pursed, and she jabbed him swiftly in the ribs with her elbow.

It was impossible to forget about the Season. It was all everyone ever talked about in the weeks leading up to Midsummer. Then as soon as it was over, they were already planning for the following year. Whenever Queen Elowyn lifted the Veil, allowing anyone outside of Aeramere to enter, the whole damn continent lost their minds. Everyone who was anyone was suddenly in the market for a mate. For two straight weeks, mothers tried to marry off their daughters, sons were beseeched to take wives, alliances were formed, and for some unlucky bastards, souls were fated. Midsummer was a frivolous celebration of mundane courtship encouraged by overzealous matchmakers who chose their victims with precision. Though Asher supposed it wasn't such a terrible situation for those who actually believed in love.

Another wretched notion.

Love was a lie forged for the fools. For the weak.

He'd witnessed the suffering of such an affliction firsthand. Love was the reason his mother was dead.

Cyra cast a hasty look around them, then rose on her toes, whispering into his ear. "You won't believe some of the rumors I've heard."

"You're probably right." He'd rather dance naked in a faerie circle in the dead of winter than participate in any kind of gossip.

"Ash," Cyra chided, swatting his arm once more.

"Okay, fine." He couldn't be too insolent, she was all he had left. "I'll indulge you."

She bounced on her toes, positively beaming with eagerness to divulge every last confidence while participating in the spread of rumors that likely held zero truth. "I heard Calfair Skyhelm from House Galefell wants to take a mortal bride. Can you believe it? A human."

Cyra's face scrunched at the unpleasant thought.

"A mortal?" Asher considered Calfair's reasoning. He was the heir to House Galefell and no doubt under pressure from his father to find a wife. While there were plenty of females to choose from in Aeramere, it made little to no sense for Calfair to choose a mortal. It wasn't unheard of, plenty of fae and mortals joined together. More often than not, male fae took human lovers. Some were voluntary and some were coerced. It made Asher's skin crawl to think of some of the humans he'd seen, trapped and entranced, dancing for fae lords and ladies like enchanted puppets. The glazed look in the humans' eyes always set him on edge. Even then, they never married. The mortals were merely paramours, toys the fae could play with on a rainy day. For Calfair to want to marry a human, the woman must be of noble or royal birth, come with a hefty dowry, and a possible trade agreement.

Maybe it wasn't such a poor decision after all. Still. "Wouldn't she age?"

Fae were more or less immortal. They could die...eventually. An interesting choice for Calfair.

Cyra shrugged, peering around the observatory. She noticed every detail, every mistake. "I don't know. The humans some of the fae keep as pets don't age, but they've been spelled. I imagine she'd begin to wither away, shriveling up like the petals of a dying rose." She snorted. "I've heard that when women in the human kingdoms age, their moon cycles stop completely and their breasts sag down to their navels."

"Cyra, that's hardly appropriate conversation for a lady of House Emberspire." His attempt to scold his sister was foiled by the grin tugging on the corner of his mouth. "Is that all?"

"Of course not."

"Damn." He was hoping they were done with all the talk of hearsay and whispers.

Her laughter rang out, drawing the attention of those around them. Their answering smiles were sincere enough. Let anyone look at his sister the wrong way and he'd end them on the spot.

"Lilith told me the Prince of Brackroth is attending the Season this year."

Lilith Vylera was Cyra's best friend. Though she was a notorious gossip, she was also incredibly reliable. She claimed to have a skill for being in the right place at the right time, though Asher surmised her real power was her blatant sexual prowess and the ability to pry the truth from willing lips through dreams and sex.

"The Prince of Brackroth?" Asher yanked on the tie knotted at his neck, loosening it. The observatory was suddenly stifling. It had been some time since he'd heard the prince's name in passing. "As in, Prince Drake Kalstrand of Brackroth?"

"The very one," Cyra confirmed, tucking a loose strand of fiery hair behind one pointed ear. "I hear he went to war for Faeven against one of their own."

Asher wouldn't trust Drake Kalstrand in a battle if they were wearing the same colors and fighting on the same side. He'd sooner expect a blade through the back than stand alongside him in a war. "Is that so?"

"Mm." Cyra made a noncommittal noise. "Apparently, some queen went rogue and tried to overtake Faeven with dark magic. But Prince Drake owed the High Queen of Winter a favor and she called it in, asking for his assistance in saving their realm. Quite a heroic story, actually."

Something cold and dark twisted inside of Asher. "There is nothing heroic about Drake Kalstrand."

"Considering most of the speculation surrounding him seems to be of a nefarious nature, I don't doubt it." Cyra kept her voice low, the barest of murmurs beneath the teeming buzz of uninteresting conversation. "Is he really a shadowblade assassin?"

"He is *the* Shadowblade Assassin. The only one left." Asher happened to know it for fact and would venture to say that all the stories Cyra heard about Drake were probably true. But he wasn't about to tell her as much. Though with Drake arriving for the Season, Asher's gut clenched. It could only mean one thing...he owed the Shadowblade Assassin a favor, and Drake had come to collect. "I suppose it is time for him to return to Aeramere."

"Return?" Cyra's brows quirked at his choice of words. "You mean he's been here before?"

"Once." And it was enough. Drake Kalstrand was merciless. Calculating and cutthroat. No one ever crossed him and lived to tell the tale. It was a wonder he hadn't yet murdered his father and taken the crown for himself. The last time Drake was in Aeramere, he'd forged a deal with Asher, and now he would have to uphold his end of the bargain.

Asher scowled at the dais where the inlaid moonstones were beginning to glow and the Starstorm fae were starting to assemble. The thought of Drake coming to Aeramere sent a spear of tension straight through him. He glanced over at Cyra and gripped her hand. "You must promise me something."

"Of course." Cyra smiled up at him, the mirror image of their mother. Something sharp and acidic wrenched inside of Asher. "Anything for my darling, older brother."

"If and when Prince Drake arrives, I want you to stay as far away from him as possible." He squeezed his sister's hand in warning. "Do I make myself clear?"

Her eyes widened, curiosity causing the gold of them to ignite. "Why? Is he—"

"Cyra." He took her by the shoulders so she faced him, ensuring she understood the gravity of the situation. "This is not a game, it's not another one of your scandalous amusements. I want you to swear it right now on our mother's grave."

Cyra paled. All the vibrancy and color drained from her face at the mere mention of their mother. "Okay. Yes. I'll swear it."

Asher didn't release her. "Say the words."

She bobbed her head and the beaded earrings she wore swung back and forth. "I swear on our mother's grave that I will stay far away from Prince Drake Kalstrand of Brackroth."

It wasn't much, but at least the vow would keep Cyra safe from the Shadowblade Assassin, whose moral compass had been destroyed long ago, if it ever existed in the first place.

Asher's gaze was drawn to the dais where the Starstorm family stood in a line from oldest to youngest, or more accurately, from the most pretentious and haughty to the rather pleasant and amiable. Lady Trysta Starstorm, the matriarch of House Celestine, was at the forefront of the dais, the wide sleeves of her dress swallowing the numerous bangles dangling from her wrists. Then there was her eldest son, Ariesian, the current Lord of Celestine and Asher's peer, followed by Solarius, Novalise, Sarelle, Nyxian, Tovian, and lastly, the twins— Caelian and Creslyn.

He hated that Cyra had dragged him all the way to the front of this spectacle. He would've preferred to loiter near the back of the observatory for a quick and easy escape. At least then he wouldn't be entranced by Novalise and her starstruck eyes. He wouldn't be forced to wonder if she was wearing lace or silk, or anything at all beneath her encumbering gown. He wouldn't be curious if her lips still tasted of starberry sparkling wine, just like when they shared that stolen kiss in the alcove of her family's ballroom.

"Oh! And I have one more bit of information." Cyra's voice lured him away from the dangerous thoughts smothering him. "One that even you might find interesting, Asher."

"Oh, really?" he drawled, entirely uninterested.

"Yes." Her voice dropped and she leaned in conspiratorially. "Queen Elowyn is looking for a mate...for her *son*."

Asher stared at his sister, dumbfounded.

"For Prince Aspen," she clarified when he didn't respond.

"And why would I find that interesting?"

"I would think it's obvious." Cyra folded her arms across her chest, arching one pointed brow. "You're the Lord of House Emberspire. You already serve as one of her High Councilors. Much as I'm loath to admit it, you are rather dashing. But most importantly, I'm your *sister*. And I can't live at home forever."

"It's out of the question."

"But why?" Cyra pouted.

"Because the prince is..." Asher hesitated. He couldn't disgrace the Prince of Aeramere in public. Rumors would circulate and then he'd find himself in a dungeon beneath the palace, on trial for treason. Unless, of course, they killed him outright. Neither outcome sounded like a pleasant experience. So he spun her imagination, twisting it away from thoughts of marrying a prince, and focusing on why the notion of falling in love was dangerous in the first place. "Love is a death trap, Cyra. A manipulation of the heart, and a mockery of the mind."

Cyra's eyes flicked to the dais where Queen Elowyn glided forward to address them, regal and aloof, her expression always one of cautious indifference. "But Aeramere needs an heir."

"Your sister is right."

Asher turned around and came face to face with Lord Reif Marintide.

The seafaring fae ran a hand through his unkempt hair and

flashed Cyra a winning smile. His sister flushed beneath the lord's attention, and Asher gritted his teeth. "Queen Elowyn needs to marry off Prince Aspen and produce an heir sooner rather than later to quell the potential for any uprisings."

Cyra gasped. "Uprisings?"

"The likes of which were extinguished years ago," Asher interrupted smoothly, "and haven't been heard from since."

Reif made a dismissive, scoffing sound. "So says the hermit who never leaves the safety of his library."

"Right." Cyra drew the word out, either blissfully unaware or pointedly ignoring the strain between them. Just as quickly, her focus was back on Reif and his too-bright smile. "Enough about the queen and the prince. Are you in the market for a bride, my lord?"

"If my mother has it her way, I'll be married off by the end of the Season." Reif shook his head once, then adjusted the rolled sleeves of his shirt, intentionally drawing Cyra's gaze to the tattoo of cresting waves wrapping around his forearm. "But I prefer to be the one to break the rules, not make them."

Obviously.

That wasn't surprising in the least, given Reif's careless nature.

"In any case," he added, rocking back on his heels, a smug kind of expression yanking the corner of his mouth upward into a smirk. "I'm sure my mother will be pleased to know I've already set my sights on someone."

"Really?" Cyra clasped her hands together, near giddy with the prospect of being the first to hear who the legendary Reif Marintide planned on choosing for a bride. "Who?"

Reif grinned, then nodded toward the dais. "That one."

Asher followed his line of sight and every muscle in his body tensed with apprehension when his gaze landed on Novalise.

Over his dead fucking body.

CHAPTER FIVE

The observatory was teeming with nobles from all five houses, and the air was charged with weighted expectations. Novalise shifted, uncomfortable in her own skin. It was too warm, too crowded. The bodice of her gown was crushing her ribcage. She felt as though her breasts were on full display, and with every ragged inhale, she struggled to catch her breath. Pinpricks of anxiety crawled up her spine, causing her gut to clench and seize. Her palms grew damp, and she swore every soul in the room could hear the erratic beating of her heart.

Calm down, she scolded herself.

She could do this. She could face her fate in front of all these people. After all, she was a Starstorm. Her entire life was spent in the spotlight, under Ariesian's watchful eye, ensuring she never took a single step out of line. The dutiful oldest daughter who did everything expected of her. She attended every party with a smiling face, completed everything that was asked of her, and held herself to the highest level of perfection. Novalise could handle a simple star reading. It wasn't like her entire destiny was hinged on this one night, like every hope and dream she'd held close to her heart was all culminating in this singular event when the stars finally aligned.

Novalise sucked in a shaking breath.

No pressure. Absolutely none. All she had to do was stand there and look lovely, ignore the fact that every pair of eyes in the room were focused on her, and the stars would take care of everything else. She had nothing to worry about, not a concern in the world.

Her heart skittered uncontrollably.

Then why did she feel like it was all about to come crashing down upon her like a violent rogue wave? Like a swift undertow ready to drag her beneath the surface of the relentless sea?

Her chest rose and fell in rapid succession.

Her breathing grew shallow.

Queen Elowyn, rigid yet lovely in her own way, stood off to the side of the dais, the edges of her beauty blurred.

Novalise blinked. Her mother appeared before her, and the delicate scent of her perfume was suddenly too cloying to tolerate. The intense fragrance of rosewater and bursting florals caused a dull ache to pulse at the base of Novalise's neck, all the way up to her temples. Her mouth was dry and papery, her stomach a mess of tangled knots. But her mother, Trysta Starstorm, the renowned Reader of Stars, seemed oblivious to her eldest daughter's turmoil.

"My darling," she crooned, beckoning Novalise from the safety of her siblings. Lifting her arms, the sheer fabric of her sleeves tumbled to her elbows and the stack of bangles she wore on each wrist clinked together like the chords of a tragic strain. Her mother's hair, white like freshly fallen snow, was twisted back from her face, and pinned into place by a comb of shimmering selenite. She motioned for Novalise to join her. "Come forward."

Novalise forced her feet to move, urging herself closer to her mother's side while attempting to smile. The ground was unstable beneath her feet, the inlaid moonstone seeming to tilt and whirl with every step. Or maybe she was the one who was struggling to remain upright while the world around her started to spin out of control.

Fingers curling into her palms, she bit her nails into her skin until the initial pinch of pain went numb. Another heaving breath caused her blood to rush. It echoed in her ears, loud and reverberating, drowning out all other sounds. Everyone was staring at her. Watching her. Waiting for her to crumble. Her strength was wavering. Panic sluiced through her, shredding her confidence, leaving her stricken. From beside her, she knew Queen Elowyn was speaking, addressing everyone in the observatory, but her words were garbled. Disoriented, Novalise couldn't hear anything over the thunderous beating of her heart. The outskirts of her vision darkened, fading into an unfocused smear of color.

She thought she heard her name.

Novalise pulled her gaze from the queen to her mother.

Trysta's mouth was moving, but no words were coming out. Her dark brows pulled together, lips pinching. Again she opened her mouth, but it was too slow, like time had stilled altogether.

Novalise shook her head and the room swayed. She needed to escape. To run from away from here. To flee.

There was a strange tug on her heart, and she scanned the crowd of onlookers only to find him staring up at her. Concern rippled around him in waves so dense, she was surprised he didn't knock over everyone around him.

"Breathe, Novalise."

That voice. Asher's voice. It took up residence in her mind, weaving in and out of her dreams, haunting her heart.

Her knees began to quake.

"Breathe," Asher repeated through the bond, quieting her mind.

She inhaled sharply, but her bottom lip trembled. *"I can't do this."*

"Yes, you can." His eyes, dark gray and rimmed with gold, held onto hers, refusing to let go. He nodded toward her mother, the faintest of gestures. *"Look at your mother."*

Novalise dragged her gaze away from Asher, blinking rapidly until the image of her mother gradually came back into focus.

"Now, go stand beside her." Asher's voice was gentle yet firm.

Carefully placing one foot in front of the other, Novalise walked across the dais to where her mother was standing. The furrow of distress lifted from her mother's forehead, and she smiled, tilting her head back as the bronze constellations hanging overhead started to move, spinning in a slow circle until the whole of the evening sky was visible through the glass dome ceiling.

Novalise clutched at the bond, clinging to it as though it was the only thing that would keep her from drowning in an ocean of panic.

This was it, the one reading she'd been looking forward to for her entire life. Every breath, every decision, every moment led to this pinnacle of time. Her birthright and all that she was promised would be granted to her. She would take her mother's place as the next Reader of the Stars. The magic coursing through her blood would enable her to forecast fates through the blessing of the sight. And her soul match, her mate, the one who *wouldn't* reject her, would finally be revealed.

Novalise rolled her shoulders back, determined to remain unflustered and composed. But a collective gasp echoed through the observatory. The hushed whispers and rising murmurs were too difficult to ignore.

Her mother's eyes were glazed with uncertainty and darted

all over the sky as she murmured a stream of unintelligible words.

"Mother?" Novalise reached for Trysta's hand. Her fingers were clammy and damp.

"Lady Celestine?" Queen Elowyn stepped forward, layers of emerald silk floating around her like they moved in their own separate space of air. Glinting eyes of rich brown narrowed, latching onto Trysta. "Is something wrong?"

Not once in Novalise's life had she ever seen her mother rendered speechless. Until now.

"No, no. Of course not." Trysta glanced over at the queen, then looked upon Novalise, the haze of bewilderment suddenly clearing as though she was seeing her daughter for the first time. When she smiled, it was pained. "Novalise Starstorm Celestine, tonight the stars reveal the path to your destiny will lead you to—"

Her mate.

Just please, say his name.

"Great change and heartache."

"What?" Novalise shrieked and jerked backward, her gaze swinging up to the sky.

Icy cold fear licked its way down her spine.

She'd never seen anything like it. Shooting stars streaked across the heavens, a tail of iridescent colors bleeding behind them. Moonlight cut through the clouds like silver daggers. Stars tumbled toward the earth like flickering orbs, burning out and turning to ash right before colliding with the mountain peaks surrounding Celestine. Madness had descended upon the skies. The constellations were in chaos.

"This isn't right." Novalise shook her head, pressing her fingers to her temples. She squeezed her eyes shut. "This isn't what I was promised. I was supposed to find love. This reading should have confirmed that. I can't possibly—"

"Darling." Her mother's hands wrapped around her wrists,

drawing her close. Novalise opened her eyes and found Trysta staring at her, the age lines of her face etched in sympathy. "The stars make no promises."

The admission went against everything she learned, everything she studied, everything she thought she knew about her magic. Novalise staggered back. "But mother, you said—"

"Yes, yes." Trysta's tone was flippant as she cupped Novalise's face with her hands, then ran her thumbs along the apples of her cheeks. "I know what I said, but the stars have spoken. As of tonight, your fate is sealed. I can offer you no more answers."

"No." Her voice was raw. "This can't be right."

Lost.

Everything was lost to her.

She could handle not becoming the next Reader of Stars. If she was meant for something else, then so be it. But she was supposed to wed in a fortnight, and time was not on her side. There was only one male she longed for, and he currently wanted nothing to do with her. The other lords of Aeramere who deemed themselves worthy of being suitors took no interest in her. They either wanted alliances and the reputation that would follow with claiming her as their own, or they were only interested in her for her magic.

Novalise didn't matter to them. They weren't invested in her as a wife or an equal, they viewed her as property.

She twisted her hands together in front of her, squeezing her fingers. If she couldn't find a male on her own, the decision would fall to Ariesian and her mother. Ariesian, well, she at least trusted her brother's judgment. But her mother...Trysta would likely marry her off to the highest bidder.

Novalise drew in a ragged breath, pressed her palm to her stomach in a desperate attempt to suppress the acidic rise of anxiety bubbling up inside of her. A loud, rushing sound exploded through her mind, followed by a stabbing twinge in the center of her chest. Trepidation raked its claws through her, and Novalise doubled over. She couldn't catch her breath, and the damned dress she wore only seemed to further compress her lungs. She swatted away the hands of those who tried to help her, shoving past the onlookers without a second thought as she staggered down the steps of the dais. In the distance, she could've sworn she heard someone call her name over the deafening noise clamoring inside her head.

All she wanted was the calm. The quiet. The solitude.

She reached for the one male she knew could give her all of that and more. Asher. If she could hear his voice, if she could connect to the steady beating of his heart, then maybe she would remember how to breathe.

Stumbling to a stop, she tossed a glance over her shoulder to where he'd been standing earlier, before the reading, but there was no sign of him.

Asher was gone.

She was alone. Gasping for air that wouldn't come, she turned on one heel and started running. The sting of humiliation slapped her across the face, but she burst through the doors of the observatory, out into the warm summer night. The path she took veered left, away from the main house and toward the gardens. She could hide there, among the arches of wisteria and the walls of lilac. In the garden, in a haven of winding pathways, trickling fountains, and blooming flowers, she could find solace in her despair.

Because beneath the overhang of delicate purple wisteria and concealing vines, the chaos of the stars would not be able to find her.

So, Novalise ran. Hot tears streaked down her cheeks and twice she tripped, not caring when the gown snagged on a bush with thorns like teeth, ripping the satin she wore to shreds. The vicious plant snared her skin too, as the warm trickle of blood slid down her thigh. But she didn't stop.

She would run until she had nothing left. Until she could no longer feel anything at all.

CHAPTER SIX

*A*sher cursed under his breath and roughed a hand over his face.

What the hell had he been thinking, slipping into her mind like that?

But damn if he'd been able to stop himself. She'd been almost paralyzed with a kind of quiet delirium. Her thoughts were a cacophony of turmoil, rendering her terrified. He couldn't stand there and watch her suffer. Especially not in front of so many people who would undoubtedly spread rumors about the unfortunate turn of events.

He'd been perfectly content to live his own life for the past six months while Novalise lived hers. They were better off away from one another. Sure, he saw her face every time he closed his eyes at night and sometimes being separated from her was physically painful, but he didn't want her. He didn't want anyone. What happened between them was primal, a fusing of their magic. There was no love there. No affection or intimacy.

The mating bond between them was a lie.

True love only brought pain and heartache, and he was

entirely too familiar with both emotions, thanks to the virulent relationship of his parents.

He stood before one of the fountains in the gardens of House Celestine. Smooth slate granite was shaped into a tower of stacked stars, ranging in size from large to small, but instead of water flowing from them, it was some sort of sparkly, silvery liquid. He reached out to touch it, to run his fingers through the strange substance, when a rather feminine yelp sounded from behind him.

Asher wheeled around just in time to see Novalise tumbling down the path toward him, arms flailing. Her hair unfurled behind her like ribbons of lavender silk and her eyes were wide as she tumbled toward him. He reached out, snaring her quickly by the waist as she toppled into him, the force of her impact enough to send him off balance. Her elbow slammed into his abdomen, knocking the air from his lungs. He staggered backward, grappling to remain upright, when the heel of his boot caught the bottom edge of the fountain.

"Oh, shit."

There was no recovering.

Asher locked one arm tight around Novalise, hauling her against his chest. With the other, he covered her head, protecting her, preparing to take the full brunt of the blow. The back of his knees hooked onto the ledge of the fountain and down he went, landing on his ass with Novalise in his lap. Pain splintered through him, but it was fleeting, his main concern was the coughing female he held in his arms. Shimmering water sloshed all around them, pouring from the stone stars and soaking them thoroughly.

She gasped and sputtered, chest heaving, shoving wet strands of hair back from her face.

"Are you alright?" he asked, lightly running his hands over her to check for any obvious wounds.

"I'm fine." She winced when he grazed her thigh, where her

dress was practically falling apart. The fabric was stained a darker color than the rest. She smacked his hand away. "I said I'm fine."

"And I can clearly see that you're injured." He lifted the soaked pieces of satin from her skin. "May I look? To make sure you're okay?"

She huffed in annoyance. "If you must. But it will heal fast enough."

Of course it would. Fae healed naturally and usually at a rapid pace. But that didn't mean it didn't hurt. The gown looked as though it had been torn from her body. Angry red scratches marred her pale flesh.

Alarm fired through him.

With one hand, he cupped the side of her face, assessing her.

Her cheeks were flushed pink and so was her nose. Damp lashes framed her swollen, red-rimmed eyes.

She'd been crying.

And he would kill whoever was responsible. "What happened? Did someone hurt you?"

"No." Novalise shook her head and droplets of the iridescent water slid down her neck and arms. She stuck some of the damp strands behind her ear and looked away from him. "I got caught by a thorny bush."

"A bush," he repeated, arching a brow.

"Yes. With thorns."

"So, no one attempted to...harm you?"

"No." She ran her fingers beneath her eyes, clearing away the smudges of kohl. "No one hurt me."

"Good." Asher let his hand fall away from her face. "I'm not above seeking revenge, but I'd prefer to avoid it."

"You prefer to avoid everything," she muttered, toying with some of the crystals dotting the sleeves of her gown. "And everyone."

"Don't pretend to know or understand me, my lady. My

reasonings are my own." He hooked her chin with his thumb and forefinger, forcing her to meet his gaze. "Just because we're bonded doesn't mean I owe you an explanation for anything."

"I'd expect nothing less." Novalise jerked free from his hold and a familiar flame of indignation ignited in her eyes. "I can think of plenty of other places where my company is both desired and appreciated, and none of them involve you."

"Is that so?" Asher countered. He hadn't realized she was full of so much fire.

"Yes. That's so." She crossed her arms with a sigh of indifference, turning away from him. But all she did was wriggle that perfect ass of hers right against the seam of his pants. His cock pulsed to life, and he swallowed a groan.

Asher clamped both hands on her hips to still her.

"Then why," he asked, leaning closer, his lips hovering above her ear, "are you still sitting in my lap?"

At once her mouth fell open, but just as quickly she snapped it shut.

Shoving away from him, Novalise struggled to her feet.

"There." She sniffed. "Problem solved."

Asher stood, raked his hands through his hair, and climbed out of the fountain. He didn't miss the way her eyes roved over the damp shirt molded to his abdomen and chest, or the way they widened when her gaze dipped lower still. Her heartbeat quickened, echoing in his ears, matching the pace of his own. He was acutely aware of her, of everything about her. Of the celestial magic flowing through her veins, calling to him like a siren's song, of the way her full lips barely parted, like she was waiting to be kissed.

He held out his hand to her.

Novalise scowled at his proffered hand.

"I don't need your help, my lord. I am perfectly capable of exiting a fountain on my own."

She clutched her skirts, lifting them to reveal miles of silky flesh. Then she hiked one leg over the ledge of the fountain. Planting both hands on the edge, she teetered back and forth, on the verge of falling back in, before she finally heaved herself out onto the path. Her breath left her in a rush and she staggered forward, but one of her heels wedged itself between the crevice of the stone pathway. Sighing, she slipped her foot out, and abandoned the shoe completely. She looked half-drowned, like she'd been dunked into a tub of water or washed up on the shore after a shipwreck. The sodden gown clung to her, leaving little to the imagination, and her lavender hair fell around her, plastered to all of her curves. Kohl was smeared beneath her eyes, but the glimmering water made her look as though she'd been forged from the stars.

She cast him a withering glance over her shoulder, and when she realized he was staring, her gaze sharpened.

"What?" she asked, thoroughly exasperated.

Asher shoved his hands into his pockets to keep himself from dragging her against him and kissing that scowl off her pretty face. "Just thinking."

"About?"

"About whether I want to kiss you again or..." He closed the distance between them in two strides. Her answering gasp was near breathless and when her starlit gaze landed on his mouth, it took everything in his power to keep him from devouring her whole.

"Or?" she prompted softly, her tongue darting along her bottom lip, causing Asher's blood to burn.

"Or whether I want to toss you back into that fountain."

"Oh, piss off." Novalise whirled away from him and started back up the path through the garden, her gait uneven with the loss of one shoe.

Asher let out a low whistle, admiring the distinctive sway of her hips. "Impressive. I never knew Lady Novalise Starstorm had such a mouth on her."

This time when she turned back to face him, it was slow. Intentional. Her smile was pure seduction laced with poison. "Yes. And it can do more than just spout off naughty words, too."

Without warning, images slammed into his mind. The smooth velvet of her skin beneath the palm of his hands. Her waves of lavender hair splayed over his black silk pillows. Hips moving to meet his every thrust. Stars bursting between them in a shower of midnight flames. Nails scouring his back. That mouth of hers taking every last inch of him.

But then she was up on that dais again, looking like she was crafted from porcelain. Fragile. Breakable. Nothing at all like the faultless projection she displayed to the rest of the world.

Asher rocked back onto his heels, wondering what could've caused her emotions to swell with disquiet, to leave her trembling with dread. The apprehension growing within her had nearly strangled him. Only when he worried she might actually collapse did he slip into her mind to calm her. "Do you want to tell me what happened back there?"

He nodded toward the observatory in the distance, and her face instantly shuttered.

"Why? So you can ridicule me?" Her voice broke, and it wrecked something inside of him. She wrapped her arms around herself, her pace slow and uneven as she hobbled up the path. Long shadows crawled over her, and she shivered. "So you can tell me I'm nothing but a spoiled princess who didn't get her way?"

Asher strolled toward her, casually flicking his wrist so a sphere of black and silver flames erupted in his palm. Magic throbbed through the air as he manipulated the flames into a glowing orb of heat that followed Novalise, warming her. "What do you mean, you didn't get your way?"

"I mean…" Her eyes followed the orb of faerie fire as it encircled her, the corners of her mouth barely lifting before turning down once more. Another sigh escaped her, and her shoulders fell. "I mean, I lost everything, my lord. Now leave me alone."

Nope. That wasn't going to happen. He was too invested.

"There's a number of things you could lose. Your shoe, for example." He dropped onto a bench beneath an overhang of wisteria blossoms. "Care to be more specific?"

She fisted her hands on her hips. "Are you always so intolerable?"

"I suppose that depends." He stretched his legs out, crossing one ankle over the other. "Are you always so dramatic?"

"You really have no idea, do you?" Novalise was pacing now, her steps fitful and uneven. She paused, yanked off her other shoe, and tossed it into the gardens. "My star reading was disastrous."

Asher bit the inside of his cheek. He didn't believe in star readings or signs, but figured now probably wasn't the best time to mention it.

"You're right," he mused, tucking his hands behind his head. "You didn't get your way, but it's not the end of the world. You can control your own destiny."

Novalise gaped at him. "No, I can't. That's the one thing I have no control over."

"Says who?" he countered.

"Everyone."

"Everyone meaning your mother?" He hit his mark and her mouth snapped shut.

She dropped onto the bench beside him. Moonlight flickered through the wisteria, highlighting the iridescent water on her face. It was like liquid stardust. Slowly, he reached out and gently swiped his thumb along her cheek. She usually projected radiance. Confidence. But now, she looked crestfallen, as though everything she loved had been taken from her.

Asher leaned back, letting his hand drop. "What happened in the observatory?"

"I already told you." Her face pinched in anguish. "I—"

"No." He grabbed her hand, smooth and unmarred, soft against the calluses of his skin. "Tell me what happened before your reading."

"I don't know." Again, her perfectly crafted exterior faltered, and for a moment, he saw the shadow of fear lurking beneath the surface of her flawless skin. "I've had this burning doubt in the back of my mind, like this ever-present sense of dread."

She ducked her chin, angling her face away from his view. "For a moment, I thought it was you."

He couldn't blame her. Not really. The bond ensured they felt each other's emotions with astute clarity. Yet over the past few days, his emotions had ranged from harbored resentment to plain disregard. Which could only mean her feelings were more substantial.

"And then up on the dais, with everyone staring at me, I started panicking." Novalise rubbed her lips together, hastily swiping away the smudges of kohl beneath her eyes. "I was so close to having everything I wanted, but all this anxiety bubbled to the surface. It was like I was drowning, like I couldn't get to the surface for air. My palms were sweating, my chest was tight, the blood was rushing in my ears, so loud I couldn't hear anyone or anything."

She inhaled a shaky breath, her gaze sliding to him. "Until you."

Asher couldn't tell her she nearly broke him. That seeing her fracture left him undone. It was something he could hardly admit to himself. "You looked terrified."

"I was…" She startled, jolting up from the bench. She stared at him, wide-eyed. "Oh gods, what if that's why?"

Asher stood, a line of concern furrowing across his brow. "I don't follow."

"I wasn't strong enough to accept my fate. I'm not worthy of being the next Reader of Stars." She pointed a finger at him, bottom lip trembling. "You knew it. You told me so yourself."

The reminder of his insult was a punch to the gut. "Novalise..."

"The stars knew it, too. That's why my destiny changed. That's why I'm standing in a garden, soaked to the bone, with no shoes, crying to the one male who doesn't want me." Pure heartbreak was etched into the smooth planes of her face. "I'm not good enough."

The tears started falling. Hard and fast.

Shit.

He grabbed her by the shoulders, hauling her close. He hated the way she shook in his arms. Hated himself for caring. "Listen to me. You *are* the stars."

Cupping her cheeks with his hands, he leaned forward, pressing his forehead to hers.

Her nearness set his soul on fire.

Again, the beating of her heart belonged solely to him. Her breath, every inhale, every exhale, was an extension of his own. His magic strained for her, pined for her. The longer he held her in his arms, the more difficult it would be to walk away.

With one finger, he traced the constellation of stars on her skin. The flesh right above her heart was soft, like velvet. "You bear Estrela's crown. You were born with the constellation of it tattooed upon your flesh. The magic of the stars courses through your veins."

Her palms came to rest on his chest, her fingers curling into the dampened fabric of his shirt. The bond drew her closer to him, reeling her in. Magic pulsed around them, causing the air to thicken with undercurrents of desire. But the attraction was superficial, forged by the unfortunate connection between them.

Such a clever reminder wasn't enough to keep his arms from

sliding from her shoulders to her waist, dragging her against him. She was warm and pliant in his arms, melting into him. He wanted to peel off every layer of damp clothing, to feel her move against him like silk, to hear her gasps and moans of pleasure.

She rose up on her toes, leaning into him.

Gods, he wanted to kiss her.

"What do I do, my lord?" Her whisper floated between them.

Steeling his reserve, Asher bent forward. He pressed his lips to the corner of her mouth, breathing in the intoxicating scent of her. Faint rose, dark berries, and lush vanilla. Then he pulled back and brushed his thumb along the line of her full bottom lip.

"Prove your worth," he murmured, releasing her completely. The space between them was suddenly cold. Empty and desolate.

Asher forced himself to step back. "Defy the stars."

Novalise stared at him, bewildered. He turned around, away from her, and headed back up the path toward House Celestine. She watched him go, he could feel her eyes boring into his back. But it was nothing compared to the frenzied desperation of the invisible thread binding them together. Each step was a knife to the heart, a painful agony that caused his chest to ache.

She deserved to be with someone who could love her, with someone who actually accepted mating bonds. And definitely not with someone who would rather be chained in iron for the rest of his days than be shackled to a female who believed in the very thing responsible for his mother's death.

The stars had claimed his mother would only have one love for the whole of her life. She'd loved Asher's father uncondi-tionally, and his father...well, he loved wine, doling out vicious punishments, and the company of other females. When his father died, it ruined his mother, and she followed his demise shortly after.

Love for her children, for Asher and Cyra, was obviously not enough for her.

Asher shoved his hands into the pockets of his pants and ducked his head, putting as much distance as possible between himself and Novalise. It didn't matter if every time he closed his eyes he saw a world of midnight flames and glittering stars. There was only one logical thing to do.

He had to find a way to break the bond.

CHAPTER SEVEN

*T*he stars lied.

Disappointment sank its claws into Novalise's spine.

Again, Lord Asher Firebane had walked away from her.

Disheartened and dejected once more, Novalise trudged back up the sloping mountainside. Her family's home was built into the side of the Moonfall Peaks, as close as one could get to the heavens. Open air corridors lined with ivory pillars met in pointed arches where constellations were etched into frosted glass windows. Crystal stars floated along the ceiling in every hall, illuminating the blue goldstone floors like the night sky. Outside, the house was like twilight watercolors, bleeding in shades from the deepest purple to turquoise. Curving spires pierced the low-lying clouds and winding staircases led to sweeping balconies that overlooked the gardens and all of Celestine—the city of stars.

The sight of it always managed to leave her a little breathless.

Except this time, she was struggling to breathe because her feet were bare and aching, she was drenched in liquid stardust, and every step Lord Firebane took caused her heart to yank in agony.

Overhead, the silhouette of carriages being pulled by Eponians passed through the clouds and dull moonlight. The winged horses were majestic against the catastrophic sky of falling stars. At least everyone was finally leaving, no doubt heading to Queen Elowyn's palace for the lifting of the Veil. Perhaps they would have forgotten all about her botched star reading once the opening of the Season was underway. Then maybe if she was lucky, she could avoid the snide remarks and pitying glances.

All she needed now was for Lord Firebane to take to Ember-spire so she wouldn't have to face him again. He was hardly one to relish in the frivolities of court, much less the Season. His sister, however, seemed far more interested in participating in all the seasonal activities. Even if he wasn't already on his way back home, the lifting of the Veil was an immense celebration. It would be crowded with fae from all over Aeramere, not to mention all the visitors from neighboring kingdoms and realms. She supposed there was as good a chance as any, that even if Lady Cyra did force him to attend, Novalise wouldn't even see him.

It wasn't nearly as intimate of a gathering as her reading.

A tiny sigh of relief escaped her.

The threshold to her house was empty save for the two guards positioned on either side of the vaulted door, and though she was keenly aware of their gazes tracking her every movement, she knew they wouldn't alert anyone to her pres-ence. If she was careful, she could avoid running into any of her family members at all.

Novalise slipped through the towering door as silently as possible, only to find herself in the brightly lit entry hall where it seemed as though a spotlight had been cast upon her. Twin spiral staircases leading to the second level split the entrance in half and standing in the center, on the inlaid crest of House Celestine, was Ariesian, Solarius, and her mother.

Gathering up the shredded remnants of her courage, Novalise padded toward them. There were no alcoves in this room, nowhere to hide away and wait for them to leave.

She put on a brave face, trying not to wince when they caught sight of her.

Her mother saw her first. "Fates divine! My darling girl, are you alright?"

"Novalise." Ariesian took one look at her torn gown, at her disheveled appearance, and pure rage erupted in his eyes. His magic, a raw and powerful expanse of shadows and stars, permeated the air. The entire house seemed to shudder beneath the force of his might.

"What happened?" he demanded. "Who did this to you?"

"No one did anything to me." She attempted to smooth her hair, spraying droplets of iridescent silver everywhere. It was confounding how males were so concerned with *who* hurt her instead of caring about *how* she was feeling. "I lost my balance and fell into one of the fountains in the garden."

Disbelief hardened the lines of his stern brow. "I see."

"Nova, it's good to see you've got some of your color back." Solarius stepped out from behind their oldest brother, a crooked smile on his face. "You were looking at little unwell before the reading."

She wouldn't tell them the real reason her cheeks were flushed. In fact, she wouldn't think of Lord Firebane again. Absently, she rubbed the spot on her chest where he'd traced Estrela's crown. The binding between them twisted, a painful reminder of his dismissal, and she bit her bottom lip to keep from crying.

"Do not worry, my sweet child." Trysta bustled forward, mistaking the pain of heartbreak for humiliation. The bangles on her wrists jingled along with the swishing of her skirts. "I'm sure the stars will sort themselves out eventually. Until then, you will continue to carry on, as you've always done."

Ariesian studied Novalise, his face a mask of his true emotions, but it was Solarius who offered her his arm. "Are you well enough to attend the lifting of the Veil? If not, I will gladly escort you back to your rooms."

"Of course she'll go." Trysta waved one hand through the air, easily dismissing the notion. "She'll have to clean up, and she'll need a new dress, but Novalise wouldn't dare miss such an important opportunity."

"Opportunity?" Novalise echoed as another tremor of anxiety itched its way across her skin.

"We can't allow the misfortune of your star reading to set us back." Ariesian adjusted the cuffs on his shirt, then straightened his coat. He was impeccable, the epitome of nobility. "You are the eldest daughter of the Starstorm fae and of age. Queen Elowyn and Mother have already set a date for your impending wedding. Therefore, it stands to reason you will still be required to marry by the end of the Season."

In other words, she was expected to pretend as though her entire world wasn't tossed upside down. To act like all she was promised hadn't been ripped away from her. She would do it, of course. She would go through the motions, continue to smile and be obliging, because she always did exactly as she was told. She abided by the rules, never stepped out of line. Just like the eight-pointed star beneath her bare feet, she knew her direction, understood her purpose. She would wed by the end of the Season, but with no guidance from the celestial skies, Ariesian and her mother would choose her mate for her.

Unless Novalise found one on her own.

Defy the stars.

Lord Firebane's words echoed in the far recesses of her mind.

She trembled, shaking the warmth of his voice from her thoughts.

"Solarius." Her mother's prim voice cut through the air. "Take your sister upstairs and ensure she's presentable for the opening of the Season. The rest of us will leave for the palace. We don't want to be late for the lifting of the Veil, and we'll meet the two of you there once Novalise is ready to attend."

Solarius bowed. "As you wish, Mother."

Ariesian stalked off without a backward glance while their mother followed closely behind, shaking her head and murmuring to herself until their footfalls faded completely.

Novalise climbed the stairs to her room, careful to avoid eye contact with any passing servants. But her gaze snagged on Solarius.

"Do you think he's mad at me?" she asked, stealing a look at him from beneath her damp tresses. "I know there's a considerable weight upon his shoulders and I feel like I've only added to it, what with my blunder of a reading and now having to find a husband."

"Mad at you? Never." Solarius shook his head and wisps of silver hair fell across his brow. "Ariesian is under considerable stress, yes, but not because of you. If anything, I think he's more agitated with himself for not preparing for every possible outcome. We all foolishly assumed the reading would foretell your mate, especially since you were originally promised everlasting love at your birth. Now it's Ariesian's duty to find you a potential match and if I know anything, it's that the well-being and happiness of a most beloved younger sister is not something he takes lightly."

Novalise paused in the corridor, a few feet from her bedroom. "He's worried I'll be unhappy?"

Solarius strode past her and opened the door, gesturing for her to enter. "He's worried he'll be the one at fault for making you unhappy. It's an important task, marrying you off. I imagine most older brothers would only care about the impending benefits like trade, fortified alliances, and things of that nature. But Ariesian is not like most. He cares for *you*."

"Because I was promised a love match."

Her brother simply flashed another boyish smile and said nothing. She stepped into the room where a new gown and shoes were already waiting for her.

"Freshen up and dress quickly." Solarius nodded toward the bathing suite. "I'll wait for you downstairs and then we'll ride to the palace together."

Novalise scrubbed herself clean in the copper basin and when she finished, two maids were already waiting to help her dress. The gown was navy blue and strapless with a fitted bodice that cut to her waist. From there, the skirts ballooned out into puffy layers of periwinkle silk and a train of shimmering lace overlay trailed behind her. It was excessive and ostentatious, undoubtedly the work of her mother. The maids pulled her thick hair into place, braiding it off her shoulders, then pinning it into place with hairpins of moonstone and pearls. They helped her into a pair of heels that pinched her toes, and when she finally ventured back downstairs, Solarius was there waiting for her. Exactly as he promised.

"Sister." He tucked her hand into the crook of his elbow. "How is it possible for you to look even lovelier than ever?"

She let her head fall onto his shoulder. "Dare I say magic?"

He grinned, then led her out the front entrance of the house to where a carriage was out front, waiting to take them away to Queen Elowyn's palace.

The pair of winged stallions stomped at the earth, tossing their heads with impatience. Their midnight coats glistened like onyx as they stretched their wings. The Eponians were a gift to every house from the Skyhelm fae of House Galefell, since no faeries within Aeramere had wings of their own. Though Novalise had heard stories about fae in other realms possessing wings, she wasn't entirely certain if it was true. Not even the Skyhelm fae had been gifted with the blessing of flight, though their command of the wind and skies lent them quite the advantage.

Solarius helped her into the carriage, and she slid onto the sleek leather cushion as he took the seat across from her. Once the door was securely closed, there was a rumbling like the call of thunder, and the Eponians took to the night sky. The ground vanished from beneath them, giving way to moonlit clouds and mountain peaks. Novalise peered out the window as the landscape shifted from the twinkling illumination of Celestine to the rich, jewel tones of Emberspire's city. Novalise had heard stories about waterfalls and faerie pools located deep within the surrounding lush forest.

Her heart twinged within the tight walls of her chest at the sight.

More than anything, she hoped the fates would be on her side for the remainder of the night. She didn't want to see Lord Firebane again. She didn't want to feel the constant pull to him, she didn't want to suffer through the persistent longing to be near him. It was positively excruciating. Maybe it was good for her to attend the start of the Season. Perhaps Ariesian would find her a mate tonight, someone who wouldn't discard her like she was nothing more than a thorn in his side. Certainly, a love match would be strong enough to sever the futile bond between herself and Lord Firebane.

She never should've kissed him on Winter Solstice beneath Caelian's enchanted mistletoe.

Solarius leaned forward in the seat across from her, resting his elbows on his knees. "Are you sure you're okay? I can ask the coachman to turn us around."

Novalise almost told him, she almost opened her mouth and told him that no, she would never be okay because Asher, her mate, had rejected her. She sucked her bottom lip under her teeth to keep it from trembling, to keep from telling her brother the one thing she was destined for would never belong to her.

Instead, she offered him one of her best, most practiced smiles. "I'll be fine. Thank you, Sol."

A line formed across his brow, as though he didn't believe her. But then he leaned back and pressed the subject no further.

Glancing out the window once more, Novalise dared to look up at the sky. It was the same as before. Shooting stars, hazy clouds, and chaotic constellations.

Novalise settled back against the soft leather of the bench. Soon enough, all would be right in her world, even as a tiny, insignificant voice continued to whisper in the back of her mind.

Defy the stars.

CHAPTER EIGHT

*A*sher had every intention of leaving House Celestine and returning home, but Cyra had other plans. She'd dragged him into a carriage and they'd taken flight, joining the other fae at the queen's palace for the start of the Season.

Tonight was no different, though the queen seemed intent on outdoing herself year after year. The theme looked to be an enchanted forest, and no expense was spared to ensure everyone attending the revelry for Midsummer was both dazzled and overwhelmed. Each fae in the realm who was available for pairing was forced to wear a crown. The males were given wreaths of laurel with gold-dipped leaves while the females donned circlets of roses and peonies.

Asher scowled as Cyra placed the crown of laurel on his head.

Music floated through the woods and glowing faerie lights of soft blue and green danced upon the ground, illuminating the paths into the surrounding forest where the Veil glimmered like a thin layer of gossamer. In the shadows of the beyond stood clusters of figures and carriages, the outlines of people from other realms waiting to gain entry to Aeramere. Lanterns of faerie fire hung from archways formed by trees, their trunks wrapped in vines of crawling ivy, while flowers of pale purple and white cascaded around them. Streams of turquoise wound their way through the forest, the riverbeds filled with smooth stones that sparkled in the reflection of moonlight. Woodland creatures darted in and out of the shadows, tempting partygoers with their adorable faces and fluffy tails.

Cyra was no exception. She reached down to pet a passing chipmunk as it scampered away from a group of fae children attempting to lure it with handfuls of acorns.

"This is ridiculous," Asher muttered, carefully avoiding making eye contact with any eligible female in their general vicinity. "I shouldn't have to wear this absurd crown if I have no intention of marrying."

Cyra ignored his complaints.

"Let's just hope this isn't a disaster like Lady Starstorm's reading." She adjusted her crown of white roses, ensuring not a petal was out of place. Her gaze swept through the forest, then up the small hill where the queen's palace was set against a backdrop of sage mountains. "Then again, I heard she already has a line of suitors waiting to court her, so—"

"Sorry?" Asher coughed, smacking his chest with his fist to quell the sudden rise of anger flaring there. "What did you say?"

"Lady Novalise Starstorm," Cyra repeated, oblivious to his increasing vexation. "Honestly, Ash. It's like half the time your mind is in another world altogether."

Asher dismissed her valid accusation with a wave of his hand. "You mentioned something about suitors?"

"Yes, it's most likely she'll have a surplus of them." There was a tinge of jealousy in his sister's tone. But then she sighed, and it vanished. Cyra pursed her lips, tapping one finger to the corner of her mouth. "Since her star reading was a failure, males from all over Aeramere will try to win her hand. If you ask me, I think they only want her for her magic."

"Why the sudden interest?" That burn of anger morphed into a ravenous, gnawing pang of resentment. "In her, I mean."

Not that he should care. Because he didn't. At all.

"Do you live under a rock?" Cyra's brows pinched together and she shook her head, her wild red hair tumbling around her. "Novalise is the eldest daughter of House Celestine. Since the stars didn't reveal her true match, she's fair game. She can read the stars, and I imagine her magic is exceptionally powerful. Not only that, but her brother is a High Councilor to Queen Elowyn. She's an ideal mate for anyone with something to gain, which means every male in Aeramere wants their opportunity to wed and bed her."

"Not a chance," Asher growled. Blinding wrath stole through him and the source of it was that damned bond. He didn't want to care about her, he didn't want to have anything to do with her, yet he wanted to rip the head off any male who dared to look her way.

"Agreed." Cyra was flippant, completely unsuspecting of the fact that Asher was about to erupt with untempered fury. "None of the males here stand a chance against anyone coming to Aeramere for the Season."

His gut hollowed out. The fire inside him turned to ice. "You think there will be more competition?"

"Absolutely. Novalise is like a rare jewel." Cyra strolled closer toward the forest's edge where the queen and her royal guard were gathering in preparation, motioning for him to follow. "She's coveted."

There was a tug as the invisible thread binding him to Novalise pulled taut. Then it yanked. Hard.

He whipped around, only to see Novalise standing back behind them, ensconced by the tightly knit circle of her family.

Their gazes locked and it was rapturous.

His blood sang, and his magic raced toward hers in a reckless collision of black flames and bursting stars. He wanted her, all of her. He wanted to take her away from this extravagant gathering and drag her deep into the forest, where only the most ancient trees would be privy to their darkest secrets. Beneath the cover of moonlit branches and overgrowth, he'd unravel every layer of her, starting with that elaborate dress, until she came undone in his arms. Desire filled him, lording its might over him. The bond sizzled and sparked, alive with energy. A blush bled into her cheeks as she stared back at him, as he imagined laying her down in a shallow stream, cradling her on a bed of smooth river stones, and driving himself into her over and over again until she forgot her name.

Asher's cock throbbed, urging him to make good on his imaginary promises. He took a step forward to do just that when someone snagged his arm.

He blinked, Novalise looked away, and the spell was broken.

Cyra held onto him, her eyes lit with curiosity. Her gaze darted back and forth between him and Novalise. "How did you know that Lady Novalise was behind us when—"

A surge of relief spread through him as his sister's inquisitive nature was silenced by the blaring of horns announcing the start of the ceremony.

Queen Elowyn glided toward the forest's edge, flanked by six guards on each side. Her golden crown shaped like twigs and embedded with shimmering topaz glinted in the wash of moonlight. Slowly, she turned to her subjects. Despite the rush of excitement spreading through the crowd, her face remained impassive.

"Welcome, everyone, to the annual Midsummer Season." Her eloquent voice coasted over them as tendrils of woodsy, earthy magic unraveled in the air. A radiant aura glittered around her as she spoke and her magic billowed. "As many of you know, the tradition of lifting the Veil began years ago in an effort to promote peace and prosperity between our land and neighboring realms. What started off as a celebration of the summer season soon became a fortnight of marriage proposals, alliances, and dare I say, love."

Applause erupted while Asher casually stood with his hands shoved in the pockets of his pants.

Love was a tragic sentiment, promising only heartbreak and misery.

"Tonight marks the beginning of a festival spanning fourteen wondrous days." The queen's smile held an edge, like she was privy to a secret. "Without further ado, let the Season begin!"

Cheering rang in Asher's ears as Queen Elowyn faced the forest. The Veil was a strange and magical thing, a faintly iridescent, translucent shield that spilled over every corner of Aeramere. No one could enter and no one could leave, not without express consent from the queen. He watched as she raised both arms, creating an opening within the Veil. Ribbons of magic rippled and pulled, shifting so an elaborate entrance took form with illuminated pillars and dancing orbs of faerie fire.

The music crescendoed and dozens of bodies filed in through the pulsing gates. There were mortals from human kingdoms clad in their most expensive attire. Some arrived on horseback or in carriages, their trunks loaded with gifts and offerings to earn Queen Elowyn's favor. Other creatures mingled among them, humans who weren't quite mortal at all. Asher spied a handful of witches, unmistakable given the way their scarlet cloaks swirled around them, and the way the other humans gave them an exceptionally wide berth. Fae from other realms arrived as well, many he didn't recognize. It was a conglomerate of the occult and mystical, all coalescing together under the unbearable impression of finding a mate.

Or at the very least, pretending to want one.

There was no doubt in Asher's mind that some partygoers in attendance were merely here to sleep with as many willing participants as possible, then leave once the Season ended without another thought.

At least that was a concept he could support.

Having sex purely for the intent of pleasure and release made sense. It was when one started to confuse the idea of lust with affection that things got complicated.

Asher stole a glance at his younger sister.

Cyra's eyes were wide, full of hope and anticipation. For a moment, she resembled the image of their mother, before her infatuation with the stars and the false prophecy that she would only ever have one love got her killed.

He would do whatever he could to protect Cyra from the same fate. Marriage didn't need to have intimacy or romance to work. It could be based around more logical wants and needs, like communication, compromise, and maybe even friendship. To assume that a marriage would only be successful if love was the focus was asinine.

"There he is," Cyra breathed, the awe in her voice drawing his attention back to the festivities around them. "He actually came."

"Who?" Asher scanned the forest, but Cyra pointed to the skies.

"Prince Drake Kalstrand of Brackroth."

Asher lifted his gaze and something acidic settled in his gut. Sure enough, cutting through the clouds folded across the sky was the silhouette of a dragon. It swooped down low, sending a gust of warm wind barreling through the forest. The force of it battered the treetops, causing the lanterns hanging from the branches to flicker in fear. Its body was covered in diamond-shaped scales as black as obsidian. Wings of the same color stretched wide, with dagger-sharp claws protruding from the tips of its wings. Spines lined its whipping tail and two horns protruded from its head, where pale yellow eyes glowed like the first breath of a flame. The beast circled overhead, releasing a deafening cry, drawing the attention of every soul in attendance. And atop its back sat a rider, cloaked in darkness and shadows.

Drake Kalstrand. The Shadow Assassin of Brackroth.

There were gasps and shouts as the dragon lowered itself to the ground, taking up residence in a clearing entirely too close to where Novalise was standing. The prince jumped down from his dragon, his sharp gaze unnerving all those who dared to move close for a better look. He tugged off his riding gloves, shoving them in his back pocket. Power emanated from him, dark and merciless. Fae and humans alike took a collective step back, parting for him like he was some kind of god, with shadows following in his wake. He strode through the path they made for him, heading straight for Novalise.

"See?" Cyra yanked on the sleeve of his shirt. "I told you. Novalise Starstorm's failed star reading has made her the most sought-after female in Aeramere. Even Prince Drake thinks so."

Asher watched in dismay as Novalise adjusted the crown of pale pink peonies on top of her head, her eyes following Prince Drake's every move. But when the shadow prince stormed right past her and headed for Ariesian, clasping the fae lord's hand in greeting, Asher's paranoia lessened.

Barely.

Novalise seemed enraptured. Not once did she glance at the flock of males surrounding her, eyeing her like she was a piece of freshly ripened fruit. She paid them no mind. Only Prince Drake held her captivated.

Damn it.

Absolutely not.

There was no way he could allow Novalise to attach herself to the Prince of Brackroth. He was powerful and dangerous. Vile. He relished in the chaotic, he hunted in the shadows. The male was born without morals, willing to perform the darkest of deeds if it meant he remained in control. Drake was a trained killer, proficient in the art of death, skilled to never leave a trace behind. Only he was arrogant enough to flaunt his reputation.

Asher shook his head.

He would have to talk to Ariesian. Novalise's eldest brother was sensible. Rational. He would explain to Ariesian that the prince was a poor match, that Novalise deserved someone more mundane. Someone who wouldn't use her for her magic, someone *she* could control.

Right. That's exactly what he would do.

Asher would warn Ariesian about Prince Drake, find her someone more suited to be her mate, then he could purge Novalise from his life for good.

With that, he yanked the absurd crown of laurel from his head and tossed it to the ground.

CHAPTER NINE

*N*ovalise had never seen such a magnificent beast. Nor had she seen such a magnificent man. The dragon itself was intimidating, sleek and stunning, a most fearsome creature to behold. But its rider? He was terrifying. He acted as though he owned the night, like he stole the sunlight wherever he walked, like the dawn trembled in his presence. Like death was his closest friend. She could've sworn he was a human and yet he wasn't quite…mortal.

There was something otherworldly about him.

He wore all black, from the leather armor protecting his muscular build to his boots with studs along the toe. Silver stitching was emblazoned across his chest, taking the shape of a fearsome dragon. A blood-red sash lined his trim waist, and tiny onyx daggers pierced both of his ears. Linked chains draped from his shoulders, clinking softly in the silence that followed him. His brows were drawn into a scowl and a scar cut through the one on the left. He had a stern yet smooth jawline and prominent cheekbones that were slightly flushed from the wind. Hair the color of the darkest night slanted across his forehead, messy and unkempt, as he shoved a hand through it, walking toward Ariesian.

Then he paused, but only for a moment. It was barely anything at all, nothing more than a brief passing of time, but his gaze flicked to her. A cursory once over. But long enough for Novalise to commit the color of his eyes to her memory— evergreen and ringed with pale gold, like a mysterious forest shrouded in a layer of fine mist. Cold and bleak. Mysterious. Haunted, even.

A delicious shiver of excitement and something akin to fright slid down her spine.

Everyone moved out of his way as he passed. Not out of respect, out of fear.

Solarius stepped up to her side, angling himself so he was directly in front of her. Blocking her from the newcomer's view. The dragon rider approached Ariesian and Novalise gripped Solarius's arm, expecting the worst.

"Kalstrand," Ariesian murmured, bowing. She'd only witnessed her brother bow to the queen. Not once had he bowed before anyone else. Ever.

"Starstorm." The striking male inclined his head.

She watched as they gripped each other's forearms in greeting. Ariesian didn't look angry, nor did he look pleased. Instead, his reaction was effortlessly calm. He kept his face schooled into one of complete neutrality, never wavering beneath the heavy weight of all those who stared at him.

Conversation and music slowly returned to life, drowning out the murmurs and whispers that hummed below the surface like an annoying insect. Novalise rose up on her toes and whispered to Solarius, "Who is that?"

"That, dear sister, is Drake Kalstrand, Prince of Brackroth." He leaned toward her, lowering his voice, all the while never taking his eyes off Ariesian. "The Shadowblade Assassin."

She smothered her gasp behind the back of her hand. "Are you serious?"

She'd heard rumors of their existence, that Shadowblade Assassins wielded blades so powerful, one strike was the same as a killing blow. There was no cure. No recovery. Poison filled the victim's bloodstream, turning their veins black, ruining them from the inside out until they died a most slow and painful death. The assassins moved like wraiths in the night, blending with the shadows, skilled in stealth and combat. No one ever saw them coming and no one ever saw them leave. It would appear, however, that the Prince of Brackroth was the only one left.

Another tremor jolted through her.

"Quite serious," Solarius muttered, snatching a frothy beer from the tray of one of the queen's servants.

Novalise peered around her brother to catch another glimpse of the assassin prince. He was in a deep, rather serious conversation with Ariesian, judging by the grave look on his face. Ariesian nodded once, considering whatever Prince Drake said, but Novalise didn't miss the way her brother's gaze cut across the rising hill to the palace.

"What do you suppose he's doing here?" Novalise shifted, a knot of dread forming in her stomach. The crowd of people around them was swelling and needles of anxiety pierced her, heightening her awareness. She clasped her hands before her, giving the appearance of mild interest. But in truth, she laced her fingers together tightly, and squeezed until her knuckles turned white.

"Well, if I had to guess, I assume he's here to do what's expected of him." Solarius took a healthy swig of beer, surveying the enchanted forest. His mouth pressed into a hard line. "Find a wife."

"You think so?"

"I do. The Prince of Brackroth isn't known for wasting his time on social frivolities." He stared down into the glass, gently swirling the amber liquid. "If he's not here to take a bride, then it's possible he came to negotiate trade or an alliance of some kind."

"Hm." How curious. A flicker of an idea glimmered to life in her mind.

"If you'd excuse me, Nova." Solarius bowed and she released his arm. "I have a few matters to attend."

"Of course." Novalise barely had time to respond. She nodded, slightly jarred by her brother's abrupt departure. It wasn't in his nature to abandon her mid-conversation.

But the moment Solarius left her, his loss was immediately occupied by four males. Two she recognized from House Galefell, another from House Terensel, and not surprisingly, Lord Reif Marintide.

He maneuvered his way to the front of the group, elbowing those in his path to reach her.

"My lady." He snatched her hand, pressing a firm kiss upon her knuckles.

Her spine stiffened at his nearness. She would not be so foolish as to fall for his charms again.

"My lord." Novalise forced herself to smile, setting her teeth on edge.

"Lady Novalise." One of the males moved closer, nudging Reif out of the way, and she used the opportunity to yank her hand from his hold. "Would you care to dance?"

"Oh, I—"

"No, she does not. She's already promised me the first dance." Reif stood in front of her, glowering at the opposing male. His green eyes hardened. "Perhaps you should go find another female with a shorter skirt to chase. This one is out of your league."

"I made no such promise to you." Novalise attempted to scold him, but her words lacked conviction, coming out of her mouth as nothing more than a harsh whisper.

The four males were crowding around her, smothering her, vying for her attention.

The lanky male from Galefell shifted himself to the forefront of the circle, nearly stepping on her gown in the process. She clutched at her skirts, yanking the train out of the way. Her damp palms crushed the fine fabric, wrinkling it in the process. "My lady, since your star reading revealed no answer, are you still in the market for a mate?"

She bit the inside of her cheek so hard, the thick tang of metal coated her tongue.

"Y-yes." Tugging at her gown, she stumbled back a step, trying to put some distance between herself and the overbearing would-be suitors. "That is the proper course of action."

Ambition shone bright in his eyes.

"How wonderful," he murmured, his gaze dropped to the constellation marking her heart, then lingered on the fullness of her breasts.

Novalise shrank into her skin. It was suddenly too hot. Beads of sweat glided down her back, the fluffy layers of silk clung to her slick skin. She was positively stifling. She tried to swallow the burn of alarm, but her throat was dry, like she'd been forced to gulp a bucket full of sand. "I suppose it would seem that way to you."

"Don't be so offensive, Kyren. The lady isn't a prize to be won. There's far more to consider when choosing a mate than their appearance." It seemed as though the lone fae from House Terensel had come to her rescue. He shoved the male from Galefell out of the way, but then his smile sharpened. "Isn't that right, Lady Novalise?"

Anxiety twisted through her, like the tightening vines of writhing bane—death flowers with blossoms of black that wrapped around the trees deep within the forest, slowly strangling them until they died. She pressed her lips together, pleading with herself to maintain some semblance of composure.

"That's right," Reif snapped, his magic flaring like a tidal wave ready to sweep her out to sea. The air was charged with the scent of the ocean, of salt, brine, and sandalwood. "But the power Lady Novalise possesses is none of your concern. Her magic is her own, nothing the likes of you will ever control."

They continued to bicker about her as though she wasn't even there. Arguing about which one of them would be a more suitable husband, fighting over who stood more to gain from the marriage. Not once did they consider her feelings, instead they quarreled like she was a choice mare up for auction, going so far as to declare which house was more desperately in need of an heir. Love didn't matter to them. Mating bonds were never even mentioned. They carried on, contending with one another in a verbal sparring match, until the sound of their rising voices melded into a hostile discord.

"Well?" Reif demanded. He crossed his arms, expectant.

Novalise's heart pounded against the strict walls of her chest. Tension frayed the edges of her nerves, leaving her wrought with a bubbling sense of panic. "Well, what?"

Her voice was too breathy, her lungs were too tight.

"Your choice, my lady." One of the males of Galefell urged, impatience hardening his jaw.

"Ch-choice," she repeated softly, blinking rapidly as their imperious faces blurred in and out of focus.

Reif stepped closer and the others followed suit, swarming her until she could no longer focus. "Who do you choose, my lady? As your husband?"

Novalise's heart stuttered as alarm coursed through her, causing her knees to tremble.

"I..." Darkness crept in along the outskirts of her vision as the music faded and the ringing in her ears amplified. "I need a moment."

A second later, Novalise's body swayed of its own accord. Her floral crown slipped from her head, the petals fluttering around her slowly. Tingles spread throughout her and then she was falling, unable to save herself. Right before she hit the ground, she was swept into a pair of strong arms and lifted off her feet. Cushioned against a muscular chest, she inhaled the scent of frosted pine and cold mountains. It reminded her of gray winter skies, right before the first snowfall.

"I believe the lady said to back off." The masculine voice dripped with ice, his accent heavy, tainted by the Northernlands. "It would seem the males of Aeramere need to be taught a lesson. We do not harass females in Brackroth."

Brackroth.

Novalise held her breath and gradually tipped her head back, daring a glance at her rescuer. She was being carried by Prince Drake Kalstrand, the Shadowblade Assassin.

And *everyone* was staring at them.

Reif staggered backward into a low bow. "Deepest apologies, Your Highness. I can assure you that none of us meant Lady Novalise any harm."

The prince tightened his grip, keeping her close, his fingers digging into her thigh and waist. "If *any* of you come near her again, your death will belong to me."

The promise hung in the air, the words taking on a life of their own. If there was one thing Novalise knew about shadow assassins, it was that they kept every vow. They wasted no time with empty threats.

Reif paled, his bronze skin turning ashen. He didn't say another word, he simply continued to back away one small step after another, until he disappeared into the crowd completely.

Novalise peered up at the prince. "Thank you, Your Highness, but I'm feeling—"

His menacing gaze locked onto her, and she snapped her mouth shut. Prince Drake ignored her as he stormed through the cluster of people who'd gathered to witness her torment. He carried her past a clearing where dancers twirled beneath an overhang of ribbons and floating flowers. Not one of them moved. They were all frozen in the midst of their revelry, watching the renowned assassin as he gently set her down on a wooden bench covered in cushiony blossoms.

"Are you well?"

He may have meant it as a question, but it came out as more of a demand.

"I am." Or she would be, eventually. Novalise planted both hands on the edge of the bench in an effort to keep herself upright. Her head swam and nausea caused her stomach to roil. "Thank you, Your Highness."

"Are you certain?" He folded his arms across his chest, his brows drawn in contempt. "You look as though you might be ill."

"I'm not ill." Her nails bit into the soft wood. Damn him for seeing right through her. Though it probably didn't help that beads of sweat had formed along her forehead as well. She blew out a low breath. "I was overwhelmed."

"Indeed." He didn't look at her. Instead, he kept his gaze steeled upon the celebration, disdain marring his handsome features. "You looked as though you were drowning."

Interesting.

That was exactly how she'd felt at the time.

"Novalise!"

Her head jerked up at the calling of her name, and Ariesian appeared. He darted over to her, gently clasping the side of her face with one hand. Crouching before her, his silver gaze raked across her face, the blue flecks of his eyes nearly black. "Novalise, what happened?"

Before she could respond, Prince Drake cut Ariesian down

with a singularly caustic look. "You should be more mindful of your sister."

At the slight, Ariesian stood, clenching his jaw. The cordiality between them from before had evaporated, and he grew rigid. Austere. Drawing himself to his full height, he went head-to-head with the shadow prince. "I assure you, I'm fully aware of my sister's wellbeing. As well as the rest of my siblings."

"Then you should learn to read body language." Prince Drake took one step closer. "Because your sister was clearly in distress."

Novalise rolled her eyes to the star-ridden heavens. She was exhausted from having males argue over her and speaking for her, especially when they acted like she wasn't even there. Would this wretched night never end?

Pushing to her feet, she smoothed her excessive skirts, gliding effortlessly into the role of a lady from House Celestine. "Ariesian, if you have no objections, I think I'd like to return home now."

Her brother continued to face Prince Drake, the tension between them thick and palpable. If she wanted, she could stab at it with a sewing needle. After a few strained moments, Ariesian reluctantly jerked his head toward her. "If you so wish."

"Find her an escort," the prince demanded.

"I don't need an escort." Novalise moved to her brother's side and Ariesian's arm shot out, halting her from coming any closer. "I've moved freely within this realm my entire life. There is nowhere safer than Aeramere."

But the prince disregarded her completely, like she hadn't said a word. His eyes only darkened and energy crackled around them, causing her to shiver despite the warm night.

"An escort," he repeated to Ariesian, his voice low and ominous. "Or you can consider my business here done."

Ariesian's shoulders grew taut. His jaw clenched, and Novalise caught sight of the faintest twitch. Though his arms remained by his sides, his hands were curled into fists, and power throbbed around him in intimidating waves like midnight stars.

"Business?" Concern entangled Novalise. She couldn't imagine what sort of affairs her brother would need to conduct with the shadow prince. "What kind of business?"

"It is none of your concern, Novalise. Go home." Ariesian nodded, and Solarius was by her side a second later. "Solarius will escort you."

"I am not his charge." Novalise struggled to keep her voice from pitching, fought to maintain her flawless exterior, as was expected of her. She inhaled sharply. "I am not in need of a chaperone, Ariesian. I'm not—"

He whirled on her. Though his face concealed any emotion, his eyes were a torrent of fury. "You wished to leave, now do so." He enunciated each word with suppressed anger. "At once."

Shock radiated through her.

Never before had she witnessed Ariesian lose his temper. He was always calm and righteous, in constant command of his reactions. Whatever sort of contract he and Prince Drake intended to sanction, it must have been immensely significant.

Novalise backpedaled from him and Solarius quickly caught her hand, tucking it into the crook of his elbow, holding her in place.

"Shall we?" he whispered, his voice kind.

"Y-yes." Novalise nodded, ducking her head. "Of course."

"Come along then, darling sister." Solarius led her away from Ariesian and Prince Drake, both of whom had once again resumed their hostile staring contest. "Let us leave this tedious social gathering and find our own pursuits."

With her head held high, Novalise walked with Solarius

toward one of the waiting carriages. The Eponians stomped the soft grass, as though they too were annoyed by the whole ordeal. But an unwanted feeling of apprehension continued to poke at the back of her mind, needling itself deeper. She could only hope that Ariesian knew what he was doing, and that it was for the benefit of House Celestine, and not just himself.

CHAPTER TEN

"You can't hide in your study for all of Midsummer, Asher." Cyra's voice carried through the door, incessant and tinged with annoyance. She would rap the hardwood three times, then call his name, repeating the process as though he didn't hear her the first time.

"I'm not hiding."

In fact, he was doing quite the opposite. Solace within his study granted him a peace of mind, and it was a welcome distraction. A reprieve from the societal norms. Surrounded by books, spending hours reading and dissecting magical histories helped him make sense of the world. Not only that, but losing himself in the archaic helped to keep a certain female fae from clouding the forefront of his mind. Here, he was safe to dwell in his solitude. Faerie fire lights sparked to life in their stained glass enclosures along the wall and filled the space with a cool, silver glow.

Asher leaned back, and the leather chair groaned beneath his weight. He adjusted his black-framed spectacles—they'd been a gift from Cyra. She picked them up at one of the shops in Terensel. The lenses were forged from crystal dust, and coated with a fine layer of magic that assisted with deciphering runes. Stretching, he motioned toward his wall of ebony bookshelves, and the pile of books on the desk in front of him returned to their proper places among the shelves.

"You *are* hiding," Cyra insisted through the door. She rattled the knob with the impatience of a child. "It's been two days since Queen Elowyn lifted the Veil and I've scarcely seen you."

Asher made a noise of disbelief.

Two days, and Drake Kalstrand had yet to pay him a visit. It was only a matter of time until the shadow prince came knocking on his door, ready to demand the terms of Asher's repayment. Terms that he'd spent the last two years mulling over in his mind. He knew what Drake would require of him, and it wasn't as though Asher had been wasting his time since he last saw the prince. No, he'd been scouring books and poring over notes, researching as much as possible about the powerful gemstone Drake sought, including its potential whereabouts.

"I would've thought you dead were if not for the lingering scent of your magic," Cyra grumbled, her words echoing in the hall outside of his study.

"Not dead either," Asher called back.

"Would you please open the door?" His sister huffed in exasperation. "I feel like we're children again and you've locked me out of your bedroom to keep me from coloring inside one of your favorite books."

At this, Asher chuckled.

He'd been furious at the time. The book was a thoroughly detailed collection of wars through the ages with inked drawings and maps. Cyra had colored red hearts over half the continents and seen fit to give everyone purple crowns. At least now he could look back on it with a shred of humor.

"Fine." He waved his hand toward the door, and it unlocked. "Enter if you must."

Cyra waltzed into the room and posed, planting one hand on

her hip and lifting her chin to a stubborn angle. Her fiery hair fell over one shoulder. "Well?"

He studied her. "Well what?"

"What do you think?" This time she did a small twirl, spinning once.

"I think about a great many things, as is my nature."

Her brows drew together and the scent of golden amber, apple blossom, and creamy sandalwood filled the air. "Of my dress, Asher."

He gathered up the papers on his desk and shuffled them together, sparing her a brief glance. "It's lovely."

"You didn't even notice, did you?"

There was pain in her voice. Raw hurt.

He looked up sharply.

"It was Mother's. I found it in her closet, and Lilith helped me make a few small changes for a better fit." Cyra fiddled with the edges of the scarlet gown trimmed with topaz and onyx.

Asher stood, coming around his desk for a better view. He hated that he had upset her and silently cursed himself for not making more of an effort. Cyra was the only family he had left, and she deserved better than he'd given her as of late.

"It's the dress she wore the night she met Father." His sister's voice was softer now, yet each word weighed heavily upon his heart.

"You look so much like her," he murmured, noticing the way Cyra's eyes were suddenly glassy. She blinked rapidly, holding her emotions in check. "Sometimes the memory of her beauty escapes me, until I see you."

Cyra beamed, then gave a little sniffle. "So, does that mean you'll accompany me to the Yavanna Ball in Terensel this evening?"

Asher groaned. She'd played his emotions perfectly, filling him with guilt because of his quick dismissal, then attempting to trick him into going to another Midsummer celebration at the expense of his remorse. Somehow, she always got exactly what she wanted, but not this time. Asher stood his ground. "Absolutely not."

"But I don't want to go alone." She crossed her arms, sticking out her bottom lip to pout. It was a ploy, and one she used often whenever she wanted to get her way.

"I don't want you to go by yourself either." Asher stole a glance at the study door, then at the small mountain of books on his desk. He had a great deal of runes to sift through. "Ask Lilith to go to the Yavanna Ball with you. She'd be far much better company than me."

Cyra heaved a sigh and sprawled dramatically onto the black leather sofa across from his desk. She pressed the back of her hand to her forehead, feigning distress. "Asher, I don't think you understand the importance of this situation."

He leaned his hip into his desk and crossed one ankle over the other. Slowly, he lifted his spectacles, positioning them on top of his head and off his face. Arching one brow, he eyed his sister. He really ought to work with her on the proper manners of a lady. "I imagine I understand more than you think I do."

"It's the Season and I'm of age. At some point in the near future, I'll have a suitor, maybe more than one if I'm lucky, and they'll want to court me." She bit her bottom lip, hesitant. Her gold gaze latched onto him. "Maybe even love me."

The mere mention of the word put him on edge.

"Love is—"

"A weakness, yes, I know." She drew the last word out, emphasizing it more than was necessary, and flung one hand through the air. "You've stated as much for as long as I can remember. I'm not saying I should marry for love, though the possibility is always there. But if I find a match, I'll need your permission."

He straightened, then shoved his hands into the pockets of his pants. "You think I would deny you?"

"You might," Cyra ventured, sitting up. "If it was someone like Lord Marintide."

Asher scrubbed a hand over his face. "Reif Marintide is out of the question."

Though even he had to admit, there were worse choices. Reif might have been fond of the ladies and not always so discreet in his endeavors, but he was a safer option in that he would never raise a hand to Cyra. Or any other female, for that matter.

"Which is exactly why I need you with me at the Yavanna Ball." She gestured vaguely around the room, her brows lifting. "To ward off any unlikely suitors."

Tapping his fingers restlessly along the edge of his desk, he considered his sister's reasoning. "I suppose you make a valid point on the matter."

"Of course I do." She flashed him a brilliant smile, and he knew he lost the battle against her. "I've had an excellent teacher."

"Flattery will get you nowhere with me." But the corner of his mouth curved anyway.

"I'm just grateful you're allowing me to be a part of the decision instead of choosing for me." Cyra shook her head. Her hair tumbled forward as she clasped her hands in her lap, her eyes suddenly taking a keen interest in the floorboards. "Poor Lady Novalise."

Asher jolted like he'd been struck by lightning. "She's betrothed?"

Cyra glanced up at him, lifted her arms, then let them fall by her side. "Not yet. But she will be sooner rather than later. I heard Lord Starstorm is choosing her mate for her himself, since her star reading didn't name anyone in particular. Lilith said there's a possibility they'll announce the engagement tonight."

The bond connecting him to Novalise warped into a mass of fury. Black flames tainted with streaks of silver scoured down the binding, reaching for the explosion of glittering stars. His magic roared, his blood boiled. Every thread tying him to her thoughts, her feelings, her voice, her soul, grew taut. Frenzied. He clamped down on the severe sensation, shielding himself from her.

"Who?" He ground the word out.

"I don't know." Cyra ran her finger along the seam of the sofa, ignorant of his inner turmoil. "She received no less than four marriage proposals last night."

He loosed a stream of unsavory curses that left his sister blinking in surprise.

"Why are you so upset?" She peered up at him, her eyes glinting with concern. A small frown creased across her brow. "You don't even like her."

"You're right." Asher grabbed his coat from the back of his chair, then headed for the door. "I don't."

"Where are you going?" Cyra asked, scrambling off the leather sofa after him.

"To the palace." Because if there was anyone in Aeramere who could break the bond between him and Novalise, it was Queen Elowyn.

"But what about the Yavanna Ball?"

Asher turned back to face his sister. The look on her face was nothing short of despair, and so reminiscent of their mother, it pained him. "I'll be back in time to escort you. I swear it."

She nodded, but he wasn't quite certain she believed him.

It made no difference. He wouldn't let her down. No matter what, he would return from the palace to take her to Terensel in the hopes of finding a mate. Unfortunately, he was faced with another priority. More than anything, he had to request an audience with Queen Elowyn and ask her to break the bond tying him to Novalise. He should've done it months ago. For some reason, he thought Novalise would have taken care of it herself, seeing as how furious she'd been when he'd rejected her on the Winter Solstice. But bond-breaking was no easy feat. It required consent from both parties, as it was a torturous and harrowing experience.

He'd heard stories. How it felt like one's soul was being ripped in half, how it seemed like the heart fractured into a thousand pieces before being haphazardly thrown back together once the bond was severed. The pain was insufferable. Recovery could take days, sometimes even months, and it was not something even the most gifted of healers could repair. He supposed that was why most fae either accepted the bond, or if they chose to deny it, lived the remainder of their days knowing they would never truly be whole again.

Asher threw on his coat, stalking down the hall to the outer courtyard where his carriage was waiting.

Breaking the bond would free Novalise of him. Yes, it would be painful. Yes, she would probably hate him for all eternity, but eventually, she would persevere. Of that he had no doubt. And with her wedding now less than a fortnight away, he could easily plead his case to Queen Elowyn.

Asher told himself he was making the right decision, that their reactions to one another were purely physical, fueled by lust, and fused by magic. There was no intimacy. No shared emotions. And there would never be any love.

Perhaps he would've been more inclined to believe such a lie before he so stupidly kissed her. Before he realized he would never be worthy of the one fated to him.

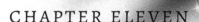

CHAPTER ELEVEN

The observatory was always quiet in the afternoon. Glowing light spilled onto the dais from the glass dome overhead, dousing the bronzed architecture in a wash of gold. But the rest of the space remained untouched, bathed in shadows and the flickering of starlight along the alcoves.

Other than on the highest balcony at night, the observatory was Novalise's favorite place. Here, she didn't need to be exemplary. There wasn't a voice in the back of her mind ridiculing her over every misstep, and there was no one watching to ensure she didn't place a single toe out of line. She didn't need to placate those around her with a well-practiced smile and a kindhearted demeanor. She didn't have to be the obedient eldest daughter of House Celestine, ready to play hostess and offer honeyed words at a moment's notice.

No, here it was just her and the stars.

Even in the blinding light of daytime, she knew they were there. Watching. Waiting.

Her footfalls sounded softly against the glittering, dark blue stone. Tucking her hands behind her back, she slowly paced the room, tracing the constellations with her mind. Memorizing every angle, every shape. Each one told a story, a marvelous tale of interwoven fates and grand designs. Eight of the most prominent constellations in the sky were engraved into the gilded Wheel of Stars overhead, and each of the Starstorm siblings had been born under a different one—even the twins.

The Great Stag for Ariesian, and Cervo the Lone Wolf for Solarius. Novalise, of course, had been born under Estrela's Crown. Azuralis, the sea goddess, was for Sarelle. Tovian had been born under the sign of Caelifera of the Mountains, while Nyxian came a little more than a year later under Aedes, the Fae Warrior. Lastly, the twins, who had been born minutes apart but on different days. Vespira the Druid had been the main constellation when Caelian was born, but the constellations shifted at the midnight hour, and Creslyn had been born beneath the Tree of Life.

As far as Novalise knew, her brothers and sisters were the only siblings in generations to not share a star sign with one another. Perhaps it was fate, or maybe it was simply because there were so many of them.

On the ground in the center of the room was the Faerie Star. Made of selenite, it shone as bright as moonlight against the deep navy granite. The Faerie Star was the focal of the Starstorm crest, the very same one that was flanked on both sides by a crescent moon.

Carefully, Novalise stood in the center of the star. This was where she drew upon her power. This was where she came alive, where she felt at one with the universe. So long as the thrum of starfire within her blood stayed quiet.

Starfire was a thread of ancient magic bound to the fierce starstorm, from which her namesake was derived. It was magnificent, an explosion of dazzling celestial force that made it look as though one held the entirety of the universe in the palms of their hands. Starfire magic could be traced through Novalise's father's lineage, though it had seemingly vanished from the bloodline over one hundred years ago. Rumors surrounded the mysterious disappearance of the starfire— stories claimed the power was hidden away as a means of protection after the Starstorm fae were dethroned during the Battle of Falling Stars. Others seemed to think the starfire and its coinciding starstorm were more of a curse, and Queen Elowyn was somehow to blame for its dormancy.

Protection or curse, it made no difference to Novalise.

All she knew was starfire now slumbered within her, and every so often, it awoke with a vengeance.

"Show me," she murmured to the skies. "Show me what remains unseen."

She was enough. She was worthy of the blessing bestowed upon her. Wishes upon stars were Caelian's magic, but maybe if Novalise was fortunate, she could tweak the reading a little. Adjust the outcome in her favor.

Novalise listened.

The stars whispered.

Spreading her arms wide, magic exploded around her. Beams of moonlight shimmered, enclosing her in a globe of celestial power. Trails of iridescent shooting stars swirled around her like a vortex, scattering stardust like confetti. Constellations took shape, aligning as the night sky engulfed her within the observatory, amplifying her magic. Aedes the Fae Warrior appeared, his notched bow and arrow stretching out over her head. Emerging from Novalise's left was the Great Stag, his mighty antlers twinkling against the darkened sphere of her creation. The last constellation to appear was Vespira the Druid, her staff of vines shining bright, dulling everything else around it.

Novalise studied the constellations as her mind fired with a dozen thoughts, trying to piece them together. Aedes. The Great Stag. Vespira. Individually, she knew what each of them meant, understood what they represented. But she'd never seen these three particular constellations gathered together before. Placing her palm over each one, Novalise drew from their power, allowing their force to fill her, their energy to enlighten her. The bow and arrow, antlers, and the staff. She recalled all the books she'd read about deciphering the stars, and while there were many passages on decoding them, her mother told her books were the most basic form of understanding the heavens. The innate ability to hear them, to master them, came from inside her.

She closed her eyes.

At once, the stars came alive.

Aedes launched blazing arrow after blazing arrow across a war-torn land. Fires ravaged this place and the scent of death hung heavy in the air. Gray skies roiled and the dense plumes of smoke cleared to reveal the Great Stag, with his gleaming white coat thundering across the horizon. A crowned figure sat gallantly atop his back, a cloak unfurling behind them as a feminine battle cry pierced the silence. From the earth, Vespira rose, her emerald staff in hand. Swathed in furs and flowers, she grasped her staff in both hands, hoisting it high in the air. Vines unraveled around her, reaching out like the hands of the Mother Goddess herself. Vespira slammed the staff into the ground and the world trembled. The landscape shifted and blurred, and the shimmering Veil protecting Aeramere shattered.

Novalise's eyes flew open, and she gasped. She swayed against the vision that rocked her, leaving her shaken. Tumbling forward, her knees hit the granite ground, but the pain of the stone was nothing compared to the fear harboring in the depths of her heart.

A war?

She shook her head, struggling to catch her breath.

It was impossible.

But the stars never lied.

Aedes was a direct representation of overcoming strife or impending war. The Great Stag symbolized power and leadership. Vespira was a sign of change. Separately, these constellations could mean a great many things, could be interpreted any number of ways. But together, there was no mistaking the validity of their truth.

War was coming to Aeramere.

The sphere surrounding her fell away and she drew her magic inward as twin streaks of starfire erupted from her fingertips. They soared over her head like broken rainbows, singeing the ceiling. She shook her head, trying desperately to quell the erratic beating of her heart.

Once she was certain there would be no more mishaps, no more glimpses of a forbidden magic, Novalise gathered up her skirts.

She needed to speak to Queen Elowyn at once. She rushed from the observatory, chest heaving as she bounded down the winding staircase. All her training to become the epitome of perfection screamed at her to walk, to look presentable, to maintain the decorum of a lady. But the corridors of her house bled together in a mix of golds, blues, and purples as she ran through the halls. She'd never been more grateful to have traded in her heels for a pair of soft leather flats. Not that she couldn't sprint in heels when necessary, but she'd rather not take any chances.

If she cut through the courtyard, she could bypass most of the estate. The shortcut would empty her out into the gardens along the side of the house, where she'd be able to grab a carriage and fly to the queen's palace without question.

She darted around a corner and sprinted into the courtyard.

Dark shadows swarmed her, stealing away her senses, and a gust of frigid wind set her teeth to chattering. She tumbled into a solid frame and all the air expelled from her lungs on impact.

One strong arm snagged her by the waist and whipped her around, lifting her feet from the ground.

"Do you make it a point to find yourself in my arms now?" a smooth, masculine voice asked as he swiftly set her down.

Novalise looked up to find Prince Drake Kalstrand staring down at her. Despite the slight tease in his tone, all humor was gone from his severe expression. He kept his arm firmly planted around her waist. The grip of his fingers would leave a mark.

"Forgive me, Your Highness." She couldn't break the intensity of his gaze. Those evergreen eyes were shrouded in mystery, dark and tempting like a forbidden forest. Her throat was suddenly far too dry. "I was in a hurry, and I wasn't paying attention to where I was going."

"Perhaps you should," he murmured.

His eyes flicked down between them. At first, Novalise thought he intended to stare blatantly at her breasts, to which she debated the level of punishment she might receive if she slapped him for his vulgar behavior. But then she caught sight of the dagger.

The prince's hand was wrapped around the edge of his Shadowblade, the tip of it mere inches from her chest. He gripped the blade so tightly it was a wonder the weapon hadn't sliced open his palm. More interesting, however, were the tiny scars covering his knuckles.

"You're lucky I was here to catch this before it pierced your heart." He flicked the dagger upward, caught it by the hilt, then sheathed it.

"If you caught it..." She stole a hasty glance behind her, but there was no one in the courtyard except the two of them. "Then who threw it?"

The shadow prince smiled, slow. Ruthless. It was terrifying. Fear lanced its way through her and she couldn't stop herself from shivering in his hold.

"It's called training, Lady Novalise." His hand moved from

her waist to beneath her chin. He tilted her head up, like he was inspecting her. "You should try it."

Novalise looked away from him, toward the corridor. Arching windows with paned glass shaped like stars lined every wall, and she wondered how many servants, how many of her siblings, were peering out, gauging their interaction. She shook her head, morphing back into the image of a regal lady.

"I could never."

"Why not?" he countered.

"I don't know anything about weaponry or swordsmanship. My studies were very particular, and none of them included books on how to fight." She snagged her bottom lip with her teeth, and his eyes instantly dropped to her mouth. Another shiver of warning tingled down her spine. "Besides, I doubt I'd be any good at it."

"Says who?" He shifted closer and the shadows of the courtyard moved with him.

"Everyone." Disappointed by her own answer, Novalise pulled her long braid of hair over one shoulder, fiddling with the sapphire ribbon tied at the ends. "That is, I'm a lady, Your Highness. The eldest daughter of a prestigious house of Aeramere. Learning how to wield a dagger or sword isn't exactly within my realm of expertise."

This time, he moved so quickly, she couldn't even track him. It was as though he was everywhere at once.

"I could teach you." His roughened whisper floated past her ear, and she whirled around to find him standing behind her, another wicked smile turning up his full lips.

Goosebumps pebbled down her arms.

She imagined he could probably teach her a lot of things.

"Nearly all the women in Brackroth are trained to fight. They choose their own weapons, of course. Daggers. Swords." Those eyes of his raked over her. "A bow and arrow might be fitting for you."

"Thank you for the offer, Your Highness." Novalise swallowed, forcing her throat to work. If she even so much as took an interest in a sword or a bow, her mother would have her head. "But I really must get to the palace. I need to speak with the queen."

His grin darkened. "Do you need a ride?"

"A...ride?"

"I have a dragon." Prince Drake jerked his head toward the other end of the courtyard. "And I can guarantee you he's faster than those absurd flying carriages you use."

"I don't know." Twisting her hands together, her teeth skated along her bottom lip once more. "I've never ridden on a dragon before."

He inclined his head, his wolfish smile all but vanishing. "Is that a yes?"

"Um...yes?"

Novalise had no time to regret her decision. The shadow prince led her from the courtyard through the sloping gardens. Her heart gave a significant twinge when they passed by the fountain where she'd fallen into Asher's lap. Two days had passed since the last time she saw him, and she wondered if he'd found a way to barricade himself from their bond. The thought left her simmering, and wishing she'd been the one to think of it first. But she had little time to dwell on the matter as the Prince of Brackroth stalked through the gardens at a clipped pace, not bothering to make sure she hadn't fallen behind. Following the winding path, his boots clicked in time to each measured step, until the floral archways and blooming shrubberies opened to a jutting mountain ledge off the Moonfall Peaks, right along the outskirts of House Celestine's walls.

There, perched and sitting like a statue carved from obsidian, was the shadow prince's dragon.

Novalise clamped her mouth shut, covering it with both hands, to keep from making any sudden noises.

The dragon was the most stunning yet frightening beast she'd ever beheld. His black scales glittered like stars on a moonless night. Rocks and small boulders tumbled down the cliffside as he lowered himself to the ground, preparing for flight. The claws along the bottom edge of his massive wings were like curving spires, carving little grooves into the face of the mountain with their sharp points. Glowing yellow eyes with slits for pupils watched her every move, as though he tracked her every breath. He thrashed his tail once and Novalise leapt, clutching Prince Drake's arm.

"Wh-what's his name?" Her attempt at polite small talk did little to ease the bundle of nervous energy tightening inside of her.

"Svartos." Prince Drake approached the dragon with ease. He checked the beast's underbelly, tightening a strap on something that looked incredibly similar to a horse's saddle, then turned around to face her. "Ready?"

"Ah, I was actually going to ask why you were here. That is, at my house." She couldn't tear her gaze away from Svartos—if she made one wrong move, he could crush her, turning her bones to dust. If she could distract the prince a little longer, then maybe she could find a way to get herself out of this situation.

"Negotiations." Prince Drake moved like lightning, leaving her no time to react. He plucked her off the ground, then lifted her up into the seat on the dragon's back, hauling himself up behind her. "Hold on."

"To what?" Her voice pitched with panic. She couldn't move, she couldn't breathe.

"Here." The prince reached around her and wrapped both of her hands around a set of sleek, black leather reins.

She doubted they actually did anything.

He pulled on a pair of worn riding gloves, tugging the leather up over his scarred hands. Then he was whispering words in a language she didn't understand. The prince grabbed the reins, gripping the section between her hands, and Svartos rose from the ground. Novalise's body went rigid, paralyzed with fear. She sucked in a strangled breath, squeezing the reins so tightly she nearly lost all feeling in her fingers. The dragon moved with a speed far faster than she imagined for his size. His wings beat steadily as he sprinted toward the edge of the cliff. Her heart thundered, her stomach dropped. She was going to die. This was it, climbing on the back of a dragon with the Shadowblade Assassin was going to be her demise.

The ground fell away from beneath them, the dragon soared, and Novalise screamed.

She squeezed her eyes shut, digging her nails into the fine leather of the reins, and held on for her life. Warm air rushed past her, hollowing her out. She pressed herself back into Prince Drake's firm body, grateful for his reassuring presence, but petrified that if she couldn't feel him sitting behind her she would inevitably fall to her death.

"Open your eyes," he demanded.

She did as she was told, tossing him a look from over her shoulder. "How did you know they were closed?"

"Your entire body is tense." His jaw ticked and he kept his gaze trained on the skies. "It's making it difficult to...concentrate."

"My apologies, Your Highness." Novalise wiggled backwards, further nestling herself against him. She'd never made anyone uncomfortable before—his words emboldened her.

He grunted. "You're only making it worse."

"Oh, I am quite sorry." She sat up, straightening her spine, ensuring her lower back curved so her bottom rubbed against the stiffening bulge in his pants. Glancing back at him once more, she tossed him her best smile. "Better?"

"Do not play innocent with me, my lady." Prince Drake's

glare was icy, and he captured her chin with his thumb and forefinger, holding her in check. "You're flirting with death."

Novalise laughed, though it was forced and lacking her previous confidence. "Unlikely."

She couldn't be certain, but he might've growled.

"Let's be honest, Your Highness." She gave him another coy smile. "When it comes to mild flirtations, I win."

Prince Drake released her then and Svartos tucked in his wings, diving straight down. They streaked through the clouds while the land beneath them morphed into nothing more than a smear of messy watercolors.

Novalise's heart shot into her throat. Svartos loosed an ear-splitting screech as the world careened past her, so fast she couldn't seem to breathe. She dragged the reins to her chest, clutching them, urging the beast upward, but he continued plummeting toward the ground in a sickening spiral. She knew those damned reins wouldn't make a difference.

"Stop!" she cried, tears streaming from her eyes. She shook her head violently as fear coursed through her. "Please, stop!"

Prince Drake wrapped his hand around the back of her neck and even through the gloves his touch was cold, like death. He angled her back to face him, his lips less than a breath from her own. "Are you frightened, *kearsta?*"

Her head bobbed, but she couldn't tear her gaze away from him. His evergreen eyes held her captive.

Slowly, Svartos leveled out. Spreading his wings wide, he flew upward toward the mountains once more, effortlessly gliding through the late afternoon sky as though he hadn't terrified her beyond belief.

"Good. Now, let's make one thing perfectly clear." The shadow prince nipped her bottom lip with his teeth, tugging firmly. "I never lose."

CHAPTER TWELVE

Queen Elowyn's palace was southwest of Emberspire, along the border of Terensel and right at the edge of the Chycarlin Forest. It was rumored the queen was once a druid, and since she favored the fae of earth magic, she built her palace at the base of a small mountain range.

Spires from the palace rose higher than the mountain's steepest peak and the forest bloomed around its lowest point. The rooftops were varied in color from deep green to dark slate, blending seamlessly with the scenery of its backdrop. Stained glass windows depicting images from the five houses of Aeramere lined the outer walls of almost all the corridors, reflecting history in the form of artisanal glass. Each scene was handcrafted by fae from Terensel, who used their magic to bend each pane of glass to their will before painting them with lavish designs. Within the palace walls, turquoise pools were filled with rainbow-hued fish and waterlilies, each of them interconnected with small ivory bridges that led from one area of grandeur to another.

Though beautiful, it was also well protected. Guards

patrolled the grounds, from the forest to the bustling city surrounding the palace, while archers manned the many balustrades and balconies.

Asher was fortunate enough that as a councilor to the queen, his access to her was easily granted. As opposed to the other fae he passed lining the small street leading up to the palace, waiting to see her. He supposed most of them were local citizens, but others were definitely visiting from neighboring lands, no doubt to ask for her favor for some ill-suited marriage. During the height of the Season, it seemed the queen's energy was focused on blessings and weddings. Everything else was shoved aside to be dealt with another day.

The doors to the queen's sitting room opened, and Asher was greeted with the scent of rosewater and ferns.

Queen Elowyn sat primly on a dark blue velvet sofa with her hands folded in her lap, her gown of emerald silk unfurling around her. She wore no crown today, but her hair was piled high on top of her head in a series of intricate braids tugged so tightly, her brows looked permanently raised. Though her movements were austere, the pale glow of her magic softened her severity. Her rich brown gaze flicked over to the decadent windows along the far wall of the room. There stood her son, Prince Aspen, with his hand tucked behind his back, his cold gaze fixated on something far beyond the horizon.

"Lord Firebane." The queen lifted one hand in greeting. "What an unexpected surprise."

Asher bowed deeply. "Your Majesty, I must apologize for my unannounced visit."

"Nonsense. It's always a pleasure to see you." She dismissed his regrets with a wave of her hand. "Please, sit."

He obliged her by sitting in one of the high-back chairs across from her. The cushions were stiff, nearly as hard as stone, and he wondered if anyone had ever actually used them before. Her fingers flitted through the air once more, except this time a servant scurried over carrying a silver tray with a glass teapot and two porcelain cups. She quickly poured the steaming amber liquid for both of them, and the lovely scent of freshly brewed herbs filled the space.

The queen accepted her cup, then took a sip, holding Asher's gaze the entire time. She inclined her head the barest of angles. "How are things at House Emberspire?"

"As well as can be expected." Asher held his teacup, silently debating asking for cream, then thought better of it. "My sister finds herself in want of a husband, so I will be assisting her in her endeavor."

Again, the queen's keen gaze flitted over to her son. "Is that so?"

Asher's entire body went on alert. There was no way the queen could be considering Cyra as a bride for her son. Not that his sister lacked any of the necessary qualifications, because she was most decidedly accomplished, but Prince Aspen...there was something about him that set Asher's teeth on edge. It was a constant prodding at the back of his mind. There was something oddly peculiar about the prince, about his overall nature, but Asher hadn't been able to place it.

"Yes," he agreed, withholding all interest from his tone. "Apparently, she fancies herself finding a love match."

The lie coated his tongue with a bitter tang, but it was done out of necessity. He had no problem helping Cyra find a mate, but her husband would require his approval, and as far as Asher was concerned, the Prince of Aeramere did not meet those expectations.

Not that he would ever say as much in front of his queen.

"Mm. I'm sure you'll help her find a desirable match." She glanced down at her teacup, sighed, then returned it to its saucer. When she smiled, the outer corners of her mouth were pinched. "Now, what can I do for you?"

"I've come to you with a request," Asher began, leaving his tea untouched. "Of a private nature."

"Oh?"

Curiosity filled the queen's brown gaze and from the corner of Asher's eye, he saw Prince Aspen snap to attention. He would have to walk this line extremely carefully. Asking the queen to break the bond between himself and Novalise was no easy feat. Just because he asked the favor of her didn't mean she was inclined to grant it. Queen Elowyn could easily deny him, leaving him bound to Novalise forever. If word got out that he dismissed Novalise, it could ruin her. Questions would start to arise, and inquiries would be made about her reputation. Everything Asher did would require the utmost care, because there was more than his desires at stake. Novalise's happiness and her future rested on his shoulders.

The queen leaned forward with an air of intrigue. "Tell me more, Lord Firebane."

"Of course, Your Majesty." Asher placed his cup on its saucer, then leaned back in the rigid chair. "You see, I—"

He was interrupted by a clamorous rise of shouts and voices coming from the palace's courtyard.

Queen Elowyn stood immediately, and Asher quickly followed suit. Her gaze snapped to her son. "What is it? What's happening?"

Prince Aspen stalked across the room and bent down toward his mother, whispering something into her ear.

"Is that so?" She arched one prominent brow. "Forgive me, Lord Firebane. It would seem I am rather popular today."

The prince straightened, and Queen Elowyn smoothed the invisible wrinkles from her gown. She strode toward the door with Prince Aspen on her heels, and the guards standing on either side of it moved into position beside her. Following behind the queen and her entourage, Asher kept his pace steady as they turned the corner and entered the grand hall of the palace. Ornate floor-to-ceiling mirrors lined both sides of the hallway, and he couldn't help but steal a glimpse of the prince's reflection. He might be royal and used to maintaining a sense of propriety, but behind his carefully crafted mask was raw fury. There was no mistaking the hard glint in his eyes.

An obnoxious creaking sound echoed up into the towering ceiling as a set of massive oak doors at the end of the hallway slowly groaned open. Their surfaces were engraved with artfully crafted whorls and runes designed to resemble the Tree of Life, and the leaves of the tree glowed a shining jade color as the newcomers made their entrance into the palace.

Something angry and furious twisted inside Asher's gut, and the bond connecting him to Novalise contracted and tugged, urging him forward.

Then she walked in on the arm of none other than Drake Kalstrand. Tendrils of lavender hair had fallen loose from her braid, framing her face. Her cheeks were flushed, pink from the wind, and her bottom lip was slightly swollen. Like she'd just been bitten. Or kissed.

Damn it. If she'd only walked in with someone other than the shadow prince, then Asher wouldn't care so much. But not him. *Anyone* but him.

"Lady Novalise, Prince Kalstrand." The queen's curious gaze slid between the two of them. "You arrived together...on a dragon."

Prince Drake bowed, Novalise curtsied.

"Svartos is far more expedient than a carriage, Your Majesty. Even ones that fly." His face remained impassive, void of expression. "And Lady Novalise wished to speak with you right away."

Queen Elowyn smiled but it was pinched, like she tasted something sour and was trying to hide it. She clasped her hands together, one finger tapping a merciless rhythm. "How kind of you to bring her to me."

"I find myself unable to refuse her." The prince slid his arm around Novalise's waist, and though she didn't appear distraught, Asher could've sworn she shivered.

"Yes. She seems to have that effect on people." The queen inclined her head, her heavy pile of braids tilting slightly. "What is it, Lady Novalise? You look most distressed."

"The stars, Your Majesty." She dropped into a low curtsy and Asher found himself unable to look away from her. "I've seen something terrible."

"Oh?" Queen Elowyn gave the barest of gestures, beckoning Novalise to continue. "Go on."

Asher shifted, edging closer to the conversation, and when Novalise's gaze flicked to him, his soul caught fire.

"I fear war is coming." Novalise threaded her fingers together, pressing her palms to her abdomen. Her magic flared, and Asher became keenly aware of her emotions as they fired through him like they were his own. She was nervous. But more than that, she was afraid she was right. "The constellations were Aedes the Fae Warrior, the Great Stag, and Vespira the Druid. Individually, they're symbolic of Aeramere, a blessing even. But they were shown to me as a trio, an impossible alignment."

Asher knew enough about the stars to understand that reading them was less a kind of studying than it was an innate sense of magic. Of divination. Supposedly, it was the sort of gift only a few fae ever possessed and Novalise was one of them.

"Aedes, the Great Stag, and Vespira?" Queen Elowyn pursed her lips, considering. "Those are some of the greatest and most ancient constellations in our sky."

"I'm aware it seems absurd for all three of them to appear given the chaos of my own reading, but I assure you, I know what I saw." Novalise tucked an errant strand of hair behind one ear, and Asher fixated on the way it curled softly against her cheek. "I could never misinterpret them."

Prince Aspen laughed. Loudly. His mother shot him down with a sharp look.

"Do you find something humorous about this situation, Your Highness?" The queen's brows drew to a point as she narrowed her gaze on her son.

He chuckled, crossing his arms. His eyes roved over Novalise, and his upper lip curled in disgust. "Lady Novalise claims she could never misinterpret the stars, yet her own reading was an absolute disaster."

Novalise ducked her head, her cheeks flushing bright pink at the prince's crude remarks.

Asher opened his mouth before he could stop himself. "Her reading is of no consequence. It simply foretold her fate, not that of Aeramere. Studies of the stars have proven that specific constellations coincide with one another throughout certain moments in history. Not once have Aedes, the Great Stag, and Vespira ever been mentioned together. Such a discovery should warrant an investigation."

Even if Asher considered the stars and their meanings to be an utter waste of time and complete garbage, that didn't mean he hadn't read up on their significance in terms of magic. Celestial readings might be nothing more than ludicrous musings, but books were factual, and logical reasoning was a validity Asher couldn't deny.

"Great," Prince Aspen muttered, crossing his arms over his chest. "Now I have a hermit fire fae who imagines himself a philosopher *and* an insufferable star reader who thinks herself worthy of her mother's acclamations trying to tell me what to do."

Asher waited for Novalise to break, willed himself not to catch her when she crumbled, but she stood firm. "I may not be the Reader of Stars, but the magic of them runs through my veins." Her gaze flicked to Asher, then landed back on Prince Aspen with cool determination. "They speak to me."

"And the Royal Guard speaks to *me*," Prince Aspen snapped

back. "If war was on the horizon, trust I would be the first to know."

Queen Elowyn bristled. "Mind yourself, Aspen."

"Apologies, Mother." The prince bowed, but it was stiff and curt. "Perhaps Lady Novalise would find it more amiable to discuss the weather and marriage rather than matters of conflict."

"An excellent idea." Drake moved closer to Novalise, tightening his grip around her waist. He turned slowly, facing Asher. "Warfare is overrated, especially when there are more romantic ways to die. Isn't that right, Lord Firebane?"

The barb hit its mark, digging deep.

The memory of his mother's death was still fresh, so clear he could visualize every last detail. From the way her limp hand hung off the edge of her bed, down to the scarlet drop of blood that slid from the corner of her mouth before she took her final breath.

Asher bowed. "If you'll excuse me."

His words were terse, each one of them forced through a clenched jaw.

"But my lord"— the queen lifted one hand, stilling him— "weren't you in need of my assistance?"

"Another time, perhaps, Your Majesty." Preferably when he wasn't so keenly aware of the grip Novalise's emotions held on him. When her heartbeat wasn't so perfectly in sync with his own. When the rushing of her blood and the symphony of her magic didn't captivate him like a siren's song. A time when, maybe, he could guarantee the breaking of their bond wouldn't kill them both.

Novalise attempted to disentangle herself from Prince Drake, but Asher was done. He turned abruptly, heading toward the open doors at the end of the grand hall, frostfire and smoke brewing in his wake.

"Lord Firebane!" Novalise's voice carried after him, but he paid her no attention.

He was too busy trying to ignore the hole that continued to burgeon within his heart. He stalked from the palace, more determined than ever, and only certain of one thing.

Bonds and soulmates be damned.

Asher would rather die than fall in love.

CHAPTER THIRTEEN

*N*ovalise watched Asher retreat, his heartbreak palpable.

She had no idea what sort of torment he suffered, and she doubted he'd ever let her get close enough to him to find out. She chased after him, but only made it as far as the entrance to the grand hall. Her dress was too long and his stride was too quick, she simply couldn't keep up.

Her magic ached for him, and a desperate longing filled Novalise. She wanted to comfort him, to soothe him. All the power of the stars yearned to be consumed by a riot of silver and black flames. Though she could sense his loss like it belonged to her instead, Asher shielded himself, barricading his heart from their bond. He was guarded, keeping his emotions under lock and key. Like a fortified stone fortress, one she would never be able to breach. Whatever hurt him, whatever was broken inside of him, was something she wouldn't ever be able to make whole.

Standing on the threshold, she watched as he climbed into his carriage and the Eponian stallions ascended into the early evening sky. They banked to the northeast, cutting through wisps of clouds, then vanished from sight completely.

Novalise startled when the shadow prince appeared beside her. She didn't even hear him approach. He was far too stealthy for his own good.

Prince Drake leaned casually against the considerable door-frame and crossed his arms. He stared at the swell of clouds, the same ones that obscured Asher's carriage from view. "You have a history with that one?"

"Not exactly." She lifted the hem of her gown and followed the smooth stone pathway away from the palace toward the wide courtyard where Svartos waited. "We kissed once."

And in turn, it ruined her for anyone else.

No one's kiss would ever compare to Asher's, of that she was sure.

Prince Drake took up an easy pace beside her. "If you want, we could make him jealous."

"It won't work. He doesn't want me." She carefully tucked back the pieces of hair that had fallen loose from her braid, pinning them into place. "Besides, I want to marry for love, and Lord Firebane thinks such a notion is futile."

She supposed she could always ignore the bond between them. Eventually it would grow weary, withering away like a summer rose before the autumn harvest. The stars would die, the flames would dampen. His voice would fade from her mind, becoming nothing more than a dull murmur in the darkest part of her heart. Then all this agony, all this suffering, would subside. She would move on, find someone who was worthy of her, someone who wanted her, and hope to the Mother Goddess herself that the one she picked loved her with a fierceness only she could match.

Prince Drake chuckled darkly, drawing her from her wishful thoughts.

"And you think you'll fall in love in less than two weeks?" His remark was caustic and the truth of it stung.

Mostly because he was right. Midsummer had already begun. Time was not on her side. Her wedding would take place at the end of the Season, exactly eleven days from now, and she hadn't any idea who she would take as her husband. An unfortunate matter indeed, because if she didn't pick someone soon, Ariesian would undoubtedly choose for her. Though Solarius had claimed Ariesian would do her justice and attempt to find her a love match, she wasn't mindless enough to realize those things took time. It could be a last-ditch effort, a final straw, and then she would be forced to settle for someone not of her choosing.

Someone who might be callous or cruel. Or just mean.

Her stomached twisted with dread but she kept her chin held high.

"Think what you want, Your Highness. But I am determined to find a love match." All her life she'd been told what to say, how to act, what to want. This was the one thing she wanted for herself. The one thing she could finally control if she moved quickly enough. "I couldn't imagine having to spend the rest of my life with someone who found me fairly tolerable."

A strange glint sparked in the shadow prince's eyes. "I have a proposal for you, Lady Novalise."

He continued to stroll alongside her, down the sloping hill of the courtyard, his long stride easily keeping up with her hastened pace. "I came to Aeramere to meet with your brother, Ariesian. I'd like to form an alliance. A trade deal, if you will."

Interesting. Solarius was right. Prince Drake had arrived in Aeramere to strike an accord with Ariesian. Strange, however, that he wouldn't immediately go to Queen Elowyn for such things, but she could only presume that whatever he sought in return couldn't be granted by the queen.

She peered up at him, curious. "What kind of proposal did you have in mind?"

Prince Drake leaned closer, overwhelming her. The scent of him caused her head to spin, and she took a steadying step back. "Let me court you."

Novalise blinked. "I'm sorry?"

"It's fairly simple. I'll pretend to court you for the remainder of the Season, giving you free rein of suitors while intimidating the ones undeserving of you. That way you can have your pick." He spread one arm wide, gesturing to the courtyard, the forest, and everything beyond. "In exchange, you'll help me secure a deal with Ariesian. In the end, we both get what we want."

"I don't know." She worried her bottom lip with her teeth, debating. "I don't see how that could possibly work in my favor. Everyone is afraid to come near you."

Her gaze slid back to him.

Prince Drake smiled, ruthless and cold. "Everyone except Lord Firebane."

Novalise opened her mouth to retort, then clamped it shut. It *could* work. If she wanted Lord Firebane to acknowledge the bond between them, maybe she would have to do something daring. Something reckless. Something like pretending to court the notorious Shadowblade Assassin.

Defy the stars.

"Very well, Your Highness." She held out her hand. "You have a deal."

He accepted her hand, brushing a featherlight kiss across her knuckles. "So long as you uphold your end of our bargain, then I'm at your service, my lady."

"Will you be at the Yavanna Ball tonight?" she asked.

"I wouldn't miss it for the world." Prince Drake bowed, gesturing to Svartos, who once again sat poised like a statue carved from onyx on the queen's expansive courtyard.

"Ah, I think I prefer to fly by carriage this time." Novalise took a tentative step back, clasping her hands together tightly. Not that she didn't trust the majestic dragon. On the contrary, she didn't trust his rider.

The corner of Prince Drake's mouth curved. "Suit yourself. I'll see you tonight, Lady Novalise."

With that, the shadow prince strode off across the courtyard, leapt upon the back of his dragon like it was the easiest thing in the world, and took to the skies.

Svartos cut through the clouds like a black blade slicing through silk, weaving in and out of the darkening heavens until he was no longer visible. Novalise watched him go, then turned to summon a carriage when she came face to face with Prince Aspen.

"Your Highness." Novalise dropped into a low curtsy, unaware of how long the prince had been standing directly behind her.

Curving lanterns hung from posts all throughout the courtyard and the amber light flickered across him, dousing half of him in shadows. He didn't look *at* her, instead his cold gaze was trained on the night sky.

"Be careful there," he warned.

With the hues of dusk settling around them, the prince looked downright nefarious.

"Wh-what do you mean, Your Highness?" Unease hung heavy around Novalise's shoulders.

Prince Aspen's dark gaze flicked to her. "The Prince of Brackroth always gets his way."

NOVALISE ALMOST FORGOT how much she loved visiting Terensel.

Even though the sky was painted in watercolor shades of amethyst and sapphire, Terensel was a lush landscape of emerald and gold. Cascading waterfalls dropped into sparkling faerie pools, breaking up the spiraling trees twisting up from the ground. Homes were built into the rolling hillsides and covered with vines, blending in with the earth. Dirt paths wound throughout the city, illuminated by strings of glowing orbs to light the way.

Unlike House Celestine, which was built into a mountain face, House Terensel was built around a massive tree. Fuchsia flowers blossomed from nearly every branch, its majestic height towering over every other tree. Rooms were on multiple levels, the entrances easy to spot with their pointed doorframes, and wooden balconies jutted out from the trunk, covered by blankets of lilacs.

The Yavanna Ball was being held in the clearing within the woods, an elegant choice meant to coincide perfectly with Queen Elowyn's enchanted forest theme.

"Have you ever seen anything so magical?" Sarelle leaned over, sipping her berry wine, her eyes a reflection of the dazzling faerie fire lights twinkling around them.

"It's even more lovely than Queen Elowyn's party, if I dare say so." Novalise glanced around the clearing. A ring of vibrant blossoms and glittering light surrounded the forest floor. Everywhere she looked, fae, mortals, and all manner of beings danced with lively merriment. A stage had been constructed at the edge of the woods where musicians played a spirited tune, tapping their feet in rhythm while couples twirled within the circle. "The music is definitely superior."

"Oh, I agree." Sarelle fiddled with the strand of teardrop diamonds dangling from her ear. "Where are Nyxian and Tovian?"

"They're not here tonight." Novalise scanned the crowd, spying the rest of her siblings.

Ariesian and Solarius were standing across the way in a deep conversation with Lord Everland, and none of them looked pleased about it. Caelian and Creslyn were in the center of the faerie ring, dancing without a care in the world. Moonflowers rained down upon Caelian, their silver petals sparkling like droplets of moonlight as her magic rose and fell to the cadence of the song. Her head fell back in laughter as she sang along. Creslyn spun right beside her, holding the skirts of her pale pink gown, as sparks of sunlight and ribbons of rainbows twirled around her.

"Nyxian and Tovian never miss a party." Sarelle took another sip of her wine. "I thought for sure they would be here tonight."

"Ariesian sent them off on some errands. Apparently, they're to sail with a High Prince of Faeven to one of the eastern realms." Novalise would be lying if she said she cared much for political dealings, but Ariesian had been oddly discreet, and that in particular had snared her attention. "It sounded as though they will be gone for quite some time."

"How strange." Sarelle's brow furrowed. "It's not like them to leave without saying goodbye. Whatever adventure they're on must be quite important."

Novalise turned to face her sister and leaned over conspiratorially. "I thought so, too. Aeramere doesn't have ships of any kind. I wonder if maybe they're sailing to set up a trade route or researching the possibility of establishing a naval fleet."

Sarelle's eyes sparked with mischief. "Or maybe they're going to fight fae pirates."

Novalise snorted. It was a decidedly unladylike noise, but she couldn't help herself. "Don't be ridiculous. There's no such thing as faerie pirates."

Sarelle's smile fell away, her pallor blanched, and her gaze lingered on something behind Novalise.

"Sarelle? I didn't mean it, of course fae pirates exist." Novalise hadn't intended to hurt her sister's feelings, but when

Sarelle failed to smile, and all the blood had drained from her face, Novalise turned to see what caught her attention.

It was Prince Drake.

He stalked through the crowd and was heading straight for her. His attire wasn't nearly as formal as the other males in attendance. Instead of a trim coat with elegant pants and shining boots, he wore a gray collared shirt with the top button undone and the cuffs rolled, tucked loosely into a pair of riding leathers. Riding leathers, Novalise noticed, that clung to his rather sculpted lower half.

Her gaze snagged on Sarelle, and she reached over, gently lifting her sister's chin to ensure her mouth didn't continue to gape open in awe.

The bodies of people dancing swirled to a standstill, parting for Prince Drake as if on command. The musicians stumbled through the final notes of their refrain, then stopped playing completely. Every set of eyes in the forest focused in on her, watching her, waiting to witness their interaction.

That tiny, all-too-familiar bubble of panic lodged itself somewhere in the back of her throat. Her palms grew damp and anxiety crawled all over her like a cluster of spiders. She knew pretending to have the Prince of Brackroth court her was a terrible idea.

Unfortunately, it was too late for her to change her mind.

In the next breath, he was before her. He captured her hand, dragging her flush against him. Most gentlemen would've stopped with a gentle brush of their lips across her knuckles, but Prince Drake was not like most gentlemen. In fact, she wasn't sure if she would qualify him as one at all. He flipped open her hand, palm up, pressing a firm kiss to the center. Then he proceeded to kiss the inside of her arm, from her wrist to her shoulder.

A shiver of trepidation left her trembling and goosebumps pebbled over her skin.

"Lady Novalise," he crooned, tucking her into his side, offering a cutthroat smile to anyone who dared look their way. "Might I have this dance?"

She nodded and handed her wine glass off to Sarelle, though following the shadow prince out into the faerie ring of flowers felt like she was agreeing to meet her end.

Prince Drake's hand glided effortlessly around her waist, dipping dangerously low to the small of her back. Then he pressed her scandalously close, so her chest was flush against him. He let one finger trail over the rise of her breasts before tracing the constellation of Estrela's crown marking the flesh above her heart. That same finger slid down her shoulder, to her elbow, then finally to her wrist, where he grabbed her hand and swept her into a dance.

"I have to admit, Your Highness..." Novalise rose up on her toes, whispering into his ear to make sure no one else heard them. Without the music, the forest was eerily quiet. So silent, even the rustling of the leaves seemed too loud. "I'm not sure this is going to work."

"Trust me." Prince Drake spun her around so she could see over his shoulder. "It already is."

Sure enough, standing outside the circle of flowers with his arms crossed, looking ready to set fire to the world, was Lord Asher Firebane.

Perhaps dancing with the Shadowblade Assassin wasn't such a bad idea after all.

CHAPTER FOURTEEN

*E*nough.

Asher couldn't take it anymore. If Cyra was right, if they were going to announce Novalise's betrothal tonight, then he would do everything in his power to ensure it wasn't to Prince Drake of Brackroth.

When he first arrived, he'd caught sight of Ariesian exchanging some choice words with Lord Everland, but now the lord of House Celestine was nowhere to be found. Queen Elowyn wasn't in attendance either, which was fine. Granted, it meant he couldn't demand she break his bond to Novalise, but it also meant she wouldn't be approving any engagements in person, which was her preference.

But then he saw Prince Drake stalk through the forest like he was one of the Ancient Ones, revered and worshipped, and it had taken every last shred of his willpower not to launch a bolt of frostfire at the shadow prince. Now, Novalise was in his arms. Her wedding would be at the end of the Season and if Asher didn't do something to stop it, she'd be forced to marry Prince Drake. If for no other reason than the fact that every other male in the general vicinity was terrified of him.

There was no more time to waste.

He had to take matters into his own hands.

Asher rolled his head from side to side, cracking his neck, then started for them. He didn't care if it was in the middle of a dance. He didn't care if everyone was watching him, if interrupting two partners on the dance floor was considered a terrible offense. He didn't care about any social cues or proper decorum. His agenda had been set.

Apprehension locked itself around him, slowing his movements. It was like being chained to the bottom of the sea and struggling to walk along the dense ocean floor. His fate was officially sealed. But he was sparing her, he reminded himself. Saving her.

In order to keep Novalise safe from Prince Drake, he would do the one thing he feared above all else.

He would marry her himself.

"If you'd excuse me, Your Highness." Asher cut the Shadowblade Assassin down with a glare of steel. "I need to speak with Lady Novalise."

Prince Drake stilled, keeping Novalise pulled snugly against him. His features were schooled effortlessly into place, and he showed no sign of emotion. No mockery. No anger. Not even a sliver of surprise. He wore a mask of indifference. "And such matters can't wait until after our dance?"

"I'm afraid not, Your Highness." It was one thing to walk the line of disrespect, it was something else to cross it completely. Right now, Asher was dangerously close to that border. "It's of utmost urgency."

A beat of silence passed. And then another.

"Very well." Prince Drake stepped aside, releasing his hold on Novalise. "My lady, I'm afraid I must release you to Lord Firebane. Unless you have any objections?"

Asher finally looked at Novalise and his magic surged, racing toward hers. He held tight to the reins of his control, relenting slightly when she shook her head once.

"If you change your mind," Prince Drake said, leaning down to whisper into her ear without breaking eye contact with Asher. "Just call my name."

His lips brushed the pointed tip of her ear, a silent threat. A warning.

Asher offered his arm, holding the prince's hard stare, and the moment Novalise slipped her hand into the crook of his elbow, the musicians started playing once more. Without a word, he took her hand and guided her out of the faerie ring, towards the forest's edge. When he was certain everyone had taken their fill of them, and no other prying eyes continued to wait for another spectacle to unfold, he stepped into the woods, taking Novalise with him.

Once they were fully concealed, he hauled her along deeper into the forest. The path here was sodden and uneven, but he kept his stride at a clipped pace, determined to get Novalise as far from the party—and Drake—as possible. They climbed over hollowed-out logs that had fallen across the dirt path and dodged bushes filled with fluttering wildlife and whispering branches.

"Where are you taking me?" she finally demanded, her breathy voice sending a rush of desire straight to his cock.

"Away from him," Asher snapped, refusing to look back at her.

"Oh, really?" Novalise wrenched herself free from his hold. "I don't think you're entitled to make that kind of decision. I am perfectly capable of choosing the company I keep."

"I'm more entitled than you think," he muttered, stalking off ahead of her. He couldn't bring himself to face her, not yet. He wasn't sure if it was because of the hope he might see reflected in her gaze, or if it would be something worse. Like resignation. "Is this your decision, then? Is that who you're choosing to marry? Prince Drake of Brackroth? The fucking Shadowblade Assassin?"

"What do you care?" She huffed and her magic crackled, causing his to damn near combust. "I don't see why you're so upset. I'm doing exactly as you suggested, aren't I? I'm *defying the stars*. And since you've made your stance on the matter perfectly clear, who I choose as my husband is none of your concern."

He whipped around on her then, consumed with desire and rage, his mind and his heart at war with one another. "So long as your soul is bonded to mine, so long as your magic calls to mine, *everything* you do is my business."

She fisted her hands on her hips, chest heaving. "You don't want me, remember? You *rejected* me."

Gods, she was infuriating.

Asher turned back, heading deeper into the woods where the moonlight sliced through the treetops like blades of glass.

"Go ahead and walk away then, just like you always do. I've noticed that about you." She was panting now. He could hear it in every sharp inhale, felt it in the rapid beating of her heart. But he didn't stop. "You walk away from situations you think you can't win. You hole up in your house, inside the safety of your study whenever things get hard, whenever there's something you don't want to face. You're a coward, Lord Firebane."

His nails bit into the roughened palms of his hands, but he didn't care. If he faced her now, there was a good chance he'd explode, unloading all of his barely contained fury, all of his anguish and hurt, all of his raw power on her. He would lash out at her. Kiss her. Then fuck her, if she let him. There would be no recovering from it. He would be lost to her forever.

"Can you *please* slow down?" From behind him, she sucked in a ragged breath, but it was edged with anger. "I can't keep up with you in this dress."

"Then perhaps you should take it off."

Her stunned silence was deafening.

At least that shut her up long enough so he could figure out what the hell he was doing. But he did slow down, glancing back at her.

Novalise trudged up the small hill behind him. The hem of her dress was caked with mud, and the heels she wore dug into the soft earth and stuck with every step. Her cheeks were flushed, and a scowl marred her brow. Pieces of her lavender hair had fallen from her braid once again, curling in the thick heat. She looked exhausted. Agitated. And downright miserable.

A twinge of guilt stabbed at him. He should've been more mindful of her. She was a lady, after all, and he was completely disregarding her well-being.

"Why are you carting me off into the woods?" Novalise spread her arms wide, annoyance flooding her once more. She huffed, attempting to smooth away the wrinkles of her silk gown. "This is absurd. We're far enough away now, no one will be able to hear you confess that you're horrified by the idea of being my soul mate. Even if you made a mistake, which we both did—"

Asher crossed the distance between them in two strides. He gripped her by the waist and tugged her against him. Her eyes widened when he pulled her close, but he didn't kiss her. He couldn't. Not again. His gaze betrayed him, dipping down to her mouth.

"Would you just be quiet?" He slid the words into her mind, and a frown furrowed across her brow.

Novalise shook her head, absently tucking a strand of hair behind her ear. "No. I'm tired of being told what to do, where to be, and how to act. I'm never allowed my own opinions, I'm never given an option or a choice. And I'm tired of it, Asher. I'm sick of letting everyone walk all over me while I stand here and take it. While I simply do nothing."

Tears pooled at the corner of her eyes, and he held her closer, fighting against his better judgment.

"And more than anything," she said, her bottom lip quivering, "I'm sick of wanting you."

"You don't want me, my lady." She opened her mouth to object, but he kept going, refusing to let her get another word in, unable to let her smart little mouth wreck him further. "The bond is the only thing tying the two of us together. What you feel is purely physical. There's no hidden emotions there, no intimacy. The tether between us is magical, wrought together by powers beyond our control. Hell, you don't even know me."

"That's not true."

A single tear slid down her cheek, and though he longed to wipe it away, he let it fall.

"I know you hate the idea of love, though I don't understand why. I know you think you want to be alone, but your isolation keeps me up in the late hours of the night, leaving me wanting to do nothing except comfort you." She arched into him slowly, grinding her hips against him. Her palms slid from his forearms up to his shoulders, locking behind his neck. Her scent teased his senses, rolling over him, layering and melding with his own. "I know you have a brilliant mind. I know you look for logical explanations everywhere, including why you were somehow bonded to me. And I know it scared you. So much so that because it was something beyond your understanding, you felt the need to reject me instead."

"There's no love here, Novalise." His words were quiet, lacking conviction.

"Then why does it ache when I'm not near you?" She rose up on her toes, leaning into him. Her eyes were like pools of liquid starlight, flecked with iridescent rainbows. They owned him.

"And why does it feel like my soul is on fire whenever you're by my side?"

"Because..." Asher bent down, pressing his forehead lightly to hers, knowing he would regret whatever he did next. "Because your heart is tied to mine."

Shoving all rational thought from his mind, Asher kissed Novalise in a storm of stars and fire.

CHAPTER FIFTEEN

*N*ovalise was aflame.

Asher's mouth crashed over hers, his tongue seeking entry along her lips, and she opened for him readily. His hands slid from her hips to her ass, gripping her, grinding her against him. He broke their kiss and she gasped, her head falling back as his mouth left a trail of burning kisses down the column of her neck. Curling her fingers into his hair, she held on as the tension between them ignited, sending a wave of energy skittering across her skin.

He adjusted, hiking up her skirts and wedging his knee between her legs, holding her against him. She practically crawled up his muscular thigh, eager for any shred of friction. His knuckles grazed her shoulders. Delicious shivers left her trembling with anticipation. He wanted her, *finally*, he wanted her.

Slowly, Asher hooked one finger, then another, under the satin straps of her dress. The soft fabric slid against her skin, and he took hold of the center bodice of her dress, nudging it down so her breasts tumbled free. Glints of silver spilled across her pale flesh, bathing her in moonlight. She curled her fingers into his shirt, fisting the material with both hands, and praying to the goddess that he didn't stop.

"Perfect," he murmured, lowering his head to her.

Novalise squirmed against him, desperate for him to touch her. To taste her. She didn't care if she was wanton in his arms, she longed for him. Ached for him. Again, she rubbed herself along the length of his strong thigh, silently begging for more.

He bent his head lower, his lips hovering above the valley of her breasts.

"Tell me what you want." Asher's words skated over her flesh, warm and sultry. She arched into him, a silent entreaty.

His tongue flicked her nipple, just once, and she whimpered.

"You." She bit the word out on a gasp.

He reached one hand up, cupping the back of her neck, drawing her close to him. With his free hand, his thumb idly toyed with her nipple—he traced slow, lazy circles, gently brushing his calloused skin back and forth across the sensitive bud at an excruciating pace. Her magic sparked and spiraled, desperate for his flames to consume her. The bond thrummed between them, beating and pulsing with a life all its own.

Shocks of pleasure rippled through her, teasing her until she thought for certain that every star in the sky would blink out of existence.

Asher nuzzled her neck, inhaling the essence of her soul, trailing whispers of featherlight kisses along the column of her neck. Novalise dragged one leg up to his waist, locking herself against him. She needed him closer. She didn't want any space, not even a breath, to be between them. Fates divine, what she wouldn't give to have the entirety of his sculpted, naked body on top of her right now. Controlling her. Dominating her. She wanted all of him, all his days and nights, from now until forever.

His fingers molded around her breast, squeezing lightly, and he softly pressed his mouth to the corner of her lips. A reminder he could be gentle. "I can't give you what you want, Novalise."

She forced herself to meet his gaze. In the dim forest, his eyes were smoldering embers, blazing with hunger. She reached up, twirling his streak of silver hair around one finger. "I only want you."

There was the slightest upturn of his mouth. He shook his head, his hair falling free from her fingers, shadowing his face. "No, you don't. What you're feeling right now is desire. Pure lust."

Asher reached down, gathering the fabric of her gown, easily shoving it out of the way. His palm slid along the underside of her thigh, holding her in place, and heat coursed through her like wildfire. Then he grabbed her other leg, repeating the movement, and hoisted her up into his arms. She was anchored against him, locking her ankles around his waist. The feel of his hands against her bare skin sent a rush of blinding ecstasy straight to her core.

"You want love." His whisper floated past her ear as he moved through the forest, carrying her. Something smooth and solid pressed against her back—one of the twisted trees. Her breath hitched as he pressed another painfully soft kiss on her neck, where her pulse leaped for him. "That is something I can never give you."

"Why not?"

This time, his mouth found hers and their tongues collided. She could lose herself in his kiss, drown in him, and never need to come up for air. Magic crackled like kindling, a riot of flames and stars. She wanted that wicked tongue of his everywhere. Licking her nipples until she broke beneath him. Trailing a path from her throat to her abdomen, then further still. Delving deep between her thighs, soothing the ache there.

Asher leaned back, his fingers digging into the flesh of her thighs, and she shifted, rubbing herself against his rather prominent erection. "I took a vow."

She leveled him with a challenging glare. "Vows can be broken."

"So can bonds," he fired back, the threat hanging between them.

Yanking his shirt, she pulled him flush against her, so there was no space left between them. "You wouldn't dare."

"Oh, believe me, I would. In fact, I almost did so today." Asher leaned down, his tongue gliding up her neck, marking her. Branding her. "Why do you think I was at the palace?"

Novalise should have felt that familiar flare of annoyance, the flooding heat of humiliation. But all she could focus on was Asher pressing her back into a tree while his hand worked between her legs, slowly unbuttoning his pants.

She'd never been more grateful to loathe lacy undergarments in her life.

He tightened his hold on her. The tip of his cock was poised at her entrance, nudging her slick folds, tempting her with the promise of release.

"Breaking bonds is dangerous." Her voice was a harsh whisper.

"So is fucking the one who rejected you." Asher pushed forward, the barest of movements, gently prying her open. She strained for him, her chest heaving. His stern gaze raked over her, scalding her. "Unless..."

She stared at him, unable to break his smoldering gaze. "Unless what?"

"Unless you marry me."

Novalise's breath hitched. There was no humor in his eyes, no mocking ridicule. He was serious. Intent. "You want to marry me?"

"Understand me, my lady. I am incapable of love." He urged his cock deeper, another inch, and she almost came undone. His touch was torture. "When I say this is all I can give you, I mean it."

Novalise told herself it would be enough. Whatever he was willing to give her, she would accept. There would be time later to sort through her feelings, to deal with the remorse of her decision, to manage the shame that came with knowing he would never completely choose her, even though their souls were bound to one another. Because she swore to the heavens that if he walked away from her now, she would die.

"Okay." She bobbed her head, spread her hands over his solid abdomen, then let her nails scrape against his shirt.

Asher groaned. "I don't love you."

She swallowed down her cry of regret. His words were a frostfire blade to her heart. "I understand."

"I don't love you." His mouth slashed across hers, his teeth nipping her bottom lip. "Say it, Starlight."

She trembled in his arms. "I don't love you."

Asher shoved himself into her, stretching her, and his name fell from her lips on a startled cry. Another adjustment and he situated himself even deeper inside of her, ensuring she felt every glorious inch of him. With devastating slowness, he slid out, then buried himself into her once more. His hips rocked back and forth, the rhythm sensuous and steady, and Novalise couldn't look away from the glow of magic pooling in his eyes. Each thrust was timed to leave her dangling on the edge before he filled her again, raising her higher. Letting her soar.

Power erupted around her and Asher in a whirlwind of stardust and midnight fire. Her braid lifted from her shoulder as the melding of their magic intensified, pulsing through the air. It thrummed between them, spurring them, beckoning to them give themselves to one another. Asher groped the back of her thighs, his fingers inching upward with each pump until his hands were molded to her ass.

He squeezed hard and she clenched, wanting more. She

clawed at his shirt, needing to feel his skin. But there were too many buttons. Why were there so many buttons?

"Fuck. You're so wet for me." He jerked forward, adjusting his grip. In one movement, he lifted her higher against the tree, jolting her into a state of agonizing bliss as his cock teased her into oblivion. "I need more of you."

He picked up the pace, pumping faster. Harder. She held onto his shoulders while her breasts bounced in his face. He lowered his head and nipped at them before finally catching one with his mouth.

Asher's teeth sank into her flesh, and their magic exploded. Stars ruptured, whipping into a dazzling storm of light. Icy flames of silver and black licked her heated skin, growing higher, threatening to combust. Their bond magnified, until the rapid beating of their hearts became one, until Asher was the only air Novalise needed to breathe.

But he didn't love her.

He would never love her.

Her soul shattered. A swelling ache strangled the desire siphoning through her. The agonizing sensation flayed her open, left her raw and bare. Despair rose like a rogue wave out at sea, crashing into her, drowning her.

"Gods. Fuck." Asher stilled, his jaw locked. A severe line cut across his brow, and just as swiftly as he slammed into her, he withdrew. "I can't do this."

Novalise's body teetered on the edge of devastation. She clutched at him, the loss of him from inside her left her shaking. "What?"

Asher stepped away from her, shoving his still throbbing erection back into his pants. He ran a hand through his mussed hair, then shook his head. He wouldn't even look at her, the bastard.

"But I agreed. Plenty of people marry for reasons other than love." Novalise's heart hammered, her chest rose and fell, but her lungs were too tight. The forest was stifling, the air suddenly too perfumed. Too stagnant. "Reasons like what you were just doing to me, for example."

Asher's scowl only deepened. Her attempt at humor failed miserably.

He shook his head. "This was a mistake. It won't work. I was a fool to ask for your hand. You will always want the one thing I can't give you. Your mind may think you capable of such a union, but your heart has shown me otherwise."

There was something in his voice, like an overwhelming sadness he couldn't form into words. But it made no difference. Once Novalise touched the forest floor, the world came crashing down, and the twisted tree was the only thing left to keep her upright.

"It's only marriage," she pleaded, hating the fact that she was begging him to choose her. To want her.

"I know you, Novalise Starstorm. You believe in fairy tales and you trust the stars to make all your dreams come true." Asher looked back at her, and the magic ebbed, but the longing in his gaze held true. Even though he tried his damnedest to hide it. "If we were to marry, you would tell yourself you're happy at first, and I have no doubt I'll be able to pleasure you beyond your wildest fantasies."

The sting of a blush bled into her cheeks.

"But eventually, you would come to resent me. You would grow to hate me because you desire a love match above all else. What will your stars tell you then? You'll become lonely and seek solace in the arms of another man, likely one more deserving of you than me." He shoved his hands into the pocket of his pants and stepped back, away from her. "I am many things, but I am not quick to forgive a transgression against me. I do not share what is mine."

"Then make me yours." She stumbled forward, dragging her dress back over her shoulders to conceal herself.

"I can't." He shook his head, his tumble of hair concealing half of his face from her view. "There has to be another way."

When he spoke, it was a murmur, like he was talking more to himself than to her.

"But you said you needed more of me." She couldn't help it, her bottom lip trembled.

"Yes. I did say that. But wanting to fuck you and wanting to marry you aren't the same thing. I shouldn't have forced either upon you." Roughing a hand along his jaw, he looked down at her, shadows haunting the planes of his handsome face. "I can't marry you."

This time, she was faster.

Novalise slapped Asher across his face.

CHAPTER SIXTEEN

The sting of Novalise's hand across Asher's face only made him want her more.

"Novalise." He reached for her, but she dodged his grasp.

"That's *Lady* Novalise to you." She whirled away from him in a flurry of satin, her braid of lavender whipping behind her.

He snatched it, grabbing a fistful of the silky strands in his palms before yanking her backward.

"My lady." Asher didn't tug hard enough to hurt her, just enough to have her back flush up against his chest. Just enough so the hasty beating of her heart caused his blood to pump with desire all over again. The curve of her body molded to his perfectly, her uneven breathing a balm to his broken soul. Gradually, his fingers trailed down the length of her neck, skimming over her jumping pulse. "Let me explain."

She turned in his arms, and for a brief moment, he thought he'd convinced her to stay. Then she shoved away from him, nearly tripping over a tree root in the process. Her eyes were on fire, like shooting stars on winter's coldest night.

"No. It's my turn to walk away." She bit her bottom lip, and he knew it was to keep herself from crying. "Now you get to see how it feels, to experience the agony I suffer every time you reject me."

Asher stood there, dumbfounded, as she stomped through the forest back to the call of music and laughter. As soon as she was no longer in his line of sight, the bond yanked tight, stealing the air from his lungs. The strength of it was overwhelming, excruciating. He would have been no less surprised if a thousand blades fell from the sky and plunged straight into his heart. The pain was enough to bring him to his knees.

Untempered anger welled up inside of him, his fury directed at himself.

This was all his fault.

He thought marrying Novalise was the best option, the only option really, to keep her safe from Prince Drake. The whole situation was made worse by the fact that she foolishly agreed. It made no difference if he warned her beforehand that he couldn't give her what she wanted, he should've known better than to believe her. Novalise was the darling of Aeramere. Perfect. Poised. As flawless as a coveted diamond.

Except for when he had her pinned to a tree with her legs wrapped tight around his waist while he drove himself into her over and over again. Her breathy gasps echoed in his mind, the way she cried out his name still rang in his ears. He'd been so close to watching her orgasm, so close to emptying himself inside of her. Fuck if his balls didn't ache just thinking about it.

But then her emotions melded with his own. He'd felt her heartbreak, her soul-shattering despair so keenly, it was like those same sensations belonged to him. He knew then he couldn't go through with it, he couldn't marry her only to see her miserable for the rest of her life. It didn't matter if their magic was a perfect match, if the power they created together was unlike anything he'd ever felt. Her sorrow almost broke him. It was pure torture, knowing his inability to love her destroyed her soul.

Unfortunately, he was out of options. No matter what choice he made, he would ultimately break her heart. Because Trysta Starstorm read as much in his stars. He'd only ever had one reading, one his own mother forced upon him, and when Trysta predicted Asher would be exactly like his father, he knew then he could never allow himself to love anyone.

Or better yet, never allow himself to be loved.

He wouldn't be worthy of affection. His temper would seek to ruin all he ever cared for and if he raised a hand to Novalise, he would never be able to live with himself.

Asher walked back through the forest, following the sounds of merriment until he was once more along the outskirts of the faerie ring. Magic swelled as he stepped over the flowers and into the circle where the music pitched to a crescendo and everyone danced as though they had not a care in the world. Even the trees seemed to sway in time to the lively beat. Boisterous laughter and the harmonious folk tune did nothing to alleviate his rotten mood.

"Asher!"

He turned to see Cyra and her best friend, Lilith, walking over to him.

"Where have you been? I was looking everywhere for you." There was a faint sheen of sweat across her brow and a sparkle in her eyes. He didn't dare ask what she'd been doing while he was gone. Cyra reached up, trying to smooth his wild hair. "And what happened to your hair?"

He gently swatted her hand away, shoving it back from his face.

Lilith watched the exchange, the corner of her deeply painted lips curling. "From the looks of it, I'd say he was slightly indisposed. A bit delayed, if you will."

Asher stiffened, brushing his hair from his face again. "You don't know what you're talking about."

Lilith looked pointedly at his dick, then let her eyes wander back up the front of him before finally meeting his gaze. She smirked, crossing her arms beneath her chest to boost her ample bosom. "Oh, I know exactly what I'm talking about."

He glowered down at her, but she didn't flinch under the severity of his stare.

The damn fae.

Of course, she would know what he'd been doing. It was time for a deft change of subject.

"Have you had any luck finding a match, Cyra?" He glanced around the party carrying on around them, carefully avoid any more interactions with Lilith. "Anyone who strikes your fancy?"

Lilith's seductive laughter rang out, garnering the attention of multiple males and more than one female. "No one you would approve of, my lord."

Cyra sent Lilith an admonishing look, nudging her lightly with her elbow. "Not yet, darling brother. Though a fae lord from House Galefell did ask me to dance. Twice."

Ah. At least that explained the flush in her cheeks. He was relieved her rise of color was not some other activity.

"That is something," he agreed, glancing out over her head once more to see if he could spy anyone lurking between the dancers, waiting for him to walk away. He'd been told on more than one occasion he wasn't exactly approachable, and he saw no reason for that sentiment to change, even if Cyra's future was on the line. He didn't exactly possess the same intimidating demeanor as the shadow prince, but he wouldn't be at all surprised if his sister had to drag her future husband before him to ask for Asher's blessing.

"What about you, my lord?" Lilith sauntered closer, her hips swaying. She used her sexual prowess on many a male for her own wicked ways, and Asher was grateful he'd always been immune to her advances. "Will you be choosing a bride this Midsummer?"

Asher made a derisive, scoffing sound. "Absolutely not."

"I imagine such a notion would be impossible, considering..." Lilith's allure faded, her voice trailing off.

"Considering what?" he prompted.

Cyra tugged on his sleeve, staring at something behind him. She'd gone terribly pale. He turned to see what captured their attention.

"Evening," Prince Drake murmured, the dancers around them backing up, giving the Shadowblade Assassin a wide berth.

"Your Highness." Cyra and Lilith greeted him in unison, dropping into elegant curtsies.

Asher afforded the prince a stiff bow. "Kalstrand."

Prince Drake eyed him coolly, inclining his head. "Firebane."

Without looking away from the prince, Asher spoke to his sister and Lilith. "Ladies."

"Come on, Lilith." Cyra grabbed Lilith's hand, tugging her close to her side. "Let's go dance."

He waited until his sister and Lilith disappeared into the safety of the crowd before addressing Prince Drake. "I thought you'd seek me out sooner, Your Highness."

The shadow prince clicked tongue, shaking his head. When he smiled, it was cruel. "You fuck up everything, don't you, Firebane?"

A flicker of annoyance fired through Asher. "What the hell is that supposed to mean?"

"I gave you something on a silver platter and you ruined it." He took an intimidating step forward, malice radiating from him. "You of all people should know I never make the same offer twice."

Unease slithered down Asher's spine. He knew the day would come when he would have to face the Shadowblade Assassin again. Inhaling, he steadied himself, calmed the trepidation coursing through him like a rapid current.

Asher lowered his voice, aware of those who pretended to

ignore them, but who listened for any significant detail from their conversation, anything that could be plucked and twisted into a rumor. "If this is about our deal, I only need a little more time. I've narrowed down the location of the *virdis lepatite* to three regions."

The prince arched a dubious brow. "Only three?"

Bastard.

"Considering the vastness of the world, yes. Only three. A mortal kingdom in the Northernlands, the Kethwyn Woods, or the bogs of Fenmire."

At the mention of Fenmire, the prince's lip curled in disgust. "Fenmire? That place reeks of tainted witch blood and ancient curses."

"All the more reason for a stone of great power to be hidden there." Asher crossed his arms over his chest, a silent provocation. "Don't you agree?"

Prince Drake was steel. Frigid air engulfed the space between them. "You have until the end of Midsummer."

Eleven days.

Asher nodded once. "Done."

They met each other's harsh glares. Unblinking. Unwavering.

"Don't let me down, Firebane." Prince Drake's voice dripped with disdain, and another menacing smile graced his glacial expression. "I remember how devastated your mother was at the loss of your vile father. I'd hate to see Lady Novalise or your precious little sister suffer the same fate."

The icy hand of fear gripped the back of Asher's neck. "Is that a threat, shadow prince?"

The barb struck true. Prince Drake loathed the nickname coined by his father and his body grew rigid, taut with rage. He sneered. "It's a promise, frostfire fae."

Asher clenched his jaw, swallowing the growl of fury threatening to erupt from inside him.

With that, Drake turned and stalked right through the group of dancers, chuckling darkly as they stumbled and tripped to get out of his way.

Frustration clouded Asher's mind. He was running out of time. He only had eleven days left to find this mysterious green gemstone while also trying to ensure Novalise stayed as far away from Prince Drake as possible. Pressure compounded along his shoulders and back, coiling into tight springs of tension. His temples throbbed as the mounting stress slicked his palms with sweat.

He couldn't handle both tasks on his own.

Knowing there was no other way, Asher went in search of the one female who was a mastermind of persuasion.

His sister.

CHAPTER SEVENTEEN

*N*ovalise paced outside of Ariesian's study, waiting patiently for any sign of her brother.

He'd not yet returned from the Yavanna Ball, assuming he was even still there. She'd seen him speaking with Solarius and Lord Everland, but then he'd disappeared. She could imagine he had more important matters to attend to, but a prickle of concern lodged itself deep within her spine.

Massive windows lined the wall on her left, each of them reaching to a fine point where faceted glass constellations hung from the center. In the dawn hours, they reflected dozens of tiny rainbows along the floors and down the hall—one of Creslyn's many fantastical creations. Now, however, the corridors were dim, lit with only the golden glow of faerie fire that flickered within the crescent-shaped sconces nestled on the wall between each window.

It was late, even for Ariesian. The skies were dark, the stars invisible behind a dense layer of clouds.

Novalise yawned, leaning back against his door. Her body sagged from the weight of exhaustion, the fire engulfing her from before had gone cold. She'd taken the entire carriage ride back to Celestine to cool off, focusing all her anger, all her frustration, and developing it into a solid plan. After her disastrous encounter with Asher in the forest, she knew she'd have to take matters into her own hands.

But fates divine, she'd been *so* close. Not only to release but also to finding a husband. To convincing her mate they were the perfect match. She'd been willing to accept the fact that Asher would never love her, but he was bound to her. The second he'd buried himself inside her, she'd known within the deepest part of her heart she would never be able to give herself to another. She'd been an absolute fool to think she could ignore the bond, to think that eventually it would lessen, perhaps even cease to hurt so damn much. If anything, the moment they'd joined together, the power rippling between them had intensified. When their magic fused, it was potent. Unrivaled. The feel of those icy flames of his licking her skin was intoxicating. Frostfire was tempting, alluring. When they kissed, it was overwhelming, as though she was being consumed by stars and flames.

Then there was that devastating nickname he'd called her.

Starlight.

She slumped against Ariesian's door, her shoulders drooping. A yawn escaped her, and she quickly covered her mouth with the back of her hand out of habit.

Certainly Asher had to feel the same things. Despite his aversion to love, they were a completion of one another. She just had to make him realize it. There had to be a way for her to help him overcome whatever held him back, whatever made him feel the need to abandon her.

Eleven days.

Novalise told herself it was plenty of time. She'd made a deal with Prince Drake, and if their plan was going to work, it would require Ariesian's assistance. She would convince her brother to draw up a trade agreement with Prince Drake, exactly as he'd asked her to do. Once she succeeded, the shadow prince would be compelled to help her secure a mate for her marriage, exactly as he promised. And not just any mate. Asher.

Because the prince had certainly been right about one thing, Asher was probably the only fae in all of Aeramere who didn't fear him. She had no doubt Prince Drake would hold up his end of their bargain. Despite being a ruthless assassin, he hardly seemed like the type to go back on his word. If anything, he would be more likely to enforce it with scrupulous consequences.

Heavy footfalls sounding down the hall snagged her attention, and she drew herself up, smoothing her rumpled skirts so she at least looked somewhat presentable.

"Novalise." Ariesian appeared at the end of the corridor, walking toward her. He glanced up and down the hall, a line of concern furrowing across his brow. "What are you doing up this late? I would have thought you'd be in bed by now."

Right. Because that was expected of her and she never did anything rebellious. Granted, staying up past her apparent bedtime wouldn't exactly start a rebellion, but this was all new for her and she was going to take it one step at a time.

She straightened, smiling to greet her eldest brother. "I need to speak with you."

Ariesian blew out a breath, the ends of his silver hair fluttering across his forehead. "Regarding?"

Novalise steeled her backbone. "A trade deal with Brackroth."

Ariesian reached behind her, opening the door to his study. Unease rippled around him. "Negotiations with other realms are none of your concern, Nova." He gestured for her to sit, and she seated herself on the plush navy velvet sofa. "Especially ones involving Prince Kalstrand."

"I understand." Novalise settled against the soft cushions, folding her hands in her lap. She couldn't back down, not this time. "But I'm also aware he seeks an accord with House Celestine."

She wouldn't mention the fact she thought it completely mind-boggling that Prince Drake would want to bargain with House Celestine and not all of Aeramere. But Queen Elowyn had never limited the reach of the houses when it came to bettering their livelihoods or improving relations among other realms. Her primary concern was that of her crown. So long as she maintained the integrity of the Veil, she would never need to worry. Unless, of course, another uprising occurred, though there hadn't been one of those in years. Not with Prince Aspen at the helm of their defense.

Ariesian dropped into the leather chair behind a desk covered with marked pages in books and stacks of paper. He was usually so orderly, and everything had its place. He leaned back, pinching the bridge of his nose. "Prince Kalstrand told you this?"

That information she was definitely keeping to herself.

"Ariesian, I'm no fool." She leaned forward, trying to make her point. "He mentioned a contract the night the Veil was lifted when he demanded I be escorted home."

Glowing faerie fire bounced off his features, covering him in a swath of light and shadow. Her brother looked exhausted. He squeezed his eyes shut, gently rubbing his temples. "His terms, Nova...they can't be taken lightly."

She would expect nothing less. This was the Shadowblade Assassin they were talking about. He moved with purpose, spoke with precision, and never said anything he didn't mean. She could only assume his mannerisms and demands would be reflected in every negotiation.

"Understandable." Novalise nodded. "What is he offering us?"

"A trade." Ariesian opened his eyes. They were dark and haunted. "Protection."

Protection? That seemed a little excessive. She wasn't involved in the intricacies of politics surrounding the houses of Aeramere, but she knew they were safe. She knew the Veil safeguarded them from any outside threats.

"Protection from who?" Novalise prompted and Ariesian sent her a withering look. "Let me guess, it's none of my concern."

"You know how I feel about you partaking in such burdensome conversations."

"The stars spoke to me in a reading, Ariesian, and the constellations that were shown to me?" She shook her head, crossing her arms. "They should *not* have been in alignment."

He leaned across the desk, lifting one brow in concern. "What did you see?"

"Aedes the Fae Warrior, the Great Stag, and Vespira the Druid."

"Holy shit." He winced, sparing her a glance. "Apologies for my coarse language, Novalise."

She waved him off, dismissing his nonsense.

"But you're right." She was on the edge of the sofa now, her fingers digging into the soft velvet. "You know what they mean as well as I do. Overcoming strife or possibly even impending war. Power and leadership. Great change. Ariesian, I couldn't possibly have misinterpreted them. Their meanings hold true, do they not?"

"They do." He dropped his head, muttering to himself. The words were unintelligible, and all she caught was the trail of a sentence ending with, "I should've known."

Suddenly, he stilled and his head snapped up. "Who else knows?"

Novalise reared back. "I'm sorry?"

"Who else have you told about your reading?" He grabbed a pen and a blank sheet of parchment from beneath a stack of books. "Your most recent one, not the one that mother conducted."

He stared at her, intent.

"Queen Elowyn and Prince Aspen." She swallowed, her throat dry and gritty. "Prince Drake and Lord Firebane may have been in attendance as well when I announced my discovery."

"Damn."

Two foul words in one night. Her brother was in a strange mood indeed. He never swore in front of her. Ever.

Ariesian sighed. He sank lower into the leather chair, kicking up his legs. Propping his feet on the desk, he crossed his ankles. His fingers drummed lightly on the arm of the chair, tapping a restless rhythm she didn't recognize. She'd never seen him so ill at ease. Ariesian was usually the embodiment of a well-bred lord. Classy. Composed. Unostentatious and reserved. But right now, he looked ready to crawl out of his skin. The tension rolled off him in thick, suffocating waves.

"He makes a tempting offer, but what he wants in return…" Ariesian unbuttoned the top two buttons of his collared shirt, yanking on them. "I'm not sure it's something I can give up."

"Why not?" She heaved a sigh of frustration, instantly regretting the action. Apprehension hardened the angular planes of his face. "Apologies, dear brother. I suppose I don't understand why you can't relinquish something in return for protection."

"Because it's valuable, Novalise." He shook his head, his expression almost pained. "It's something very precious to me."

Oh.

Oh.

Prince Drake wanted the Celestinian wayfinder, Ariesian's astrolabe. As children, they called it the Star Thief, though it was essentially a compass for the skies, but it only ever pointed to the Great Stag, Ariesian's star sign.

Novalise shifted, uncomfortable. She should've known the

shadow prince would want something that was handcrafted with ancient magic, incredibly rare, and had been in their family for generations.

"Ariesian, listen to me. I've looked up to you for the entirety of my life. You are noble. Intelligent. Loyal to a fault. But most of all, every decision you have ever made has always been for the good of our house and our family." She met her brother's weary gaze. "Do you believe the protection of Brackroth is something we might need in the future?"

His lips pressed together in a firm line. "It's a possibility."

A tingle of unease prodded along her spine. She didn't particularly care for the idea of battles and wars. Or lands ripped apart by turmoil and strife. All the more reason for Ariesian to not sleep on this trade agreement. "If Prince Kalstrand's offer will keep us safe, then you know what you must do."

Ariesian ran a hand through his hair, leaving it sticking up and out of sorts. "I'll consider it."

"Please do." Novalise stood and headed toward the door. "Good night, Ariesian. Try to get some rest."

He flicked his wrist, a pitiful attempt at a wave if she ever saw one, and then she left his study, closing the door behind her.

The halls of the house were quiet, save for the soft clicking of her heels against the dark stone floor. Windows of fused colored glass displayed her reflection, elegant and poised if not slightly disheveled. But there was not a trace of selfishness. She'd upheld her end of the bargain with Prince Drake, and now it would be up to him to keep his word. All he had to do was help make Asher fall in love with her.

Novalise slowed her steps as she neared her bedroom. With a quick glance over her shoulder, she checked to make sure she was entirely alone. Then she cupped her hands together, drawing on the magic coursing through her veins, summoning the power of the Estrela's crown. Energy flowed over her, illuminating her skin with an iridescent glow. Her magic crackled, bursting from the center of her palms, taking on the shape of an inky cloud of night. Tiny streaks of starfire sprinkled throughout it, shimmering like diamonds against a swath of black silk. Blazing brightly in the middle of it all was the spark of frostfire flames.

CHAPTER EIGHTEEN

*A*sher silently ate his breakfast, all the while being entirely too aware of his sister's movements. Cyra stirring her tea, the clinking sound of the spoon against porcelain echoing throughout the dining room. Cyra reaching for a second helping of bacon. Cyra scooping out the last of the blackberry jam for her toast when she didn't think he was looking.

They'd spent countless hours in this room together every morning, the topic of conversation always varying, never having to struggle to fill the silence with inconsequential statements. Not too long ago, this room was teeming with tension. Meals were taken in stony silence and laced with fear of their father's wrath. There was a faint blemish on the rug, where the tips of auburn leaves were blackened. That was from the night his father tried to set him on fire. Asher still bore the scarring from it on his back. His father was boasting about his fire magic, claiming that Asher's frostfire was polluted, going on about how only his shrew of a mother could possess cold fire. His words had incinerated Asher.

They fought, and when his bastard of a father tossed a fire bolt at him, he'd warned Asher not to yell or he'd end him.

He'd dropped to the ground, rolling to put out the flames. He could still smell the stench of his own burning flesh, could feel the heat from the fire as it charred his skin. All while his father stood over him, watching. Chuckling.

Asher's mother had rushed into the dining room then, screaming. His father warned her to stay away, that Asher was receiving the punishment he deserved for being unable to hold his tongue. She hadn't listened. She ripped one of the drapes off the window and threw it on top of Asher, smothering the flames.

For two months, there was a hole in the wall from where his father had thrown her into it.

Asher had done everything in his power to shield Cyra from their father's cruelty. Anything to keep her safe, to keep her blind to the violent cloud that shadowed their house.

He thought that once his father was dead, some semblance of happiness could be restored in their lives. They no longer had to live in fear. He could study and read without having to worry his father might come along and knock him upside the head with one of his own books. Or worse, use them as kindling for bonfires. But he'd been gravely mistaken. While he and Cyra tried to fill the hostile space left behind by their father with warm memories, their mother spiraled into a state of despair.

She blamed the stars for her misfortune, for stealing the supposed love of her life. And then one day, when they were finally done with "mourning" the loss of their father, their mother took her own life.

It was then Asher realized love would have no place in his heart.

Love was selfish. Brutal and harsh.

He never wanted to be subjected to its bitter ways again. Which was why he needed to enlist his sister's help.

"Cyra." Asher leaned back in his seat and took a sip of tea. "I have a favor to ask of you."

"Anything." She stole one more piece of bacon from the platter. "What is it?"

"First, I need you to understand that what I'm about to tell you is incredibly important and second, you cannot tell a soul." He watched her carefully over the rim of his teacup, expecting her eyes to flash with curiosity.

Instead, she bit off a piece of the bacon, not nearly as interested as he thought she would be in such an exchange. "Let me guess. You've discovered a way to control all the elements and need me to cover for you while you plot to overthrow the queen."

Asher coughed, choking. Then he leveled her with a grave look. "Cute. But treason is nothing to laugh about and I'm being serious."

"As am I." She looked up at him then, her head tilting. She pointed her half-eaten piece of bacon in his direction. "You're brilliant, Asher. Sure, you're a bit of a recluse who prefers the company of books to anything that breathes, but there's no doubt in my mind that if anyone could find a way to master all the elements of Aeramere, it would be you."

Asher didn't know whether he should be flattered by Cyra's compliment, or bothered by the fact that she'd apparently given thought to the prospect of him committing treachery.

"Ah, thank you...I think." He frowned, setting his tea down. It was too cool to be enjoyed, anyway. "What I actually need from you is—"

"You know," Cyra continued, taking a bite of her jam-covered toast, "I have heard rumors of an underground organization attempting to rise against Queen Elowyn."

Asher intended to chide her for interrupting him, but the information she gave so freely was disturbing. As a councilor to Queen Elowyn, he was usually privy to such matters. But the queen had a rule, politics and the like were not to be discussed during Midsummer. It was the one time of year she strictly enforced a recess from all court discussions.

He propped his elbow up on the table, leaning forward. "I'm sorry, what did you say?"

Cyra glanced around to ensure none of the servants were lingering too closely. But it was just the two of them in the room, as always.

"It's true. There is word circulating through the houses that Prince Aspen is a tyrant, and he's just waiting for the most opportune moment to get rid of his mother."

"And by 'get rid of,' you mean…?"

Cyra slid her finger across her neck, imitating the slitting of one's throat.

He grimaced. He was going to have to make more of an effort to correct her demeanor and social etiquette if he ever expected to find her a suitable match.

Shaking his head, he reached for the teapot, topping off both of their cups. "Where did you hear such a thing?"

"Males talk. Drunk males talk even more." She smoothed her hair, running her fingers along the strands of fiery red that faded to a pale gold. "But it doesn't matter where I heard it because I believe it might be true."

"How do you figure?" He couldn't quite believe he was having this conversation with Cyra, but if there was any truth to what she was saying, then he needed to stay informed. Whether it was murmurings of a rebellion or embellished gossip that could easily be dismissed, he'd rather not take any chances until he knew for sure.

"Lord Nyxian and Lord Tovian of House Celestine have recently set sail with a High Prince of Faeven." Her lips pursed, as though considering her next words. "It was all very hush-hush."

Indeed.

He'd not heard anything about it. But Nyxian and Tovian were Novalise's brothers, and if what Cyra said was true, then perhaps he could gather a bit more information from Novalise. Assuming she ever spoke to him again.

"Do you happen to know where they're sailing?" he asked, curious how his sister could come across such pertinent information while he knew absolutely nothing. Maybe there was a benefit to attending all these absurd social engagements after all.

Cyra heaved a sigh, thoroughly disappointed. "Unfortunately, I haven't figured that part out yet."

Asher rapped his knuckles lightly on the table, musing to himself out loud. "Sailing...but Aeramere doesn't have a naval fleet."

"Not yet," Cyra countered, though it sounded more like a warning.

She was being incredibly ominous.

"I want you to promise me you won't talk of such things with anyone else." Asher reached for her hand, squeezing it gently. "The last thing I want is for you to get caught up in any sort of political intrigue."

It was one thing if Queen Elowyn or Prince Aspen asked something of him, but he would not allow his sister to be used as a pawn. By anyone.

Her smile was too bright. "Of course."

"Swear it," Asher demanded. "This isn't another one of your silly amusements. If you get caught up in any of this, there could be severe repercussions."

"Fine. I swear it on mother's grave." She pulled her hand out of his hold and picked up her piece of toast. Though she seemed content, a faint line etched its way across her usually smooth brow. "Now, what is this favor you need from me?"

"I need you to befriend Lady Novalise Starstorm."

Cyra's golden eyes widened like orbs, her lashes fluttering back. "*The* Lady Novalise Starstorm?"

"The very one."

"Whatever for?" Cyra snatched her napkin from her lap, dabbing at the corners of her mouth. "I'm sure she has plenty of friends."

"That may be, but how often do you ever see her with anyone?"

Cyra opened her mouth, then closed it. Her lips pursed. "Now that you mention it, hardly ever. She is always by herself. I imagine she's quite lonely."

Her unsaid words hung in the air between them.

Like you.

"Exactly," Asher agreed, shaking off the uncomfortable sensation. "I'd like for you to keep her occupied over the next few days. But mostly, more than anything, I need you to keep her far away from Prince Drake Kalstrand."

"The Shadowblade Assassin?" She gaped at him. "But why?"

"This is the part where you must not tell a soul." Asher held her gaze, willing her to understand. "Do I have your word?"

She nodded. "Yes. Yes, of course."

He swallowed, hoping she would stay calm. "I may have accidentally kissed Lady Novalise during Winter Solstice."

Cyra's face was blanketed. Expressionless. "And?"

"And in doing so, bound us to one another."

She stared at him, unblinking. When she spoke, her voice was eerily steady. "You're telling me that your soul is bound to that of Lady Novalise Starstorm? That your magic chose each other? That she's fated to you?"

"Yes. Yes. And also…" Asher cleared his throat. "Yes."

Her eyes darted from him to her plate and then back again. Her lips were pinched, her cheeks high with color. It was like watching a child walk by a candy store for the very first time.

He could see the excitement building inside of her, and her smile widened with pure elation.

"Asher!" she squealed, snatching his arm and shaking him. "Why didn't you tell me?"

"You know exactly why I didn't tell you." She was damn near bouncing in her seat. He gestured toward her, flicking his fingers up and down. "This is why I didn't tell you."

"Are you going to marry her?"

"No."

"Don't you love her?"

"No."

"Ash..." Cyra frowned, slumping into her seat. "You can't mean that."

He tugged at the collar of his shirt. He needed Cyra's assistance, needed her to keep Lady Novalise far away from Prince Drake's vicious clutches. "Will you help me or not?"

Resigned, Cyra stood from the table. She held her head high, kept her shoulders pulled back. She looked every inch the lady, with her hands folded neatly in front of her, and her gown of scarlet silk shimmering in the soft glow of morning light. "Yes. I'll help you."

She excused herself from the table, retreating from the dining room. Pausing, she grabbed the doorframe and turned to look over her shoulder at him. "It's not fair, Asher. To either of you. Rejecting the bond to Lady Novalise is no way to live your life, and it's cruel of you to make her suffer."

Asher's jaw clenched, and he held his breath, releasing it slowly until the swell of frustration ebbed away. He could not turn into his father. He would rather die before lifting a hand to a woman or child.

"You know I can't love her, Cyra."

"Can't? Or won't?" She glanced out the curving window of the dining room, her gaze chasing something he couldn't see. When she looked back at him, sympathy softened her features.

But whether it was compassion or pity, there was no way of knowing. "No one chooses to fall in love, just as no one can fully control a bond once it takes form. It's curious though, is it not? Stars and frostfire..."

Her lips pressed together. "Reminds me of a story you told me long ago. Perhaps you should read it again."

She turned to leave, and Asher stood.

"Cyra, wait. Where are you going?"

"I'm going to do what you asked of me." This time her smile was cunning, a devious upturn of her lips. "I'm going to see if Lady Novalise would care to join me for tea. In the garden."

"Here?" Asher stepped forward and almost tripped over his own feet. "You're going to invite her *here*?"

Cyra shrugged, ignoring his concern. "I can't think of a safer place, can you?"

His sister slipped out of the dining room then, humming to herself, her lighthearted footsteps carrying her down the hall. Asher continued to stand there, dumbfounded, suddenly regretting his decision to mention anything to her at all.

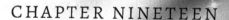

CHAPTER NINETEEN

*N*ovalise stared at the invitation.

The letter was written in gold ink with elegant script flowing across the cream parchment. It was folded neatly in an embossed envelope, but what surprised Novalise more than anything was that it was delivered by a firebird.

The beautiful creature swooped overhead, its stunning crimson feathers glittering like rubies in the afternoon sun. It dropped the letter into her hands, then darted back into the startling blue sky. She gazed up at it from the front entrance of her house, watching as the magical bird flew in and out of ribbons of white clouds.

Breaking the seal, Novalise skimmed the contents.

"What's that?"

She glanced up to see Sarelle walking down the path from the gardens to greet her.

"Oh, it's an invitation." Novalise read it once more, just to be sure.

Sarelle peered over her shoulder, rising on her toes. "To another party?"

"No. Actually, it's a letter...asking me to come for tea."

"Tea?" Sarelle leaned back, her midnight hair glittering like onyx, and laughed. "Who invited you to tea?"

Novalise shot her a look, and her sister had the decency to grimace.

"I *have* friends, Sarelle." It was a partial truth. The ladies she usually associated with at events and gatherings never called upon her and only seemed to make an appearance in her presence when it was a clear benefit to them.

"Of course you do," Sarelle amended quickly, ducking her head. Pink colored her cheeks, and she blew out a harsh breath. "I didn't mean to imply—"

"It's okay. I know what you meant." Novalise tucked Sarelle's hand into the crook of her arm and guided her back into the house. "If it makes you feel any better, you're not wrong."

She held out the invitation for Sarelle to see. "It's from Lady Cyra Firebane."

Sarelle blinked up at her, a line of consternation furrowing across her brow. "Lord Firebane's sister?"

"Yes."

"Are you going to respond?" Sarelle glanced around the great hall, smiling pleasantly as a servant carrying a vase of peonies and ferns bustled past them.

"Obviously." Novalise absently ran her thumb over the raised black wax seal depicting twin blades crossing over one another, each one ensconced in flames. "It would be audacious to do anything less."

"Let me ask that a different way." Sarelle fiddled with the ends of her hair, wrapping the silky strands around her finger, and then releasing them. "Are you going to accept?"

"I think I might. Cyra Firebane is rather lovely, and this is the first time I've ever been invited anywhere with no strings attached." She didn't want to think of all the times she'd been asked to attend parties and teas at the homes of her "friends" only to learn they were either using her to better their reputation or they wanted details about whether or not any of her brothers were in the market for a wife.

It was incredibly disheartening to come to terms with the fact that her company wasn't so much appreciated as it was manipulated.

"Do you think that's wise?" Sarelle prodded, her face composed and schooled into one of perfect calm despite the lingering questions in her eyes.

Definitely not.

In fact, attending tea with Lady Cyra was far from wise, but she *was* Asher's sister. If he was home when Novalise showed up, it would afford her the chance to make him squirm. Especially after he left her dangling on the edge of combustion with no relief in sight. Not only that, but Cyra was best friends with Lilith Vylera, a distinguished lady of the night. Perhaps Lilith would be willing to teach Novalise a thing or two in the art of seduction. The sooner the better, considering she was running quite low on time before she would be forced to choose a husband. There were only ten days left and her mother was already making the necessary preparations for her wedding at the end of Midsummer.

Novalise headed toward the sitting room off the grand hall where her mother kept a desk filled with stationary for correspondence. Sarelle followed, gnawing at her bottom lip, a habit she formed whenever she worried. Seating herself, Novalise grabbed a piece of parchment, a deep blue envelope, and some shimmering navy ink. She would pen her response herself and join Lady Cyra for tea.

"If Lord Firebane wishes to avoid me, then he should be the one to leave." Novalise signed her reply, then fanned it so the ink would dry. She folded it in half and wrapped it in a ribbon of stars. When she opened her hand, the stars twinkled, glittering brightly in shades of iridescent purple and blue. At once they shot upward, swirling around the letter, carrying it with them as they streaked through the open window, leaving a trail of stardust in their wake. In a few moments, Lady Cyra would be made aware of her expected arrival. And so would Asher, whether he liked it or not. "I will not refuse his sister's invitation in order to make him more comfortable."

Sarelle gaped at her, lashes fluttering. Then a beaming smile spread across her face.

"Look at you, Nova." She swatted at her playfully. "Wherever did this fierce independence come from?"

Novalise dabbed the pen into some more ink and started to doodle a crown of stars. She connected them easily enough, having committed the constellation to her memory. It was Estrela's crown, the same design of angular lines and stars tattooed over the flesh of her heart. "Let's just say I've finally decided to take charge of my own fate."

"Well done." Sarelle squeezed her shoulder, then bent down and pressed a light kiss to her cheek. "I'm so proud of you."

It warmed her, having Sarelle's approval. If only the rest of her family would take notice and realize she was more than a precious diamond. She didn't want to be displayed, or coveted, or treasured. What she desired above all else was to be *loved*, something she would never find among the males of Aeramere. To them, she would always be Lady Novalise Starstorm Celestine, a symbol of power, wealth, and the source of unrivaled celestial magic. None of them could offer her love, because none of them could ever see past their own greed.

"So." Novalise pressed the tip of the pen a bit too firmly and the ink blotted, then smeared. She glanced up at Sarelle, offering her best smile. "I don't suppose you'd want to join me for tea in Emberspire, would you?"

Sarelle's laughter echoed through the grand hall. She shook her head and walked away. "Absolutely not."

"Fine!" Novalise called after her, unable to help her widening grin. "See if I help you the next time you're covered in stardust!"

"There you are," a masculine voice sounded from the other side of the sitting room and Novalise turned to see Ariesian standing in the doorway. His large frame took up a majority of the space, his presence always seemed too much for any room. He stepped inside, adjusting the cuffs of his dark violet shirt, his boots clicking softly against the stone floor. "Do you have a moment?"

"Actually." Novalise stood from the small writing desk and handed him her invitation. "I was invited to tea by Lady Cyra Firebane."

"Mm." Ariesian's gaze skimmed the contents of Lady Cyra's letter, though Novalise wasn't even sure he read the words at all. "Prince Kalstrand is on his way here to discuss the terms of the alliance. I was hoping you'd be able to join us."

"Me?" Novalise inhaled sharply, taken aback. She'd never been asked to attend important meetings of any kind. Instead, she was expected to stand around, look pretty, and respond agreeably to any question asked of her. She doubted Queen Elowyn ever had to lower herself to such pathetically weak requirements.

"Yes, you." Ariesian tugged on the collar of his shirt, then tucked his hands behind his back. He looked every inch a lord prepared to endorse a pact of great significance. His hair was styled so it swooped down over half of his face, but not a single piece was out of place. The shirt he wore was crisp, impeccable. A trim belt wrapped around his waist, though it wasn't for the gray pants he wore. It was there to display the two swords at his side.

"I figured it would be good to have a feminine perspective." Ariesian offered his arm and she accepted, allowing him to guide her back through to the grand hall. "To ensure everything is agreeable."

"Ariesian, I have complete faith in your competence to draw up a trade agreement and an alliance with Prince Kalstrand."

She patted his arm, looking up at him. His face instantly shuttered. "Do not doubt yourself. You don't need me there to remind you that you're making the right decision."

His lips pressed into a tight line, but he nodded once, relenting. "Very well. I'll see you upon your return."

Novalise released his arm when Ariesian spoke once more. "So, Lady Cyra called upon you? I didn't think the two of you were friends."

"Neither did I." Novalise's shoulders rose, then fell. "But I've no other plans for the day. Maybe she wants my assistance in discussing preparations for the Firelight Festival? Emberspire hosts one every Midsummer, and it *is* a two-day-long event. I imagine it's overwhelming for her to take care of all the planning by herself."

"Yes, I suppose it would be quite the undertaking."

Novalise bit down on her smile.

That coming from a male who'd never had to organize anything a day in his life. All he had to do was arrive on time and show face.

"Quite," Novalise agreed.

He looked beyond her then, to the front of their estate. "Do you need me to call a carriage for you?"

"I'm sure I can manage well enough on my own."

Only then did she glimpse one of Ariesian's rare grins. It illuminated every plane of his face, causing him to glow from within. He looked so much like their beloved father, it nearly caused her heart to burst. "I never doubted it."

He left her then, and she headed toward the front door. Only once did she pause to consider changing, as there was a chance she was underdressed for afternoon tea. Her lavender dress was one of her favorites, though it was one of her less extravagant pieces. The bodice fit like a corset, cutting low in the front, and was trimmed with pale gold lace. Sheer, flowing sleeves draped from her shoulders, the chiffon fabric decadent and cool, perfect for summer weather. And the skirts were made of the same material as the sleeves, soft and flowing, but layered enough to offer a tad more modesty.

Honestly, it was the perfect gown to entice Lord Firebane and get him to realize he was making a grave mistake by rejecting her.

She carried herself down the stone steps as a carriage rolled to a stop in front of her. A footman appeared by her side a second later to help her climb inside. Once she was safely seated, the door closed, and the thundering of hooves filled her ears as the Eponians took flight, carrying her into the skies.

Novalise sank into the cushioned leather bench of the carriage, gazing out the window as wisps of white clouds and streams of golden sunlight swept by her. Below, the vast beauty of Aeramere spread out like a glorious watercolor painting—a wash of beautiful colors in shades of emerald, silver, sapphire, gold, amethyst, and rose, all divided by stunning mountains, rivers, and forests. It was picturesque, perfection in every sense of the word, and for now, it was safe.

At once, the landscape was swathed in shadows, and a chill crawled across her skin. It stole the light, flooded the world in darkness. She peered out the window and caught sight of what shrouded her world in darkness.

Soaring through the clouds, then banking northeast toward Celestine, was the outline of a colossal dragon.

Novalise couldn't be sure, because he was too far away and of course such a thing would be ridiculous to see, but she could've sworn the shadow prince looked right at her.

And winked.

CHAPTER TWENTY

*A*sher leaned back in the chair and raised his arms over his head. The muscles in his back ached, furious with him for sitting all day. He rolled his neck from side to side until it cracked, then popped, alleviating the building tension there. For most of the day, he'd been at his desk, locked away in his study, poring over books and papers for Prince Drake Kalstrand and the green gemstone he desired.

He stretched out his legs, crossing one ankle over the other.

All things considered, he'd made decent progress.

The *virdis lepatite* was definitely not located in the Kethwyn Woods. That forest was tainted. Cursed. A forbidden gateway to the realm of the goddess of life, it was treacherous to any living soul. Only the worthy, only the most dauntless and courageous, could traverse its perilous landscape and then live to tell the tale.

Which left only Wintervale in the Northernlands or the bogs of Fenmire.

Asher pinched the bridge of his nose beneath the rim of his spectacles and squeezed his eyes shut. He didn't know how long he'd shut himself in his study, but the hours had bled by in a blur of research and ancient rune readings. It was getting to the point where he was reading the same paragraph over and over again, yet no matter how many times he tried, he simply couldn't make sense of the words. His usual retention of information was declining.

He told himself it was because he'd been at his desk since before sunrise. In fact it had nothing to do with that and everything to do with the bond tying him to Novalise. He pretended not to see her carriage when it arrived at the front of his home, he ignored the distinctive tug on his heart when she walked past his study, and even now he dismissed the musical sound of her voice as a melody he couldn't quite place. She was seated on a wooden bench next to Cyra, directly across from where he was trying his damnedest to focus. But any time she laughed, any time she spoke, any time she *drew breath*, it was as though time ceased to exist. If she was the stars, he was her sky. If he was the fire, she was his frost.

She captivated him. Completed him.

He shook the irrational thought from his head, but again, he found himself staring at her from out of his window.

The bench she sat on was shaded by a hedgerow bursting with dark red flowers, shielding her from the sun. She was a vision in her pale purple gown, almost ethereal. It moved around her like silken clouds, floating and graceful. There was something different about her, something he couldn't pinpoint. It might've been the way she wore her lavender hair, pulled back from her face with opals pins instead of in one long braid. Maybe it was the way her eyes glittered like stardust when Cyra said something amusing. Her emotions floored him. She was happy. Radiant. Perhaps she was relieved not to be suffocated by her duties any longer. Either way, he didn't care, so long as her smile remained effortless.

Asher supposed it wouldn't hurt to take a small break. Maybe he would casually pass by the gardens and ease some of the ache in his chest. Her nearness left him with a sense of calming peace. A comfort he couldn't explain.

Without thinking about the consequences of his actions, he stood and headed for the gardens. He would probably need an excuse of some sort, something believable. He couldn't simply show up without an explanation. Then again, Novalise was likely still furious with him. Not that he could blame her. When he'd had her up against that tree, it had taken every ounce of willpower to stop mid-thrust and simply pull out of her when her torment became too much to withstand. His cock still hadn't forgiven him.

Their voices drifted over to him, and Asher stopped dead in his tracks.

"And *then*," Novalise was saying, her voice in a conspiratorial whisper, "Prince Drake took me to the palace on his dragon. It was terrifying, I thought for sure we would fall from the sky."

Cyra gasped. "Did he try to calm you or is he as callous as everyone says?"

Asher watched as Novalise tilted her head, quietly considering his sister's question. "He's cruel, but in a dangerously appealing way. When he bit my bottom lip with his teeth, I'd never been more terrified or thrilled in my life."

Bitter envy coursed through Asher, blinding him. There was something about Novalise's tone that set his teeth on edge, like she'd enjoyed the shadow prince's attention. Claws of jealousy sank into him, carving through his stomach and squeezing his heart in a vise.

"Asher?" Cyra's voice drew his attention.

He jerked his head up only to realize he stood less than a few feet from his sister and Novalise.

"What a pleasant surprise." Cyra offered him a cool, even smile. "You remember Lady Novalise?"

Damn her.

"Of course." He bowed, never taking his eyes off Novalise. "My lady."

She dipped her head, the coyest of smiles playing along the edge of her lips. "My lord."

Asher snapped straight. He hadn't expected her to be kind. It left him...uneasy.

Cyra broke through his muddled thoughts, patting the space on the bench in between herself and Lady Novalise. "Would you care to join us? You've been holed up in your study for hours. I don't even think you've eaten. Or taken tea, for that matter."

There was a flash in Novalise's eyes.

He placed a hand over his heart. "I'm afraid I'll be unable to join you. I'm on deadline for a...project and I've just realized I've neglected most of my duties for the Firelight Festival."

"Then you're lucky you have such a wonderful sister to help you." Novalise folded her hands in her lap, demure and unbothered by his quick refusal. She looked up at him, fluttering her lashes, but a sheen of ice left her eyes frosty and cold. Novalise angled herself away from him, returning her attention to Cyra. "If you want, I can see if Prince Drake can join us? I'm sure he'd be more than willing to offer his assistance. Despite his vicious nature, he can be quite...*giving*."

"That will be unnecessary." Asher stepped closer, tucking his hands behind his back to keep himself from throwing his fist into the nearest wall. His gaze slid to his sister, who watched him like he was a child about to snatch a lollipop from a candy store. "What else do you need for preparations, Cyra?"

"I think I have everything under control. Though perhaps we should divide and conquer?" His sister stood, mischief sparking like wildfire in her gold eyes. "I'll go into Emberspire for some last-minute decorations and you can show Lady Novalise to the cellar so she can select some wines for the Firelight Festival. How does that sound?"

Like he'd fallen headfirst into one of his sister's traps.

"Like a carefully crafted plan," he muttered.

"You know me so well." Cyra's smile only widened. "Lady Novalise, does that sound agreeable to you?"

She didn't seem at all bothered by the proposition. He would've expected her to offer a counter suggestion or find a way to get out of being alone with him completely. Instead, she seemed charmed by the idea.

"I am quite fond of wine."

"Then it's settled." Cyra clapped her hands together, far too giddy for Asher's liking. "We'll meet back here in two hours. Lady Novalise, would you care to stay for dinner?"

Asher maintained an expertly tight grip on his expression, though his jaw clenched until it ached and he was a breath away from strangling his younger sister.

He couldn't believe Cyra was tempting fate. It was one thing to invite Lady Novalise to stay for tea, but *dinner*?

"I'm sure she has plans, Cyra. It's enough that she's already taken time out of her day to have tea and plan the Firelight Festival with you." The silent challenge expanded between. "Lady Novalise is very busy. After all, she has a wedding to plan."

This was it, he was offering her an out. A way to extend her gratitude and leave without causing any harm or insult. A means to be free from the guilt of being raised as a polite lady who never turned down an invitation to a social gathering.

"It's true, my wedding is approaching rather quickly," Novalise agreed easily. She moved, sidling up closer to him, and Asher's lungs drew tight. "But since my opinion is of little consequence, it is my mother who takes care of such things." She looked pointedly at Cyra. "I would love to stay for dinner."

Lovely.

"Lovely!" Cyra clutched the hem of her skirt and dashed down the path, kicking up a few stones in her wake. "I'll be back soon, but not *too* soon!"

He was really going to have to work with her on projecting the manners of a lady.

Then again, he wasn't much better by blatantly attempting to ignore the female currently in his presence.

Asher held out his arm. "Shall I escort you to the wine cellar, my lady?"

"I'd like that very much."

Novalise tucked her hand into the crook of his proffered arm, and his world tilted on its axis. She was too powerful, too potent. Too much. He inhaled sharply, struggling to remember to breathe, but the scent of her overwhelmed him. She reminded him of midnight roses wrapped in silk, of ripened dark berries, and mouthwatering vanilla. He could devour her whole.

The second the thought entered his mind, images of his deepest desires flashed in front of his eyes. Novalise's beautiful body writhing beneath him, her legs wrapped firmly around his waist, her hips rising to meet his every thrust. Stars would fall around them. Flames of frostfire would consume them. He pictured her curled into his side, the softness of her hair tickling his chin and chest. Her lips teased him, her kiss ruined him. One blink and her nails were digging into his headboard, and in the next moment they were scouring his back. His cock jumped, pulsing to life. He wanted her splayed on a bed of wildflowers, naked in the cool waters of a faerie pool, but more than anything, he wanted her in the one place he knew she belonged.

His bed.

He gritted his teeth together until a dull ache formed at the base of his spine.

He'd be lucky if he survived spending the next hour with her.

"We'll both be lucky to survive with an imagination like yours, my lord."

Asher choked, barely finding the courage to spare Novalise a glance. Though she maintained a sense of effortless calm, her cheeks were flushed a beautiful shade of pink and her heart beat in time to his own.

Far too fast for such a leisurely stroll to the cellar.

The bond had shown her everything. Every thought, wish, and desire.

Damn it, he would have to be more careful.

Tugging on the collar of his shirt, his skin suddenly too warm, Asher tried to focus on anything to distract himself from the female on his arm. No matter how hard he tried, he couldn't force her from his mind.

Though he was reluctant to admit it, Novalise was becoming everything he never wanted.

CHAPTER TWENTY-ONE

*N*ovalise busied herself with trying to think of anything except ways to make Asher fall in love with her. If he caught the slightest glimpse of her thoughts, her entire plan would fall apart. It was proving to be difficult when the closeness of him sent her heart skittering out of her chest and muddled her thoughts with elusive fantasies.

Like spending the rest of her life with him.

She dared a glance up at him.

His angular jaw was set, as though he was counting down the minutes until he could rid himself of her company. In the sunlight, his eyes were a lighter gray than usual, but the gold rimming the outer edges flared with power. His raven black hair was swept back from his face, but that stubborn silver streak curled forward, looping lazily across his forehead. She longed to reach up and smooth it back, then clenched her hand into a small fist to keep from doing it.

And the spectacles he wore? He looked painfully handsome in them. They were enough to make her knees wobble.

His burning ember gaze slid to her.

He'd caught her staring, so she said the first thing that came to her mind. "I didn't know you wore spectacles, my lord."

"I usually don't. These particular ones are helpful in reading runes." Asher reached up, adjusting them. He swept the fallen lock of silver from his face and set the black-rimmed spectacles on top of his head.

Novalise melted.

He had *no* idea what he was doing to her.

The corner of his mouth twitched.

Okay, maybe he knew exactly what he was doing to her.

They rounded a corner and came to a stone door built into the side of Asher's house. Vines of ivy crawled from the base, stretching up over the brick, and each stem burst with a pretty golden flower. He turned the bronze handle and the door groaned open. Instantly Novalise was hit with the smell of musty, damp air and oak. A set of narrow wooden stairs descended into a cellar ensconced in darkness.

"Here, allow me." He removed her hand from his arm, taking hold of her fingers instead to guide her down the dim stairwell. "It can be difficult to navigate in the dark."

She swallowed a sigh when his thumb brushed across her knuckles as they started their descent. With each step, cool air assaulted her and long shadows stole across her vision. The stone door creaked shut, diminishing every fragment of light. She tightened her grip on his hand. "Don't you control fire, my lord? I would assume you would be capable of producing light with a mere flick of your wrist."

His answering laughter was low and rumbling.

"I don't know, my lady." His whisper floated past her cheek, and he released his hold on her hand. "There's something exciting about losing a sense we've become reliant upon. When one of them is taken away, the others are acutely heightened."

Novalise ignored the way her blood roared, rushing to every sensitive part of her. It didn't matter if they were in the dark, and he was possibly only mere inches from her. If she wanted to lure him to her, then she would have to convince him that perhaps she had a change of heart. Perhaps she did have an interest in Prince Drake and was considering marrying him instead. In order to make it believable, however, she would have to shield her mind and her heart from the bond tying her to Asher. She clamped down on the pitch of anxiety, and when she sucked in a breath, it was shallow.

She reached out, hoping to find a railing to help guide her down the rest of the stairs. But only slightly damp, rough stone grazed her outstretched palm. Squinting into the darkness, she strained to see Asher, but she couldn't tell if he was even standing next to her anymore. She took what she thought was one more step, but the wooden staircase ended abruptly and she pitched forward.

A yelp escaped her as she flung her hands out in front of her, bracing herself for when she hit the ground. But a pair of strong arms captured her instead and kept her from falling.

Asher hauled her against him, and his free hand cupped the back of her neck, dragging her closer. The tip of his nose brushed against hers, his mouth so close she could feel the warmth of his breath upon her lips.

"Are you alright?" he murmured, his free hand lightly coasting up and down her waist.

"Never better." Her knees buckled.

Her magic spiraled in a blaze of stars, desperate for him. She wanted to tear off his shirt and run her palms over the chiseled planes of his bronze body. She wanted to lay him back and straddle him, then ride him until his fingers left bruises on her hips. Heat pooled between her legs and goosebumps shivered across her skin.

Asher hissed on an inhale and a thousand lights flickered to life within the cavernous walls of the wine cellar. He released her at once.

Inwardly, Novalise cursed herself for being so foolish. She would *have* to at least make an effort not to want him every second of every day if she actually planned on winning his heart.

Novalise blinked, shielding her eyes. Eventually, her vision adjusted, and though it wasn't quite as bright as she originally imagined, she could see dozens of candles and the chandelier overhead ignited by frostfire flames. Some burned silver, others pitch black, but all cast the cellar in a cool, moonlit glow. She stared, walking in a slow circle and gazing around the magnificent space.

The walls were made of stone, each one housing hundreds of bottles of wine. A thin, grimy layer of dust covered many of them, the wax seals still intact. There were shelves of bottles stacked neatly on top of each other and yellowing placards listing the flavor profiles and regions of each wine. Most were local to Aeramere, but a number of the wines were from places she'd never heard of before.

"This is wonderful." Her whisper floated between them, and she sensed Asher the moment he came to stand behind her.

"Does House Celestine not have a wine cellar?" His voice was low and mild. Not teasing or dripping with ridicule. Simply curious.

"Oh, I'm sure we do." She looked over her shoulder at him, the corner of her mouth lifting slightly. "But I've never seen it."

Asher studied her, his gaze slowly trekking over her as though he was committing her to memory. Either that, or he was merely trying to figure out the best way to get rid of her. She squirmed under the scrutiny, forcing herself to find something else of interest. Something other than him. Something like...frostfire.

She skirted around him, fully aware of the way he tracked the sway of her hips. Jutting out from the wall of wine was a smooth ledge of ebony, likely to host tastings and to consider which wines pair well with what, but all she cared about was the half-melted candle burning cold with a sparkling silver fire.

Novalise reached out to touch it, her finger hovering at the edge of the flame.

"No!"

Asher moved so quickly she didn't have time to react. One minute she was about to run her fingers through the icy sparks and in the next, he'd snared her by the waist and clutched her to him so her back was pressed firmly against his chest. "That's frostfire, Novalise."

"I *know*, Asher." She untangled herself from his grasp, swatting at his hand when he tried to reach for her again. "It can't hurt me."

"Yes, it can. Unless I make it warm, the flames are severely cold and—what?" His brows knit together in concern as he watched her.

"Look." Cautiously, she extended her fingers once more.

"Novalise, no. It's not safe, you'll—" But his words died as he watched her fingertips play with the fire, as the icy cool flames licked her skin. Staring, eyes wide, his mouth opened once, then closed just as quickly. He blinked. Stunned by her, by what he witnessed.

"How did..." Asher stepped closer, pulling her hand back from the flame to analyze it. His fingers traced the faint lines inside her palm, and he ran his thumb along each of her fingers, drawing tiny circles on the back of her hand. "How did you do that?"

He was intent. Serious. He had no idea.

Novalise gave him her best smile, then planted a hand over her heart, feigning shock. "Are you saying I know something the notoriously clever Lord Firebane hasn't yet figured out?"

His mouth pressed into a line, and he ducked his head.

He *almost* smiled.

"Alright, my lady." Asher folded his arms across his chest and

Novalise ignored the way his ivory shirt stretched and pulled over his muscled arms. Those damn spectacles were still pushed back on top of his head, and every lustful nerve in her body came undone at the sight of him looking so incredibly composed. "Enlighten me."

He was going to hate himself when she told him the news.

"It's because we're mates, Asher. Because our magic chose one another." She didn't look at him when she said this, instead she fixated on the glimmer of the frostfire, watched as it almost sputtered out completely. A bead of crimson wax slid down the side of the candle, pooling at its base like a small puddle of blood. "It's impossible for you to physically hurt me. Just like this—"

She flipped her wrist like an afterthought. Magic coursed through her and she hurtled a bolt of shooting stars directly into his chest. He staggered back, grasping at his chest on instinct. They ricocheted off him, cascading around the cellar like bits of iridescent glitter.

"Doesn't hurt you," she finished, lowering her arm.

"Fascinating," he muttered, catching flecks of stardust in his hand.

If only he'd look at her that way.

Novalise stepped closer toward him and the bond fusing them together flared to life. His thoughts were a torrent, a jumble of doubts, worries, and fear. She longed to soothe him. To comfort him. But she held fast to her resolve, however much it dwindled.

"It's interesting the things one can learn when they open their mind to new ideas."

Asher stared at her, a tumultuous emotion darkening the slate of his eyes.

"For example," she continued, refusing to be dissuaded by the power banking deep within his gaze, "I thought all hope was lost for me the night of my star reading. But then someone mentioned I should defy the stars...and that gave me an idea."

"Novalise," he warned, but there was no vehemence in his voice.

"A wonderful idea, like choosing my own mate." She shimmied her shoulders, flippant. This was her opportunity to make him realize he was meant to be with her. "Either that, or Ariesian will choose for me. And with the arrival of Prince Drake, I feel like it seemed serendipitous that—"

"No," Asher growled. He shook his head, violence and magic bubbling around him, building, cracking through to the surface of his once calm exterior.

"Honestly," she drawled, shrugging off his concern. "I think you're being dramatic, my lord."

"Stay away from him, Novalise."

"Easier said than done." She sighed wistfully. Asher's jaw ticked. Tension pulled taut between them, like the strings of a violin stretched to its limit. Ready to snap. And Novalise was going to pluck the final chord. "He's handsome, wealthy, a prince...oh, and how could I forget? He rides a dragon."

Magic erupted around them, an explosion of power, a force of black and silver flames. All the air was pulled from Novalise's lungs as she was thrown backwards. She winced, bracing herself, but she never slammed into the stone wall. Asher was there, faster than lightning. One arm wrapped around her waist, the other tucked behind her head, protecting her. His chest rose and fell, each breath he drew harsh. Painful. A blaze of frostfire danced around them, sparking and glinting as every other glowing light in the cellar was snuffed out completely.

There were only the two of them together, surrounded by a storm of flames.

Pulsing. Glowing.

Asher lowered his head, his forehead coming to rest against hers.

"I'm warning you, my lady. Prince Kalstrand is dangerous. If you think to court him..." His words were gritty and raw, like he'd spent hours screaming. His gaze latched onto hers, then dipped to her mouth. "You're playing with fire."

"No." Novalise raised her chin. She wouldn't back down, not from him. Lifting one hand, she floated her fingers through the flames like a lover's caress. Capturing a tiny spark of frostfire, she cupped her hands together, blowing lightly. The sphere encircling them wavered, throbbed with a life force all its own. She smirked. "Now, I'm playing with fire."

Asher squeezed his eyes shut, a line of pain marring his brow.

The bond amplified, anchoring them to one another. She knew he fought against its control, struggled to shutter his thoughts from her mind, to block his emotions, to close off his heart.

Novalise reached up, trailing her fingers along the underside of his smooth jaw. "You'd really stand by and watch me marry someone else?"

His eyes flew open, dark and fierce. His hand slid from the back of her head to her neck. He grazed his bottom lip with his teeth, then said, "If it meant they would love you unconditionally, then yes."

"Even if you knew it would be another male touching me. Kissing me." She rocked her hips forward, grinding herself against him. Rising onto her toes, she pressed her lips to the corner of his mouth, then lingered. "Making me beg until I scream his name and not yours."

A noise erupted from him, like nothing she'd ever heard. Part anger, part agony, she couldn't be sure. But Asher reared back and slammed his fist into the wall next to her head. Novalise jumped, her eyes widening as she stared at him in surprise. She never expected the broody Lord Asher Firebane to be so...violent.

Rock and stone splintered, tumbling down, crashing onto the floor. Glass shattered and wine poured from the broken bottles, staining the stone, pooling on the ground in a river of red. Asher shoved himself away from her. Blood spilled from his knuckles, the skin ripped and torn. The trail of red dripped down his fingers. He wiped his hand against the fabric of his pants like the wound was nothing. Like he felt nothing.

"*This* is why I cannot marry you." Asher pointed to the crumbling stone where the broken wine bottles used to be stored. "This is why I will never allow myself to love you."

"Why? Because you punched a hole in the wall?" Novalise spread her arms wide. Not a single stray rock had hit her. Not a drop of wine had spilled on her. Despite his temper, he'd kept her safe from his wrath. "You didn't hurt me, Asher. You *can't* hurt me."

At least, not with magic.

Emotionally...well, that was another matter entirely.

"Because I cannot always control myself, Novalise. I am full of anger." He yanked his spectacles off his head and shoved his hand through his hair, pacing. "Do you have any idea how difficult this is for me? I never wanted this, yet now I'm being driven to insanity by the desire just to be *near* you."

He stalked back and forth, his boots clicking harshly against the cellar's uneven floor. "Every night, I dream of you. Every morning, I wake up wanting you. From the moment I kissed you on Winter Solstice and every second after, I have *yearned* for you. And when you look at me like that..." His hand cut through the air between them. "Like I am all you will ever desire in this life and the next, it kills me that I—"

Asher stopped abruptly, pinching the bridge of his nose. He shook his head, then turned from her.

She reached for his hand, but he pulled away, heading toward the stairs on the opposite wall. The ones that would lead to the first floor of the house. To his study.

"Asher, wait."

"Pick some wine, please." He didn't look at her again. He flicked his wrist and a handful of candles sputtered back to life. "I'll meet you upstairs for dinner."

He trudged up the stairs, and when the door closed soundly behind him, she examined the hole he'd left behind.

Novalise didn't know what Asher had suffered that left him so distressed, so resentful. Whatever happened to make him loathe the thought of showing any kind of affection must have been dreadful indeed. He was at war with himself over his feelings for her, and though it may have been a singular spark of hope, there was enough there to coax the fire of his feelings to life. But first, she had to figure out why he was so tormented, why he couldn't simply let himself love her. And there was likely only one person in Aeramere who could help her uncover what kept his heart from hers.

Novalise's new best friend, Lady Cyra Firebane.

CHAPTER TWENTY-TWO

*A*sher stalked down the hall, bypassing his study, and headed straight out onto the terrace. He took the steps leading into the garden two at a time as a sense of unease, of restlessness built along his shoulders. He had to put distance between them. Being trapped in the cellar with Novalise was too much. It was agonizing being in the same space as her. To make matters worse, he'd lost his temper in front of her.

Raking a hand through his mussed hair, he treaded through the gardens, weaving a footpath through the ornamental trees and flowering rosebushes.

He could have hurt her, and Trysta Starstorm would have been right. He would be exactly like his father.

The thought alone caused his insides to twist, a ball of acidic frustration rolling in the pit of his stomach. He blew out a low, shaking breath.

Gusts of wind blew through the flowers and trees, shaking blossoms and leaves from their limbs and scattering them in all directions. The sun dipped behind a wall of ominous clouds rolling in across the horizon, casting long shadows as far as the eye could see. Puffs of gray roiled with smoldering black, stealing away all the ribbons of blue. The birds had gone silent, and in the distance, there was the low, menacing rumble of thunder.

"Asher!"

At the sound of his name, Asher whipped around to see Cyra rushing toward him with bundles of paper bags in both arms. The wind snatched at her hair, unfurling it around her like an inferno of flaming red and pale gold.

"Where's Lady Novalise?" she demanded, her brows narrowing.

He jerked his head toward the house. "In the cellar."

"You *left* her down there?" Cyra shifted the bags in her arms, huffing out an annoyed breath. "Honestly, Asher, and you call yourself a gentleman."

"I thought—shit." He tugged on the collar of his shirt, the sting of embarrassment crawling up the back of his neck. "Apologies, Cy."

Her scowl only deepened. "I'm not the one in need of your apology."

She turned on her heel, marching toward the house, a cloud of indignation hanging over her as a light rain pelted from the sky. Asher darted in front of her to grab the door just as her leg swung back to kick it open. The point of her heel connected soundly with his shin.

He grunted, wincing as pain shot up and down his leg.

"Serves you right," she mumbled in lieu of an apology, striding past him. "I am *mortified* that you would leave her all alone, in the cellar of all places, while you—oh."

Cyra stumbled to a stop and Asher almost plowed into her, hauling himself back before knocking his sister over.

There was Novalise, seated on the burgundy sofa in their sitting room. Her legs were tucked underneath her, and an open book was in her lap. Not just any book, he realized. One of his books. A storybook. The same one he'd read to Cyra when she couldn't sleep at night.

"I've never heard of this story before." Novalise's voice was soft as her fingers lightly skimmed the first few pages.

"It's one of my favorites." Cyra glanced pointedly in Asher's direction. "My brother knows it by heart, don't you, Asher?"

"Ah..." Asher shoved his spectacles into the pocket of his pants, shifting his weight from one foot to the other beneath Novalise's steady gaze. "Yes. I do."

"Will you tell it to me?" she asked, her eyes darting anxiously to the window, where the skies continued to darken.

"Of course he will," Cyra responded for him, setting down the bags she carried. She dropped onto the cushion next to Novalise, a daring smile painting her face. "Won't you, Asher? There's plenty of time before dinner."

There was no escaping them.

"Very well." Asher spread his palms open and two glasses of red wine appeared. He handed one to Novalise and the other to his sister, then he moved to the gilded cart in the corner of the room where a variety of liquors were stored. He poured himself a shot of whiskey and downed it in one gulp, savoring the burn. "Once upon a time, before there was life, before any being of this world took their first breath, the Mother Goddess created both the day and the night. But when the beauty of twilight stole across the skies and nightfall blanketed the land, she thought the world was too dark. Too lonely without the light."

He ran his thumb along the rim of his glass and walked in a slow circle as he wove his words together.

"To remedy this, she collected the darkest waters, the cresting waves, the currents and tides. She used frostfire to freeze the sea and create a glowing light for when darkness fell. The Mother Goddess hung the midnight sun high in the night sky, but it was too heavy to remain in the heavens." He swallowed as Novalise watched him, thoroughly enchanted. "The midnight sun fell, shattering into thousands of pieces that became the stars and with the largest fragments she could find, the Mother Goddess forged the moon."

"Asher…" Novalise sighed, his name a whisper between her lips. "That was wonderful."

He rubbed the back of his neck with his hand. "It's only a story."

"Is it?" Cyra pinned him with a hard stare, the weight of her words settling around them like a challenge.

"I picked out the wines for the Firelight Festival," Novalise said abruptly, cutting through the strained tension. She closed the book and stood, her pale purple gown gliding around her like a waterfall of satin. "One of your servants helped me bring them upstairs. Oh, and don't worry. The mess was cleaned up as well."

Cyra's cheeks flamed, appalled. "What mess?"

"Nothing," Asher interjected quickly. "It was an accident."

"Oh?" His sister's eyebrow quirked, the annoyance in her eyes flashing to amusement.

Novalise smiled, demure as ever. "Not that kind of accident."

Cyra laughed and stood. "I don't know about the two of you, but I'm famished." Her gaze snagged on Novalise. "Do you want to change before dinner?"

"I didn't bring another dress." Novalise dipped her head, stiffening when the howl of the wind echoed outside of the house, causing the rooftop spires to groan.

"That's nothing a little glamour can't fix." Cyra cocked one hip to the side and crossed her arms, a scheming smile turning up the corner of her mouth.

"It's fine, really. I don't mind wearing my day dress." Novalise took a step back, bumping right into the sofa. "I wouldn't want to impose."

"Nonsense. You're not imposing at all." Cyra looked down-right conspiratorial. "Is she, Asher?"

"Not at all," he agreed, keeping his expression neutral.

"I really don't think—" Novalise's voice trailed off as Cyra's magic danced around her in a cloying cloud of shimmering smoke.

The scent of amber, apples, and sandalwood hung heavy in the air, causing Asher's eyes to water, and when the mist finally cleared, it was all he could do to keep his jaw from hitting the floor.

It was still Novalise, but instead of moonstone and stars, she was rubies and fire. Scarlet satin draped from her shoulders, the front of the dress cutting down all the way to her navel. The smooth fabric wrapped around her like a vise, hugging each of her curves. Black diamonds lined the hem of the slit that rose to her hip, but the scrap of black lace clinging to her thigh was enough to cause all the blood to drain from his head and pump straight to his cock. Her lavender hair was unbound, the silken tresses falling to almost her waist, showcasing tiny crimson and gold charms. He hadn't realized her hair was so long, or that when dressed in red, her eyes sparkled like silver flames. Magic thrummed between them, the bond carefully winding its way around his heart, coaxing him to take one step forward. Then another.

Seconds passed, maybe minutes. He couldn't be sure. He didn't know, didn't care. But he was standing in front of Novalise and she was staring up at him, her lips painted a deep, sinful red. It was a shade that reminded him of illicit fantasies, like her mouth taking every inch of his cock, and all he could see were those fucking perfect red lips.

Her audible gasp jerked him from his daydreams, rooting him back in place.

"Come to think of it..." Cyra yawned. Loudly. Excessively. "I think I'll take dinner in my room tonight. You two go on without me."

She tossed a flippant little wave over her shoulder and strolled out of the sitting room.

Novalise didn't move.

Asher didn't breathe. He couldn't. She'd stolen the air from his lungs and he'd all but forgotten what it meant to live.

Outside, rain slashed against the windows. Darkness had fallen abruptly, and lightning streaked across the sky, distant thunder answering its call.

"It's too dangerous for the carriages to fly." The words he spoke were soft, a bare murmur. His hand moved of its own accord. His fingers slid through her hair, twisting the locks around one finger, letting them fall away like ribbons of silk. "You should stay, at least until it passes."

She nodded in agreement, but her body trembled. Unease shivered down the bond, and Asher cupped her chin with his hand, urging her to look at him. Something was wrong. He stole a glance out the window where the skies were murky and roiling, where distant thunder rumbled, growing louder with each passing minute.

Perhaps she was afraid of the storm.

"I have some work to do in my study. You're more than welcome to join me if you would like." He offered his arm, and her hand came to rest in the crook of his elbow. "We can take our dinner in there."

"Okay." The room was illuminated by a flash of lightning again and Novalise drew herself close to him. Energy radiated from her, snapping and crackling like the kindling of a bonfire.

Asher led her back down the hall to his study, then nudged open the door, allowing her to enter first. The temperature outside had dropped drastically, making it cooler in the house. He flicked his wrist so the hearth ignited, drenching the dark space in a warm, comforting glow. Long shadows stretched across the slate walls and when he turned to face Novalise, she shuddered.

Her arms were wrapped tightly around her body, but he knew her well enough to know it had nothing to do with modesty and everything to do with the tension causing her hands to clench and unclench. She worried her bottom lip—that *tempting* red lip—and with every rise and fall of her chest, her heartbeat quickened. The air was charged, electric. Stars fell around her like rain, fizzling from her fingertips, scorching the white rug at the hearth so the fibers turned to blackened ash.

"I should go," she whispered, stepping away from him. "I shouldn't be here. Not now."

Panic lanced through her and the bond quivered. Power thrummed through her body, swelling to a crescendo. Sizzling beams of violet and indigo swirled around her like a maelstrom. Thunder rattled the heavens, and she squeezed her eyes shut.

Concern clouded his thoughts, and he closed the distance between them in two strides. "Novalise, what's wrong?"

"Stay back!" She flung her hands out in front of her to stop him and her eyes flew open. They'd turned a bright sapphire blue. "It's the storm. It does something to my magic, something horrible, and I can't—"

Another blinding flash lit up the study and the answering crack followed, so loud it rattled windowpanes. A bolt of blazing starfire erupted from her palms, striking him right in the chest.

"Asher!"

Her screams were drowned by the starstorm.

Burst after burst of starfire slammed into him, knocking the air from his lungs. Her magic owned him, ruled him. His shirt was shredded, nothing more than charred clumps of fabric. By all rights, the attack should've killed him, but all he could focus on was the sheer terror etched into the soft lines of her beautiful face. He held firm against the assault, never once taking his eyes off her.

Tears slid down her cheeks, shimmering droplets of iridescence.

"I can't…" Her chest heaved and she gasped, broken. "I can't control it!"

He lunged toward her, and she stumbled back. But he didn't relent.

Asher grabbed her, hauling her against him, accepting the full brunt of her force. It reverberated through him. He clenched his jaw to keep his teeth from rattling while she thrashed in his arms. The starstorm crashed into him, an archaic force of celestial magic, explosive and radiant. He took every blast, every surge of star beams and fire, as her wild magic coursed through him. It encircled them both, exploding from her.

"Let me go!" she cried, her voice pitched with fear. "It's too dangerous."

"You can't hurt me," he murmured. He held her closer, tucking her head beneath his chin. "Your soul is mine, your magic is mine. Nothing you can do will ever hurt me."

"Too much." Novalise leaned back, staring up at him. She shook her head violently. "It's too much."

"I can take it." He grabbed her chin, holding firm, forcing her to meet his gaze. "I'll take all of it. Always."

Asher knew he shouldn't comfort her. He shouldn't care about the fact that a sphere of uncontrollable ancient starfire erupted around her. But she was terrified. Whatever she'd experienced, whatever he'd witnessed, had left her panicked and afraid. It didn't matter if she might misinterpret his consolation for affection, he couldn't very well stand there and do nothing. He might not be able to love her, but that wouldn't stop him from caring for her.

If there was one thing he'd learned from the toxic marriage of his mother and father, it was that he would *always* protect a lady in distress.

And Novalise was most certainly in distress.

She crumpled against him, and he scooped her into his arms,

her power ebbing, the stars gradually winking out. Outside, the summer storm slowly subsided, the thunder nothing more than a distant rumble. She buried her face in his chest, and he ran one hand down her velvety hair, soothing her. "It's alright, Nova. You're safe with me."

But her racing heart didn't calm. Her fingers curled into the scorched remnants of his shirt, clutching him like he was an anchor and she was drifting out to sea. Fright bubbled inside of her, and goosebumps pebbled across her flesh. Asher held her tighter, sliding his hands beneath her hair to rub her back.

"Breathe, Starlight." He spoke the words through their bond to her mind.

A tremor raced down her spine.

"So long as you're with me, you're safe. Do you understand?" He pressed a gentle kiss to her temple, then cheek. Warning sirens fired through him. He was toeing a dangerous line. *"You will always be safe with me."*

"I'm...I'm s-sorry." Novalise sniffled. When she looked up at him, her beautiful eyes were starlit once again. Puffy, but starlit. Tears stained her cheeks and his skin.

"You have nothing to apologize for, Novalise." He cupped her face in his hands, wiping away the stray tears with his thumbs.

Her head came to rest against his shoulder, and slowly, her body relaxed, the fight fading from her. "When it storms...I lose control."

"We all lose control." Asher sat down on the sofa, cradling her in his arms. "No one is perfect. Though you're pretty damn close."

She laughed, but it was a weak, feeble sound.

Novalise tilted her head back and looked up at him, then her gaze dipped down to his mostly bare chest. She collected what remained of the burnt fabric from his skin, dropping the singed clumps of material onto the floor. "Your shirt..."

"Think nothing of it."

Then her hands were moving slowly over his exposed flesh, exploring. He stilled, surrendering to her touch. There was no scar, no bleeding. No burn marks. Not a single trace of the power she inflicted upon him.

Carefully, she wrapped her arms around his neck. Hesitant.

The softest of sighs escaped Novalise and though Asher swore he didn't love her, there was no doubt he felt *something*. So, he did the only logical thing he could think of.

He kissed those red fucking lips.

CHAPTER TWENTY-THREE

*A*sher's mouth crashed against Novalise's and currents of pleasure rippled through her. Cushioned in his lap with his strong arms wrapped tightly around her, coherent thoughts seemed to slip from her mind. With her eyes closed, however, all she could see was him taking every hit of her magic, every agonizing bolt of starfire. He'd simply stood there and taken it all. He should have been dead, would have been dead, were it not for the fact that their magic, their souls, were bonded.

But his chest was unblemished, with no trace of a scar, unlike her brother Nyxian. The last time it stormed, he hadn't been so lucky to escape her power unscathed.

"You're thinking too much." Asher's voice rumbled through her, his teeth nipping at her bottom lip.

She opened her mouth to respond, but he seized the opportunity to slide his tongue over hers instead.

"No apologies," he murmured.

Novalise nodded, keeping her arms entwined around his neck. She didn't want a single sliver of space between them.

Asher ran his hands lazily up and down her sides as he

kissed her, his palms coasting along the curve of her breasts to the flare of her hips. The rub of cool satin against her skin sent delightful shivers coursing through her, riddling her flesh with goosebumps. Threading her fingers through his hair, she angled their kiss, desperate for more of him.

His thumbs brushed back and forth across her nipples, pebbling them into tiny peaks. The friction of her gown and his touch worked her into a frenzy. She strained against him, each nerve heightened to a new level of awareness, sensitive and raw. He broke their kiss, moving his lips to her cheek, then jaw, then down the column of her neck. Desire ricocheted through her, straight to her core.

Novalise arched into him to grant him better access, wiggling in his hold until the hardened length of his erection gently nudged her bottom. She clenched her thighs together, squirming, and the overwhelming need simply to *feel* left her nearly breathless. A deep, rumbling noise echoed in his chest. Feral. Primal. He tugged the sleeves of her dress down her arms, freeing her breasts from the confines of the restrictive scarlet satin. His gaze darkened, shimmering with power, those deep gray eyes of his reminding her of midnight flames. He snared her by the hips and lifted her from his lap, leaning her back against one of the soft, feathered pillows.

Then Asher devoured her.

His lips left a scorching trail across her heated body. He grazed her skin with his teeth, biting her breasts just enough to sting, only to soothe the pain away with his hot tongue. Pulling her nipple into his mouth, he sucked—hard—so she arched and writhed beneath him. She clutched at his shoulders, her nails digging into him, relishing the way his muscles flexed beneath her touch. His skin was a golden bronze, like he'd been kissed by fire. She inhaled, breathing in the scent of him. Sandalwood and amber with some tempting kind of spice. He peppered her with searing kisses down through the valley of her breasts, to her abdomen, while pushing aside the long length of her gown. His hands slid beneath the fabric, and he took his time, curling one finger beneath the black lace garter strapped her to her thigh. He pulled it, then let it snap back against her skin.

Novalise jerked, spasming at the shock of the pleasure induced by pain.

A single flame of frostfire ignited from the tip of his finger. In one fluid movement, he scorched the lace from her skin.

"This dress." Positioning himself between her legs, he gathered a fistful of satin, shoving it out of his way so it pooled at her waist, leaving her bare for him. "I can't decide if I want to see it on you or on the floor when I taste you."

"Both?" The question squeaked out of her.

Asher's smile was slow and deliberate. "Who am I to deny such a request?"

He lowered his head between her legs, his breath hot on her exposed flesh. He blew lightly, the rush of cool air forcing her to lift her hips in a silent plea.

Thunder rumbled outside, causing Novalise's insides to quake and tension to coil through her.

"Breathe, Starlight." Asher's voice drifted over her, easing the wave of apprehension threatening to drown her. He cupped the back of her knee, gently lifting her leg over his shoulder.

She sucked in a harsh breath, and Asher's tongue skated over her slick folds.

Novalise unraveled.

He splayed one hand over her stomach to hold her down, keeping her firmly in place. Every flick of his tongue sent her careening toward the edge of ecstasy. His mouth moved over her, licking at her wetness, taunting her. Teasing her. He sucked her clit into his mouth, and she cried out, gripping the edge of the sofa with one hand and snatching his hair with the other.

"Ash, please," she begged, panting.

She struggled, attempted to shift her hips, needing more.

"Is this what you need?" He swirled his tongue over her throbbing clit, then shoved two fingers deep inside of her, curling them.

"Yes." She lifted her other leg, locking it around him. "Yes, please."

He worked her hard and fast, taking her higher until she soared. Until the orgasm rocketed through her like dozens of shooting stars.

She melted into the sofa, her legs going limp.

Asher drew back and stood, kicking off his shoes. Propping herself up on her elbows, she watched as he unbuttoned his pants. They fell to the ground, and he nudged them aside, so he was standing before her in nothing but a pair of black shorts that left little to the imagination. They were snug, hugging his sculpted ass and the erection that looked ready to burst free from them. A distinctive flush bled into her cheeks. His broody and studious exterior, coupled with his lavishly modest clothing, disguised the gorgeous specimen hidden beneath. He was all hard lines and sinewy muscle, and she wanted to touch every inch of him.

"You know," he drawled, "they call you the darling of Aeramere."

"Who is they?"

"Everyone." He removed the black shorts, the full length of him on display for her viewing pleasure.

Novalise's tongue darted out, sliding along her bottom lip.

Lust brewed in Asher's gaze, and he stepped toward her, the tip of his bulging cock barely a breath from her lips.

"You're a princess on a pedestal, worshipped and adored by everyone. They call you a diamond, whisper that you're flawless." He gripped his dick with one hand, jerked it twice. "Because you're a good girl, aren't you, my lady? You're a good girl who always does exactly as she's told."

She nodded, gazing up at him, and opened her mouth.

Asher chuckled. "Stand up and take off your dress for me, Starlight." His gaze dropped to the heels she wore. "Take off those damned shoes as well."

Novalise did as she was told, sliding the gown down her body. She thoroughly expected Asher to stand there and watch her, to revel in the caress of the satin against her skin. But when she stepped out of the puddle of red fabric at her feet and slid off her shoes, he was sprawled on his back on the white fur rug by the hearth, firelight reflecting off his golden skin. One hand was tucked behind his head, the other patting his chiseled thigh.

She took a hesitant step forward. "Are you sure? Because you said—"

"I know what I said. But right now, I want the darling of Aeramere to ride me until she sees stars."

Excitement skittered down her spine.

Dropping onto her hands and knees, she crawled up his solid body, maneuvering herself so she straddled him, the tip of his cock poised at her entrance. Bracing her palms against his chest, she hovered above him. His dark eyes glinted like smoldering embers. She brushed a lock of silver hair back from his face, her fingers coiling around the smooth strands.

"You know what will happen if we do this, don't you, my lord?" The words fell from her lips in a hushed whisper.

His face remained impassive, cool and steady. "I'm well aware."

"And are you quite certain? If we—"

Asher's hand cupped the back of her neck, drawing her face close to his own. His gaze dipped to her mouth, then back to her eyes. "Lady Novalise Starstorm, I understand that taking you fully, completely, will secure the bond between us. Just as I know that once we do this, I will have accepted it...and you."

His hand slid from around her neck, coming to rest on top of her heart. There, he traced the constellation marking her skin. "But I am prone to rage and silent suffering. My fate is one of unpredictable violence, and I would rather die than see you on the other end of my aggressions. I cannot...cannot love you in the way you deserve. I am not an ideal mate. But for you, I will try."

It would be enough. She had an eternity to make him fall in love with her.

"I accept you, Lord Asher Firebane Emberspire."

An emotion she didn't recognize flashed in his eyes, then he blinked and it was gone. "I accept you, Lady Novalise Starstorm Celestine."

With that, she lowered herself onto his thick shaft, inch by delicious inch. He groaned, taking hold of her hips, until she was fully seated on top of him. He filled her, stretched her, eased that agonizing ache of longing only he could satisfy.

"Very well, my lord." She rocked once and his fingers dug into her, certain to leave bruises. "Make me see stars."

Asher guided her up and down, slowly at first, helping her find the perfect rhythm. Each time she sank onto him, he'd jerk upward, forcing himself deeper inside of her. Her nails scoured his chest, clawing at him for purchase while he let her take the lead, increasing their pace as she saw fit. She rode him exactly as he'd demanded while a thousand sensations fired through her, sending her into a spiral of lust.

For once, she was in control. She made the decisions. She was in charge.

But then Asher smiled.

He adjusted, drawing his knees up behind her, forcing her back to arch. Suddenly, he lifted his hips from the rug, thrusting further into her. Over and over, he rocked his hips, never touching the ground, reaching the most intimate part of her core.

Novalise gasped, a rush of euphoria leaving her spellbound. She could do nothing but hold on as he plunged his cock into her, the magnitude of his strength, of his skill, causing a cascading waterfall of stars to rain down above them.

Asher's grin only widened, and he tucked one hand behind his head, his hot gaze drinking her in as she edged closer to a state of reckless bliss. Again, he surged into her, driving her higher and higher. This time her head fell back on a cry as waves of pleasure tingled across her flesh. He snared a fistful of her hair, gently tugging, holding her in place as he carried her to the devastating crush of release.

"Ash!" She clawed at his chest, the orgasm tightening inside of her, ready to snap.

"Come for me, Starlight." His voice was strained, breathless. "Be a good girl."

Again, she did exactly as she was told.

Novalise came undone as a flurry of silver stars. Midnight flames erupted around them, the bond between them flaring to life.

"You're so damn perfect." Asher groaned, emptying himself inside her, their joining tying the two of them together for an eternity. Magic exploded like a symphony, a crescendo of starfire and frostfire cocooning them in a state of euphoric bliss.

She collapsed on top of him, tiny, twinkling stars dancing across her vision.

He rolled her over so her back was to the hearth, curling her into him, tucking the top of her head under his chin. She could think of nothing more pleasant than the way she fit perfectly against him.

Novalise nuzzled her face into his neck, their hearts beating in time with one another. Their emotions—elation, contentment, arousal—were entirely in sync. A melody of stars and the harmony of fire.

She sighed. "It's late."

"Mm." His arms only tightened around her, his fingers drawing idle circles along her spine.

"My family might be worried." She shivered, enjoying the way his cock, still nestled between her thighs, twitched to life again.

"Ariesian knows you're here. He also knows it's too dangerous to take a carriage in such a storm."

Novalise didn't mention that the storm had already passed. "You want me to stay?"

"Correction," he muttered, his voice thick with drowsiness. "I'm not allowing you to leave."

She couldn't stop the smile, so bright her cheeks ached. "That's rather bold."

His chest rumbled. "So is marrying someone you've never met."

Then his sleepy voice was in her mind, tickling the bond between them. *"Rest now, Novalise. You're safe with me."*

Comfortable silence filled the sliver of space between them. Eventually, Asher's heartbeat slowed alongside her own. His breathing grew even and deep, the rise and fall of his chest slowly luring her to sleep.

Novalise closed her eyes, but before she succumbed to the world of dreams, she whispered two words through the bond, wondering if he would ever hear them.

"Choose me."

CHAPTER TWENTY-FOUR

*C**hoose me.*

Novalise's words echoed in Asher's mind. She'd sent him the soft, simple plea through their bond, thinking he was asleep. But he'd heard them clearly, and an uncomfortable sensation squeezed in his chest.

Even now as he disentangled himself from her sleeping form, there was another twinge in his heart. This one was deeper. Stronger.

Not love but...something.

Affection? Endearment? It was a strange sentiment he couldn't quite place.

He pressed a kiss to her forehead, and she snuggled further into the plush rug, the edges still singed from her explosive magic.

He was definitely going to ask her about that whenever she woke up.

Asher stood and tugged on his pants. He waved his hand over Novalise, glamouring a gray blanket to cover her, then flicked his wrist toward the hearth, stoking the fire to ensure she stayed warm.

Absently, he rubbed his chest.

Turning away from her, he walked over to sit at his desk. Everything was exactly as he left it—opened books filled with runes and scribbled notes, stacks of sifted papers—all in its proper place before he abandoned his work to go find Novalise in the gardens. He lowered himself into his chair, put his spectacles back on, then ran one hand through his rumpled hair.

Valuable time had already been lost, even if it was incredibly worth it, but now he had to get back to work. He had only days left to find this *virdis lepatite* for the shadow prince. Reading runes was one thing, deciphering them was something else altogether. They were an archaic language, written in the old tongue, and their translations weren't always clear.

He didn't know how much time had passed. It could've been hours or possibly even minutes, they all blurred together. The moon was still high when Novalise stirred from her sleep.

"Ash?"

His heart stuttered, clenching.

He'd always hated that nickname, but when it fell from her lips, it was like a lullaby.

Asher glanced over at her, and all the air was siphoned from his lungs. She was sitting up, the fire behind her caressing her pale skin in a warm, fiery glow. The blanket had fallen to her waist, but her hair tumbled around her, so he caught glimpses of her flesh beneath the lavender strands. She stood, rubbing the sleep from her eyes.

He glamoured her a soft black shirt, one of his own, that skimmed the middle of her thighs. She looked down, and when she met his gaze again, her smile set his heart racing.

"Couldn't sleep?" she asked.

She was so far from the truth. He could've slept next to her for days.

"I only have nine days left to locate this gemstone." Asher leaned back in the chair. The muscles along his shoulders were tense, pulled tight from the strain of exhaustion. He rolled his neck, stretching out his legs, and crossing one ankle over the other.

Novalise walked over to him. In his shirt, he'd never seen anything more tempting in his life. Already his cock pulsed, wanting her again.

Suddenly, the tips of her fingers grazed the skin of his back, following the scars marring his flesh. "What happened here?"

Concern weighed down her every word.

His throat tightened. "My father."

Novalise tensed, but she didn't pry, and he was grateful for it.

"Is there anything I can do to help?" She moved next to him, peering over his shoulder.

"Unless you can locate and obtain a mystical gem..." He slid one hand between her legs, his fingers curling around her thigh, stroking her soft skin. "Then I doubt it."

She picked up some of the papers and flipped through them. Then she leaned in closer, a tiny line furrowing across her brow. "I can do this."

Asher sat up straight, staring at her. "What?"

"I can help you find this stone." She shuffled the papers, her lips pursing in concentration. "I'll have to do a reading, but I can't imagine it would be difficult."

"A star reading?" He didn't think they were good for anything except the foretelling of fate. It never occurred to him star readings could be useful for other things as well.

"Yes, it's fairly simple. Granted, it will have to take place within the observatory..." She cocked her hip to the side, leaning into him. "But once I call upon the stars, any question I ask will be answered. For example, where to find this gem."

Well, damn.

If he had known it would have been that easy, he would've asked her months ago for her assistance.

"Who needs this...*virdis lepatite*, anyway?" Novalise handed the papers back to him. "It seems like it could be dangerous if it falls into the wrong hands."

Asher already had a slightly gray conscience when it came to researching the gem. He shoved back from the desk and stood, stretching. "The one who seeks it hails from the Northernlands. He'll be gone by the end of Midsummer and then will no longer be any concern of mine."

"Oh?" The corner of her mouth lifted into a coy smile. "Is it a secret, then?"

"Perhaps." The lie tasted bitter on his tongue.

Asher scooped Novalise into his arms. It was time for a change of subject and sleep. He couldn't tell her the *virdis lepatite* was for Drake, that locating the stone was part of a bargain Asher struck with him two years ago. Just like he couldn't tell her he was the one who hired the Shadowblade Assassin to kill his father.

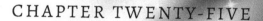

CHAPTER TWENTY-FIVE

*T*he mouthwatering scent of bacon lured Novalise from sleep.

She stretched against the soft rug, her body pleasantly spent and comfortably warm. Reaching her arms over her head, she arched her back, delight humming in the back of her throat.

"If you keep making those cute little noises and extending yourself like that..." Asher lifted the hem of the shirt, pressing a kiss to her abdomen. "I'll be forced to take you again."

Her lashes fluttered and she peered up at him. "Forced?"

Morning sunlight spilled in through the windows of his study, dousing them in a haze of gold. He was seated on the rug next to her, propped up with one arm, his gaze lazily skimming up and down the length of her. His eyes were heavy, banked with the fire of desire, and he lightly trailed the curve of her breast with one finger. She wanted nothing more than to savor every inch of his gloriously naked chest, kissing a path all the way down below the waistband of his pants. If this was what it would be like to wake up next to him every day, she wanted to do it for the rest of her life.

As though sensing where her mind had wandered, he arched a brow in amusement. "Your breakfast will get cold."

Novalise eased herself up, planting her lips at the base of his neck. "What if I'm not hungry?"

"Then your stomach betrays you." The corner of his mouth lifted in a knowing smile.

"Fine," she grumbled, tucking her legs under her. As much as she loathed to admit it, Asher was right.

She was positively famished, and before her was a spread of delicious food. Two trays were set on the ground filled with bowls of fresh berries and cream, along with plates of crispy bacon, fried eggs, and a pile of biscuits with jam. A carafe of juice was accompanied by two glasses of water, as well as a steaming pot of tea.

"I wasn't sure what you preferred." Asher shoved one hand through his hair, not quite meeting her eye. "So, I asked for an assortment."

"Lucky for you, I'm not picky." She grabbed some of everything and filled her plate. "And I also love to eat."

"Even better." He poured her a cup of tea, and the next few minutes passed in comfortable silence.

Until Novalise realized his brow was pinched in that studious, brooding manner again. "Is something wrong, my lord?"

He stirred his tea, and it was as though she could see his mind working. Considering. Thinking. "Are we going to discuss what happened last night?"

Doubt grazed the back of her neck like the touch of an unwanted advance, and she shuddered. Last night was... wonderful. All she ever wanted, really. To be seen. To be appreciated and cherished. Unfortunately, there was a very real chance he did not feel the same. He accepted her, yes, but that didn't mean he didn't regret his actions. If he was remorseful, she might recover from whatever he said next. However, if it was resentment he felt...well, then. There would be no hope of her ever surviving another stinging blow of dismissal.

Asher replaced his teacup on the tray and stretched out his legs, watching her. "Do you always lose control of your magic when it storms?"

Oh.

He wanted to talk about *that*.

It was a secret she kept well-guarded. Only a handful of people knew she possessed the ancient starfire magic. Nyxian, obviously, because he'd been the one struck down by it. Solarius knew as well, because Novalise had run to him as soon as Nyxian had been hit, and then their mother. Trysta was the one who told her to conceal it, to keep the starstorm a secret. She claimed it was because fae from other houses might spread rumors and false prophecies, like the return of a powerful magic that was once lost. But Novalise thought Trysta worried that if Queen Elowyn discovered she could call upon the starfire, the queen would see it as a direct threat.

The thought left her unwell.

Now, however, Asher was among those who'd witnessed her spiral. In fact, he'd taken on the full brunt of her power without batting an eye.

"The starfire appears out of nowhere. When it storms, the starstorm is violent, like what you witnessed. Other times, like during a star reading, it's just glimpses of starfire. Sometimes only a few sparks. Lately though, it's almost as though it's waiting for something. I can sense the magic flowing through me, lurking, watching...it's difficult to explain." She carefully spread some raspberry jam on a biscuit, refusing to look at him as she spoke. "Usually, I'm prepared for it when it happens. When I'm home, I try to find a place to hide where I can't hurt anyone."

Like the lower levels of House Celestine. The cold, desolate halls deep within the mountain's base, where no one could see her torment or hear her cries of anguish. Where she's not a burden or an oddity. Where her unpredictable exploits can be fully ignored. Starstorm magic was ancient. Fabled. Though it was her family's namesake, no one in their bloodline had possessed such magic for a long time. It was thought to have died out years ago, before her father's father was born. For Novalise to be blessed with the starstorm was unthinkable. For her to be incapable of controlling it was a curse.

Asher's brow knitted with concern. "Have you hurt someone before?"

"You mean besides you?" Her pathetic attempt at humor failed miserably.

"That was nothing, nor was it what I meant." He reached over, tucking a lock of hair behind her ear. "And you know it."

"My brother. Nyxian." Novalise swallowed around the lump in her throat, remembering the first time her magic attacked of its own accord. "We were out in the gardens, collecting starberries. We were young, then. Nyxian was barely seven and I was twelve. We knew a summer storm was coming, the thunder was causing the ground to tremble. The mountain peaks vanished behind a wall of dark clouds."

He continued to stir his tea, his face void of judgment.

"It was the first time it ever happened, when I knew something was wrong with me. It wasn't the same magic I've had since birth. This was different. Stronger. The moment lightning shattered the sky, I felt power unlike anything before. It was terrifying." She squeezed her eyes shut, trying to will the memory away. "Nyx tried to help me, but it was too dangerous, like nothing we'd ever seen or faced. Starfire exploded from my palms in a blinding slash of light. Streaks of dark purple and the deepest blue. The hairs along the back of my neck stood on end. And then Nyxian was on the ground."

She thought she'd killed him.

Novalise opened her eyes, reminding herself to breathe.

Asher nodded slowly. "That explains the scar. I always wondered how he got it."

The scar would mark her brother for the rest of his life. It cut down from his brow across the left side of his face, straight through his eye. He'd worn a patch over it for months while the best of Aeramere's healers fought to save his sight. When he was finally healed, the scarring had faded, and his sight had returned. Except where his eye should have been a dazzling silver, a streak of sapphire ran through it, as though his pupil had been slashed down the center.

Trysta had been able to keep the incident silent and kept within the walls of House Celestine. When Nyxian could finally walk about without a patch over his eye, Trysta told everyone he was "star-touched." The phrase stuck with him throughout his childhood and if Novalise was being honest, it was probably the reason for his rather obnoxiously conceited attitude. He wasn't haughty by any means, but rather smug and annoyingly charming.

"Perhaps we should find some way to get you a protective bubble or shield, something to protect you during storms?" Asher took her hand, distracting her from her thoughts. He interlaced his fingers with hers, and she tried not to overthink the gesture.

While it was sweet of him to suggest she protect herself, her primary concern was for those around her.

She couldn't avoid storms forever. Or using her magic. At some point, the starfire would show itself for all to see, and Novalise would have to make sure she was ready to face the consequences.

"Perhaps," she agreed.

Asher leaned in to kiss her when the door to the study burst open.

"Asher? Do you know where my—" Cyra stumbled to a stop, her gaze darting back and forth between them, to the dress on the floor, and back again. "Oh. Good morning, Lady Novalise."

Her golden eyes twinkled, sparkling with mischievousness.

Novalise took a sip of her tea, pretending to be unruffled and poised, despite the fact that her hair was a mess and she was wearing one of Asher's shirts. "Good morning, Lady Cyra."

A beat of silence passed between them, while Cyra's smile only widened.

"What were you looking for, Cyra?" Asher asked, deterring his sister. He kept his tone surprisingly even, nonplussed by the idea that she'd walked in on their shared moment of intimacy.

"Oh, um, I needed something for the Firelight Festival. But I'll find it on my own." She waved, backing out the door. "You two just...carry on."

Once Cyra soundly shut the door behind her, Novalise finished her tea. "I should go."

Asher rose to his feet, offering her his hand. She accepted, and he pulled her up so she was flush against him. Standing so close to him caused her heart to flutter. Her blood to rush. Her thoughts to empty. It was impossible to remember what to say, how to act, what to do.

"We can prepare for the star reading to find the *virdis lepatite* at your convenience." Novalise flinched. She sounded so formal. So dull and droll.

"After the Firelight Festival then?" His hands moved to her waist, brushing up and down the soft material of his shirt. Each motion caused the hem to inch higher. The heat of his touch burned through the fabric, scorching her skin. Tantalizing warmth pooled low in her belly, pulsing, filling her with need.

She clenched, unsure how to say goodbye.

A curtsy was too absurd. But a kiss could be seen as a gesture of affection, one Asher might not be willing to return. She supposed she could hug him, a fairly neutral deed.

"You could start," Asher said, his voice low and tempting, "by putting on something less revealing. I might be on friendly terms with Ariesian now, but I have no doubt he'd come for me if I sent you home in nothing but one of my shirts."

A flush crept up Novalise's neck, bleeding into her cheeks.

She quickly glamoured herself a dress, nothing fancy. Just a simple gown of ivory cotton and embroidered silver stars.

"And what of my purple dress?" she asked, twisting her hair into a thick braid. "It is my favorite, after all."

"I'll have it cleaned and placed in my room for safekeeping." He hooked a finger under her chin, angling her face up to his own. "Should you decide to stay again."

Excitement bubbled inside of her, like a hundred butterflies fluttering wildly.

Asher's lips brushed over hers. Once. Twice.

For the first time, walking away from him didn't hurt so badly. For the first time, Novalise thought her plan might actually work.

The entire carriage ride home, she kept two fingers pressed to her mouth, savoring the feel of him.

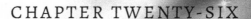

CHAPTER TWENTY-SIX

*N*ovalise's gaze darted around the gardens of House Celestine and to the edge of the mountain cliffs.

There was no sign of a dragon.

She steeled her spine into place, clasped her hands in front of her to keep herself from fidgeting, and strode into the foyer of her home. Head held high, she smiled politely and nodded in kind, but she was absolutely certain that every servant she passed knew she hadn't slept in her own bed last night.

Which was fine.

Completely acceptable, actually.

So what if she'd stayed with Asher last night? Plenty of other respectable ladies had lovers, some had more than one. They weren't expected to be prudes or chaste, yet no matter how many times she told herself her actions were justifiable, she couldn't keep the warmth from her cheeks. It was one thing to be discreet in such matters, it was something else altogether if her entire household knew about her dalliances.

She aimed for the staircase on the right that would lead her straight to the safety of her bedroom, when a door swung open from the far wing, and Solarius sauntered into the grand hall.

His silver hair was pulled into a knot on the top of his head, the black tips sticking out in all directions. The tie he wore hung loose around his neck and the sleeves of his shirt were haphazardly rolled, as though done so in haste. His pants were terribly wrinkled, and he strode toward her with a crooked smile on his face. From the looks of it, he didn't sleep in his own bed last night either.

"Good morning, darling sister." He slung a casual arm around her shoulders and winked. "I won't tell if you won't."

Novalise grinned, leaning into him. "Deal."

"Okay, if anyone asks, I was in town playing a few rounds of crystal spades." They climbed the stairs together, and his gaze darted up and down the hall. He lowered his voice to a whisper. "I lost too much money, drank too much wine, and fell asleep on the side of the road while trying to make it back up the mountain."

Novalise looked up at him sharply as they reached the threshold of the hallway. "Is any of that true?"

"Not in the least." Solarius laughed. "What's your excuse?"

She thought for a moment, trying to compose a plausible explanation for her absence. "Well, I was—"

Her mouth snapped shut.

Ariesian was at the opposite end of the hall, stalking toward them, consternation deepening the frown across his brow.

"Solarius. Novalise." He glanced between them, then studied her, his keen gaze taking in her tangled braid and ridiculously plain dress. "Did you stay at House Emberspire last night?"

Anxiety lodged her voice somewhere in the back of her throat. From beside her, Solarius reared back, his brows arched in surprise.

"Really, Nova?" he whispered conspiratorially. "Lord Firebane? And how is the book-loving fire fae in bed?"

She jabbed him swiftly in the ribs with her elbow, glaring up at him with silent condemnation.

"Nova?" Ariesian prompted. He crossed his arms over his chest, his displeasure expanding the longer she stood there without speaking.

"Of course not." She laughed, but it was forced. Strained and slightly off-pitch. She clenched her hands together. Panicking under pressure, she blurted out a stolen excuse. "I was in town playing crystal spades. I lost too much money, drank too much wine, and found a safe place to sleep for the night."

Solarius might be able to get away with sleeping on the side of the road, but she most certainly could not.

"What?" A scowl marred Solarius's face, but his eyes danced with laugher. "That was *my* reason for strolling back home in the early morning hours."

Ariesian sighed, pinching the bridge of his nose to disguise his growing vexation. "You don't have anything to be ashamed of, Novalise. I merely want to ensure you're being careful."

Careful? Did he think so little of her as to assume she might be with child before marriage? She was *always* careful.

Novalise fisted her hands on her hips, the urge to defend herself against his assumptions rising. "I'll have you know, my moon cycles are none of your concern. I drink a special blend of herbal tea regularly to prevent—"

"Gods, no!" Ariesian threw his hands up to silence her, his eyes widening. "That is *not* what I meant."

Solarius chuckled, coming to her rescue. He planted one hand on her shoulder, lowering his voice. "Ariesian was inquiring whether you're certain traipsing around with Lord Firebane is the best course of action, since your wedding is only a few days away."

She huffed. "I am not innocent. I'm allowed to enjoy the company of whomever I choose."

Solarius turned red.

Ariesian turned stone cold.

"I'm aware." His voice dripped with disdain. The stars

trembled, despite being eclipsed by the glowing sun. "But I also know that everyone in Aeramere is watching your every move, waiting to see what will happen. After your star reading..."

He trailed off, the unsaid words hanging between them like the cloying scent of heady perfume.

Right. Of course, her disaster of a star reading would be at the forefront of his mind. Nothing had gone according to plan despite the effort she put forth to achieve the fate promised to her. She'd worked so hard, she'd been so diligent. She never stepped out of line, did everything that was asked of her, and allowed decisions to be made for her. The artfully crafted pedestal she'd been placed upon had given way beneath her, sent her careening back toward the ground, only to be caught in a web of risky bargains and unpredictable chance.

And what did she have to show for it?

She'd made a deal with the Shadowblade Assassin, she'd yet to take her place as the Reader of Stars, Asher had finally accepted her but refused to love her, and worse, her wedding was days away and she wasn't even sure he would agree to marry her.

"I'm sure everything will fall into place." Solarius broke the strained silence, giving her shoulder a gentle squeeze. "Our Novalise is going to the have the wedding of the Season."

Ariesian grunted, shaking his head. "At least the stars got something right."

With that, he stalked past them, his brooding temperament hanging over his head like the clouds of an incoming storm.

Solarius's hand fell away, and he faced her, tugging lightly on her braid. "Don't worry, Nova. Ariesian has a lot on his mind as of late."

"Is finding a suitable husband for me something that plagues him?" She ran the toe of her shoe along the line of constellations inlaid against the smooth stone floor. Exasperation burned in her stomach, acidic and volatile. "Because I am quite capable of doing that on my own."

She was competent at a great many things, if only she was ever offered the opportunity to prove it.

"Not in so many words. Our discussions are usually centered around court politics and things of that nature." Solarius tilted his head, running his thumb along the hard line of his jaw. "What about Lord Asher Firebane?"

Novalise bristled. "What about him?"

"Does he want to marry you?"

He did...and then he didn't.

"Not exactly."

"Then maybe that is why Ariesian is concerned about you spending time with him." He bent down and planted a kiss on the top of her head. "It is a useless endeavor to pursue someone who doesn't reciprocate your feelings. Trust me, I know."

She leaned back, looking up at him. For a moment, all traces of his amiable, good-natured demeanor had vanished. Shadows crept into his eyes and his mouth was drawn tight, like he was lost to a memory she couldn't see. Solarius looked forlorn. Regretful, even.

"Novalise!"

She glanced past Solarius to see Sarelle heading toward them, her cheeks flushed pink.

"There you are." Sarelle sucked in a breath, then smoothed her skirts. "I've been looking everywhere for you."

"Is something wrong?" Novalise asked, disquiet coursing through her.

"Of course not." Sarelle gave a flippant wave of her hand, sprinkling stardust everywhere. Solarius wiped a smudge of it from off her cheek, his smile returning once more. "Your wedding dress has arrived. Mother wants you to try it on to see if any adjustments need to be made."

Her wedding dress.

The one thing she chose was finally here.

"Come along, Nova." Sarelle snagged her by the hand, attempting to tug her down the hall. "She's waiting."

"I'll leave you to it, then." Solarius inclined his head, and Novalise followed Sarelle through the corridor leading to their mother's room.

Trysta's quarters were spacious and decadent. The walls were papered a dark navy and etched with dazzling constellations. Deep purple draperies were peeled back, fastened in place by bands of gold to allow streams of sunlight to spill in through the soaring windows. The furnishings were all made from dark walnut, the surfaces gleaming. Her mother's vanity was tidy, with bottles of perfume and jars of ointments organized by size on one shelf. In the center of the room was an expansive four poster bed. The right side was fully made, with not a single pillow out of place. On the left side, however, was a single white rose. A new one was placed upon the bed each morning, as a doting gift to the memory of Zenos Starstorm, Novalise's father.

"Ah, Novalise, my darling." Trysta swept forward, the bangles on her wrists jingling. She pressed a featherlight kiss to each of her cheeks. "Now, I've spoken to Queen Elowyn, your wedding will take place at her palace in the grand ballroom."

"But I wanted to get married outside, under the stars." Novalise swallowed her irritation, and it roiled in the pit of her stomach.

"Don't be silly. It's far too warm to have the ceremony outdoors." Trysta swatted her argument away like an annoying fly. "Everyone will be miserable."

Novalise would be the one who was miserable.

Trysta flitted about the room, prattling on about the decorations Novalise didn't like—gaudy glass stars that mimicked the real ones Sarelle could create and bouquets of pungent dahlias even though they made Novalise sneeze. Then there was the guest list, an assembly of some of the highest ranking fae in Aeramere, along with House members, relatives, and friends, many of whom Novalise had never met.

Novalise twisted her hands together as an uncomfortable sensation caused her skin to crawl and itch.

Her mother's voice carried from the closet.

"And finally," she exclaimed, wheeling out a dressing form with a cape thrown over it. "The dress."

Trysta pulled the cape off the form, and Novalise stared in horror.

The gown was hideous.

It was nothing like she'd imagined or dreamed. Not at all what she'd decided upon. The dress she'd chosen was supposed to be deep violet, made of luxurious silk and chiffon. Both elegant and simple in style. She wanted thin straps with a modestly low neckline across the bosom and a starburst of rainbow moonstones exploding from her hips all the way down the delicate hem.

But this…this was a monstrosity.

Novalise shook her head. "It's not what I wanted."

Trysta smiled, gazing at the dress as though it was every-thing *she* could've hoped for. "I made a few modifications after your last fitting."

"A few?" It was an entirely new design.

"Be a good girl and go try it on." Trysta gestured toward the door of her bathing suite.

Without warning, Novalise was flooded with memories of the night before. Sprawled on Asher's sofa with his mouth fused to her core while she was helpless to do anything but let him send her into oblivion. Asher thrusting into her over and over as she rode him, teetering on the brink of sheer ecstasy.

His words echoed in her mind.

Because you're a good girl, aren't you, my lady? You're a good girl who always does exactly as she's told.

Warmth spread across her chest, and she fanned herself, suddenly too hot to breathe.

"Nova?" Her mother's voice drew her from her sensual thoughts.

She tore her gaze away from the gown and met Trysta's questioning gaze. "Hm?"

"Go try it on."

Novalise ducked her head. "Yes, Mother."

She shuffled into the bathing suite, loathing every second she undressed. The gown her mother had chosen for her was wretched. Morose gray and painfully repulsive, it draped over her like an oppressive cloud of disappointment. The sleeves were sheer but long, and there were a thousand onyx buttons up the front, the last one stopping at the base of her throat. A high collar sprouted around her neckline like a pruning peacock, making it nearly impossible to move her head, while dense layers of puffy tulle suffocated her.

Just like every other aspect of her life.

Again, she couldn't quite breathe.

Gathering up handfuls of the irritating fabric, Novalise stalked out of the bathing suite.

Trysta's expression morphed from one of tiresome patience to absolute rapture. She plastered one hand to her heart, gasping obnoxiously. "You look like a dream."

Novalise spied her reflection in the ornate floor to ceiling mirror. "I look like I'm a week away from coming out of mourning."

"Nonsense." Trysta bustled around her, fluffing the absurdly long train, dismissing her complaint. "I'm meeting with Lady Everland of House Terensel later today to discuss the final arrangements for the flowers. The dahlias are *such* a lovely choice. I had the very same ones at my wedding. But I think if she can provide them in a dark burgundy, possibly even black, then white lilies would be the perfect complement."

Bitter frustration clawed its way up Novalise's throat. "Are you planning my wedding or my funeral?"

Trysta's nostrils flared and the look that flashed across her face was nothing short of scorn. "What has gotten into you?"

"I'm sorry, Mother. I just..."

Say something, a tiny voice inside herself pleaded.

She needed to speak up. To use her voice, to make herself heard. She was allowed to make her own decisions, to choose for herself. This was *her* wedding. She was allowed to have an opinion, to disagree, to argue, and to be combative. Otherwise, she would lose herself, becoming nothing more than the idyllic darling of Aeramere. Always agreeable. Always obedient. Always lacking in conviction.

Her courage failed her.

"I'm just nervous." The lie spilled from her, leaving a foul taste in her mouth.

But Trysta's expression softened. "It's understandable. Marriage is a milestone in life, and not one to be taken lightly. But your future husband is...somewhat kind, has exceptionally powerful magic, and is heir to the throne. I have no doubt he will take excellent care of you."

Warning fired through Novalise, causing her throat to close.

"I'm sorry, what did you say?" But she heard the exact words her mother had spoken, and she knew they held significant meaning.

Your future husband is...not your future husband will be...

"Oh, child. You must get your head out of the clouds." Trysta opened an ebony box on her vanity and rummaged through it. "His Highness won't appreciate it if you fail to listen—"

"What?" Novalise shrieked, panic causing her blood to thrum and her palms to sweat.

"Novalise, have you not heard a word I said?" Trysta turned toward her, a black diamond solitaire ring surrounded by a halo of rubies pinched between her fingers. "His Highness will not approve of your constant daydreaming."

His Highness.

Prince Aspen.

Oh gods, no.

Trepidation turned her skin to ice as tiny beads of panic-induced sweat slid down her spine. Her heart hammered, pounding against the wall of her chest. Her lungs seized, her throat closed. Fear clouded her mind, and she stumbled backward a step, suddenly lightheaded. Empty and hollow, she felt as though she'd been carved from the inside out.

Novalise was too late.

She hadn't picked a husband in time, so one had been chosen for her. And not just any male, a prince. The Prince of Aeramere.

No.

She shook her head, backing away from her mother, away from the fate that doomed her.

"Where are you going?" Trysta demanded, closing the distance between them.

Out. Novalise had to get out.

Without responding, she turned away from her mother and ran.

"At least take off the dress before you ruin it!" Trysta called after her, anger lacing her tone. "Novalise!"

But she didn't stop, and for once, she didn't listen.

Novalise sprinted through the corridors of House Celestine toward Ariesian's study, gasping as dread urged her on, begged her to hasten her steps. She couldn't marry Prince Aspen. She couldn't marry anyone. Not so long as her heart belonged to Asher.

CHAPTER TWENTY-SEVEN

*A*sher stared at the shadow prince sitting across from him, trying to maintain a sense of calm. Novalise's emotions were a torrent inside of him, a swelling rush of agony and despair. Yet there was nothing he could do to reach her, to try to soothe her. Not so long as the Shadowblade Assassin sat in his study, watching his every move with a vicious eye.

Drake had shown up with no notice. The only warning Asher had was the beating of wings and a dragon's call before the Prince of Brackroth was standing at his door. Now he was in his study, tapping his fingers idly along the edge of Asher's desk, his cold gaze intensely focused on something near the hearth.

Asher craned his neck to see what had snagged Drake's attention.

On the ground by the sofa was a pool of scarlet silk— Novalise's dress.

Coughing lightly, Asher drew Drake's focus away from the discarded gown. "I still have eight days left."

"I'm aware." Drake leaned back in the seat, flicking away an invisible fleck of dust from the collar of his shirt. "Just as I'm certain you've made progress on the task at hand."

Asher nodded. "I have indeed."

Drake stared at him, waiting with tense patience for him to continue.

"I've eliminated the Kethwyn Woods and Wintervale as possible locations for the *virdis lepatite*. I'm fairly certain the gem can only be found in the bogs of Fenmire…"

A scowl pulled both of Drake's dark brows downward.

"I know that's not what you wanted to hear, Your Highness." Asher thumbed through the stack of papers on his desk, all riddled with scribbles and notes. "But I'll be able to give you a more precise location in a few days."

Namely, after Novalise conducted a star reading to tell him where exactly to find this blasted gemstone. Then he could rid his life of the shadow prince once and for all.

"I trust you will." Drake's expression remained one of cool composure even as a beat of weighted silence passed between them.

Then another.

Asher straightened in his seat, leaning forward to match the prince's indifferent countenance. "Is there anything else, Your Highness?"

Drake's face was a void, vacant and impassive. The Shadowblade Assassin thrived on being unreadable. There was no way to gauge his intent. He was calculating, precise, and lacking any obvious tell. "What do you know of Lady Novalise Starstorm?"

Asher tightened the reins of his control. "What of her?"

"What are her likes? Her interests?" The prince ran his thumb along the underside of his signet ring, a silver band emblazoned with the emblem of a dragon. "Her favorite color? Favorite book?"

Shuttering away the brewing rage pulsing beneath the

surface of his skin, Asher feigned nonchalance. "I don't make it my business to know the whims of females."

Drake stoked Asher's temper, setting fire to the kindling of his anger. "It seems you don't make it your business to know much of anything."

Asher locked his jaw, clamping his teeth together so tightly, a dull ache formed at his temples. He was in no mood for the shadow prince's games. "What are you getting at, Kalstrand?"

"Only that for someone who spends his time surrounded by the knowledge of the worlds, you're far more ignorant than I would've thought."

Asher was on his feet a second later. He slammed his hands on the desk, toppling over a pile of books and sending a stack of papers askew. His magic burned, imploded, and bled from his palms into the hardwood. He knew without a doubt the scorch of frostfire would leave behind an irreparable blemish.

"Insult me again," he warned.

The prince rose, matching his intimidating stance. "Or you'll what? Challenge me to a duel? Invite me to take part in a battle till the death? If so, I gladly accept. Because we both know I would win."

Drake bared his teeth, the truth of his nature revealing itself. Callous and ruthless. An assassin to his core.

"Out," Asher demanded, pointed toward the door of his study. "Now."

Drake eased back, the corner of his mouth twisting up into a smug smile. As though he knew something Asher did not, and it gave him a sick kind of satisfaction. Knots of unease twisted in Asher's gut.

"Are you aware she's engaged?" Drake asked, his voice eerily calm.

"I know her wedding is at the close of Midsummer." It was all everyone was talking about since plans for the event were in motion. All of it beyond his control, and likely beyond Novalise's as well. "But she is not yet engaged."

"How wrong you are, old friend." Drake chuckled, the sound of it hollow and bitter. The tiny hairs along the back of Asher's neck stood on end. "I have it on good authority that the engagement will be announced at the Firelight Festival."

Drake tilted his head, pretending to consider his own words. "I believe you're the one hosting that particular little celebration, are you not?"

Impossible.

Novalise was with *him* last night. If she was engaged to someone else, Asher would've sensed it. He would have known. He shook his head. "I don't believe it. She would have told me if that was truly the case."

"Why? She owes you no explanations." Drake inhaled deeply, all traces of complacent taunting vanishing from his face. "Curious the way her scent clings to you, the way it mingles with your own. Did you honestly think I wouldn't find out? That I wouldn't *know*? Novalise is your mate, and you don't even love her."

The blade of insult struck true, piercing Asher. "Why should I believe anything you say?"

"For one, I never lie." Power seemed to magnify around the shadow prince. Darkness fell around him like a cloak, making it almost impossible to discern the difference between him and the shadows. "But if you don't want to believe me, then perhaps you'll take the word of your sister, who's lurking in the shadows of the hall outside your study, listening to every word of our conversation."

Asher reared back just as a wall of understanding slammed into him.

Drake tossed his arm out, and the door to the study swung open.

Sure enough, there was Cyra, her golden eyes wide in shock.

She toppled forward, flinging her arms up to catch her balance. "I'm so sorry, Asher." She spared the prince a hasty glance, fear mirrored in her gaze. "Your Highness."

"Lady Cyra, are you aware it's a crime to eavesdrop on royal family in Brackroth?" Drake turned toward her slowly, stealing all the light from the room until the entire place was cloaked in crawling shadows. She paled at his advance. He moved closer, one intentional step at a time. "Do you know what the punishment is for such an offense?"

In one fluid movement, he opened his hand and a dagger appeared. The handle was wrapped in black leather, at the hilt was a bloodred jewel, so dark it looked almost black. And the blade was shrouded in shadows, like the deepest part of the ocean where the light could never reach.

The Shadowblade.

A strange noise came from Cyra, a choking, startled cry. Her eyes widened in terror.

"Stay away from her, Drake." Fury erupted inside Asher, a well of uncontrollable wrath. Frostfire sparked at his fingertips, the silver and black flames snapping. Crackling. Ready to ignite.

"Save your pathetic little flames for someone who cares." The shadow prince glared at Cyra with a menacing smile. "I think I'd enjoy teaching your darling little sister some manners."

Cyra screamed.

Drake moved so quickly Asher couldn't even track him. In less than a second, he was standing behind Cyra, jerking her head backward, the flat edge of his Shadowblade pressed firmly against her throat. She whimpered, clutching at his forearm, struggling to put space between the skin of her neck and his weapon. Tears slid down her cheeks, her watery gaze silently begging Asher to save her.

Asher moved around from behind the desk.

"Watch it, Firebane." Malice coated Drake's tone like ice. "We wouldn't want my blade to slip across her pretty little throat, now would we?"

Cyra was sobbing now, her shoulders shaking uncontrollably.

Asher took another intimidating step forward, ready to set the shadow prince on fire. "You wouldn't dare."

"You're right. I wouldn't." Drake laughed, but it was vicious. Heartless. The laugh of a man with no soul. "I'll leave her for some other bastard to discipline."

He swiped the blade across her neck.

"No!" Asher jerked forward, then froze.

The Shadowblade didn't break Cyra's skin. Instead, it cut clean through a lock of her hair. Drake captured the fiery curl in one hand, then rubbed his fingers together, letting the strands of red and gold fall to the ground like loose threads.

"Let this serve as a reminder to you both." Drake stepped away from Cyra, the scowl deepening across his brow. "Do not cross me. Ever."

Then he vanished, blending into the shadows as though he'd never even been in the room.

"Cy!" Asher darted toward her, catching her before she crumpled to the ground. "It's okay, Cyra. I've got you."

She cried in his arms, trembling. He would kill that fucking prince for threatening her, for making a game of her life. Holding his sister close, he ran a hand down her hair, barely containing the might of his fury when his fingers entangled with the strands that were severed by the Shadowblade.

Cyra sniffled, pulling back from him.

"Don't worry. It's only hair." He tucked the short pieces behind her ear. "It will grow back. Better your hair than your flesh."

She shook her head, swiping hastily at the tears that continued to fall. "It's true."

Asher lowered himself to the ground, tilting her chin up to face him. "What's true?"

"Everything Prince Drake said about Lady Novalise." She sniffed again, then hiccuped, attempting to regain her composure. "Lilith said we're expected to hear about her engagement tonight at the Firelight Festival. Queen Elowyn and Lord Starstorm signed her impending marriage contract."

Her words were a sharpened sword to the gut. Severing. Carving him up from the inside. Asher's hands curled into fists, clenched tightly as all the air was pulled from his lungs. The bond tying him to Novalise blazed in his chest, the threads binding them urging him to go to her. To free her from this fate. Flames reached for the stars.

"Who?" he bit the word out.

"I don't know." Cyra struggled to her feet and Asher stood, helping her find the solid ground beneath them. She sucked in a harsh breath. "There are rumors, of course, but no one is certain."

Damn it.

He had to do something. It was one thing for Novalise to pick a mate on her own, to choose someone else besides him. But for that decision, that eternal commitment to be made for her...it pained him. Left him gutted. She'd been so ready to marry whoever the stars revealed, and then when her world had been turned upside down, she'd been more than prepared to find a husband on her own. But now...

"You have to stop it, Asher." His sister's voice cut through his thoughts. "You can't let her marry someone else. She is *yours*. And you...you belong to her. Ever since the Winter Solstice, ever since that kiss bound the two of you together. Your magic will suffer, you will be afflicted for the rest of your days if you allow this to happen."

Dropping his head, he refused to meet her earnest gaze. He'd accepted the bond to Novalise, he'd accepted *her,* and now it was too late. He should have gone straight to Ariesian and asked for her hand in marriage. There was no way he could live with himself if he put Novalise in harm's way. Especially if Trysta Starstorm was right. That damned star reading haunted him most days, served as a steadfast reminder that he would never be enough. Perhaps this was for the best, and he should be grateful Novalise had found a match. Someone who wasn't fated to be an abusive bastard.

"I'll never be able to give her what she wants, Cy."

"Then give her all you have, give her all you are." Cyra grabbed his hands, fervent and demanding. "I know you've sworn off love because of Mother and Father, but not every relationship is undesirable. Not every relationship ends in loss."

Asher shuttered his emotions, closing up. She had no idea the violent chaos that was their father. She didn't know he was vile, that he beat their mother until she could barely walk, that he wielded her love for him like a weapon. Just like she would never understand that it was their mother's desperation to be loved that ultimately ended her life. Asher had protected her from those harsh truths and kept her safe from a reality of despair.

"You don't know what you're talking about," he muttered, pulling his hands from her grasp.

"Then tell me," Cyra demanded, throwing her arms out wide. "Tell me why you deny her heart?"

He opened his mouth, then snapped it shut. No good would come of reliving the past. It would only hurt Cyra more.

"It doesn't matter." He shook his head, backing away. "What's done is done."

"So that's it, then?" She huffed out a breath, rolling her eyes to the ceiling. "You're going to give her up to someone who doesn't deserve her?"

"She was never mine."

"Sure." Cyra spun away from him and headed for the door.

She paused, glanced over her shoulder, and tossed him the most scathing look. "Keep telling yourself that, Asher. Then you can watch as the two of you spend an eternity miserable and heart-broken, because you're too stubborn to see the truth of some-thing, even if it's right in front of you."

She stormed out of his study, leaving him alone to wallow in his thoughts. In his regret.

He could marry Novalise, but doing so would subject her to a lifetime of violence. He could try to control his temper, to restrain the volatile nature of his birthright, but one day he wouldn't be able to hold back. One day, he would snap. And when that happened, he'd rather end his own life than watch her suffer by his hand.

Guilt ravaged him.

He'd promised her that she would be safe with him, always. But he would promise her the moon and the stars, the moun-tains and the oceans, if it meant he could protect her. If could find a way to open his heart to her.

It wasn't that he was incapable of love. Not truly.

He adored his mother, once. He cherished his sister. And Novalise...she was the beating of his heart, the calling of his soul.

No, he knew he could love her, and he would, fiercely. For as long as he drew breath, and in the lifetimes after.

But Asher...well, he simply wasn't worthy of *being* loved. By anyone. Especially not by Novalise.

CHAPTER TWENTY-EIGHT

*N*ovalise burst into Ariesian's study unannounced, no longer caring if her arrival was deemed inappropriate or less than dignified. She'd already wasted enough time.

She stomped into the room, chest heaving. "Ariesian."

Her eldest brother startled at the sight of her, nearly tipping out of his chair.

"I must speak with you at once." She closed the distance between them, steeling her spine in preparation for the impending argument.

His gaze took her in from head to toe, his mouth falling open slightly. He blinked once, gave his head a small shake, his brows furrowing in question. "What in the name of all the constellations are you wearing?"

"It's my wedding dress," she snapped, as if it was the most obvious thing in the world.

"It's..." He swallowed, and given by the way he tugged on the collar of his shirt, she knew it was taking every ounce of his good breeding to remain polite. "Interesting."

"It's abhorrent and we both know it. But that is entirely

beside the point." She rounded the desk, jabbing her finger into his chest. "What have you done?"

Ariesian clasped her hand firmly, pushing her impudent finger aside.

"I'm afraid I don't know what you're talking about." He turned his attention back to the tidy pile of papers on his desk. "I've done a great many things."

She ground her teeth, annoyed with him for being so apathetic toward her.

"My future husband," she prompted, hoping to jar his memory.

"What of him?"

Ah, so he didn't even deny it.

"I thought we..." Novalise hesitated, framing her words carefully. Ariesian might be her brother, and he might have made a terrible mistake, but he was still the Lord of House Celestine. "That is, I thought you valued my opinion. I was of the mind that I would choose my mate."

Ariesian nodded in agreement, not looking up from his paperwork. "And you did."

She gaped at him. "I most certainly did not."

He ran a hand over his face, rolling his neck back so he looked up at the ceiling. She hated it when he did that, hated it when he treated her like a child, as though she were sullen and waspish for no reason. It was infuriating.

After a sharp inhale, he faced her.

"Novalise, you told me yourself that you were fine with the contract, even when I questioned you." His hand cut through the air. "You told me you were sure I was making the right choice by signing the agreement."

He was speaking nonsense. Not once had they ever discussed a marriage contract.

"That is not true." She crossed her arms over her chest, glowering down at him. "I would never—"

"But you did!" His voice boomed, his patience with her evaporating. She jumped back, stunned by the outburst.

"I would never agree to marry Prince Aspen!" Novalise cried, her hope at convincing Ariesian to change his mind becoming weaker by the second. "And I would assume you cared for me enough not to marry me off to some cruel, inconsiderate, cold-hearted royal!"

His eyes widened, his brows lifted.

"What?" he asked, the word croaking out of him.

Novalise faltered. She knew Ariesian, she understood his mannerisms and was quite good at predicting his moods. One glance and she could easily determine his temperament. Right now, he was shocked.

"Am I wrong?" She clutched her hands together to ward off the inevitable shaking, to disperse the unease crawling down her spine. "I mean, you did agree to wed me to Prince Aspen, did you not?"

Ariesian paled, all the color leached from his face. "I did not."

An icy shiver brushed across her shoulders like the hand of death.

When she spoke again, it was a hoarse whisper. "Then who am I marrying, Ariesian?"

"I hope you're not too disappointed." A rumbling voice cut through the weighted tension between them.

Novalise looked over her shoulder and there, lounging in the doorway of Ariesian's study, was Prince Drake Kalstrand.

The Shadowblade Assassin.

NOVALISE STARED AT PRINCE DRAKE. A full minute passed before she mustered the courage to say anything, before she finally found her voice.

"No." She spoke the word with conviction.

Ariesian pushed up from his seat, coming to stand beside her. "It's done, Novalise. We've already signed the—"

"I said *no*." She glared up at her brother, silently challenging him. Ariesian's brows, constantly in a semi-permanent state of frowning, lifted for a moment before returning to their usual glower.

She strode over to where Prince Drake was lounging against the door and speared him with a look of pure loathing. "This was not a part of our agreement."

"What agreement?" Ariesian called from behind her, but she ignored his question.

The shadow prince spread his arms, offering her an impassive shrug. "I don't recall the specifics."

Anger boiled inside of her, bubbling and hissing, threatening to overflow. It was like a storm gathering off the coast of Aeramere. Dark clouds piling on top of one another, roiling in the sky. Sinister, building with each lash of lightning. Except she was the gale, ready to unleash havoc on those around her. Years of frustration, of being silenced, converged and reached a breaking point. She trembled, but not from fear.

From rage.

Novalise shoved past Prince Drake, intentionally ramming her shoulder into his arm. The bastard didn't even give an inch, and it was like running into a brick wall. To make it even worse, she caught the uptick of a smile from the corner of her eye.

Wretched man.

"Novalise, wait!" Ariesian's voice echoed, pleading with her to come back, but she stifled the obedient, dutiful sister inside of her.

She was seething. Outraged. She was furious with the

shadow prince for taking advantage of her dilemma and angry with herself for failing to see right through his plans. Resentment fueled her. Ariesian had blindsided her, he'd signed her life away, and by the time she realized what happened, it was far too late. And Asher...damn her mate for being unable to find it in himself to love her. She clenched her jaw to keep from screaming at the top of her lungs.

What began as a brisk pace through the corridors of her house became a sprint. She ran, her feet carrying her like the wind, her revolting wedding dress tangling around her ankles. Mocking her. Onward she continued, rushing up the elaborate staircases to her safe haven.

She needed to breathe. To think. She couldn't spend an eternity with Prince Drake.

Bursting through the glass doors to the highest balcony of House Celestine, Novalise staggered out onto the smooth stone. The warm summer breeze surrounded her, smothered her. Each breath was sharp and painful, a blade stabbing into her side, puncturing her. She fisted one hand over her heart. Her lungs were pinched. Aching. Her thoughts were a muddled mess of hurt, anguish, and fury. Magic heated her veins, spurring her on, drawing upon the swell of emotions she couldn't control.

Gripping the edge of the railing, she held on until her knuckles turned white. Stone pillars rose on either side of her and in their sapphire glimmer, she caught sight of her reflection.

Her hair was a mess, her eyes were wild.

But other than that, she was no different. Always the same.

She was the epitome of a lady, pleasant and passive, stuffed into a pompous, hideous dress that was strangling the life out of her.

Chest heaving, she sucked in a breath. Then loosed a piercing scream of frustration.

Magic poured from her in dazzling, star-filled waves. She

curled her fingers into the stuffy collar around her neck, ripping it from her throat, and tossing it to the ground. Violet and indigo starfire exploded from her, lifting her hair into lavender ribbons, shooting up into the sky. She clawed at the buttons trapping her, yanking them off by the handful, scattering them all around her. Her magic only intensified, billowing, building into a frenzy as beams of stardust encircled the balcony. Again, she tore at the dress, wresting herself free from the confines of everything it stole from her. Pieces of the gown caught fire, and she watched in satisfaction as the scratchy material went up in starry flames, then drifted to the ground, scorched and ruined.

This time, the reflection gazing back at her was no longer her own. Gone was the practiced perfection. The epitome of a lady. She stared at what remained of herself. A Starstorm fae with shredded bits of cloth clinging to her flushed skin. She was rejuvenated, restored. All traces of who she was forced to become now burnt pieces of tulle and suffocating satin. Scraps of the darling of Aeramere curled at her feet.

The starstorm receded, and Novalise drew in a shaking breath.

"Such an interesting take on fashion." The heavily accented voice jarred her, and she spun around to find Prince Drake watching. He strode toward her, closing the distance between them, every step, every click of his boots, intentional.

This time when she shivered, it was from fear.

"I much prefer this version of you." His finger lifted one of the tattered pieces that barely covered her breasts. "Even if it leaves little to the imagination."

Another heated swell of anger washed over her. She slapped his hand away. "Don't touch me."

Prince Drake tucked his hand behind his back, but beneath his frozen, green gaze, she felt more exposed than ever. "Very well, my lady."

"I am *not* your lady." She hated the wavering of her voice but was spurred on by her own resolve, determined to stand her ground. "And I will *never* be your wife."

A slow, scheming smile spread across his chiseled face. "Oh trust me, I will be leaving Aeramere with a wife." His gaze swept over her once more, freezing her. "Whether it's you or one of your sisters is of no consequence to me."

"Excuse me?" Novalise reared back, astonished by his admission. "My sisters are out of the question."

His jaw ticked.

"Be that as it may, do you think I want a female who is mated to someone else?" He crowded her, edging her closer to the railing. She flung her hands back to catch herself on its smooth ledge before she toppled over. "Do you think I would enjoy watching you pine for another for an eternity?"

"I'm not mated—" The lie almost slipped from her tongue when a gust of frosty air slammed into her, stealing the words from between her lips. The scent of frosted pine and wintry mountains overwhelmed her, left her dizzy.

Planting both hands on either side of her, he leaned down, so close their noses nearly touched. "Mind your words, my lady. Deceit is incredibly unflattering."

Goosebumps pebbled across her flesh. The railing of the balcony dug into her backbone, a firm reminder she had nowhere else to go. No means of escape.

"You want him," Prince Drake crooned, "do you not?"

Him. Asher.

Novalise ducked her head, hiding behind the fallen strands of her hair. "My soul aches for him."

"Then I suggest you do exactly as I say." The shadow prince slid a finger under her chin, tilting her face up to his own. His skin was like ice. "From now until the end of Midsummer, you are marrying me. You're in love with me. You only want me."

She blinked. "But Asher—"

"Only. Me."

Her brows bunched in frustration. "But what if—"

He lifted one hand, silencing her. When he spoke, it was as though he'd read her thoughts, like he saw right through her.

"You ignore his advances. You avoid all conversation with him. So long as you're on my arm, your attention remains solely focused on me." He eased back, barely enough for her to remember how to think clearly. "So long as you're betrothed to me, no other will dare look your way for fear of my wrath."

Novalise opened her mouth to object, and he snapped it shut with one finger.

"Lord Firebane, however, will be the only one to defy me." Prince Drake stepped away and Novalise wrapped her arms around herself in a desperate effort to keep warm. When she met his gaze, his full lips were upturned in a smug smile. "You'll see."

She rubbed her hands up and down her arms to ward off the chill. "It will never work."

"I never fail," he countered smoothly.

She didn't believe him. This plan...it was impossible. It would only serve to push Asher further away from her, and perhaps that's what Prince Drake planned all along. Asher would never want her now. He would stand by and watch as she was taken away to Brackroth. He would never make a stand for her, never fight for her.

"So," the shadow prince drawled, his chilling gaze sweeping over her once more. "Would you like to explain that little display of magic?"

Novalise opened her mouth, and he lifted one finger, snagging it on her bottom lip. "Mind. Your. Words."

She jerked away from his touch, stiffening. "It was nothing."

"Is that so? Because it looked like a starstorm to me." His eyes roved over her, taking in every inch of her, lingering on the charred scraps of her former wedding dress strewn across the balcony. "A kind of magic that hasn't been seen in nearly a hundred years."

Novalise was unsure how Prince Drake knew anything about starstorm magic, but she was certain of one thing. She would not discuss it with him.

Maneuvering herself out from his cage, she strode past him toward the balcony doors. Pausing at the threshold, she tossed him a glance from over her shoulder, willing her spine into place. She'd finally gotten herself a backbone, and she was going to use it. "If you tell anyone about what you think you saw, I'll kill you."

"Threatening me now, are you?" Prince Drake chuckled darkly, shadows bleeding around him like the onset of nightfall. "What a wondrous, beautiful disaster you are."

Novalise refused to answer him. Swallowing her fear, she pushed through the doors, fleeing the balcony as calmly as possible. She had no clue what she'd done, or what had come over her. But she had to get away, and she couldn't look back. Walking toward the winding staircase, she allowed the tremors to overtake her, and could only pray to the goddess that she hadn't made a terrible mistake.

It was one thing to insult the Prince of Brackroth.

What she'd done, however, was far worse.

Novalise had threatened the Shadowblade Assassin, even though he could end her life in less time than it took to breathe. She shook off the sense of foreboding, a tiny beam of pride fusing inside of her. If she could stand up for herself, if she could tell off the Shadowblade Assassin, then no one could stand in her way.

The darling of Aeramere be damned.

She was Novalise Starstorm Celestine, and she would defy the stars.

CHAPTER TWENTY-NINE

*A*sher surveyed the courtyard of House Emberspire.

Trees with leaves that dripped like strands of rubies lined the walls, and bronze bowls set atop pillars were illuminated with flickering flames that would burn for two nights straight. Firebirds soared overhead, their blazing tails creating a display of fire dust and sparks. Lively music coaxed even the most timid of dancers, drawing them out to partake in the revelry. Wine flowed freely, laughter rang out above the crackling of tinder, and the courtyard came alive.

It was exactly how his mother would have wanted it. The Firelight Festival was always one of her favorites.

At least before his father ruined it for her by indulging in too much alcohol and cavorting with other females, some of whom were married with families of their own.

Asher ground his teeth, jaw clenching. Images from the last Firelight Festival when his mother and father were still alive seared into his mind.

His beautiful mother stood beneath one of the ancient oak trees, her chin lifted proudly with a tight smile on her face, while she watched her husband openly flirt with some female from House Galefell. At first, his hand would linger a little too long on the female's waist and he'd lean in too close whenever they spoke. But then the innocuous teasing went a step further with his father grabbing a handful of the female's ass and sloppily kissing her in front of everyone, with no regard to his wife's feelings.

The sight of his father's infidelity burned a hole in the pit of Asher's gut.

Only later, after the festival ended and all their guests went home, did his mother finally call out his father for his blatant misdeeds.

Asher would never forget the transgressions of that night.

In a drunken rage, his father beat his mother mercilessly. Asher heard the echo of her screams and burst into his parents' bedroom to find his father pummeling her beneath the might of his cruel fists. She'd suffered a broken jaw, a shattered wrist, infinite bruises, and a crushed spirit at his hands.

Asher stumbled into a blind rage.

He accosted his father, lashing out at the bastard who was the source of so much pain and agony within the walls of his home. Stealing the abusive attention away from his mother, he forced his father to attack him instead. What seemed like hours of explosive fury was only a few harrowing minutes of exchanging blows with one another. Asher walked away with a busted lip and two broken ribs, but it was nothing compared to the state of his father. Using his frostfire, he'd burned his father's hands, blackened the skin so severely, one wrong move would turn them to ash. Then he'd threatened to do the same to the bastard's cock.

In his heart, he knew he'd done what was right.

But his mother cried, screamed, begged him to stop. To show *mercy*.

His prick of a father had the nerve to smile. Like he knew

he'd won, like he knew exactly how much control he had over the woman he hurt time and again.

Asher decided then and there to call upon the Shadowblade Assassin. He thought that if his father was dead, he could spare his mother. Without her husband, she would be safe. She would be protected. She would be happy.

But it hadn't been enough to save her life.

The sounds of jovial music and rousing laughter jarred Asher from his thoughts.

He blinked, regaining his focus, the ghosts of his past fading into the dark recesses of his soul where they belonged.

Before his eyes, his courtyard was a swelling throng of merriment.

Fae, mortals, vampires, and even some witches, all in Aeramere for the Season, assembled into two lines for a folk dance. He spied Cyra among them, preparing to dance, her smile wide and full. No shadows haunted her face. She was simply enjoying herself, carrying on without a care in the world. Oblivious to all he'd done to afford her the life she deserved.

That, he thought with some small satisfaction, was as it should be.

Asher nodded curtly in greeting to anyone who passed him, his gaze constantly skimming above their heads. But out in his courtyard with the amber firelight gleaming brightly, contrasting the shift of shadows, there was no sign of lavender hair.

He ignored the rod of annoyance digging into his spine.

A full day had passed, and he'd not heard a word from Novalise. He'd attended Queen Elowyn's High Council meeting yesterday, and though Ariesian was there as well, he hadn't said a word, acting as though he hadn't, in fact, signed away his sister's life. Of course, there'd been more important matters to discuss. Whispers of possible rebellions to the north, and mounting frustrations and growing unrest sifted through the people of Aeramere like the chilling first breath of winter. Queen Elowyn seemed to think the only way to quell such rumors was to force her son, Prince Aspen, into marriage. She reasoned that if he produced an heir to the throne, then somehow a newborn babe would make them a stronger adversary. As though rulers, monarchs, and emperors weren't overthrown repeatedly throughout history, royal bloodlines be damned.

It was an absurd thought process.

The birth of an heir wouldn't be enough to stop the discontent spreading throughout the realm.

And last Asher checked, the furthest thing from Prince Aspen's mind was a wife.

"Ah, Firebane."

Asher's gaze slid to the male standing before him. He inclined his head. "Marintide."

"Never thought I'd see you here." Lord Reif Marintide stepped up beside him, a drink in one hand, his eyes already glassy from far too much indulgence. "I thought you hated these sorts of things."

Asher stared at him, his expression blank.

"I live here," he answered dryly.

"Hm." Reif glanced around, squinting up at the spires protruding proudly from Asher's house, as though realizing where he was for the first time. "So you do."

He took another drink of his wine, then gestured widely, the contents sloshing over the rim of his glass. "Pity about Lady Novalise, don't you think? Can't believe Starstorm is marrying her off to that bastard of a prince."

Asher's stomach hollowed out. His heart stilled, and the air evaporated from his lungs. "What did you say?"

Reif shook his head, nearly losing his balance in the process. He righted himself quickly enough, pointing with one finger while barely holding onto his glass. "Of course you haven't heard the news. You love books more than social affairs, but I'm surprised your sister didn't mention it before."

"Who?" Asher demanded, glaring down at the lord from House Azurvend. "Who was chosen for Lady Novalise?"

Reif met his gaze, the haze in his eyes suddenly clearing, as though the question had sobered him instantly. "I just told you...the prince."

"There is no way Lord Starstorm would approve a betrothal between her and Prince Aspen, he's—"

"Not our prince." Reif lifted one hand, nodding to something behind Asher. "*That* prince."

Asher turned, already knowing who he was going to see, but praying to any god or goddess that it wasn't true. He must have defied them in another life because when he spun around, there was Novalise.

She was decked in a gown that bled from icy purple to deep blue, the beauty of twilight before the sky gave way to nightfall. Rainbow moonstones dripped from her ears and her hair was woven into a braid with ribbons of silver intertwined throughout. She wore the same gold necklace as always, the eight-pointed star framed by crescent moons, the crest of House Celestine. And pressed in close, with shadows unraveling around him, was Drake Kalstrand.

That fucking prick.

Without thinking, Asher strode forward, pushing his way through the surging crowd. He had to do something. What, exactly, he wasn't quite sure. All he knew was there was no way he could allow Novalise to marry Drake. People pressed in on all sides of him, desperate for a glimpse of Aeramere's darling with the notorious shadow prince.

The music trailed off, and the dancing came to a standstill as Queen Elowyn and Prince Aspen appeared in his line of sight.

"Good evening, citizens of Aeramere and distinguished guests." The queen began her monologue about the joys of the

Season, but her words were a dull drone in the back of Asher's mind. All he could focus on was Novalise, and the unease that rippled around her in waves so dense, he was shocked no one else could feel it. "As many of you know, the end of the Season is upon us, and there's no finer way to close out the celebration of Midsummer than with a wedding."

Damn it. He had to get to her. Now.

Asher nudged his way closer to the front of the gathering, but the queen continued her speech.

"Every year, the stars align, choosing a fae of Aeramere to bestow their many blessings. This year was no exception." She gestured to where Novalise stood, fused onto the arm of Drake. There was no mistaking the way she curled into herself, preparing for the blow. "So, I am pleased to announce the marriage of Lady Novalise Starstorm Celestine to Prince Drake Kalstrand of Brackroth."

Stilted applause engulfed him. A discerning sense of dread seemed to linger in the swell of partygoers, an undercurrent of mistrust. Tight-lipped smiles were met with troubled glances, a pretense of content behind the guise of coiled tension. This wedding wasn't going to be a celebration of merriment and perpetual bliss, but rather the culmination of something far more sinister. Like a languid shadow on the prowl, ready to plunge their world into darkness.

Through the thin visible spaces between the bodies cramming into one another, Cyra caught his eye.

She mouthed the words, "Do something."

Asher was on the move a second later, navigating the dense cluster of people and barreling into anyone who wouldn't get out of his way. Just when he thought the tide would never break and Novalise would be swept away in a sea of well-wishers, the flood of fae parted, dumping him right in front of her and Drake.

"Lady Novalise." Asher bowed, never taking his eyes off the shadow prince. "Your Highness."

He could sense her eyes boring into him and, instinctively, he reached for her. "Might I have this dance?"

He didn't care if there wasn't any music playing at the moment.

Drake slid his arm around her waist, enveloping her, and Novalise sucked in a harsh breath. "I think you lost that privilege some time ago."

Asher was fuming. He would not be dismissed, especially not in his own home. Damning the consequences, he ignored Drake completely. "Novalise, you must know—"

Drake stepped between them, blocking her from his view. Taunting him. "You also lost the privilege of speaking with her as well."

He steered her away from Asher, guiding her toward the dance floor everyone else conveniently abandoned. At once, an alluring melody drifted through the air.

The bond between them was suddenly frantic. Asher's magic clawed for release as he watched Drake lead her in a series of intimate spins and steps.

No.

He wouldn't allow it.

"Nova..." He reached for her mind, calling her to him.

From across the courtyard, her gaze latched onto him. Drake spun her away from him in one fluid motion, then snapped her back into place beside him. All the while, her eyes remained locked on Asher.

"Tell me it's not true," he pleaded, more desperate to hear her voice than he realized.

"I'm sorry, my lord. The contract has been signed." Her breath caught as Drake lifted her into the air, tossing her high, then catching her as though she weighed no more than a feather. *"There's nothing I can do."*

Sorrow hung from her every word.

"There has to be a way to get you out of this." Asher couldn't give up. He couldn't let Drake win, not when Novalise was the one at stake. *"I'll speak to Ariesian."*

She bit her lips, a delicate sheen misting her eyes. *"It's too late."*

Damn it. If she cried now, every last thread of his control would come undone.

"No, it's not. I will not rest. I will not fail you. I will stop at nothing to see you safe...with me." Something wrenched inside of his heart, an unyielding kind of emotion he didn't recognize. *"Novalise, I—"*

Suddenly, it was Drake who cut into his line of sight. His eyes were cold and empty. Novalise's bottom lip trembled.

"Perhaps I didn't make myself clear the first time, Firebane."

Asher clamped his mouth shut, stunned. It was impossible. There was no way Drake could interject his own thoughts between that of their bond. Such a feat was incomprehensible. Yet there he stood, pinning Novalise to him, as though he'd heard every word spoken. Novalise gasped, wincing as he hauled her into his arms. She shoved her palms against his chest, but he refused to release her.

"You had your chance." The shadow prince's voice exploded into Asher's skull, scraping along his mind like sharpened talons. He gritted his teeth against the onslaught, and Novalise whimpered in response. *"And now, she's mine."*

Drake gripped Novalise by the chin, dragging her mouth to meet his in a severe and punishing kiss.

"Novalise!" Asher roared down the bond, but there was no response.

Nothing.

As though she couldn't hear him, could no longer sense or feel him.

Alarm stole all rational thought from Asher's mind, and for

the first time in a long time, he recognized the emotion bleeding him out from the inside.

Fear.

Music faded into the background, the voices and conversations floating around him died. The only answer Asher received in return was dark, rumbling laughter echoing through the deepest recesses of his mind.

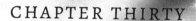

CHAPTER THIRTY

"What did you do?" Novalise gasped as Prince Drake led her into another dance. Asher's voice was quiet in her mind, as though the bond tying them together was somehow muted.

Drake guided her effortlessly across the makeshift dance floor of House Emberspire's courtyard. "Nothing that won't entice him to pursue you further."

She went through the movements, the steps and spins, hating every second of it.

"But how?" she rasped over the hypnotic melody, plastering a practiced smile on her face. Other couples danced with them, around them, but the curious gazes of those who watched bored into her spine. "You intruded upon our bond, you silenced our thoughts. What sort of magic is that?"

Light played across his hardened features, but he moved with the shadows. "The dark variety."

Her mouth fell open. Prince Drake slid one finger beneath her chin and gently closed it, sweeping her across the floor in a complex series of footwork.

"Come now, Lady Novalise. Don't look so appalled." His

smile was venomous. He was poison in the flesh. "I've never pretended to be something I'm not."

She scowled, her own smile sharpening. "And what are you?"

"An assassin forged from the shadows. A prince with a soul as black as the darkest night. A villain, not a hero. Always an enemy, never an ally. A nightmare come to life." The music slowed and they stopped moving, but the world around her continued to spin. The prince's deadly grin vanished. "In other words, my lady, a monster."

Another song picked up almost immediately, a hauntingly slow melody, and Prince Drake wasted no time gathering her back into his arms for the next dance.

Every muscle in her body screamed at her to run, to put as much distance between herself and the Shadowblade Assassin as possible. The space between them was magnified with the presence of danger, an underlying sense of precarious doom. He was vile. Wicked. Worse than even Prince Aspen, which spoke volumes considering the Prince of Aeramere was a vicious snake by trade. Her gaze swung from one cluster of onlookers to the next, seeking out any sign of Asher. But he was nowhere to be found.

"Your attempts to find your knight in shining armor are futile." He glared down at her. "He'll come to your rescue…eventually."

Prince Drake crushed her against him, his grip so strong, she swore he might snap one or two of her ribs. She winced against the assault, her chest tight. The closeness forced her to look up at him until he spun her away, his ironclad hold linking their fingers as he twirled her again and again, each spin faster than the last. Colors blurred together along the outer edge of her vision. Her stomach twisted into dizzying knots, and with every turn she found herself desperate to find his terrifyingly hand-some face, fearful that if she missed her spot even once, she'd either faint or vomit.

Finally, the relentless spinning ceased, and he yanked her back into his arms.

Novalise sagged against him, sucking in a haggard breath. Squeezing her eyes shut, she waited until she could stand on her own two feet without toppling over before opening them.

Meeting his remorseless gaze, she attempted to disentangle herself from him. But Prince Drake's arms were a fortress, and for her, there was no way out.

"I came to Aeramere for two things, Lady Novalise. Thanks to your brother, I already have one." His evergreen eyes flared with power. "The other is on the shoulders of Lord Firebane. If he delivers, then I'll be on my way. If he does not..."

Prince Drake chuckled darkly.

But something pulled at the back of Novalise's mind. A memory, a conversation.

The one who seeks it hails from the Northernlands.

Asher's words replayed in her mind, and she stared up at the shadow prince in horror. *He* was the one who wanted that green gemstone. The one jewel capable of amplifying his malicious intent. Of intensifying his dark magic. Of exaggerating his already overinflated ego.

"You'll ruin us." She spat the words out, bitter and angry.

"Are you always so dramatic? It's only a game, *kearsta*." He dipped his head toward hers, his lips barely a breath away. The wintry scent of him caused icy beads of panic to drip down her back. "You want to make him jealous, do you not?"

"No. I mean yes, but no." She blinked rapidly, trying to form a coherent thought. "That's not what I meant."

The shadow prince merely lifted a brow.

"I mean, you'll ruin all of us." Her chest rose and fell, her breathing hitched. "If Asher finds that jewel—"

At the word, Prince Drake faltered. It was barely noticeable, the faintest of missteps. But then his gaze narrowed and his hold on her tightened once more, bruising. Cruel.

"You'll be unstoppable," she breathed. Her heart thundered, the sound of her rushing blood echoing in her ears.

He edged back, pulling himself up to his full height, his gaze skimming over the top of her head. "You know not of what you speak."

"Yes, I do," she hissed. No longer would she endure being subjugated. She was more than *just* a lady. She was a Starstorm fae of House Celestine and she would *not* be ignored. "I know you seek the *virdis lepatite* for its extreme power. I know you're forcing Asher to find its location before the end of Midsummer."

A sinister laugh escaped him, and his eyes turned as cold as a forest in the dead of winter. "Is that what he told you? That I'm *forcing* him to do my dirty work?"

"I...he didn't say anything at all. Not exactly. But I know you—"

"You know nothing," he growled.

Magic emanated from him. Raw, dense power. It pulsed around them, pressing in like a wall of indestructible stone, until her jaw ached and her temples throbbed. All around her, time slowed to the point of impossibility. Every movement, every laugh, seemed to take ages to progress. It was as though she was attuned to every event unfolding around her, but each second was suddenly the length of a minute, if not longer. Even the music was a languid pull of drawn-out melodies to the point of pain.

Yet Novalise remained fluid. Only she and Prince Drake were immune to the might of his power.

"And did your precious mate tell you that the reason he must find this stone for me is part of our deal? It's he who must hold up his end of our bargain." Prince Drake leaned in close, enveloping her in a swath of shadows. They swallowed the light, blotting out the amber beams of faerie fire until they were nothing but streaks of muted gray. The swirls of inky darkness swarmed her, stealing the warmth, leaving Novalise chilled and trembling.

"After all," he mused, as an afterthought, "I've already fulfilled mine."

Terror ricocheted through her, muddling her confidence. "B-bargain?"

"Ah, another piece of information he withheld? Well, allow me to enlighten you, *kearsta*."

Her nails bit into her palms as Prince Drake drew her into a dance of melding shadows and infinite time.

"The reason Lord Firebane searches restlessly for the *virdis lepatite* is because he asked a very dark favor of me." Each step across the entranced dance floor brought him closer to her.

"A favor?" she asked, her voice barely an audible squeak.

Prince Drake's slow, intentional smile left her palms damp. "That I be the one to kill his father."

At once, his magic receded and the courtyard tumbled back into motion. The music was suddenly too loud, and the voices grated against her flayed nerves. No one seemed to notice that the shadow prince took control of time, how he'd held authority over their every breath. She swallowed hard, the contents of her stomach burning like acidic bile, threatening to pour from her at any second.

Sweat beaded along Novalise's forehead. "I don't feel well."

"No one ever does after a timestruck." Drake looped one arm around her waist. "Come with me."

Novalise clung to him like he was a rock and she was stranded out in the middle of a turbulent sea. It didn't matter if every set of eyes tracked her as she passed by. Their thoughts of her meant nothing. Because in that moment, the shadow prince was the only one holding her up, and she couldn't let go.

CHAPTER THIRTY-ONE

*A*sher prowled through the gardens, far from the courtyard, unable to clear his mind.

Disembodied voices floated toward him from the right side of the gardens, beyond the wall of flowers, but he ignored them. He needed to think, he needed to find a way to save Novalise from the shadow prince.

Damn it.

Why had he been so foolish? He paced past the rosebushes, venturing further into the elaborate maze of flowers and ferns. Already he'd wasted too much time.

Asher rounded the corner, nearly colliding into a couple hidden in the shadows of ornamental blossoms hanging from one of the many arbors. At first glance, they looked to be in the throes of a heated argument, exchanging harsh words with one another.

"Apologies," he muttered, "I didn't see—"

He stopped short, recognizing the male almost instantly.

It was Solarius Starstorm, Novalise's second eldest brother. But the female standing next to him, with faint lines furrowing across her brow, was not a fae like Asher expected. She was most decidedly mortal, with plain brown hair and a button of a nose. She folded her arms across her chest, and though most would be annoyed with his intrusion, she looked almost relieved.

Asher glanced between them.

Solarius bent down, whispered something in her ear, and the mortal huffed in vexation. She rolled her eyes to the starlit heavens, then turned on one heel, stomping off back toward the courtyard.

"I apologize for the interference." Asher raked a hand through his hair, shoving it back from his face. "I've been distracted most of the evening."

Solarius adjusted the cuffs of his sleeves, his gaze never leaving the retreating female. "I can imagine."

"Everything alright there?" Asher asked, nodding in her direction.

"Perfect. Just letting go of the past." An emotion flicked across Solarius's face, but in the faint play of light and shadows, it was practically unreadable. He turned to face Asher, and it was gone completely. "Have you figured it out yet?"

"Figured out what?" He spoke each word with caution, unsure of Solarius's motives for such a peculiar question.

Solarius didn't even blink. "How you are going to wed my sister."

Instantly, Asher opened his mouth to object, but Solarius cut him off.

"Don't play dumb with me, Firebane." He shook his head, a barely perceptible smile tugging at the corner of his mouth. "I know that look. Your scents mingle, a complexity only shared by mates. You can deny it all you want, but you're in love with Novalise. And you're a fool if you let her marry Drake Kalstrand."

"You're mistaken," Asher answered coolly.

He was *not* in love with Novalise. Affection? Most likely. Desire? Absolutely. But not love.

Solarius closed the distance between them, his silver gaze glowing with power. "She deserves better than a fucking assassin."

Asher shifted, uncomfortable. He was fully aware Novalise deserved to marry someone worthy of her, but that didn't mean he merited such an honor. "I walk with shadows of my own."

The Starstorm fae shook his head, his barely there smile fading. "Everyone battles their own demons. No one is purely good or evil, just as the line of morality has never been strictly black and white. All our souls are blurred with shades of gray."

"And what of the stars?" Asher countered, his words dripping with sarcasm, agitated by having his objections toward love so easily rejected. "Do they not design the premise of our fate?"

Solarius scoffed, taking a step back. He leaned against a pillar wrapped in ivy and tiny red blossoms. "The stars never lie. But that doesn't mean they've never been…misinterpreted."

The absoluteness of his words caught Asher off guard. For as long as he could remember, House Celestine lived and breathed by the promise of the stars and celestial magic. To claim star readings weren't always fact, to assume they were somehow misconceived or swayed, went against everything they accepted as truth.

It was unthinkable.

"Are you saying the Reader of Stars," Asher ventured cautiously, "your *mother*, was wrong?"

"I'm saying everyone makes mistakes." Solarius shrugged nonchalantly. "And that star readings are the most basic form of celestial magic. Anyone can be taught how to do it, whether they possess Starstorm blood or not."

Basic?

Confusion clouded Asher's thoughts. He pinched the bridge of his nose. "Wait. What?"

Solarius stole a glance over his shoulder, his keen gaze raking up and down the path of the gardens, ensuring no one was near. "Listen to me very carefully, Firebane, for I am only going to say this once, and I will not repeat myself. And if you ever make mention you heard this from me, I'll deny it to my grave."

Asher nodded once, solemn and resolute.

"My mother is not a true Starstorm. She married into the bloodline. My father taught her how to read the stars, but she was always too emotional to maintain any kind of indifference. She allowed her feelings to guide her instead of using the clarity of mind." Solarius pushed off the pillar, the planes of his face hardening in the crawling shadows. "Do you really think someone of Novalise's power was destined to be a simple *reader?*"

Asher considered his words, and images of Novalise seared the back of his mind. The bursts of starfire that exploded from her in his study, the loss of control she suffered when the starstorm overwhelmed her.

"No," Solarius answered for him. "It was all a plan put into place by my mother to keep Novalise under lock and key. Except when it was time to enforce her premeditated reading onto Novalise, she couldn't because the constellations were in chaos. Anyone who looked up at the sky that night would have known my mother was lying. There would have been too many witnesses for her to execute her scheme."

"Novalise's fate was your mother's doing." Asher's thoughts were a collective whirlwind of understanding. The destiny Novalise had been promised at her birth was a fallacy. That dull predetermination—everlasting love—hardly matched the fiery spirit burning inside of her. "Trysta is manipulating her."

"Now, don't get me wrong. I love my mother, to an extent."

Solarius didn't agree with Asher, but he didn't outright deny his claims, either. "But wouldn't it make more sense to ask yourself why she would want to hide Novalise's true magic, a power that has been dormant within the Starstorm bloodline for hundreds of years?"

There had to be a logical reason.

Trysta used Novalise's reading as a means to control her. But why? There must be something else, some deeper motivation for wanting to keep the truth of Novalise's power a secret. Even if Ariesian was the lord of the house, Trysta wouldn't willingly give up Novalise to Drake unless she planned to gain something in return. Something worthwhile. Like an alliance. As Novalise's mother, she would have to sign the agreement as well. But no one in their right mind would ally themselves with the Shadow-blade Assassin. He thrived on the malevolent and was too volatile, too untrustworthy. Not even a contract inked in blood would hold him to his word. In fact, the only one worse than Drake Kalstrand was...

Prince Aspen.

Trysta wouldn't have worked so hard for so many years to keep Novalise's magic hidden only to give it away because her daughter had to take a mate. She had plenty of suitors. There would be too much at stake, and Asher could almost guarantee the Prince of Aeramere was behind it all. Either Prince Aspen held something over Trysta Starstorm or she was working with him to help overthrow Queen Elowyn, with the assistance of Drake Kalstrand.

It was the only plausible explanation.

"Fates divine," Asher muttered, pressing his hand to his forehead. He looked over at Solarius, and the fae's face was completely devoid of any emotion. "You think your mother is conspiring with Prince Aspen?"

To this, Solarius only gave the slightest incline of his head.

Hells, it was worse than Asher thought. "And you know about Novalise's abilities, about the starstorm."

It wasn't a question and they both knew it. Granted, Novalise had told him as much, but he wanted to glean as much information as possible from Solarius while he has the chance.

"Of course. Novalise came to me the afternoon it happened." Solarius gave a half-hearted laugh. "They needed help coming up with an excuse for such a nasty scar."

Asher wondered what other secrets Trysta kept, what other readings she misconstrued, with or without intent. Perhaps she'd fabricated his own star reading as well.

Solarius straightened, and when he spoke, his voice was gravely quiet. "There's only one way to win Novalise's hand."

Right.

Asher was familiar with the protocol when it came to interfering with a contracted marriage.

A fight to the death.

CHAPTER THIRTY-TWO

*D*isoriented and still feeling like she might lose the contents of her stomach at any moment, Novalise gladly accepted the glass of sparkling water Prince Drake handed her.

She took a few sips of the fizzy liquid, slowly letting its light citrus flavor quell the queasiness as the shadow prince kept one arm locked tightly around her waist to hold her upright.

Gradually, she regained her focus, her thoughts became more coherent, and she no longer felt like she was being tugged from one moment in time to the next. Swallowing another gulp of water, she steeled her resolve and looked up at Prince Drake.

"That magic...you called it a timestruck. How did you do it? I've never met anyone capable of manipulating the flow of time."

"I prefer to keep my secrets close." The prince's gaze drifted over the courtyard, tracking every movement with cunning clarity. He watched as fae, mortals, and the like glided closer, as though debating whether or not to make a formal approach, before losing their nerve and disappearing back into the crowd. Their clandestine glances and idle speculations never went unnoticed. Prince Drake saw *everything*. His deep green eyes grew colder with each passing second, until they lighted upon Creslyn.

He tracked her every movement, the way she seemed to float through the dancers before locking arms with Caelian and tossing her head back in laughter.

Novalise clenched the glass in her hand until she thought it might shatter. The hells would freeze over before she ever allowed the Shadowblade Assassin anywhere near her younger sister.

A tingle of unease prickled the hairs along the back of her neck, and she looked to where Queen Elowyn and Prince Aspen stood upon a small dais overseeing the fiery revelry. They were joined by a few other council members, including Novalise's mother and Ariesian. While most of them seemed enthralled with the fire dancers who twirled batons ignited by flames of burning silver and icy black, only her mother and Prince Aspen seemed distracted. Their lips were moving and though they didn't face one another, it was obvious they were having a conversation. Every so often, the queen would shoot them a look of stern disapproval.

Whatever they were discussing, Queen Elowyn looked none too pleased.

From beside her, the cool presence of Prince Drake's hand against the small of her back left her chilled despite the warmth of the summer evening. Frosty tendrils from his touch seeped through the thin layer of silk, and goosebumps shivered all over her flesh. Cold emanated from the shadow prince, a stark reminder she stood in the presence of the one who was capable of stealing a life as easily as others could breathe.

"You killed Asher's father." The words fell from her.

"I've killed many." His teeth skated along his bottom lip, his fingers curling around her waist. "If you're looking for an explanation or are struggling to understand why, then I suggest you ask Lord Firebane."

"You make it sound so simple considering you just forbade him from speaking to me." Novalise rolled her shoulders back, jutting her chin up.

Prince Drake looked down at her, a strange expression on his face, as though finally seeing her for the first time. "But did I forbid *you?*"

Beats of tense silence passed between them before she tore her gaze away from the intimidating man.

She tried to recall what she knew of Asher's father. From what she remembered, he was negligent and lackadaisical, showing little to no interest in any areas of lordship save for the indulgence of alcohol. He was boisterous and indignant, carrying on with other females in a blatant show of disrespect to his wife and family, ensuring his affairs were far from discreet. Rumors circulated around the late Lord Firebane's death, but it had been shrouded in mystery, and the details never revealed. His death hadn't been one of natural causes—it took more than a common cold or old age to kill a fae—but hearsay surrounding his demise was spun from anything. Whispers of a slip of poison to taking his own life. The latter had befallen Asher's mother mere days after his father's death.

The shock of it had stunned all five houses, almost as severely as Novalise's own father's unexpected death.

But Asher had been the one to bargain with Prince Drake. It was Asher who wanted his father killed.

The real question was, why?

What could the former Lord Firebane have done to Asher that was so atrocious, so abhorrent, that Asher wanted him dead?

She wondered if it had something to do with those scars on his back.

Another thought took form in Novalise's mind, one that had been plaguing her for several days.

"Why did you want a contract with Ariesian?" she asked, drawing Prince Drake's attention away from the celebration and back to her. "Why not forge an arrangement with Queen Elowyn, with all of Aeramere?"

"Because House Celestine has something I want," he replied too easily, his lulling voice laced with venom. "Something your queen cannot give me."

"And what's that?"

"A wife."

Novalise made a derisive sort of noise. There had to be a more profound interest for the shadow prince than a mere marriage pact.

"I don't believe you. You could have your pick of ladies, willing or not, given your stature." She gestured vaguely toward all the eligible females currently within their vicinity. "Why my house, why my family?"

The shadow prince considered her. She watched him as he silently debated, forming a strategic response and choosing his words with extreme discretion.

"Great change is coming, my lady. A war of the ages, unlike anything this world has ever seen." He leaned in, crowding her. She attempted to swallow, but her throat was rough and gritty like sand. "I have witnessed firsthand the atrocities, the destruction we will face."

So claimed the man who was searching for a gemstone of diabolical power, a jewel that could cause the ruination he just described. She shifted and leaned back, giving herself some leverage against the frightening aura of his demeanor. "Why should I think you wouldn't be the cause of it?"

His answering laughter was low and evocative. "You really don't know me at all, do you?"

"You're avoiding my question," she fired back, hating the telling tremble in her voice.

"Am I?" Beguiled, Prince Drake grinned. The sight of his smile, a real one, nearly wrenched her heart from her chest.

It was unfair that someone so vile could be so devastatingly gorgeous. Shaking off the unwelcome thought, she wrapped her arms around herself in a vain effort to stand her ground. She *would* have a proper response. "Why my family?"

Prince Drake's smile vanished, transforming him into the cutthroat villain. The one who hunted and stalked in the shadows of night. "Because Celestine is the most powerful house in Aeramere. The stars rule over every element. When the time comes, I want to ensure I'm aligned with the strongest faction."

His words caused the deepest part of her soul to shudder. "And you think aligning with one house is more beneficial than the fortitude of all five houses combined?"

This time, only the corner of his mouth lifted upward. Slow and purposeful. "How adorable of you to assume the five houses will stand together under the threat of war."

One by one, he planted seeds of doubt within her. Sowing and nurturing them with his words of warning.

"Of course we would. Aeramere is our home." Even as Novalise said it, threads of uncertainty twisted together, wrapping around her conviction like a vise. "The houses would band together to stave off an attack from anyone who tried to take it from us."

"Are you certain?"

No.

"Yes."

Smugness dripped from the shadow prince's handsome features. He crossed his arms, the black shirt he wore stretching across his muscled chest. "And what if the attack comes from within?"

Novalise reared back, stunned. Her gaze swung across the courtyard, confirming no one lingered too closely to overhear their discussion. "That's treasonous."

"That's warfare," he countered. "Rumors are already spreading, whispers of quelled uprisings and silenced rebellions. All of it taking place right beneath your pretty little nose, and by the time you realize it and accept what is happening, it will be too late to do anything. But you'll have a front-row seat to the ruin of your realm."

"You're wrong."

She staggered away from him, but he was right in front of her again in a single stride.

"Am I?" Prince Drake reached out and snared her jaw, his movements faster than lightning. His thumb and forefinger dug into her cheeks, squeezing until she nearly yelped from the pain. "Your most recent star reading, the one you summoned of your own accord, predicted such a fate, did it not?"

Shock slammed into her.

She'd almost forgotten about her star reading. She'd hastened across Aeramere on the back of Prince Drake's dragon to warn the queen about the vision, to explain the ramifications of the constellations. Yet Queen Elowyn and Prince Aspen had disregarded her claims. They'd left her feeling foolish and trite, claiming she should concern herself with her marriage and the weather rather than worry about the possibility of improbable threats.

It was humiliating.

Prince Aspen had stated in front of everyone that he would be the first to know if such declarations were true.

But he was duplicitous, which made it the more likely that he was the one behind any revolts. Of course he would proclaim they didn't exist. It was all the more reason to keep Queen Elowyn in the dark if such a coup was indeed in the works.

Everyone knew he coveted his mother's crown. He would murder her in cold blood if given the chance.

Panic crashed into her, a wave of relentless apprehension. A squeezing sensation pinched her lungs, making it almost impossible to breathe. Anxiety scoured her like a blade, carving her from the inside out, its sharpened edge serrating her with alarm.

Prince Drake released her, and she clamped her hand over her mouth, rubbing the sensitive skin now marred from his wicked hold. "Putting together the pieces of the puzzle now, aren't you, *kearsta?*"

It was unbelievable.

Aeramere had always been at peace. Her mother's star readings were always ones of fortune and beauty, all things good in the world. Until the constellations fell into chaos. Until Novalise's reading upended everything.

Her gasp was hollow, carved out of her. "This is all my fault."

"No." Prince Drake's voice was severe, cutting through her thoughts. "None of this falls on your shoulders. It has been years in the making, seen only by those who choose to believe the gravity of the situation."

She stole a hasty glance at the dais. Ariesian no longer stood alongside the other members of the High Council, and Prince Aspen was gone.

"Does my brother know?" The beating of her heart drowned out her pleas. "Have you told him what you told me?"

The shadow prince's face remained impassive, an impenetrable façade of hardened stone. "I've warned him in as many words, yes."

It wasn't an answer. Not exactly.

"If I were you," Prince Drake said, his voice eerily mild, "I'd keep a steady eye on the company you keep and listen for the hushed conversations when they think no one else is listening.

Walls have ears, trees have stories, and even rivers and lakes keep secrets of their own."

Novalise's jaw dropped open. "Are you suggesting I eavesdrop?"

Never in her life would she have considered such a thing, but the shadow prince made it sound achievable.

"If you want your house to survive." His reply wasn't a threat. It was an ominous foretelling of a promise not yet kept.

"Aeramere hasn't seen war in years." She glanced up to the night sky, where the stars burned, where the constellations danced. If what Prince Drake said was true, and this battle came from the inside, the houses would crumble. Allegiances would be chosen, they would fight one another, losing all sense of loyalty to their realm. Without Queen Elowyn, the Veil would collapse, leaving Aeramere open to invasion. Despite the warm summer night, Novalise was cold. Frozen by fright. "It could be the end of us."

"War is how all kingdoms rise and fall, my lady. Do not fool yourself into thinking they are created by the good deeds of the noble." Prince Drake plucked a flute of red wine from the tray of a passing servant. "They are built from the ashes of war, born of bloodshed and strife."

"But—"

"It cannot be avoided." The shadow prince downed the wine, inspecting the glass. His gaze snagged upon hers from over its rim. "You of all people should know the stars never lie."

He was right and she loathed him for it.

All around her, the merriment appeared too strained, like it was contrived from a false sense of happiness. She wondered how many fae from other houses knew about the depravity lurking within their realm, how many of them hid secrets behind their coerced smiles.

"If you'd excuse me," Novalise murmured, determined to

find Asher. He would know what to do and could help her make sense of this mess.

A muscle in the shadow prince's jaw ticked. "You should really let him come to you."

Snagging her last shred of courage, she glared up at him. "I'm done waiting."

He didn't even blink. "If you insist."

Prince Drake remained motionless, uncaring and uninterested in her determination. She spun away from him, anticipating the moment he would drag her back to him, but this time, he let her go. Perhaps his demands of her were all for show, a means to taunt the other houses, to parade her around like a prize.

Novalise offered small smiles to everyone she passed, keeping her pace calm and ladylike. With every inhale, the bodice of her dress became unbearably tight. The second she was in the gardens of House Emberspire and free from the inquisitive eyes of other nobles, she hoisted the hem of her gown with both hands and ran.

CHAPTER THIRTY-THREE

*N*ovalise expected to find Asher in his study, but the bond between them lured her through the gardens of House Emberspire and into the surrounding woods. She followed the tug, the familiar pull of longing, picking up her pace as she dodged low-hanging branches and avoided tripping on overgrown roots. Thorns from bushes blooming with wild roses snared her gown, shredding the fabric, their tiny points scraping across the flesh of her upper thigh. She winced, sucking in a breath through her teeth, ignoring the pinpricks of crimson dotting her skin.

Nothing would slow her down.

The terrain became more uneven, and Novalise found herself climbing over small boulders, the courtyard of House Emberspire far below her in the distance. The shoes she wore pinched her toes and rubbed her heels raw. They were fine for dancing but utterly useless for climbing hills and tramping through a forest. She kicked them off with haste, leaving them to tumble down the small hillside behind her, relishing in the feel of the cool, damp earth beneath her bare feet. Her magic sang, the fire of the stars searching for the frosty midnight flames of Asher's soul.

Higher she went, scaling the hillside and maneuvering her way around the jeweled trees, when the rushing sound of a waterfall filled her ears.

Novalise staggered out into a small clearing and stood in awe of the sight before her.

Silhouetted against the darkness, near the edge, stood Asher. His hands were clasped behind his back while he looked out over the shimmering falls. Crystalline waters, illuminated a glowing turquoise, flowed from multiple rugged cliffs. Each one jutted out from the hill, depositing the gushing streams into the faerie pool below where curls of steam danced upon the surface. Moonlight filtered in through the dense trees, casting the banks of the pool in a hazy, ethereal gleam. Soft beds of grass cushioned large, smooth gray stones covered with green moss. Fire sprites, miniature fae barely the size of her palm, darted through the woods and around the water's edge, leaving a sparkling golden trail in their wake.

It was breathtaking.

Novalise took a cautious step forward so as to not startle him. "Asher?"

He glanced back over his shoulder at her. "Novalise?"

Instantly, his gaze skimmed the tree line, looking for any sign of Prince Drake.

"It's only me." She moved closer. "I came alone."

"You're bleeding." His gaze focused on her thigh, where her dress was in pieces and her skin was scraped but slowly healing itself. The burning ring of gold around the darkness of his eyes amplified. "And you're barefoot."

"I was attacked—by a rosebush," she added quickly when silver flames ignited from the tips of his fingers. "It's fine. I'll be fine."

There was a shift in his expression then. Something in his

face softened. The stern line usually present across his brows diminished and when he spoke, his voice was quiet. Reverent. "You seem to have an affinity for being attacked by thorns and bushes."

Novalise launched herself into his arms. Clasping both sides of his face with her hands, she drew him close and kissed him.

Asher gathered her up, crushing her against him. His lips were a warm welcome, and his tongue glided over hers like velvet, coaxing breathy sighs from her with every taste. She trailed her fingers up his ears, following them all the way to the pointed tip. Asher groaned, his hands skimming down to her hips, pressing her into him so she could feel the fullness of the effect she had on him. He broke their kiss, moving his mouth to her jaw, then her neck, nipping the sensitive area with his teeth. A gentle lick, a harsh scrape, then another swipe of his hot tongue to ease the sting of pain.

"I need..." She gasped when his thumb brushed across her breast, hardening her nipple into a peak.

"Tell me what you need," he murmured, biting at her neck once more.

Novalise shook her head. Tingles spread through her and heat pooled between her legs, but she hadn't come to find him for this, at least...not yet. "I need to talk to you."

Given the current circumstances, any other male might've become disgruntled by the cooling of the heated intimacy simmering between them. But not Asher.

"Very well." He leaned back, his dark hair with its streak of silver falling into his face, and he nodded once. "I need to talk to you, too."

"I know about your father." The words tumbled from her before she could gently ease into the subject.

Asher stilled. His eyes, once burning like embers, dimmed. He released her, letting his hands fall to his side, then he turned away to face the waterfall once more.

She had yet to understand his reasoning on the matter. She moved closer and grabbed his hand, the damp grass soft and slippery beneath her feet. "Talk to me. Tell me why. Why did you have Prince Drake kill your father?"

A deep crease formed along his forehead as he gazed out over the cascading waters. Though she only held his hand, it was as though his entire body had turned to stone, hardened with resentment of the past.

"Is it because he was despicable and didn't seem to give a damn about anyone?" she pressed, tightening her hold on him. "Or is it something worse? Like the fact that he continuously betrayed your mother with little regard to the effect it would have on your family?"

Were it the latter, at least that was something she could comprehend. Though having someone killed for their indiscretions seemed like a drastic consequence, but still.

"He abused her, Nova."

Asher's words hollowed out her heart.

"He broke her. Physically and emotionally. Then he'd put her back together before doing the same thing all over again." Asher swallowed and the shadows of the night haunted his handsome features. "I did what I could to become the focus of his aggressions. I took every punch from that bastard's fist just so he'd stop hitting her. For a while, it worked. I stayed on the receiving end of his rage until I was old enough to fight back."

Novalise wrapped her arms around his waist, but his gaze was locked somewhere in the distance beyond them. Somewhere she wasn't invited. He'd sheltered himself from their bond, and she was left in the cold to wonder. She couldn't imagine being forced to witness such wretched behavior. She'd likely never recover if she ever saw her father raise a hand to her mother when he was alive. And Asher, oh gods, her heart. How old was he when he first tried to sway his father's anger? Sorrow filled her, for she knew no amount of sympathy could ever undo the trauma of his past. Tears pricked at her eyes, imagining a young Asher—a youth compelled to become an adult too soon—stepping up to deter his father and save his mother.

"My father tormented my mother. He was a vicious, vile creature. Mercilessly cruel." Asher ground out each word, his jaw clenched so tightly, the veins pulsed along his neck.

"Asher, you must know…" She ran a comforting hand up and down his arm in an attempt to soothe. "Surely, you must know you're nothing like him."

He looked down at her, his face a void. Empty from years of the transgressions against him. "The stars told me a different story."

Weighted silence stretched between them. Novalise reached up, cupping his cheek with her hand. Beneath her palm, she could feel every beat of misery, sense all his fleeting emotions. Vengeance. Desolation. Remorse. She let her fingers trace the line of his solid jaw. "What do you mean?"

"I've only had one star reading in my life, given by your mother." Asher's gaze flicked to her, fleeting, before he returned his attention to the waterfall's edge. "I'll never forget the words she spoke to me."

Unsettled, Novalise let her hand fall away. "What did she say?"

"That I will end up exactly like my father." He faced her, his gaze fraught with worry. He shoved his hair back from his face, stepping away from her, closer to the edge of the cliff. "I vowed then and there to never subject my wife to the wrath of my temper. I would never raise a hand to her. But I'm no fool, Novalise. Everyone is capable of making promises and breaking them. To ourselves. To others. Eventually, it became easier to accept the fact that not only should I never fall in love, but that I'm simply not worthy of it."

Novalise clamped one hand over her mouth, appalled by such an admission.

"Before my mother died, she told Cyra and I that the stars promised her a life filled with love. With my father's death, she thought her fate was stolen from her." He spread his hands wide, then his shoulders dropped, fully defeated. "Not once did she consider me or my sister. Her love was only for him. Not for us. She took her own life a few days after his death."

Novalise sniffled, hastily wiping away the unbidden tears falling down her cheeks. "You *are* worthy, Ash."

He opened his mouth to counter her, but she raised one hand, silencing him.

"My soul chose you. And yours...yours chose me." Grabbing his hand, she placed it over her heart, allowed him to feel the depth of her love, how her heart beat solely for him. "Ever since we shared that kiss on the Winter Solstice, I've been yours. I chose you then, I still choose you now."

Asher's hand moved to the back of her neck, drawing her close. "Nova..."

She threw her arms around him. "For me, it will always be you."

They collided in a kiss of stardust and flames. Passion unfurled between them, pulsing through the warm summer night, enveloping them in an inferno of heated lust. His mouth was everywhere at once—her lips, her neck, her shoulders, and that delicate area above her breasts. Her nails scoured his shoulders, and she leaned back to glance down between them, reveling in the way his hardened length strained against his pants. But his touch was a frenzy and this was something she wanted to savor. She wanted to pleasure him, to prove he was worthy of all she had to offer. Reaching for him, she grabbed the waist of his pants. As soon as his cock sprang free, she would draw him into her mouth. Suck him. Taste him. Worship him.

"Fuck," Asher groaned, nearly stumbling.

She swept her tongue along her bottom lip, and he tracked the movement. "I believe what you meant to say is that you want to fuck me. Am I correct in that assumption?"

Then his voice filled her mind, a balm to her soul. *"Such a dirty mouth for such a good girl."*

The corner of her mouth curved into a slow, simpering smile. *"Only for you."*

She stepped back, ready to drop to her knees before him.

"Nova! Stop!" Asher jerked forward to grab her. His hand grasped only air.

But it was too late. The soft ground beneath her feet gave way and she slipped, losing her balance. A shriek escaped her and then she was floating through the air, falling. Greenery bled past her, the spray of water splattered against her face. Bracing herself, she sucked in a final breath of air, only to see Asher diving after her, right before she plunged into the faerie pool.

Warm, glimmering water sloshed around her as she kicked, struggling to orient herself. Her gown stuck to her legs, winding around her like a thick vine, weighing her down. She swam harder, fueled by her own self-worth. She was an excellent swimmer. If and when she did die, she refused to let it be by drowning.

Suddenly, a strong arm wrapped around her waist. Asher held her to him, cutting through the water with ease, hauling her to the surface.

They broke through together, with Novalise gasping, sputtering, and coughing, while Asher muttered a rather unsavory stream of curses. He didn't let her go until her feet could touch the smooth, pebbled bottom of the faerie pool, where the water was no longer over her head. She stood up, drenched and warm from the hot springs, but alive. And more in love than ever.

Still fuming, Asher stalked toward the edge of the pool. He tugged off his tie, and she couldn't do anything but stare at the wet white shirt suctioned to his skin. Asher yanked it over his head, swearing at all the stars as he tossed it onto the grassy banks. Tiny, incandescent waves lapped at his waist as shimmering beads slid over his bare chest and down his solid abdomen. Steaming mist unfurled around him, taunting her. His entire body looked sculpted from stone, rock hard and near godly. Each dip and curve of his muscled form glistened, causing Novalise's mouth to water. He shook his head, spraying droplets in every direction before pushing the damp strands back from his face. In the radiant pool, he was the epitome of everything she ever wanted.

Right now, she only wanted one thing.

Novalise was soaking wet, and it had nothing to do with falling off a cliff into a faerie pool.

She waded over toward him, his brow furrowed in an instant. But before he could scold her, because she had no doubt those were his exact intentions, she leapt into his arms. Shock flashed in his eyes, only to be replaced quickly with untempered desire. He caught her easily, staggering back only once, and she locked her legs around his waist.

She wanted him. All of him.

Tangling her fingers through Asher's hair, Novalise pressed her mouth to his, fusing them together in a burst of starlit flames.

CHAPTER THIRTY-FOUR

For Asher, there was only Novalise.

When she'd tumbled off that damn cliff, it was the first time he'd known true fear. His soul left his body, his world shattered.

He saw the look in her eyes before she leapt into his arms, the flash of need and longing. Her mouth was on his a second later, hot and hungry. Because Novalise was the embodiment of his every desire. He would fall to his knees if only to see her smile, take a blade to the heart if it meant she would never look upon another the way she looked at him. He'd been wrong to assume she would bring chaos to his life, not when she was the reason his heart continued to beat. She was not some prized jewel or treasure to be claimed. She was layered and complex, full of fire only he could coax to life.

He relished in it, reveling in her, and when she kissed him, there was a twinge in his chest. Like an emotion he couldn't quite place.

Their tongues meshed in a dance, exploring and tasting. She squirmed in his arms, rocking her hips, grinding against his cock as it strained for release from the confines of his pants. He palmed her ass, fingers digging into her soft, round flesh, and she broke their kiss, her head tilting back in a gasp of pleasure.

Drops of luminous water slid from her shoulders to the valley of her breasts, gathering like a necklace of turquoise diamonds. She arched, her nipples hard and protruding against the fabric that shielded them from his view. She was decadent, and he ached for her. Their magic spiraled, then crested, waves of power crashing into one another in a culmination of falling stars and sparking flames. With her wet hair plastered to her cheeks and her dress clinging to her like liquid nightfall, she resembled a water nymph. A siren of the seas.

And she belonged to him.

Asher buried his face in her neck, breathing her in. Gliding his hands up her back, he wrapped his arms around her completely, embracing her.

Novalise went pliant, melting into him. "Are you alright, my lord?"

Her voice was like a song, one he would gladly follow to his death.

"You fell off a cliff," he grumbled, speaking the words into her damp skin.

"But you came in after me."

"Because I..." He clamped his jaw, every muscle seizing with dread. Those three words almost spilled from him, but fear gripped his heart, squeezing until he thought it would burst. "Because you are mine."

Asher shook his head. "You fell from a fucking cliff..."

Her fingers caressed the underside of his chin, angling his face so he looked directly into her eyes. "Are you angry?"

"Furious," he muttered, swiping a few damp strands of hair back from her face. "But mostly at myself for not ensuring your safety."

"Well, I'm safe now." She dug her heels into his lower spine, rubbing herself against him. The friction of heat between them sent his cock pulsing. "Though I must admit, tumbling from the waterfalls was quite the rush."

His gaze shot to hers, catching a glimpse of amusement. He cupped the back of her neck, dragging her face close to him. "Don't ever do it again."

Novalise's lips curved into a seductive smile. "Yes, my lord."

There was that strange twinge again, except this time it cut deeper, yanking violently.

He bent down, slashed his mouth across hers, scraping his teeth along her bottom lip. She sighed and tangled her fingers in his hair, her kisses growing more frantic with each passing second. The air between them sizzled, crackling with magic, magnifying every movement, so each touch sent pulses of heightened awareness coursing through him. He carried her through the faerie pool toward the bank along the edge as water sloshed between them and fire sprites swooped overhead.

Asher didn't care if they had an audience.

Let them watch.

Wading closer, he pressed Novalise's back into a smooth, moss-covered stone positioned along the water's edge, pinning her. He hooked his fingers under the thin straps of her silk gown and tugged the fabric down so it billowed around her waist. Her rosy pink nipples were already hard and he bent down, sucking one into his mouth, swirling his tongue around the tiny bud. She loosed a harsh gasp, her nails digging into his back for purchase.

"Ash," she cried, whimpering his name.

He moved from one nipple to the next, showering each of them with affection, sucking on them, teasing them with his teeth, until she was feverish and writhing.

Asher fitted himself between her legs, stroking his bulging erection against the apex of her thighs, fully aware the wet fabric of his pants and the warm water against her swollen slit would create almost unbearable friction. Up and down he guided her, content to draw out her pleasure as long as possible. His cock throbbed, desperate to be inside of her, to fill her completely. It took every last shred of his strength not to rip open the seam of his pants and bury himself so deep within her that she screamed for him until there were no stars left in the sky.

Novalise squirmed in his hold, shoving her hands between them as she furiously tried to unbutton his pants.

"Are you in need of something, Starlight?" he asked, swallowing hard to keep the edge out of his voice.

"Yes." Her breathing was already labored, and he glanced down, admiring the quick rise and fall of her breasts with each inhale. Her silvery, glittering eyes found his. "You, Asher. I need you."

He shifted, the faerie pool making it far more difficult to drop his pants than necessary. The warmth of the hot springs assaulted him, stealing his breath.

Asher realigned himself at her entrance, his hands gripping her thighs, spreading her wide for him. He was about to sink into her when she plunged her hands beneath the surface of the water. Her warm fingers wrapped securely around his shaft, and he expanded in her grip, her soft touch not nearly enough to encircle him completely. With delicate movements, she started to work him, fluid and effortless. The silky glide of the water and her featherlight caress would be his undoing.

His jaw locked and he ground his teeth together. "Fuck, Nova. That's enough."

"Why?" she purred, pressing dainty kisses along his neck. "Don't you like it?"

"I said, *enough*." He grabbed her wrists, hauling her arms up over her head. With one hand, he held her hands down, pressing them into the mossy stone behind her. "Tell me what you want."

Her eyes widened, damp lashes fluttering. A pretty stain of pink colored her cheeks. "What?"

He repeated the words. "Tell me what you want, Novalise."

Hesitation flickered across her face. He could easily slide into her mind and read her thoughts, then he would know exactly what she wanted him to do to her. But it would be so much more enjoyable to hear her say the words.

She bit her bottom lip, and his cock swelled again. "I already did."

"No." His smile was slow. Intentional. "You told me what you *needed*. They are not the same thing. Now, tell me, or I'm going to do what I want and make no mistake, I will not hold back."

Shadows cast by clouds drifting across the moon blanketed them both, but even in the faint light, there was no mistaking the slight curve to her lips. "Will I like it?"

"Let's find out."

Asher didn't give her a chance to respond.

Primed and ready, he drove himself into her slick folds, stretching her. Filling her.

Her head fell back against the stone and a strangled cry slipped from between her lips.

"Do you know what I want?" he asked, thrusting upward, burying himself inside her. He withdrew with agonizing slowness, then pushed in deeper, reaching the pinnacle of her desire. "I want to fuck you until you become the stars."

Each time he pulled out, she whimpered. Each time he filled her, she moaned.

His muscles trembled, spasmed, but gods, she was worth it. She would always be worth it.

"I want to mark you," he growled. "To make you mine."

Asher lowered his head, sucking the ample flesh of her breast into his mouth. Then he bit her, not too hard, but enough so that initial wince of pain sent her reeling. Novalise's body jerked, the walls of her cunt clamping around him, squeezing.

"Asher!" She thrashed, trying to break free from his grasp, but he kept his grip around her wrists firm, denying her.

She was close, but he wasn't going to let her come. Not yet.

Gently, he swiped his tongue across the reddened, sensitive skin, then slid his free hand between them, shoving the soaking fabric of her dress out of the way. His fingers skimmed her thigh, inching higher, teasing her. Until he reached the bundle of nerves begging for his touch.

He kissed her softly on the mouth, moving in and out of her in long, languid strokes.

Then he whispered, "Sparkle for me, Starlight."

Her eyes flashed. "Yes."

Asher waited one beat. Then another. And when her bottom lip trembled, he speared her hard and fast. Over and over, he surged into her, ensuring she took every solid inch of him. His thumb teased her clit, driving her closer to release. Her back arched against the stone, and her thighs fastened around his waist in a silent plea for more.

"Ash, please," she begged, unraveling.

"Anything for you. Anything." He let go of her wrists, then snared them both again, one with each hand, restraining her on the stone. Stepping closer, he pumped into her with more force, delving deep inside of her, filling her to the hilt. She clenched, squeezing his cock, sending bolts of pleasure ricocheting through him.

The rushing of the falls coupled with her breathy moans left him undone.

Stars fell, catching fire as the orgasm ripped through her. Asher groaned, slamming into her one final time as his own release exploded from him in a wave of pure ecstasy.

Thoroughly spent, Asher gathered Novalise into his arms, and carried her out of the faerie pool. He set her down upon the grassy banks, then waved his hand through the air, igniting a small fire to warm them. Silver flames danced, sparking toward the sky. Novalise situated herself on the ground, curling into his side.

Stars peeked in through the canopy of trees and she pointed up at them.

"Do you see that one there? The one that looks almost blue?" she asked, her finger tracing the line of stars against the dark of night.

Asher nodded. He already knew the star, knew the constellation she wanted to show him.

"The Great Stag," she breathed, sighing into him. "He's one of my favorite constellations. Do you want to know why?"

He leaned toward her, pressing a kiss to the top of her head. "Why?"

"Because he's representative of so many things. Wisdom, strength..." She traced the tip of her finger along the ridges of his abdomen. "Virility."

Asher couldn't help it, his muscles flexed on instinct beneath her touch.

"But mostly," she continued, oblivious to his taut stomach, "the Great Stag is my favorite because no matter where I am, he's always there. Even with all the thousands of other stars, he shines the brightest. So long as I can see him in the sky, I know I'm home."

That strange twinge returned, except this time it was like the bond itself wrapped around his heart, then squeezed, refusing to let go.

☽✳☾

"HAVE you heard the story of Estrela and the Great Stag?" Asher propped himself up on one elbow, casually draping his other arm around Novalise. A tiny frown marred her brow and she shook her head. "Most people forget they have a past," he explained, gesturing to the constellations in the shape of majestic antlers, the other much like a crown.

"After the sun god tried to control Estrela, she tossed her Wheel of Stars into the sky and fled to the heavens." He glanced down at Novalise, damp lavender hair spilling around her like ribbons of satin. The way she was looking at him…he didn't know anyone was capable of such emotion. Asher cleared his throat. "Once Estrela arrived, the night sky welcomed her, but she wandered aimlessly through the heavens with no place to call home. Lore says the Great Stag discovered her one moonless winter night. Her tears had turned to stars and led him straight to her. It's said he guided Estrela north, to her place in the sky. It's why Estrela's crown and the stag's antlers align every Winter Solstice, and always to the north."

Asher lightly brushed his thumb along Novalise's bottom lip, then bent down to kiss the corner of her mouth.

"Perhaps," he whispered, "that's why he feels like home."

"Maybe you're right," she agreed, a faint sheen glossing her starlit eyes. "After all, I was born under the sign of Estrela."

"Indeed you were."

"What about you, Asher?" She rolled onto her back and gazed up past the treetops, where diamonds sparkled against a blanket of sapphire. "What sign were you born under?"

He swallowed, his throat suddenly thick. "The Great Stag."

Her eyes snapped to his face. "Really?"

"Yes." He nodded once, his chest suddenly too tight. "Really."

She stared at him for a full minute, and it was as though he could see her mind working. Processing all he had said, making sense of the story behind the stars.

"How curious," she murmured.

Curious, indeed. It seemed the stars knew what they were doing after all.

"What did you need to talk to me about?" she asked, her question jarring him from his thoughts of fate and stars.

Asher's chest hollowed out. This conversation would not be as pleasant and wondrous as the last. "There's something you must know, but let me preface it by saying that it won't be easy for you to hear."

The faintest of lines creased her smooth brow, but she nodded. "Okay."

"I have reason to believe your mother is working with Prince Aspen to overthrow Queen Elowyn." The words spilled from him, and he stared down at her, waiting for her response.

The frown marring her forehead deepened as she processed his statement. "That...that can't be right."

He struggled to find a way to properly explain the harsh accusation. But he needed her to listen, to understand. Solarius's words jumbled together at the forefront of his mind. "Star reading is the most basic form of celestial magic, it can be taught to anyone. In fact, it was your father who taught your mother how to read them."

"Asher, wait." Novalise sat up, bracing herself with both hands in the grass. "This is absurd."

"I know it sounds ridiculous, but I need you to trust me." He covered one of her hands with his own. She didn't pull away, but her expression morphed from one of adoration into something else altogether. Something his rational mind couldn't explain. "Your mother knows the truth of your magic, about the starstorm. But have you ever wondered why she's made you keep it a secret all these years? She manipulated your reading to keep you under her control."

She yanked her hand from his hold.

Damn it, he was losing her.

"She's using you, Novalise." He hated the desperation in his voice, the way he was practically begging her to let him explain.

"No." She shook her head sharply and stood, smoothing the layers of wrinkles from her damp gown.

"Where are you going?" Asher was on his feet a second later. "Novalise, I beg you. Please listen to me. I'm telling the truth."

"No," she repeated firmly, her gaze darkening to molten silver, swallowing the prisms of rainbows. "Whatever information you've received is false. My mother would *never* lie about my star reading."

"I'm not saying she lied. She just misinterpreted it." He reached out to grab her, but she dodged him, avoiding his grasp. "On purpose."

Novalise laughed, but it was harsh. Grating. "I don't believe this."

Her lips pressed together in a hard line.

"Why else would she agree to wed you off to the Prince of Brackroth if for no other reason than to keep you under her watch? Prince Aspen and Prince Drake are working together, Nova." Asher crossed his arms over his chest, refusing to back down. "They're going to dethrone Queen Elowyn, and they're going to use you to do it."

"Enough!" she cried. Starfire burst from her in an explosion of deep purple and sapphire streaks, illuminating her from within, surrounding her like a raging halo.

Asher staggered back, stunned.

There was no storm in the sky tonight.

She flung her arms out to the side as magic poured from her. Power roared inside of him, clawing for release, flames of black and silver longing to dance with the stars that taunted them.

Novalise glared up at him, her face flush with anger. "I will hear no more of this."

He took a tentative step forward. "If you would just listen—"

"I have listened to everyone else the whole of my life, Asher Firebane." She paced the bank of the water's edge, then whirled around to face him. "Do not be like the rest of them, do not try to silence me."

"Damn it, Novalise! I would never try to silence you. Your

voice is a balm to my soul, I would die a thousand deaths before ever forcing you to bend to my will." Her cold exterior wavered beneath his words, and something akin to trust haunted the planes of her pretty face, but it wouldn't be enough to change her mind. "I'm only asking you to consider—"

"To consider what?" she countered, an array of starfire cascading around her. "That everything I've ever known is a lie? That my mother is staging a coup?"

Why must she be so infuriating?

He pinched the bridge of his nose with his thumb and forefinger, willing himself to remain calm, to undermine the mounting frustration bubbling to boil. He sucked in a sharp breath and lowered his voice. "I told you this would be difficult to hear, Nova. I know it sounds impossible, but I wouldn't even have brought it up if I didn't think you were in danger. I want nothing more than to protect you, to keep you safe. The stars may never lie, but your mother can."

Again, he reached for her, but she smacked at his arm, pulling away.

"No. Don't you dare." Her chest heaved as she backed away from him. All the love, all the desire she felt for him evaporated. The bond trembled violently. "Do you realize what you're saying is treasonous? My mother is a lady of House Celestine, a High Councilor to Queen Elowyn, and here you are making these terrible accusations that she's somehow colluding with the prince? Fates divine, Asher, are you even listening to yourself?"

He threw his arms out, flames erupting from his open palms and scorching the earth at their feet. "Tell me then, what reason would your brother have to lie to me?"

Novalise's mouth fell open. Her starfire raged, spitting at him. "Which brother?"

"Solarius!" he shouted, incensed by her lack of understanding. "Who else, Nova? The only one of your brothers who actually gives a damn about your wellbeing. The same one who knows we're mates, who told me I should marry you, who isn't blind to the fact that the last person his sister should ever be betrothed to is a fucking assassin!"

Wrath consumed him. A wave of uncontrollable violence slammed into him, spurred by her refusal to listen to him. To believe him. To trust him. He whipped away from her, blind with fury, and stalked toward the edge of the faerie pool. Releasing a shout of frustration, his fist collided with the boulder nearest him, crushing the stone to dust beneath the might of his anger.

Novalise gasped, and he spun back to face her, raking a hand through his hair. His chest heaved as she clamped one hand over her mouth, her eyes suddenly wide with fear. With understanding.

"My mother was right," she whispered hoarsely, flinching as he turned around to face her. "You are exactly like your father."

The hollowness of her words hung in the air between them.

There was a distance between them now, a gaping chasm carved by her anger, by the truth of her sentiment. His heart splintered, the pieces of it falling at her feet. He'd been a fool to give it away to her.

He grabbed his shirt from one of the smaller river stones and tossed it over his shoulder.

"Asher, wait." Novalise's voice cracked, and the bond wavered, shuddering. "I'm so—"

"Just go," he said quietly.

She froze. Silent tears spilled down her cheeks, twinkling like diamonds in the moonlight.

"Ash."

Her voice nearly broke him.

"I stayed away from you because I feared heartbreak. I was certain, with every fiber of my being, that I would be the one to hurt you, and I knew that if I did, I would never be able to live with myself." He forced himself to meet her tearstained face.

"Not once did I ever consider that it would be you who hurt me."

A strangled sob escaped her, but he stepped back, the space between them growing cold and empty.

"Do not follow me, Lady Novalise. Go and marry the shadow prince, go and do exactly what's expected of you." Asher fisted his hands, his nails biting into the flesh of his palms hard enough to draw blood. "And while you're saying your vows and swearing your fidelity to an assassin, I will ensure Queen Elowyn breaks the bond between us."

Exactly as he should've done so many moons ago.

Novalise's sobs carved out the remnants of his soul.

Asher turned then and walked away from her, rejecting her for the final time. His magic raged, the bond cracked, sending a crushing ache of despair through him. The pain was unlike anything he'd ever known. But no amount of punishment would ever be enough to make him forget the severity of the wounds left behind by Novalise's words.

CHAPTER THIRTY-FIVE

*N*ovalise dropped onto the damp grass, broken. She hugged her knees into her chest as the tears continued to fall. Beside her, the flames from Asher's fire dwindled, then snuffed out completely. Tendrils of smoke curled into the air, vanishing on the summer breeze.

What had she done?

She'd been furious with him for the claims he made against her mother, even more angry with herself for denying the fact that what he said seemed to hold a sliver of truth. But her emotions had gotten the best of her, and she'd unleashed all that pent up bitterness on him. Then she'd spat out the one thing she knew would hurt him the most. It was a malicious and cruel act, when in fact, she was more furious with herself.

For years she'd held onto the resentment, she'd tolerated it while people spoke about her like she wasn't standing in the room with them. In silence she'd suffered the condescension, she'd allowed every decision to be made for her, she'd followed the rules, and she'd kept her opinions to herself.

Now she wanted control of her life. She wanted to take it all back and prove her own worth. There was more to her than a pretty face, and she was more than perfect marriage material. She was powerful, full of an ancient magic that had once disappeared from her bloodline. Unfortunately, the one who believed in her, the one who convinced her she could defy the stars and rewrite her destiny, had just abandoned her.

And while you're saying your vows and swearing your fidelity to an assassin, I will ensure Queen Elowyn breaks the bond between us.

Novalise gasped as another strangled sob broke from some shattered piece inside her.

She'd hurt Asher. Severely.

When he walked away, the bond jerked so violently she thought for certain it would snap in half. The pain that followed was intolerable, scouring through her with a vengeance, scorching her from the inside out. Her knees gave out, shoving her to the ground in despair.

They would never recover from this, not after what she said to him.

She'd been heartless. Cruel and unjust.

The look in his eyes when he left her, the way the warmth in his eyes went cold, would haunt her forever.

A noise sounded from somewhere above her, like the clicking of a tongue.

"I told you to let him come to you."

Prince Drake's voice floated over her like a cloak of misery. She glanced up at him. The shadow prince stood a few paces off to her right, his arms crossed. He wore his riding leathers, silver chains draped across his broad shoulders, and even his hands were gloved.

She scowled at the man who'd done nothing but wreak absolute havoc the moment he walked into her life. "Go away. Please," she added, belatedly. "I just want to be alone."

"Understandable. There's solace in solitude." But he didn't leave. "Unfortunately, the Firelight Festival is almost over. You can cry yourself to sleep in your room, but not on the forest floor."

Novalise gave a half-hearted laugh. "Your empathy is astounding."

"It's one of my finest traits."

She thought she heard a smile in his voice, but when she looked over at him again, his face was a mask of indifference.

Strange silence settled between them, lacking in comfort, but not exactly hostile either. It was more of an understanding.

She stared out at the faerie pool, where the shimmering water bubbled at the base of the falls. The fire sprites had all but vanished, for they only slept during the daylight hours and dawn was slowly approaching. Scooping up an oval pebble, she slung it haphazardly into the pool. It skipped the surface twice before sinking to the bottom.

"How did you find me?" she asked abruptly, not fully expecting him to answer.

She heard the shifting of his boots over the grass, like he was stepping closer. "Your scent isn't that difficult to track."

Novalise scoffed. "So, you're stalking me now?"

"More or less."

Another beat of that heavy, all-encompassing silence passed between them, weighted and dense.

"I hurt him," she whispered, more to herself than the prince.

"It's in our nature to hurt those we love. Whether intentional or not."

She dared another glance at his mention of the word that caused her such agony. She never would've expected Prince Drake to be capable of such an emotion.

Her nose tingled with the threat of more tears.

"He will never love me after what I said to him." Her voice cracked, the pain of admittance reverberating through to her heart, fracturing it into tiny shards. She blinked and hot tears escaped from the corner of her eyes. There was no stopping them this time. "He told me to marry you. And that he'll have the queen break our bond."

Novalise's chest heaved and her shoulders trembled as the choking sob tore loose. This wasn't something she could mend with a practiced smile and pleasant charm. Asher would never love her, not fully and completely. He hadn't even wanted to hear her apology.

He was lost to her.

Prince Drake heaved a disgruntled sigh, and before Novalise realized what was happening, he'd scooped her off the ground and into his arms.

She sniffled, summoning up the last of her strength in a vain effort to prove she wasn't another damsel in distress. "I can walk."

"And I can move between shadows."

His words were all the warning she had before the world descended into darkness. Cold permeated the air around them as the shadows at his command swallowed them whole. Pressure caved in on her, crushing her against him. She struggled to breathe, her lungs near collapsing as a scream lodged in the back of her throat. The tantalizing scent of his magic, of cedar and burnt leather, assaulted her, and she weakened against the onslaught of his power.

Wrapped in shadows, she was helpless as the otherworldly coldness seeped into her bones. A profound sensation seized her, like her soul had been ripped from her body. It was as though she was being siphoned from one plane of existence to another. Blemishes of colors blurred before her eyes, but the world itself became nothing more than alternate shades of gray, masking them as they moved through the forest.

Prince Drake carried her through the shadows, the speed at which he shifted from one place to the next dizzying. Her head spun and she squeezed her eyes shut.

Terrifying emptiness slowed the beating of her heart.

There was no denying the shadow prince perfected the art of dark magic. He manipulated the occult. Whatever the source of his power, it was not entirely of this world.

Icy panic slid down her spine as the realization jarred her from her languid state.

The shadows.

That was how he moved without being seen, how he seemed to vanish without a trace. Logic slipped into place. No wonder he was the Shadowblade Assassin. It wasn't only because he had a blade of death that left behind fatal wounds.

It was because he *was* the shadows.

Novalise's eyes flew open, the shadows dispersed, and she found herself staring up at a sleeping dragon.

Mist unfurled around Svartos, and terrifying glowing eyes opened, locking onto her. The beast stretched, the might of his wings cutting through the overhang of evergreen leaves and dense branches. His claws sank into the earth as he awoke, plowing through the soil while he prepared himself for flight.

Carefully, Prince Drake set her down.

She glanced down. Shadows crawled at her feet, obscuring them. Whirling around to face the shadow prince, she jabbed him in the chest with her finger. "What *are* you?"

Prince Drake snared her by the waist, plucking her off the ground, then deposited her in the seat upon the dragon's back.

"I already told you." He hoisted himself up behind her, grabbing the reins. "A monster."

Svartos rose, twitching off his previous state of slumber. He craned his long neck, those piercing yellow eyes zeroing in on her. Novalise edged back in the seat, her back pressed firmly against the solid wall of Prince Drake's chest. Though Svartos seemed amiable enough toward her, he was still a creature capable of breathing fire and launching her off his back. She would take no chances. The dragon ambled forward, stretching his intimidating wings, and in the early hue of dawn, they glinted like decadent obsidian.

His massive claws dug into the ground as he picked up speed, kicking up dirt and debris. The trees rattled, their leaves scattering from their limbs like frightened birds. Mountains trembled as bits of rock and cliffside tumbled down from their carved peaks. At once, Svartos beat his wings, sending them soaring into the early morning sky. They sifted through rosy pink clouds, aiming east, toward the glow of dawn where House Celestine stood perched on a mountaintop, outlined in shades of gold.

Novalise turned her head toward Prince Drake, her eyes never leaving the head of the beast guiding them over Aeramere. "Can I ask you something?"

"If you must."

"You spoke earlier about an impending war and how the threat could come from within." She paused, sensing the shift behind her.

"That is not a question." His arms barely grazed hers as he steered Svartos, but it was enough for her to detect the rigidity in his motions.

"Obviously." She pressed her lips together, willing away the sigh of annoyance. "What if this supposed threat came from House Celestine?"

He stiffened, his chest expanding behind her. Dark power pulsed through the air and the breeze cooled. Shadows pooled around his hands. "What are you implying?"

"Asher said something tonight, something awful." Novalise couldn't lose her nerve. Not now. Trepidation shivered along her spine. "He thinks my mother is conspiring with Prince Aspen to oust Queen Elowyn."

She stole another hasty glance at Prince Drake's gloved hands. They were tight on the reins, the black leather pulled taut across his knuckles.

"Is that so?" His voice rumbled like distant thunder.

"Yes." Unable to look away from the shadows that slowly unraveled, wrapping around her wrists like threads of midnight satin, she swallowed down the knot of anxiety clogging the back of her throat. "And there's something else."

"Let me guess," he drawled, the darkness he summoned ebbing. "Lord Firebane thinks I'm involved as well. Because why else would your mother and brother ever agree to marry you off to a notorious assassin?"

"Yes." The word escaped Novalise on a breath, and she pitched forward slightly, angling herself so she could see his face. "That's exactly what he thinks."

His eyes, as dark as a forest in the dead of winter, focused on her. "And what do you think, Lady Novalise?"

Uncertainty warred with her thoughts. To agree with Asher was to condemn her mother and admit she thought Prince Drake was involved in the treasonous undertaking as well. But the idea of denying Asher's claims caused her skin to crawl. The entire situation kept her on edge, fraught with a continuous plague of worry. It was a dangerous, disconcerting game. One where she knew at some point, the time would come to choose sides.

"I think my mother is innocent in all of this, and I'll continue to believe as much until I speak to her on the matter." It seemed the safest option, even though the words tasted foul in her mouth. "If she is indeed working with Prince Aspen, then I need to uncover the reason behind it. He must be coercing her. She would never ally herself with him of her own free will."

She should've said as much to Asher, asked for the chance to prove her mother's innocence. Instead, she'd assaulted him with her words, spewing contempt.

"And what of me, *kearsta*?" Prince Drake asked, amusement dripping from his tone as he guided Svartos toward the cliffside near House Celestine. "Do you think I play a role in this scheme as well?"

"You make your own decisions, Your Highness." Novalise rolled her shoulders back, locking her spine into place. "I would never underestimate you."

"Good answer."

Svartos swept down from the skies, landing on a smooth ledge near the mountain's peak. Tucking in his obsidian wings, the beast lowered himself to the ground, huffing once, as though annoyed that his morning flight was forced to come to an end. She understood the dragon's frustrations. She wouldn't want to stay in one place either if she could fly whenever she wanted and never look back.

Prince Drake dismounted from the seat with skilled ease, then reached back up for her. Snagging her by the waist, he lifted her off the dragon's back and set her down. The surface of the ledge was cold against her bare feet, like walking on ice.

She shivered, clamped her jaw tight to keep her teeth from chattering, and she wrapped her arms around herself to ward off the chill.

She peered up at the shadow prince, but even with the golden rays stretching out above the mountain's peak, the sunlight never seemed to touch him. "Thank you for taking me home."

"Farewell, my lady." He nodded sharply, climbing back into the seat atop his dragon without a backward glance. "And until I see you again, mind yourself."

Novalise wasn't sure what he meant, if he intended his words as a proper goodbye or a warning. She didn't have time to ask, because in the next breath, Svartos pitched into the dawn and she scrambled back to avoid being taken out by one of his majestic wings.

The mountainside sloped as she trekked down to where the sprawling gardens glittered with beads of dewdrops. The starlight fountain gurgled in welcome, its shimmery silver waters sparking with the fire of a dozen rainbows. Not so long ago, she'd tumbled right into that fountain, landing in Asher's lap. She meandered along the winding path toward the house, admiring the ornate complexity of climbing roses and the neatly trimmed hedges bursting with lavender blossoms. Inhaling deeply, she enjoyed the mingling fragrance of multiple florals, taking the time to distract herself from anything that reminded her of Asher.

But it was a useless feat.

He was everywhere.

The scent of him lingered on her skin, and anytime she blinked, she saw him in her mind's eye. She tested the bond, softly calling to him. The only answer she received was the steady beating of his heart and a despondent sense of calm. She sifted through his emotions—remorse, melancholy, and the crushing pain of heartache—and collected them like shards of broken glass. There had to be a way to piece them back together, to make him whole once more.

A simple apology would not be enough.

She would stop at nothing to earn his trust. His love. He was more than her mate—what they shared was more than a magical kiss beneath an enchanted flower. They were not bound by the stars, but chosen, their destinies forged together by a force stronger than fate. Estrela and the Great Stag came together every Winter Solstice. It was no mere coincidence the same happened for them. Her love for Asher was endless, binding.

He calmed the unhinged panic that left her quaking with disquiet. He emboldened her sense of self, beckoned her to seize the life she wanted, not only what she was told to accept. He told her once to defy the stars, encouraged her to take the destiny she desired most and not settle for what she was given, and right now, she wanted him. For in her mind, a life without him was not worth living.

Perhaps a drastic measure was needed in order to evidence the depth of her affection.

Novalise walked in through the front courtyard of House Celestine, knowing exactly what she had to do to repair the bond between them, and came face to face with her mother.

CHAPTER THIRTY-SIX

*E*xhaustion tugged at Asher. Tension coiled in his shoulders and a dull ache throbbed at the base of his neck, reaching up to his temples.

He'd been staring at the same stack of books for hours after leaving the Firelight Festival without bothering to bid anyone farewell. After his argument with Novalise by the faerie pool, he'd been all too eager to get away from the noise, to clear his mind. But the festival was always two nights in a row, and unfortunately for him, he still had to suffer through one more evening of being socially acceptable.

At the time, sleep had eluded him, so he'd gone to his study instead. He preferred the quiet, the calm, and the soothing, albeit lonely, silence. Except now, dawn was cresting. Its rays slanted in through the window, illuminating every minuscule fleck of dust, and intensifying the ache in his head. Already he'd read the same paragraph four times, and he was no closer to uncovering the whereabouts of the *virdis lepatite* than he was a few hours ago.

He picked up his glass of whiskey, the ice long since melted, and swallowed down what remained of the amber watery contents. The woodsy flavor coated his tongue, and the hint of spice burned the back of his throat. Running one finger along the rim, he flipped the page of the book in front of him, the rune markings gradually becoming smudges of ink and blurring together.

Asher leaned back in his chair, and stretched out his legs. He adjusted his spectacles, sliding them down the bridge of his nose to rub away the fatigue from beneath his eyes. Reading and studying for pleasure were one thing, but transcribing runes was another beast entirely. It was tedious. Interesting yet draining at the same time. Deciphering their meanings was something he used to enjoy. Now it had become painstaking, if not altogether miserable.

If he'd been smart, he would've swallowed his pride and asked for Novalise's assistance.

But the thought of her was torturous.

Her harsh words drifted through his subconscious even as he tried to distract himself with work. Despite his best efforts, the cruelty of them continued to linger.

She'd carved out his heart, stolen a piece of him he'd never thought to give away.

Stiffness crept along his shoulders, causing the muscles to pull taut. He rolled his neck, the distinctive *pop* offering him a thin slice of reprieve.

A gentle tap sounded on the opposite side of his study door. It creaked open and Cyra peeked in, clad in her nightgown and bronze satin robe. "Ash?"

He lifted his head, and she stepped further into the room. "Asher, it's just after dawn. Have you even slept yet?"

"I have not."

Cyra trod across the floor and sat in the chair across from his desk, pulling her knees to her chest, her robe tumbling around her. She eyed his empty glass of whiskey with disdain, then flicked her wrist, glamouring them each a steaming cup of tea.

She blew on it, staring at him from over the rim, and took a cautious sip. "Is everything alright?"

He nudged his spectacles, returning his attention to the books spread before him. "Perfectly fine."

Cyra loosed an exaggerated sigh. "I wish you wouldn't lie to me."

Asher removed his spectacles, placing them on the desk, and leveled his sister with a stare. "What do you want to know, Cyra?" Exasperation iced his tone. "That I've been harboring the guilt of our parents' death because it's all my fault? That I've lost my mate to an assassin? Or that perhaps she hates me because I told her I think her mother is staging a coup against the queen?"

His sister gaped at him, the teacup bobbling in her hands.

He sat back, crossing his arms over his chest. It wasn't often he shared his innermost thoughts or issues with his sister, or anyone for that matter, but for some reason, everything he'd been holding onto for so long poured from him like a turbulent river. "There you have it. Nothing is fine, so please, take your pick of my troubles to discuss."

Cyra's bottom lip quivered, her eyes welling with unshed tears. She hastily blinked them away.

Damn, he'd been harsh. Perhaps too harsh.

She set her teacup down, and Asher thought perhaps she intended to leave. But then she tucked a strand of fiery hair behind her ear, and the gold of her eyes turned molten. "Do you really think I'm so ignorant?"

"Cy, I never said you—"

"Oh, but you did." She bristled, sitting up straight. Leaning forward, she planted both hands on the edge of his desk, her brows narrowing. "Not specifically, but you did. Do you honestly think I was blind to it all? I *know* Papa beat Mama senseless. I saw her bruises, tended to her broken bones, same as you. I know you hired Prince Drake to kill Papa and you know what? I'm glad."

Asher reared back, stunned by her admission.

She worried her bottom lip, considering her next words. Resolution hardened the planes of her youthful face. "The bastard deserved to die. I only wish the Shadowblade Assassin had taken his time."

He rose, the hollowness of her words hanging in the air between them, filling him with a sense of apprehension. He'd been so careful, he'd taken every possible precaution to protect his sister from their father's indiscretions, from the cruelty of his love. "How did you know about that?"

Cyra shook her head, her waves of hair falling in front of her face like a curtain, shielding her from his view. When she glanced back up at him, there was a kind of emptiness in her eyes. A dismal sort of sadness. "For someone who is incredibly studious, you don't pay much attention. It was easy for me to fade into the background, to pretend to be oblivious to everything happening around me when no one paid me any mind."

All that time, he thought he was sheltering her, but in truth, she felt neglected.

"I didn't know, Cyra." Asher rounded the desk, gently placing one hand on her shoulder. "I thought I was protecting you."

"I understand, and I appreciate you for it. But it wasn't fair of you to take the brunt of his violence in an effort to spare me." She stood and wrapped her arms around him, and he stepped into her embrace. She sighed, then leaned back. "Just like it isn't fair of you to think you're undeserving of love."

"Cy—" He tried to interject, but she held up one hand, silencing him.

"Let me finish." Cyra gathered his hands, squeezing them in her grasp. Her eyes searched his, pleading. "I could not have asked for a better brother. You love me, you care about me and protect me. And you deserve every ounce of happiness imaginable. You are capable of love, Asher. You're worthy of love, and you will *never* hold a likeness to the male who dared to call himself our father."

Asher swallowed, a knot of emotion clogging the back of his throat. It choked him, refusing to ease, even as Cyra hugged him fiercely.

"She left us for him." His words were strangled, like he'd swallowed fire. Harsh and scorched. "She chose him over us."

"I know." Cyra buried her face in his chest. "And it was her loss, not ours."

When she finally released him, her eyes were rimmed with red, but the tears hadn't fallen. She sniffed, blinking rapidly.

"You know I will always do anything I can to help you. Well, almost anything." She hesitated, a small smile pulling at the corners of her mouth. "I don't like the dark, and I have a fear of spiders."

She giggled, a glimpse of the youthful sister he remembered reappearing once more. He couldn't recall the last time he heard her laugh fully and completely. That was something he would have to remedy. Cyra turned away, heading for the door, and her hip accidentally bumped into one of the bookshelves lining the wall of his study. A leather-bound book with a tattered binding toppled to the floor. Cream-colored papers littered with markings slipped out from between the frayed pages.

"Sorry, Ash." Cyra scooped up the fallen book, collecting the discarded papers, then stacked them neatly on his desk. She turned to go, sending him one long look from over her shoulder. "Promise me you'll try to get some rest."

He nodded. "I will."

Eventually.

Asher waited until Cyra slipped back out the door and closed it behind her, then he replaced his spectacles and settled back down to examine the runes.

Something shimmered out of the corner of his eye.

He glanced over at the book Cyra had placed on his desk. Though the lettering was faded, there was no mistaking the way the embossed silver shapes shifted, morphing into a set of ancient characters.

Runes.

He grabbed the book and flipped it open, scouring the loose pages. Runes of silver appeared on the parchment, telling the history of an archaic bloodline of witches. He skimmed the collection of runes, each one revealing a piece of legend from another time. Wonder and something akin to trepidation reverberated through him, shaking him to the core. He closed the book, ran his finger along the lackluster raised letters, then opened it once more.

He stared down at the tome in his hands, a cold wash of disbelief rushing over him.

Asher had found the *virdis lepatite.*

CHAPTER THIRTY-SEVEN

*N*ovalise glanced around the empty grand hall, a slight shiver trekking down her spine. Starlight ensconced in decadent crystals hung overhead, illuminating her and her mother in a soft, pale glow. Their silhouettes stretched along the polished floor, crawling along the shimmering stone like spilled ink.

"Mother." She twisted her hands together, flinching as her mother's dark blue gaze raked over her, a disapproving frown creasing the center of her brow. "I'm surprised to see you're still awake."

"Well, it shouldn't be too surprising." Trysta planted her hands on her hips, the bracelets she wore clinking down her wrists. "After all, you're the one who vanished after the announcement of your engagement to Prince Drake."

Her mother's lips pinched together as though she'd bitten into something terribly sour. Trysta focused on Novalise, taking in her torn dress and bare feet. "What happened to you? You look as though you fell down a hill."

Off a cliff, if she wanted to be precise, but Novalise kept those thoughts to herself.

Her mother was still in her formal attire from the Firelight Festival—a navy blue frock with bell-like sleeves and silver embroidered stars along the hem. She wore her hair pulled back into an elaborate bun, not a hair out of place, whereas Novalise looked like a walking disaster. Her gown was torn at the thigh from where she'd snagged it on a rose thorn, her hair was a damp, tangled mess of knots, and her feet were filthy.

Novalise made a poor attempt to smooth away some of the wrinkles from her dress. "There were some matters that required my attention."

Trysta's admonishing frown only deepened, her lips tugging to one side in disdain. "Or perhaps it was Lord Firebane who required your attention?"

Cold spread through Novalise at the mention of Asher's name. But she would deal with her regret, with her torrent of emotions some other time. She pulled her shoulders back, willing herself to maintain some sense of calm indifference. "I am perfectly capable of handling Lord Firebane on my own."

"Yes, yes. Of course you are, darling." Her mother waved one hand through the air, flippantly. Dismissive. "However, I'm not necessarily concerned about you."

"Then who is the focus of your concern?" Novalise asked.

She didn't know her mother was aware of her relationship with Asher. Trysta had never mentioned him before. Usually, she was oblivious to such matters regarding her children, the particulars of their lives often becoming the responsibility of Ariesian instead. Yet it seemed her mother had been paying attention after all. Though she'd likely never considered Asher to be a formidable suitor, right now she seemed to be viewing him as more of a threat.

The thought hollowed out her belly, a harrowing sensation that stole its way through her, flooding her veins with panic.

"His Highness." Trysta stared at her, unblinking. "Prince

Drake," she clarified after Novalise took a second too long to respond.

"Why would you worry about Prince Drake?"

"I don't think your betrothed will take too kindly to you doting upon another man's affection." Her mother looped her arm through Novalise's, guiding her toward the stairwell.

She glanced up at the glass ceiling. The sky was already a shade of indigo, the hues of dawn approaching fast, coloring the edges gold. "I don't think Prince Drake very much cares."

Trysta laughed, full and rich. "Trust me, darling, he cares. The man is madly in love with you."

Novalise scoffed. Her mother's idea of love must be truly warped if she thought the shadow prince was in love with her.

"Besides." Trysta climbed the steps to the second level, her heels clicking on the stone, as she carted Novalise along with her. Turning slightly, her mother gestured to the paintings lining the walls, each one set in a gilded frame, the canvases displaying constellations shifting across iridescent galaxies. "The stars never lie."

Except they had for Novalise.

Unless Asher was telling the truth.

"But they don't make any promises, right?" Novalise pressed, remembering the words her mother spoke on the night of her star reading.

Trysta looked at her, startled. There was a flash of something in her eyes, an emotion Novalise couldn't quite discern, and then it vanished.

"You said as much after my star reading," Novalise continued, stopping on the landing. "When the constellations were in chaos."

Her mother shook her head, the large diamond drops swinging from her ears. "Yes, darling. It's completely plausible. It doesn't happen often but—"

"Can they be misconstrued?" Novalise interrupted, silencing her mother's excuses. "Can they be misinterpreted?"

"Where is all this coming from? Has the wedding upset your nerves?" This time Trysta laughed, but it was off, a little too sharp. She reached out, placing the back of her hand against Novalise's forehead. "Are you unwell?"

"I'm perfectly fine." Novalise pulled away, a surge of annoyance stabbing into her tone. She was tired of being treated like she was made of crystal. Fragile and delicate. "This has nothing to do with the wedding."

"Then what is it, my dear?" Trysta's brows furrowed, a line of concern harboring her forehead. She searched Novalise's face, worry darkening her eyes. "Has something happened?"

Novalise debated how much to say, how much to withhold. She couldn't outright accuse her mother of a crime, but at the same time, if Asher was correct in his assumptions, then she wanted to hedge around the subject and attempt to garner as much information as possible without coming across as suspicious. "I was just thinking that maybe the reason the stars didn't align for me is because I'm not meant to be the next Reader. Maybe my fate lies elsewhere."

She watched her mother closely for any tell, for any sign of guilt. But Trysta's expression softened, taking on that maternal gleam she often displayed to Novalise and her siblings when they were children. Trysta gently cupped Novalise's cheek. "Oh, my sweet child. The stars are more like guidelines."

"Guidelines?" Novalise almost choked on the word. She stepped back from her mother's touch, pressing her fingers to her temples. To assume the stars were more like recommendations, or mere suggestions, was deplorable. It was contrary to all she'd learned, to everything she'd been taught. The polar opposite of her upbringing and general understanding of celestial magic.

"Yes. It's pleasing to think our destinies have been forged by the heavens, but the reality is"—Trysta spread her arms wide, bracelets jingling—"we all have a choice."

A choice.

Fury ignited inside of Novalise.

She'd never been given a choice about anything. Ever. She'd always been told where to be, how to act, how to dress, what to say. For years she'd been trained to keep her mouth shut, to never speak out of turn. Every life decision had been made for her and she'd accepted it with grace. Of her own free will, she'd allowed herself to become a pawn, a trophy, an effigy. A pretty face without a voice.

Her mother captured her hand, squeezing lightly. "If you want to become something other than the next Reader of Stars, then seize that opportunity. You are capable of achieving whatever your heart desires."

There was only one thing Novalise desired…Asher.

And maybe something more.

Starstorm.

The word slipped into the recesses of her mind, the whisper of a promise.

"I could do anything?" Novalise asked.

Her mother leaned forward, placing the lightest of kisses against her forehead. "Anything."

Trysta released her hand, heading down the long hall toward her bedroom.

"But what about you?" Novalise called after her.

"What about me?"

"If I don't take your place, you'll be expected to continue on as the Reader of Stars." Novalise knew the pressure of the title was a weight upon her mother's shoulders. It was a position full of responsibility, and as with every advantageous station, a price had to be paid. "Do you enjoy it?"

A cloud drifted over the glass ceiling, diminishing the rising sun, casting her mother in long shadows. Despondency ebbed from her like a cloak of sorrow. "I did, once. When your father was alive. Now, it's merely an appointed position to be held within Queen Elowyn's High Council. It comes with its own stress and a multitude of obligations."

Curiosity plagued Novalise. Now that she finally had the courage to speak her mind and ask the questions she'd held inside for so long, she couldn't seem to stop herself. "Is it hard?"

"Trying at times, but not hard." The corners of Trysta's mouth lifted in a faint upturn, a ghost of her usual beaming smile. She waved her hand through the air, brushing off the sentiment. "I'm sure anyone could do it."

Novalise froze, trapped in a state of immobility.

Star reading is the most basic form of celestial magic, it can be taught to anyone.

Asher's words replayed in her mind.

"Try to get some rest now, darling." Trysta stifled a yawn, disguising it behind the back of her hand. "Tonight is the final evening of the Firelight Festival, and then it will be time to finalize your wedding preparations."

Novalise's thoughts were a blur, a whirlwind of confusion and mistrust. She never would've imagined her mother was capable of conspiring against Queen Elowyn, but now shreds of doubt wove their way inside her, overwhelming her with uncertainty. There was still a possibility it was all a misunderstanding, nothing more than a rumored fallacy. Yet, she couldn't quite let go of the unsettling notion that maybe, just maybe, Asher was right.

Either way, she would have to uncover the truth.

Trysta headed down the hall, then paused, turning back to glance over her shoulder. "Oh, and Nova?"

Novalise clasped her hands together to keep them from trembling, schooling her expression into one of innocence. "Yes, Mother?"

"Stay away from Lord Firebane."

Novalise opened her mouth to object, but Trysta continued, not allowing her to get in another word.

"You do recall what happens when someone interferes with a wedding, do you not?"

Novalise swallowed, her throat thick and dry. She'd almost forgotten about the disastrous aftermath when one fought for love. "A fight to the death."

"Exactly." Trysta smiled and this time, it was laced with warning. "Let's not give Lord Firebane the wrong impression. Surely you wouldn't want to be the reason for his demise."

With that, her mother turned away from her a final time and strolled down the hall, leaving Novalise alone and wrenched with fear. Icy beads of sweat slid down her spine. Her palms grew clammy and damp. Her heart thundered, pitching with panic so her breathing hollowed out, weak and uneven. If Asher fought Prince Drake, there was no way he would survive. The Shadow Prince would destroy him, end him.

Terror crippled her and she swayed, collapsing to her knees. The cold stone of the floor was jarring, biting through the thin fabric of her gown. She wrapped her arms around herself, rocking back and forth, squeezing her eyes shut. This was all her fault.

She couldn't lose Asher.

She couldn't let him die for her.

Stricken, she sucked in a gasping breath. The air wouldn't come. She tried to swallow, to dislodge the knot of hysteria clogging the back of her throat, but it was impossible. Her chest ached, her lungs were too tight.

A broken sob escaped her, breaking her.

Then she heard it. The soothing calm of a voice, a gentle caress down the bond tying her to Asher.

"Breathe, Starlight. Breathe."

CHAPTER THIRTY-EIGHT

*A*sher stood beneath the hot spray of the shower, letting the scorching water sluice over his skin.

At Cyra's request, he'd gotten at most three hours of sleep, but preparations for night two of the Firelight Festival were already underway. The last thing Asher wanted to do was to entertain the lords and ladies of Aeramere while pretending to be a formidable host all evening. Though the first night of dancing took place outdoors, the second night was usually held in a ballroom, something Asher could not stand.

He absolutely detested the idea of people milling about his private residence, cavorting with one another in a show of debauchery and affluence. Some always arrived far too early, while others often overstayed their welcome. It grated on his nerves, left his patience raw, watching them drink his wine and state their overtly obnoxious opinions on everything from the decorations to the number of books piled neatly upon most every surface in his house.

Asher turned off the shower and dried off, wrapping the towel around his waist. He stalked from the bathing suite to his bedroom, then flung open the doors to his wardrobe in search of something suitable to wear. He would've preferred it if pants and a collared shirt alone were deemed socially acceptable, but he had no doubt he would suffer Cyra's scorn if he didn't at least put on a trim coat.

Donning pants, boots, a crimson collared shirt, and a sleek black coat, Asher tossed a careless glance in the floor-length mirror next to his wardrobe. His hair was still damp, so he ran his fingers through it, adjusting the singular curl of silver so it fell in his face. Suddenly, he was flicking away imaginary flecks of dust and tugging on the sleeves of his shirt, ensuring he was more than presentable.

He'd never cared much for his appearance, but tonight he would have to face Novalise. After their argument, he'd been determined to seek out Queen Elowyn and demand she break the bond. But in the early morning hours, Novalise's emotions had slammed into him with a force greater than anything he'd ever known. Panic had consumed her, owned her. The rapid beating of her heart echoed in his ears, and her shallow breathing caused his own lungs to tighten. It didn't matter if he was still angry, it was torture to feel her suffering. He'd whispered to her then, to soothe the relentless terror washing over her. The moment he slipped into her mind, her thoughts calmed.

Eventually, her heartbeat slowed, and her breathing evened.

But she hadn't replied.

All things considered, it was probably for the best.

Asher opened the door to his bedroom and stumbled to a halt.

Cyra was there, twisting the satin ribbon of her gown between her fingers, wrinkling the fabric. Her skin was ashen, like it had been leached of all color. She stumbled backward, sending a nervous glance down the hall.

"Cyra." Asher stepped toward her, ready to catch her for fear she'd faint. "What is it? What's wrong?"

"There's someone here to see you." Absently, she reached up, touching the red strands of hair that hung shorter than the rest. "The Prince of Brackroth is waiting for you in your study."

"Don't worry," he murmured. "I won't let him near you again."

Asher strode down the hall, ready to confront the shadow prince. He didn't even bother with the handle, and with a flick of his wrist, the door swung open. Drake was sitting in the chair across from his desk, his spine impossibly straight, one ankle crossed over his knee. Cold power emanated from him, chilling the space. His demeanor projected that of an eerie quiet, like the stillness left behind in the wake of death.

"Your Highness." Asher settled himself in the leather chair across from Drake, eyeing the prince with hardened disdain. "I believe when I sent a message to the palace, I mentioned we would discuss my findings tonight."

He intentionally slid his gaze to the window. Afternoon sunlight streamed in through the sheer curtains, the beams of gold not quite touching the shadow prince, as though they avoided him completely.

Drake remained unfazed and impassive, his bored expression never wavering. "I find myself too impatient to wait."

Typical royal entitlement, expecting everyone to drop whatever they were doing in order to meet their demands.

"Very well." Asher grabbed his spectacles and put them on, then opened the drawer to his desk where he kept the book of runes he'd discovered, a chance result of Cyra's inelegant departure earlier that morning. "As promised, I found the location of the *virdis lepatite*. Unfortunately, you will have to travel to the bogs of Fenmire."

Drake recoiled, a mirthless smile coiling at the edges of his mouth. "Sinister place."

"Indeed." Asher flipped open the book to the placeholder he'd used to mark the spot where he'd uncovered even more unfavorable information. "I'm afraid it doesn't get much better, either."

The shadow prince leaned forward in his seat, a prominent frown creasing his brow. "What do you mean?"

Asher tapped his finger on the markings inked across the cream parchment, then angled the book so Drake could obtain a better view. "These aren't fae runes. They're the Runes of Caillevan, an ancient coven of powerful witches. Every witch alive can trace their lineage to the Caillevan. You've heard of them, I presume?"

"Yes. I have." Drake straightened, his gaze skimming the contents, his scowl deepening. "My father tried to vanquish them. For three years, he sent his armies to hunt down the witches of Caillevan. But killing a witch is no easy feat. He became obsessed, experimenting on them, burning them, torturing them. My father never cared much for anyone more powerful than himself."

Drake shifted in his seat, focusing on the pages of runes displayed before him. "Some of them fled, many of them perished. We heard rumors that the ones who were able to escape retreated to the Fenmire bogs, or to other kingdoms outside my father's reach."

Drake tugged on his riding gloves. "If Fenmire is where I must go, then so be it."

Asher swallowed, uncomfortable. He'd heard about the witch hunt in passing but had no idea so many had met their death. "That's not all."

The shadow prince sat back, his expression grim. "Lovely."

"There's one witch in particular you must seek. An old hag, the maker of the *virdis lepatite*. Her allegiance lies with no one. While she's neither good nor evil, she makes no qualms about offering up one of these gems to anyone willing enough to pay the price." Asher pulled the book back toward him and closed it. "If I were you, I'd suggest you make certain you're the highest bidder. I sincerely doubt you're the only one in pursuit of such magic."

Drake was on his feet a second later, agitation pulsing around him in dense waves. "Is that all?"

"No." The word cracked through the air, splintering the tension. Asher met him, standing as well. He slammed his palms onto the desk, rattling the jars of ink and causing a stack of papers to flutter to the floor.

Drake's brows lifted in mock amusement. "Something you want to say to me, Firebane?"

"Call off your marriage to Novalise Starstorm." He removed his spectacles, leveling the shadow prince with a ruthless glare.

"No," he sneered in return. "I don't think I will."

Indignation gripped Asher, spurring his resentment. It didn't matter if he was fated to Novalise or not, it was as Solarius had said. She deserved better than a damn assassin. Especially one who was quite possibly orchestrating a rebellion. Asher's nails bit into the soft wood of the desk, carving into its surface. "I know what game you play."

Drake's cutthroat smile only widened. Apprehension strained in the air, hissing and coiling around them like a venomous snake ready to strike. "And which one is that?"

Asher's tightly wound grip on his resolve frayed, coming undone. "The one where you and Lady Trysta Starstorm use Novalise as your pawn to help Prince Aspen rid his mother of the throne."

Dark, resounding laughter erupted from the shadow prince, disturbed and menacing. Clouds stole across the threads of sunlight, swallowing the room like nightfall. "Once again, Firebane, you prove to be a brilliant idiot."

He turned without another word, heading for the door.

"Don't do this," Asher warned, his magic rippling, fueling him.

"Don't do what? Marry Novalise Starstorm? Exploit her magic? Proceed with a witch hunt to search out a jewel capable of ruination?" He secured the gloves he wore, wrapping the leather bands snugly around his wrists. "You'll have to be more specific."

Damn it.

Drake knew about the starstorm magic slumbering within Novalise. If Asher didn't stop this marriage, Drake would own not only Novalise but also her power. He would wield her like a weapon against Queen Elowyn.

"You're using her," Asher ground out, an accusation more than a statement.

The shadow prince lifted one shoulder, then let it fall, unconcerned about the matter. "She's a means to an end."

Asher exploded, the might of his wrath consuming him. His muscles trembled with rage, his blood burned with fervency. Magic coursed through his veins, the space between them thrumming with violent energy. Asher would set fire to the world if it meant sparing Novalise from the Shadowblade Assassin.

"You don't even love her," Asher growled.

An unnatural calm settled over Drake, his stoic expression making him appear carved from stone. His words dripped with ice when he said, "And neither do you."

The ensuing silence was so deafening, Asher thought for sure his ears would rupture from the lack of sound.

Drake turned on his heel and left the study, his footfalls reverberating down the hall, cracking like thunder from a looming storm.

Asher remained rooted in place, his breathing remarkably calm. Clarity and understanding gripped him, anchoring him against the onslaught of realization. There were no alternatives, no courses of action that would end in victory. The truth of his destiny crept in, clouding his vision like a heavy fog rolling in from off the Chantara Sea.

Asher would either lose Novalise forever.

Or he would die.

CHAPTER THIRTY-NINE

The ballroom of House Emberspire was nothing short of magical.

Obsidian flooring lined the room, threaded with veins of shimmering gold that wove into whorls mimicking a flame. Gilded vases were positioned near the entrances, each one overflowing with vibrant red flowers with blackened tips. Frostfire sparked in sconces crafted from ruby crystals and over their heads magic pulsed as rippling waves of fire billowed, drenching the space in a golden glow.

Though Novalise told herself she wouldn't look, she'd seen no sign yet of Asher.

Sarelle stood beside her in a gown of navy, the hem faded lightly to silver, making it look as though she walked upon clouds of stardust. Novalise was nearly her opposite. In a dress of pale gold that bled into a deepened cobalt, the silk moved around her like liquid. Golden beads embroidered to look like constellations fell from her waist to the floor, like stars falling into the ocean.

"Anyway," Sarelle continued, unaware Novalise was only partially listening, "as it turns out, the poor male mortal *thought* he was falling in love with a princess from a neighboring land, but she's actually a witch. She spelled him and Queen Elowyn is not at all pleased. It's quite the scandal and apparently, she's considering closing the Veil permanently this time."

"Oh." Novalise scanned the ballroom once more, her gaze flitting over her twin sisters, Caelian and Creslyn, who were dancing in a circle, spinning and twirling with their arms raised above their heads. "How awful."

"Novalise," Sarelle scorned, the tone in her voice dragging Novalise from her thoughts. "Are you even listening to me? When the queen closes the Veil after this Midsummer, she might never open it again."

"*Oh!*" She whirled, facing Sarelle. "That is alarming."

Both alarming and slightly unnerving, if Novalise was being honest with herself. Only Queen Elowyn wielded the power to raise the Veil. If she closed it off completely as a means of protection, then that was one thing, but sealing it forever because of a love spell was something else altogether. No one could ever come in, no one could ever get out.

Novalise's heart sank into the pit of her chest. Her brothers, Nyxian and Tovian, were sailing out at sea, living lives full of travel and adventure. What if they couldn't return home?

She shook the preposterous thought from her mind. Of course Queen Elowyn would grant them entry into Aeramere. They were Starstorm fae.

Another needling thought stabbed at her.

Perhaps the queen's impending decision to close the Veil had nothing to do with the witch and the mortal at all. Maybe it was intended as a means of self-preservation, to safeguard her realm and position them against threats from within. If she cut off communication to outlying lands, then she could focus on any mounting turmoil lurking inside Aeramere. Maybe she *knew* about the plot against her.

If such a scheme existed...

Sarelle chewed on her bottom lip, her shimmering gaze sweeping across the sea of bodies. "Do you think she'll follow through with such a thing? The very idea is disconcerting and seems to be a rather extreme consequence for the use of a love spell."

"I tend to agree with you, it does seem..." Novalise trailed off, two bent heads in the far corner of the ballroom catching her eye.

Just beneath one ruby sconce lit with frostfire stood Solarius and her mother. The silvery glow drenched them in a play of faint light and shadow, but from her vantage point, it was easy to discern they were in the throes of a heated discussion. Solarius raked a hand through his shoulder-length hair, a testament to his frustration. Trysta fisted her hands on her hips, a scowl deepening her glower.

She watched as Ariesian walked over to them, attempting to diffuse the situation.

"Sarelle." Novalise lightly jabbed her sister with her elbow. "Are you seeing this?"

To make it worse, more than one bystander had chosen to hang about and eavesdrop, obviously intrigued by the argument between the matriarch of the Starstorm fae and one of her beloved sons.

"They argue all the time. Mother and Solarius have never gotten along." Sarelle rose up on her toes, peeking around a couple who stopped in front of her, blocking her view. "At least, not since Father died."

Novalise contemplated her sister's words, rolling them around in her mind. She always regarded herself in intimate confidence with Solarius, as he was the one closest to her in age. Had she always been so blind to the animosity developing between him and their mother?

"Don't worry." Sarelle reached over and gently patted

Novalise's forearm. "I'm sure they'll work it out. They always do."

But when Solarius stalked off, fury brewing around him like a storm cloud, Novalise wasn't so confident in her sister's assumption.

She headed off in the same direction as her brother.

"Where are you going?" Sarelle called after her.

She tossed a backward glance over her shoulder. "To speak with Sol."

Novalise followed Solarius's retreating frame, squeezing her way between the scuffle of bodies and yelps of shock as he shouldered his way through a line of dancers. She opened her mouth to call out to him, when a shadowy figured stepped directly in her path.

She stumbled into the solid wall of a chest, looking up to find Prince Drake towering over her.

"If you're going in search of Lord Firebane," he said, the rich accent from the Northernlands inflecting his tone, crafting each word like a provocative sin, "he isn't here."

"I'm not, I was going to—wait. What do you mean, he's not here?" Novalise skated her teeth along her bottom lip. She'd lost sight of Solarius, and now Asher wasn't even going to make an appearance. "This is *his* party."

"Be that as it may, my lady, the Lord of House Emberspire has chosen not to grace us with his presence this evening." Prince Drake took her hand, hooking it into the crook of his elbow.

"But why?"

"Well, if I had to guess," Prince Drake mused, bending his head down to whisper in her ear. "I would imagine it has every-thing to do with you."

"He's avoiding me."

"For lack of a better term."

Novalise expelled a sigh, disgruntled. She knew he was still upset with her, even though he'd been the one to pull her from the recesses of her mind when the overwhelming surge of panic left her fragmented and shattered by despair for his life. It was his voice she heard, his composure that filled her, and pieced her back together. She had to find him.

"Come." Prince Drake led her toward the dance floor, where couples twirled in time beneath the churning flames of magic. "Dance with me."

She pulled back, but her heels slid along the smooth surface of the ballroom as he pulled her. "I can't, I really need to—"

"Nonsense, *kearsta*." The shadow prince gestured around them. "Everyone is watching."

But for the first time in a long time, Novalise didn't care. "No."

Her refusal hovered in the space between them, the remnants of her confidence dangling precariously in the balance.

"Pardon?" He watched her with cool regard, his dark green eyes frosting over like a forest kissed by winter.

She would not cave beneath the pressure of his intense stare. She was exhausted from being relegated to a life not fully her own, and she would no longer stand for it.

"I said, no. I cannot dance with you right now, Your Highness." Novalise disentangled herself from his hold.

She expected backlash of some kind, perhaps even a flair of his temper or a glimpse of his ominous shadows. But a flicker of admiration passed over his handsome face instead.

"Very well, my lady." He lowered his head, placing an icy kiss on her cheek. His whisper floated past her ear, causing goose-bumps to skitter along her skin. "He's in the gardens."

Novalise dropped her shoulders and angled her face to the shadow prince, fully aware his mouth was entirely too close to her own. "Who?"

His voice was low, like a sinuous swath of velvet dancing

across her skin. "I think you already know the answer to that question."

She nodded once, dipped into a low curtsy, then excused herself. If Asher was in the gardens, there was no time to waste. Following the gentle tug on the mating bond, she slipped outside into the warm summer evening. She'd worn her hair loose so it hung down to the middle of her back, the tiny moonstone charms woven into the strands tinkling in the soft breeze.

Novalise played the part well, nodding to lords and ladies she passed on the path and offering them a pleasant smile as she kept her stride deliberately leisurely, as though she was simply enjoying a stroll through the lavish ornamental gardens. Deeper she went into the maze of climbing flame-red flowers wrapped around pillars of obsidian and hedgerows so tall and dense, they obscured the light from the floating lanterns suspended between them. Overhead, wisps of clouds unfurled before the moon, casting a halo around it, draping the gardens in a blanket of hazy darkness.

Rounding a corner, she spied an ivory stone bench situated beneath an arching wall of scarlet roses. The pull of the bond beckoned her to the path veering to the left, but a lulling voice guised beneath a veil of stealth caught her off guard.

Novalise stilled as a warm, feminine voice drifted through the towering barrier of roses.

"Another rebellion? Where?" It was Queen Elowyn who spoke, but Novalise couldn't quite tell the male whose company she kept.

"Two, Your Majesty." The mysterious, gravelly response sounded closer to the roses than before. "One in Azurvend, and another in Galefell."

Prince Drake was right, the rumors were true.

There were uprisings in Aeramere after all.

"Do we know who's behind them?" the queen asked.

"There's no proof or guarantee, but..."

Novalise had to uncover who was behind such a cryptic tone. She bent down, quietly removing her heels, then gathered the hem of her gown and climbed up onto the stone bench. The decadent scent of roses surrounded her, alluringly sweet, and she rose up on her toes in an effort to peek through the petals and leaves. She barely saw Queen Elowyn, just the back of her emerald-green cloak and the glint of a crown on top of her head. Mindful of the thorns, Novalise leaned forward for a better look at the male who accompanied her, but all she could see was a crop of golden blond hair.

"He must be growing bored," Queen Elowyn murmured, as though her thoughts were her own. "If we can find a means to distract him, something to divert his attention, then perhaps he will cease this foolish charade."

Prince Aspen.

Queen Elowyn paced in a slow circle, the click of her heels stirring the wilted rose petals at her feet. "I planned to marry him off to Lady Novalise Starstorm, but she got herself tangled up with the Shadowblade Assassin instead, likely her mother's doing."

Novalise jerked backward and nearly toppled off the bench. She threw her arms out to catch her balance, holding her breath, praying to the stars she didn't make too much noise. Queen Elowyn made it seem like Novalise's mother had married her off to Prince Drake on purpose. Which could only mean one thing...Asher was right.

She shuddered, almost grateful for her mother and Ariesian's decision to make her wed Prince Drake. He was far more tolerable than Prince Aspen. Marriage to the faerie prince would have been horrendous. Acid roiled in her stomach, but she ignored it, rising on her toes to peer through the rose wall once more. Except this time, her whole body was trembling.

The male chuckled, his quiet laughter a seductive melody.

Novalise's knees quaked and a shameful blush bled into her cheeks.

"Do you really think a wife is a sufficient distraction, Your Majesty?" he asked, a hint of amusement coloring his tone.

"For Aspen, a female is always a good time."

The queen paused, turning to face her champion. She tilted her head and the faceless male stepped closer. Novalise leaned forward, desperate to see with whom she held clandestine meetings.

"What about the other Starstorm daughter?" Queen Elowyn pondered. "Sarelle, is it?"

No!

Novalise pitched forward, the sharp tip of a thorn stabbing into her shoulder. She hissed in pain, then plucked it free from her flesh.

The voices on the other side of the rose wall had gone silent.

She had to get out of here before she got caught. If she was captured eavesdropping on the queen, there was no telling what sort of punishment she might suffer.

But before Novalise could flee, a large hand clamped over her mouth, and she was dragged further into the garden's floral maze.

CHAPTER FORTY

ith one arm wrapped snugly around Novalise's waist and his other hand clamped firmly over her mouth, Asher hauled her away from the queen and her Captain of the Guard. Novalise kicked and thrashed in his arms, attempting to fight him off, rather valiantly if he admitted as much, but she was no match for his strength.

"Be still," he commanded through their bond, and the thread binding them together quivered.

At once, she went pliant, sagging against his chest.

He carried her to the one place in the garden that was special to him, a secret place where midnight blooms wrapped in silver vines created a covered archway, safe from prying ears and eyes.

Asher released her and as soon as her bare feet touched the ground, he jerked her around to face him, grabbing her by the shoulders. "Are you *trying* to get yourself killed?"

She looked so perfect, so positively serene, but the moment he opened his mouth, her pretty face instantly shuttered. "Of course not, I was—"

"Eavesdropping on the queen?" he interjected, unable to

control his temper. "Fates divine, Nova, what if you were caught?"

"I was caught," she snapped, glaring up at him, her eyes lit with accusation.

He ran a hand through his hair, groaning. "What if you were caught by someone *other* than me? Do you have any idea what the punishment is for that kind of crime?"

He couldn't believe she'd been so absolutely foolish, so absurdly reckless. She was lucky he'd been the one to discover her. If he'd been a minute later, she would be taken away by royal guards and locked in the damn dungeon. The mere thought of it left him raging.

"I'm sure the queen would—"

"Whipping, Novalise. You would have been *whipped*. And not just once, multiple times, over and over. Until your dress was in shreds and your back was a pulpy mess." Asher squeezed his eyes shut, fought against the urge to slam his fist into the nearest stone wall. The pain would be worth it if it meant he didn't have to think about the idea of Novalise being tortured. He opened his eyes again only to find her standing with her arms wrapped tightly around her and the sheen of tears glassing her starlit gaze. He sighed, harsh and anguished. "What's gotten into you?"

"You!" She lurched forward, slamming her palms into his chest, pushing him with all her might. He didn't even stagger back. "It's you, Ash. You occupy all of my thoughts, you consume every fiber of my being."

Novalise gave a small sniffle, blinking away the tears that threatened to fall. "And I am so sorry for the vile things I said. I never meant...I never intended to hurt you. I'll understand if you refuse to accept my apology. I'm not even sure I can forgive myself."

"Starlight."

He reached for her then, cupping her face with both hands,

using his thumbs to wipe away the tears that slipped out of her control. Bending down, he pressed a kiss to her forehead.

"Tell me," she whispered.

Asher's heart wrenched and he eased back.

Those eyes of hers, silver with glittering flecks of a shattered rainbow, sought him. Captivated him.

"Tell me you don't love me," she repeated those words, *his* words, back at him.

"Novalise—"

She shook her head, refusing him. "If, after all this, you still don't love me, then I will walk away from you right now, and you can be free to break our bond. I won't look back, but I'll never regret loving you."

He pulled her in close, holding her against him. She smelled of midnight roses and dark berries wrapped in soft vanilla. Their magic reached for one another, a delicate dance down the mating bond, a rapture of stars and fire.

"Please." She buried her face in his chest. "Just tell me."

"I can't," he admitted, because his heart beat only for her. She was all he ever wanted, in this life or the next. "I have never loved another before you, and I will never love another after you. My soul chose you, and I would rather spend an eternity in the fires of hell than ever live a day without you."

Asher slid his fingers under her chin, tilting her face up to him. "All that I am, is yours."

He lowered his head, and her eyes fluttered closed. Her lips were less than a breath away, so close, and he would finally be able to taste her again. To savor her. To treasure her.

"Well." A stern female voice splintered through the silence surrounding them. "Isn't this cozy?"

Asher spun around, pulling Novalise behind him, her gasp ringing in his ears.

Standing on the other side of the secluded archway were Trysta Starstorm and Drake Kalstrand.

"Novalise, come here." Trysta's gaze flicked over Asher with harsh scrutiny. "Now."

He sensed it the moment she shifted out from behind him and into view. She stood beside him and when she answered her mother, her voice wavered.

"I don't think so."

"Do not make this any more difficult that it needs to be, darling." Trysta held out her arms, her somber features softening slightly. "Come along."

Warmth spread through Asher. Novalise clutched his hand, leaning into him for support. He interlaced their fingers, squeezing tightly.

She rolled her shoulders back and stiffened her spine, ready to face her mother down. "No. I don't want to marry Prince Drake. I don't love him."

Trysta's hands dropped to her sides, the bangles she wore clanging harshly through the air. She expelled a tired laugh, grating and pinched. "Oh, darling girl, love has nothing to do with it."

"But you and father married for love," Novalise countered.

At the mention of her late husband, Trysta flinched. It was nothing too noticeable, a slight twitch of the shoulders. But to Asher, the insignificant movement screamed of guilt.

Novalise took another small step forward, and he held tight to her hand.

"I want a love match," she declared.

That annoying twinge, that ever-present ache in his chest, expanded.

"Love is for the weak. The broken. Isn't that right, Lord Firebane?" Trysta tossed her hateful words in his direction, the barb striking true. "Your father was quite skilled in the art of seduction. He courted multiple ladies with no regard to your mother's heart, and more than one of his affairs involved females who were married."

Her loathsome gaze skimmed him up and down, revulsion curling at the corner of her mouth. "It would seem the stars were right. You are exactly like your father."

Seething, Asher released Novalise's hand, ready to confront her wicked mother. But a swarm of shadows stood in his way.

"Come with me, Novalise." Drake offered her his hand, blocking Trysta from Asher's view. "Before Lord Firebane does something he'll regret."

But Novalise was not so easily swayed. She stared up at the shadow prince, her brow knitting in concern.

"You...you sent me out into the gardens on purpose." Accusation set fire to her words, anger frothed and bubbled beneath the surface of her furious face. "You knew I'd find Asher here, and then you brought my mother to shame me. You tricked me."

"Who, me?" Drake almost looked appalled, but the dark gleam in his eyes spoke volumes about his malicious intent. "Never."

"Novalise, if you care about Lord Firebane as much as you say, then you'll walk away from him right now." Trysta's words were clipped, tinged with a foreboding promise. "Otherwise, I'll let your betrothed be the one to teach him a lesson."

Drake smiled, ruthless and cunning. The Shadowblade appeared then, its honed blade glinting like nightfall and a thousand shattered stars.

The fucking bastard.

Novalise gasped. "You wouldn't dare."

"Oh, believe me." Drake flicked his wrist, catching the sharpened tip of the dagger between two fingers. "I would."

Drake was many things, but of them all, he was not a liar. He always made good on his word, be it a threat or a promise.

"Go." Asher spoke the words into Novalise's mind, pleading with her. *"Don't worry about me. Just go."*

"Consider this your final warning, Firebane." The ice from

Drake's voice infiltrated their bond, sending a cold spike of paranoia down Asher's spine. *"Stay away from what is mine."*

He extended his hand to Novalise once more.

This time, she was forced to accept.

Her emotions were a violent force, and Asher felt every one of them explicitly. Fear swam inside of her, drowning her courage. The panic was there as well, hidden beneath layers of anger and hopelessness.

Asher watched as she walked away with Trysta and the shadow prince. Novalise glanced back once, her lips pressed together in a firm line, sheer determination reflecting back at him.

It couldn't end like this for them, not with her being sent off to Brackroth. His magic bellowed, a roar of endless torment. Finally, he recognized the merciless ache, the gnawing agony he suffered whenever Novalise wasn't near. It had nothing to do with the bond.

He was in love with her.

Damn the stars. Damn the fates.

Asher would stop at nothing to ensure Novalise remained by his side for an eternity, or he would die trying.

CHAPTER FORTY-ONE

*T*he city of Celestine was brimming with beauty, a gem among the Houses of Aeramere. Located in the valley of the mountains below her house, it was sprawling, its stone pathways designed to mimic the Faerie Star with its eight points. The buildings were all an iridescent white to enhance the shimmer of the stars at night, their beams and framework made of black opal, stark yet radiant. Glass ceilings carved the skyline, many of them coated with a fine layer of magic that tinted them a deep hue of violet that darkened during the day, then faded away completely at night.

Fountains could be found throughout the city, each one worthy of casting wishes. In the center was an extravagant courtyard where smooth, navy goldstone tiles were laid to take the shape of twin crescent moons. Between the decadent tiles was a large, round silver reflecting pool, its opaque waters reminiscent of liquid stardust. Shops lined the market area selling moonstone, selenite, and other crystal ornaments, while some sold mystical plants and flowers that only bloomed in the twilight or midnight hours. There were bakeries, cafes, and the sweetest fae who usually stood on one of the corners with her wooden cart selling jars of moonlight.

One of Novalise's favorite places was Moonbeams, the most adorable shop that sold celestial sweet treats and starberry sparkling wine. She made it a point to stop in whenever she was in the city, but unfortunately, her mother had her every move tracked and hadn't let Novalise out of her sight.

Instead of indulging in a piece of moonberry cake, she was standing on a raised pedestal, surrounded by her mother and sisters, while she was forced to try on yet another wedding gown.

Hopefully, this one wouldn't be nearly as horrendous as the last.

With her arms held out to the sides, she remained perfectly still, clad in nothing but her silk undergarments, while Astralina, the owner of the shop, wrapped a measuring tape around her waist.

"Suck in, Novalise." Her mother made a clicking noise from the side of her mouth. Trysta was seated on a blush velvet settee, with her ankles crossed, stirring the cup of tea in her hands. She had yet to take one sip. "There's not much to be done about your hips, but one deep breath should make the size of your waist more manageable."

Novalise bit the inside of her cheek to keep from snapping. What did it matter if she had full breasts and wider hips? Her waist was as narrow as it ought to be, but Trysta always attempted to squeeze her into gowns that were a smidge too tight.

"She's fine, mother," Sarelle scolded, directing her scorn toward Trysta. Smiling at Novalise, Sarelle reached out and tucked a lock of hair behind her shoulders, then whispered, "Let it out."

Novalise exhaled a sigh of relief. She was grateful her sisters had willingly come along on this excursion. It hadn't taken much convincing, but she didn't want to be left alone with her mother for any great length of time. Caelian and Creslyn were browsing Astralina's wares, toying with ribbons of every color and admiring bolts of the finest fabrics. At their mother's unjust comments, however, both of their heads snapped toward Novalise in unison.

It was rare for them to bear witness to Trysta's churlish behavior, as more often than not, the twins could do no wrong.

Astralina moved in front of Novalise, effectively producing a barrier between her and her mother's scrutinizing gaze.

"This one is my newest creations, Lady Novalise. Exceptionally fitting for a Starstorm fae." She draped a length of violet silk around Novalise. The fabric was cool against her skin, embellished with swirling diamonds made to look like falling stars. Beads of gold and onyx were sprinkled throughout. It moved around her, molding to her body for a perfect fit. The neckline wasn't too low, the waist was snug, and a seductive slit rose all the way to her upper thigh.

"Not the violet," Trysta said, her voice clipped. "It washes out her complexion."

The fabric in Astralina's hands immediately faded from lush violet to somber gray.

Novalise gently placed her hand on Astralina's shoulder. "I want the violet."

She stared at her mother, the silent challenge budding between them, expanding like a wall of insurmountable tension.

Caelian and Creslyn shifted on their feet, angling themselves toward the conversation. Sarelle moved closer to the pedestal in a show of support.

Trysta ceased the stirring of her tea, then loosed a dramatic sigh. "Fine. Since your last wedding dress mysteriously disappeared, I suppose this one will have to do lest it vanish, too."

"It didn't disappear." Novalise watched, pleased when the fabric returned to its vibrant violet shade. "I burned it."

The teacup in Trysta's hands clattered on its saucer and she gripped it, her knuckles whitening. "You did *what?*"

The irritation bubbling between them spiked, threatening to boil over. But Novalise held the intensity of her mother's stare, refusing to back down. "I said, I burned it."

There was a flicker in Trysta's eyes, but before Novalise could decipher it, her mother blinked, and it was gone. "What, with fire?"

"Yes." Novalise dipped her chin. This was her moment of truth. "With starfire."

Sarelle sucked in a breath, catching Novalise's hand. "Are you serious?"

But Novalise was too focused on her mother to respond.

"Starfire," Trysta repeated mildly. There was a heavy moment of hesitation and she laughed, loud and grating. "Darling, don't be ridiculous."

"I'm not." Novalise clamped her jaw so soundly it ached.

"But Nova." Creslyn glided forward, her eyes round like sapphire orbs. "Starfire has been dormant in the Starstorm line for years. Longer, even."

"Not anymore," Novalise countered.

Trysta's admonishing gaze slid to Astralina. "Excuse us for a moment."

"Of course, my lady." Astralina bobbed a swift curtsy, then exited through a set of gossamer curtains toward the front of the store.

Trysta set down her teacup, then stood, her chin lifted to an angle of authority. She clasped her hands together, prim and poignant. "Very well, Novalise. Let's see it."

"I..." She glanced around the space. Her sisters watched her with rapt attention, expecting her to reveal the long-lost powerful magic that died out from their bloodline before their births. Trysta knew she possessed the ability, she was the one who told her to conceal it, yet now she was acting as though she had no idea at all. Novalise's brow furrowed, she never imagined her mother would demand an exhibition. "I haven't yet mastered it. What I mean to say is, I'm unsure of how to summon it on command."

"Mm." Trysta looked her up and down, diminishing her with one callous glance. Then she turned on her heel and exited the dressing room, disappearing beyond the other side of the curtains. Dismissing Novalise, as always.

Caelian was in front of Novalise a second later, gazing up at her in wonder. "Are you really blessed with starfire?"

She nodded slowly, resigned. Disappointment and disheartenment weighed upon her shoulders, crushing her. "Yes. Ask Nyxian."

Creslyn smothered her gasp. "He's seen it?"

"How do you think he got that scar?"

Her lashes fluttered as she backed and nearly stumbled into Caelian. "You attacked him?"

"Of course not!" Novalise stepped down from the pedestal, and Sarelle helped her undress, carefully hanging the wedding gown on one of the velvet racks. "It was an accident. There was a storm, and this terrifying sensation overcame me. I felt myself slipping, losing control. Nyxian was there. He tried to help me counter it, but the streaks of starlight that burst from me turned to flames, engulfing me in this maelstrom of starfire. I couldn't control it, and one of the bolts hit Nyxian."

She shuddered, remembering the fear that gripped her when she thought she'd killed her younger brother.

"You created the starstorm." Sarelle tied the laces down the back of Novalise's day dress. There was no accusation in her tone, but no question either. It was a simple statement of fact.

"I did." Novalise adjusted the front of her dress, smoothing the pieces of lace. "It's why I flee to the lower levels of the house whenever the weather turns violent. Down there, in the darkened halls of the mountain, is safe for me."

And everyone is safe from her.

"I know it seems impossible," she continued, "but Lord Firebane has witnessed it once before." He stepped into her starstorm and took it all. The lashing of it, the intense power of it. "As has Prince Drake."

Creslyn tilted her head, a line of concern knitting across her brow. "So, it only happens during storms?"

"Or when I'm angry." Like with that first hideous wedding dress.

Creslyn jabbed Caelian in the side with her elbow. "I *told* you she wasn't afraid of storms. She was afraid of what happened *during* the storms."

Sarelle snared Novalise's hand again, giving it a firm squeeze. "I believe you."

The twins nodded furiously, speaking as one. "So do we."

Novalise's gaze slid to the curtains. There was still no sign of her mother. "Thank you."

Caelian wandered over to a wall of shelves overflowing with spools of ribbon. "Have you told anyone else?"

"Solarius knows, I needed his help after the accident with Nyx." The starstorm was a closely guarded secret. Or it was until recently. "Nyxian may have told others, but I don't know. We never spoke about it again."

Sarelle's brows shot up and she blinked. "Whyever not?"

"Well, because at the time, I thought I had killed him." The starfire had hit Nyxian in the face, carving up his left cheek to his forehead, splicing the iris of his eye. He'd carried the scar for years. "I think we were both in such a state of shock, we just never mentioned it again."

"You should tell Ariesian." Creslyn tucked her hands behind her back, browsing the display case full of rings, necklaces, bracelets and earrings, the glittering jewels attracting her gaze. She was always fond of anything that sparkled. "I bet he could help you."

"That's right," Caelian agreed, glancing over her shoulder at them. "He's incredibly powerful, Novalise. As the eldest, he has an extensive knowledge of all the Starstorm magic. I'm sure if he knew you were blessed with starfire, he would be more than willing to train you."

She'd have to consider it. Her relationship with Ariesian was...complicated. He was the eldest, and he wore the weight of all that was expected from him like armor. Heavy and impenetrable. Intimidating. Like the walls of a fortress unable to be breached. She supposed she could tell him about the starstorm. But even if he believed her, even if he never doubted her, she wasn't entirely sure he would agree.

It was almost too much to ask.

Novalise glanced over at Sarelle while Caelian and Creslyn distracted themselves with jewels and piles of satin. She kept her voice low, and a steady eye on the curtains. "Thank you for believing me."

"Of course, I will always stand by your side." Sarelle toyed with the violet silk ribbon at her waist, her gaze flicking around the shop. "But right now, we have more important things to figure out other than how you can learn to control the starstorm."

"Like what?"

Sarelle leveled her with a look of pure contempt. "Like how to stop you from being forced to marry Prince Drake tomorrow."

"I'm running out of options." If Novalise could find a way to expose Prince Aspen, then that would cause enough of an uproar that the wedding could be delayed, at least for a few days. However, as of right now, she was lacking any solid evidence and doing so also created the very real possibility of exposing her mother.

"If Lord Firebane wants you," Sarelle whispered, her gaze sliding to the twins, "he'll have to fight for you."

Novalise cringed, her stomach coiling into unforgiving knots. She didn't want a life without Asher in it, nor did she want to see him suffer at the hands of Prince Drake's wrath. It was too dangerous. Too brutal. The entire process was archaic. A battle to win a lady's hand only proved that females had no voice when it came to such matters. They were silenced and cast to the side, left with no choice but to marry the victor of a bloody, deadly duel.

"Lord Firebane won't win." Novalise squeezed her eyes shut. "Prince Drake will destroy him."

"But would he do it?" Sarelle asked. "Does he love you enough to risk his life for you?"

Novalise opened her eyes and was met with her sister's compassion. She pressed her lips together and looked away, unable to withstand Sarelle's pity. "I don't know."

CHAPTER FORTY-TWO

*I*t was the wedding of Novalise's nightmares.

All of it was wrong—the flowers, the music, the guests. And the man...the man was *definitely* wrong.

Novalise paced the stuffy sitting area outside of Queen Elowyn's throne room, where her wedding was to take place. There were two glass doors along the far wall that opened to a small balcony, just large enough for one person. Drapes of emerald hung from the windows, their centers pulled back with gold cord. Novalise was half-inclined to yank the draperies down from the rods. If she worked quickly, she could tie the ends together and craft a makeshift rope. Then she would be able to climb over the balcony and scale the palace walls to freedom.

Granted, she was fairly certain she wouldn't even make it to the border of the palace before she was caught by guards, dragged back to the throne room, and forced down the aisle. But it might be worth a try.

Novalise gnawed her bottom lip, her heels clicking softly in time against the gold-veined ivory floor, like a countdown to her demise.

She hadn't heard from Asher at all since she last saw him in his gardens. Not once had he attempted to reach her, not once had she heard even a whisper of his voice. On more than one occasion, she'd reached for him through their bond, but only silence had answered her. It was possible he'd given up on her, that he considered fighting for her a lost cause.

Not that she could blame him. It was a valid concern.

Prince Drake hardly seemed like the kind of person to show mercy.

But Novalise couldn't lose Asher. Not to Prince Drake and not to death.

She had to stall—if she could put off the wedding for three more days, Queen Elowyn would have no choice but to close the Veil. Then she could buy herself some time. Besides, there was no way the queen would allow her to leave Aeramere with the shadow prince unless they were already married.

Escape was her only option.

Novalise darted across the room and locked the door. Reaching up, she grabbed a handful of the thick drapes and tugged. Hard. Anxiety spun through her as the fabric ripped away from its bindings and the bronze rod bobbled, nearly tearing the fixtures from the wall. She repeated the process with the next set of drapes, then laid them out on the floor, tying them together with the gold cord.

Music sounded from outside the sitting room, and she stole a quick glance at the door. It would only be a matter of time before Ariesian arrived to escort her to the throne room.

Make haste, Novalise.

She fought against the tremble in her hands, urging herself to concentrate.

You can do this.

When the final pair of draperies were bound together, she stood and admired her work. She wasn't entirely sure about the length, only that the balcony was at least as high as the tree line in the distance, if not higher. She took one end of the rope and fastened it around two of the stone spindles of the balcony's ledge. Tightening it until her fingers cramped, she pulled again. The rope held.

Satisfied with the knot she'd secured, Novalise tossed the rope over the balcony. Her stomach clenched when she realized it wasn't long enough. The last length of draperies hovered about eight feet from the ground. The drop would be painful, but worth it if she could get away in time.

Already stars were peeking out from behind moonlit clouds, obscuring the courtyard in haphazard shadows. She calculated the distance from the palace to the forest's edge. She would have to be quick and stealthy, using the cover of darkness to her advantage.

Two rough knocks sounded outside the door of the sitting room.

"Novalise?" Ariesian's voice echoed from the other side. "Are you almost ready?"

"Just a moment," she called, kicking off her shoes. The heels would only hinder her.

Hoisting the hem of her wedding dress, she lifted one leg over the edge of the balcony and peered down. Bile rose hot in the back of her throat, but she swallowed it, blowing out a shaky breath to steady herself. The ground was so far away, and the rope made from drapes swung lightly in the breeze, crushing her nerves.

"Nova." Ariesian's voice threaded with impatience and this time, he rattled the doorknob. "Novalise, unlock this door at once."

"Damn," she muttered, annoyed that her brother couldn't see fit to give her a few more minutes to make her grand escape. "I said I just need another minute!"

"The ceremony is about to begin." He pounded against the door again, firmer this time. "Everyone is waiting."

Let them wait.

She dragged her other leg over the railing, teetering on the edge of the balcony on her tippy toes. The knocking on the door turned to pounding, with Ariesian's voice bellowing from the other side. Fear sliced through her, but she ignored it. Snaring a fistful of fabric with one hand, she positioned the rest of it between her trembling knees, then hooked it around her ankles to give herself some leverage. The heavy velvet grew damp beneath the grip of her palms, sliding some, but she started her descent, shimmying down the side of the palace wall.

The summer breeze was stronger now, pulling her hair loose from its pins, and stinging her cheeks. Her gown whipped around her, tangling with her legs and the rope as she struggled to find purchase. The muscles in her arms burned, aching with exertion, and her legs were cramping. It took far more effort than she realized to become a runaway bride.

Something overhead cracked. Splintered. A rush of magic, of explosive power, illuminated the room above her.

Novalise's head snapped up.

The door.

Ariesian had broken down the door.

"Nova!" His silhouette took form on the ledge, so broad he blocked out nearly all the shards of broken light from the room. He leaned over the balcony, his silver eyes glowing with intensity, the sapphire flecks blazing bright. "What, and I cannot stress this enough, the fuck are you doing?"

Novalise heaved a sigh and glanced over her shoulder. She was still about fifteen feet in the air, much too far to make a jump for it. But goddess above if her body didn't feel like quitting on her already. She looked back up at her brother.

"I believe it's rather obvious. I'm escaping."

She saw it then, the slightest twitch of his lips.

She couldn't remember the last time she saw him smile.

Ariesian rested his elbow on the stone railing, propping his chin on his fist. "And what shall I tell everyone if you succeed in this daring escapade?"

Novalise moved a few more inches down the rope, locking her ankles around the drapes even though her muscles protested in agony.

"You will tell them...that I no longer wish to marry the Prince of Brackroth. And that..." She sucked in a ragged breath, her fingers throbbing as she tried to keep a tight hold on the drapes. "And that I am absconding from this wedding ceremony with haste."

"A contract is a contract, Novalise." Ariesian reached down, clasped the rope with both hands, and heaved, hoisting her back up toward the balcony.

"Ariesian, no!" Novalise yelped, her legs slipping as her feet swung freely, kicking in the air. "Stop right now! I will *not* marry someone I do not love!"

"Love doesn't win wars." He hefted the rope again, hauling her higher into the air. "Everything we do, everything *I* do, is for the good of House Celestine. Even if that means marrying one of my sisters off to secure protection against unnamed and unknown threats."

"You're making a mistake," Novalise protested, fumbling to get herself further down the rope and closer to the ground.

"Nonsense." He blew an errant strand of hair from out of his face. "I never make mistakes."

"Ariesian, I swear to the goddess, if you don't lower me to the ground right this instant, I'll..." Desperation clawed at her. She wouldn't get another opportunity. "I'll let go."

He hesitated, his hands stilling on the rope. "Nova, we can talk this through. It's only—"

"I mean it, Aries!" At the use of his childhood nickname, he froze. She hadn't called him that in years. Her shoulders strained, her wrists burned, her fingers were wound so tightly around the knots of fabric that she swore they'd fall off at any moment. "Put me down now or I will let go and fall a dozen stories to my death!"

"It's not a dozen," he countered, his brows drawing together in a hard line. "It's only two, and your dramatics are unnecessary."

She opened her mouth to spout off some unsavory retort when the scent of sandalwood, amber, and spice wrapped around her on the breeze.

"Let go." Asher's voice was a caress down the bond, a soft brush along her cheek, a stroke of fingertips down her spine. *"I've got you. Let go."*

Novalise stared up at her brother. His eyes widened, reflecting a flicker of fear the moment he realized she intended to hold true to her word. Ariesian lunged, releasing the rope, and reaching for her hand. "Nova!"

But Novalise smiled and let go.

Time moved as though the air itself cushioned her fall. Slow and languid, like a feather or the petal of a flower floating on the wind. Stars tumbled across the sky, illuminating the look of horror, of absolute fear, on Ariesian's face. Her hair unfurled around her in streamers of lavender, her gown seemed suspended in time.

Right before she knew she would hit the ground, Novalise closed her eyes.

The impact never came.

A pair of strong arms caught her and cradled her against the sturdy wall of a chest. The heartbeat was calm and steady, unnaturally even, much like her own.

Novalise peered up into the face of her rescuer. Cold determination rolled off him in waves, forged around her like steel. His eyes were blazing, the outlying rims of gold set on fire by the passion swirling inside them.

"Ash." His name left her on a breath, softer than the stirring of leaves among the trees.

The corner of his mouth curved, but his smile didn't reach his eyes. "Hello, Starlight."

CHAPTER FORTY-THREE

*N*ovalise was in Asher's arms, she was safe, and for now, that was all that mattered.

He had no idea what the hell she'd been thinking climbing out over that balcony in a wedding dress with no shoes and no one to catch her. The end of drapes she'd tied together still hung a good eight feet off the ground and a fall like that was more than a little dangerous. She could've broken multiple bones. Asher had planned on making an imperious entrance into the throne room, declaring his love for her, and claim his willingness to fight for her hand.

Then he'd seen her dangling from the improvised rope she'd made, yelling up at her brother, and his plans had gone out the window.

Quite literally.

Novalise gazed up at him, wrapping her arms around his neck. "You came back for me."

He bent down, pressing his nose to the tip of hers. "I never left."

"Firebane."

Asher's head snapped up, meeting Drake's hardened gaze

across the dimly lit courtyard. He stood shrouded in the shadows of the entrance to the palace, a gathering of onlookers growing behind him. Cyra stood out among them, her face a blank canvas. He didn't know if she was upset, or furious, or terrified. He didn't really want her here, didn't want her to witness his death, but surely, she had to know he was doing the right thing...for once. Novalise's family gathered closer, nudging their way to the front, followed by the vast majority of nobles in Aeramere. Flanked by guards on either side of them were Queen Elowyn and Prince Aspen, their faces mirror images of one another—severe, yet lined with a vague curiosity.

Well, at least he would die with a full audience in attendance.

The queen strode out from around Drake, stepping forward. At once, faerie fire illuminated the courtyard, burning from lanterns so brightly it could've been mistaken for dawn.

"Lord Firebane." Queen Elowyn clasped her hands together, regal and assertive, her voice carrying through the night for all to hear. "You're aware of the consequences for interfering with a wedding, are you not?"

Slowly, Asher lowered Novalise to the ground. Her small hands curled into fists, clutching at his shirt. "I am."

"Ash," Novalise pleaded, her voice a whisper meant solely for him. "Don't do this."

"I won't let him take you." Asher took her hands, pressing a kiss to each of her knuckles. "Not now, not ever."

"I really don't understand why you're making this such a big deal, Firebane." Drake shoved his hands into the pockets of his pants and the shadows surrounding him expanded. "It's not as though Novalise is all...sunshine and rainbows."

Drake grinned but it was forced, edgier than usual.

Asher strode forward, ready to defend his mate. "Do not compare her to sunshine and rainbows when she is so clearly moonlight and stardust."

"Very well." Drake vanished from the doorway of the palace,

engulfed by a swath of his own darkness. Shadows swirled, never touching the light, disappearing completely. Eerie stillness settled over the crowd of guests and nobility, the unexpected realization of Drake's power dawning upon them with stark clarity, as though they suddenly remembered they were in the presence of the Shadowblade Assassin. A moment later, the air shifted, and Drake reappeared, standing behind Asher. He removed his coat and leather gloves, tossing them to the ground, then readied his stance. "Let's get this over with, shall we?"

Asher glanced over at Novalise, nodding once. Her face was pallid, as though the rose of her cheeks had been siphoned from within her. Fear stole through her, heightened by cold dread, the well of it funneling into him. She shuffled back, her bare feet padding lightly across the stone of the courtyard. Solarius stepped up beside her, his expression grave, and draped a protective arm around her shoulders, pulling her close.

Asher bowed before the shadow prince, and Drake returned the gesture.

Then Asher attacked.

Magic swelled and crackled in the air, the dense scent of sandalwood and amber permeating the space between them. Bolts of frostfire erupted from the tips of his fingers, a streak of silver and midnight aiming straight for Drake's heart. The shadow prince lifted one hand, capturing the frozen flames in the center of his palm. A crackling noise echoed in Asher's ears, the sound of splintering glass. The flames morphed in Drake's hold, solidifying into shards, each one with a honed and carefully crafted edge.

Drake drew his hand back, then his arm shot forward, sending the fragments of frostfire raining down upon Asher like a dozen sharpened swords.

He dove, rolling across the stone ground to dodge the assault.

They shattered around him, the blade of one slicing across his cheek, like ice serrating his skin. Something warm and sticky slid down the left side of his face, the metallic smell of his blood tainting each breath.

Piercing cries of panic melded with the hasty shuffle of footfalls from those who'd gathered to watch. But Asher had no time to make sure none of the innocent bystanders were injured. He had to focus on staying alive. For Novalise.

For himself.

Popping back up on his feet, he crouched low, hurtling a blaze of blackened flames toward Drake. Asher's magic struck the ground first, igniting around the shadow prince, encasing him in a ring of fire. They rose higher, licking the sky, spitting and expanding until the shadow prince was no longer visible behind the infernal wall. Anyone else would've feared for their life. Anyone else would've screamed as the flames melted their clothing, as the stench of burnt hair and charred flesh clogged their lungs.

But not Drake.

He walked right through it, smothering the magic, extinguishing it until all that remained was scorched stone and ash.

The bastard laughed, cold and cunning. "Is that all you've got, Firebane?"

Asher had no warning before Drake's fist collided with the side of his face, the crunching of flesh and bone sending his head spinning. His mouth filled hot with blood and he spat, blinking rapidly to recover his vision.

"What the fuck, Kalstrand?" Asher growled. He wiped the back of his hand across his mouth. His skin came away smeared with crimson, the swelling ache already causing his head to throb.

"Magic is for the weak," Drake taunted, circling him in a predatory stance.

He drew back, preparing to land another blow, but Asher

anticipated the move and dodged it. Cutting his fist through the air, his knuckles slammed into the underside of Drake's jaw. His head snapped back, drops of scarlet splattering across the front of his black shirt.

This time, it was Asher who smiled. "You forgot one thing, shadow prince."

Drake sneered, his teeth stained red from the blood. "What's that, frostfire fae?"

"I'm an excellent fighter." He'd had years of practice...against his father.

They collided in a storm of untempered fury. Years of unchecked anger poured from Asher in the form of bare-knuckled punches—anger with his father for being such a repulsive bastard, anger with his mother for not loving him and Cyra enough to stay alive, but mostly, anger with himself. For shutting Novalise out. For rejecting her. For being so blind, so damn stupid, that now he was going to lose her.

Drake swung again, and Asher blocked, deftly landing another hit on the shadow prince's face. He stumbled back, his footing unstable. Asher lunged, pummeling Drake in a series of swift jabs. With every strike against him, Drake seemed to become more maniacal, as though he thrived on the bloodlust of the brawl. His harsh laughter grated against Asher's fraying nerves, fueling his rage. He surged forward, but Drake spun, whipping around to avoid another meeting with Asher's fist.

"Well done, Firebane," Drake chuckled, blood dripping from his wounds, the flesh around his right eye mottled purple with streaks of black and blue. "Show them exactly who you are—a violent prick like your father."

Something inside Asher snapped.

The jeer struck true, and he rushed toward his opponent, the knowing glint in Drake's dark eyes the only warning before Asher realized his mistake.

The shadow prince launched himself into a backflip, the

metal toe of his boot connecting with Asher's chin. His teeth rattled, and blood coated his tongue. Pain erupted from the base of his skull to his temples, pounding and relentless. Bile scaled the back of his throat, but he attacked again, refusing to back down, except this time Drake blocked every strike and punch with ease. His motions were sharp and precise. Not once did he falter, his skill set in the art of fighting unrivaled.

Without warning, a blade materialized in Drake's hand, the gleam of it sending a spear of alarm straight through Asher's heart.

It was then he remembered who stood before him.

The Shadowblade Assassin.

Screams ruptured his thoughts—Novalise's screams.

Drake stalked toward him when Asher caught sight of something blue and pulsing from the corner of his eye. He tossed a hasty glance to his right, only to see Reif Marintide standing nearby, a sword crafted from the tides glowing in his hands. Reif tossed the weapon in Asher's direction. It spun through the air in a wave of power, and he caught it by the hilt, just in time to defend himself from the Shadowblade's wrath.

The intense rush of oceanic magic reverberated through Asher, the crash of the two weapons deafening. The dead silence of night met the roar of the sea. He stepped into every attack, unyielding. Again, the battle ensued, sword versus dagger, a daunting display of expert weaponry.

Sweat slid down Asher's back, fusing his shirt to his skin. Exhaustion clawed at him, a formidable foe who threatened to be the promise of his end. His muscles ached, straining and growing taut. With every breath, he reminded himself he was still alive. He was still breathing. But Drake showed no signs of such weariness. Not even with blood pooling from every gash on his face. He looked as though he was just getting started.

Suddenly, Drake flipped the Shadowblade high into the air.

Asher tracked it, and Drake's boot met him squarely in the

chest, sending him flying. His lungs caved, and he landed flat on his back against the stone of the courtyard. His head snapped against the hard ground, and spasms of pain seared through him so his vision blurred and his mind reeled.

"*Asher! Get up!*" Novalise shrieked, fear lacing her voice as it ripped down the bond.

But it was too late.

Drake was upon him, the tip of the Shadowblade aimed right for Asher's throat. "Any last words, Firebane?"

Asher's head lolled to the side to find Novalise. She was shaking uncontrollably, her eyes wild with feral vengeance. Through the torment of it all, he smiled, then said, "I love you."

Drake hoisted his blade.

"NO!" Novalise's scream shattered the stars. She sprinted toward him, bursts of starfire cascading around her in a sphere of celestial power. Arms outstretched, palms splayed open, the magic surrounding her intensified as her hair lifted from her shoulders and the streaks of starfire swirled faster in a riveting show of force. Turbulent and tumultuous, she was the starstorm, the namesake of her birthright.

Murmurs of shock and awe resounded through the crowd, but it wasn't enough to deter her.

Novalise's fierce gaze cut to Drake as she aimed the wrath of her fury at him. When she spoke, her voice was as calm as death. "Not. My. Mate."

The shadow prince met her enraged glare, then pulled back slowly, withdrawing his weapon. Cold emanated from him, an iciness that caused Asher's bones to shudder. Shadows crawled around Drake, his face a mask of barely contained violence. He wiped his thumb along his bottom lip, glancing down as it came away smeared with blood. The corner of his mouth twisted into a sinister smirk. This time, when Drake lifted the Shadowblade, he aimed it straight toward Ariesian.

"You owe me a wife."

In the next breath, the shadows engulfed him, and he was gone.

"Asher." Novalise's magic receded and she dropped to her knees. Her hands were warm as they roved over his face, gently soothing. "I thought I was going to lose you."

Asher groaned, his busted lip throbbing as the magic of his blood slowly worked to heal his injuries. "I'd be lying if I told you I thought differently."

Because in truth, he could've sworn on this night, he would've lost her forever.

Her lavender hair fell around them like a curtain, and she bent down, lightly brushing her lips over his. The kiss was soft, the barest of touches. And it set Asher on fire.

He would love her. Marry her. And spend the rest of his days worshipping her until there was nothing left of this world.

Asher eased himself up into a sitting position and wrapped his arm around her waist. Dragging her against him, he inhaled the alluring scent of her, memorizing everything about her. This dazzling female, who somehow always ended up barefoot and was often attacked by bushes, had captured the one thing he never thought to lose—his heart. She'd mended some broken part of him, but more than that, she'd saved him from himself. He tucked a lock of hair behind her ear, and knew within the deepest part of his soul, his love for Novalise would span an eternity.

Novalise cupped his cheek with one hand, and her eyes, those pools of endless wonder, filled with tears. "You love me?"

Asher grinned. "Until the end, Starlight."

EPILOGUE

*D*rake stood in the shadows of the forest of Aeramere. Some of them stretched from the towering ever-greens, some of them were of his own making. He shoved his hands into the pockets of his pants, leaning against the rough-ened bark of an ancient tree, watching through the thick grove of branches while a collection of fae, vampires, mortals, and witches gathered just beyond as Queen Elowyn prepared to close the Veil for Midsummer.

Soon, those who were invited would leave, and the rest of the world would be shut out once more.

The queen's magic would not hold forever.

In the distance, he spied Novalise Starstorm and Asher Fire-bane, dancing and looking more sickeningly in love than ever. No doubt they were already planning their wedding.

Served them right.

His gaze skimmed the revelry, his focus drawn to *her* again, despite his better judgment. She twirled with abandon, always the center of attention. Her eyes were too bright, her smile too radiant. It was obnoxious. Even from this distance, her laughter rang out like tinkling bells, the sound of it enough to cause his jaw to clench. Pretty rainbows and sprinkles of sunshine rained down upon her, a stark contrast to the blackened countenance of his soul.

Despite her sparkling demeanor, which he loathed, she was quite possibly one of the most stunning creatures he'd ever beheld.

Her hair—silver and threaded with pale hues of blue, pink and purple—was unbound. Wild and reckless, just like her. She had the body of a goddess, luscious curves and swaying hips. Large gold hoops swung from her pointed ears and a crown of dark pink flowers sat atop her head. Her lips were full, and damn, if that midnight blue dress she wore didn't display her ample bosom.

He'd love nothing more than to sink his teeth into one of her perfectly round breasts, to have her writhing, screaming, and panting beneath him.

Already his cock was aching.

Fuck that.

Those kinds of thoughts, the ones where he wanted to leave her broken and begging for him, where he wanted to absolutely *ruin* her, were exactly why he would have nothing to do with Creslyn Starstorm.

Behind him, a puff of hot air ruffled the leaves, sending the birds seeking refuge in their cover flying for the skies.

"I know, Svartos. Patience." Drake summoned a slab of raw meat and tossed it to the dragon. "I have no intention of leaving here without my future queen."

Drake called to his shadows, drifting easily between where they crawled and lingered, their stealth a cold, familiar comfort.

He appeared beside two fae males a moment later.

Ariesian Starstorm didn't even flinch.

"Prince Kalstrand," he said coolly, his gaze never leaving the celebration unfolding before him.

"Lord Starstorm." All other pleasantries were unnecessary. Ariesian knew why he was here.

His brother, however, looked downright furious. Solarius glowered. A pity his distrust was so misplaced.

"I thought you'd be on your way to Brackroth by now, Your Highness." Solarius dragged out Drake's title, his voice seething with contempt.

"On the contrary," Drake crooned. Two could play this game. "I've come to collect what I'm owed."

Solarius crossed his arms in a show of dominance. "Novalise made her choice. The contract is null and void."

A slow, intentional smile tugged at the corner of Drake's mouth. "I see your brother failed to explain to you the details of our terms."

Ariesian stiffened, his complexion paling slightly.

Solarius turned, demanding an explanation. "What's he talking about?"

Ariesian remained silent, pulling a folded piece of parchment from the inside of his coat. He handed it to Solarius without a word.

He scanned the contents and Drake watched as Solarius's face went from ashen with shock to scarlet with fury. "This is signed in blood."

"Indeed." Drake flicked his wrists, adjusting the cuffs of his sleeves. "As you can see, the contract never bound me to Novalise in particular, but to any of the Starstorm daughters."

"What the fuck, Ariesian?" Solarius shoved the document at his brother, then raked a hand through his hair. "How could you do this?"

Still, Ariesian's gaze never wavered. It tracked everything and everyone, most notably his sisters—Sarelle, Caelian, and Creslyn. "I did what is best for House Celestine."

"By selling away the life of one of our sisters?" Solarius was incensed, a simmering volcano ready to erupt, like the ones in the Wastelands.

Drake was only slightly upset he wouldn't be around to witness it when the Starstorm lord finally boiled over. "Fear not, Solarius. There's no need to be jealous. I hear your dear eldest brother has already secured you a wife as well."

Solarius's jaw dropped, but Drake had no more time to waste. Already Queen Elowyn was moving closer to the forest's edge, preparing to close the Veil for good.

"Now," Drake demanded, "Hand over one of your sisters so I can be on my way."

Solarius stormed toward him. "You can't mean to take her *now*? The Veil is closing, and we'll never see her again. She deserves a proper wedding, with her family in attendance, and there is no way I'll allow you to—"

"Enough. A deal is a deal." Ariesian stepped in his brother's path, effectively blocking Solarius from Drake. "Take Creslyn."

Drake almost choked.

Solarius roared.

"Creslyn," Drake repeated, and his gut seized.

"The contract stated I would choose." Ariesian lifted his chin, daring him to counter. "I think you'll find her a suitable *match*."

Drake's hands coiled into fists by his side. For the first time in a long time, he'd been bested.

"Fine," he ground out, acknowledging the Lord of House Celestine with the slightest incline of his head.

Ariesian bowed in return.

Darkness unfurled.

"Ariesian! No!" Solarius shouted, but Drake was already on the prowl, hunting down his future bride.

He moved through the crowd as nothing more than a flicker of doubt, an obscure glimmer of shade, hardly noticeable to anyone. Until she was standing right in front of him. He reached out, intent on grabbing her, when she spun around to face him, as though suddenly aware she was being watched.

"Do you mind? I'm trying to..." Creslyn Starstorm's eyes widened, orbs of sapphire deep enough to drown him.

Without a word, Drake stole her into the shadows.

She didn't scream or cry, she didn't flail or try to escape. Beneath the guise of his shadows, she simply let him carry her through the forest. He dodged a gathering of witches collecting fallen branches and stones, avoided the smaller group of vampires who looked as though they'd like to go sleep for a hundred years, and the mortals, goddess save them, who stumbled around in a drunkenly foolish stupor. Only when Svartos came into view did Creslyn's body tense in his arms.

Drake didn't allow her time to question or protest.

He leapt up, seated himself on Svartos's back, hauling Creslyn into his lap. The weight of her gaze fell to his hands, no doubt questioning the scars that riddled his flesh. Once she was secure, he pulled his leather riding gloves from his back pocket and tugged them on, securing the bands on his wrists. He waited a beat, and then another. Waited for her to fight him, to demand he return her to her family. But again, she remained still. Yielding. Resigned.

Damn her.

"*Vaeja*," he muttered, and Svartos took to the skies as the world shimmered, and the Veil fell.

The dragon soared under the guise of nightfall, sifting through the clouds, moonlight glinting off his sleek black scales like broken diamonds. The flight to Brackroth would take some time, hours maybe with no interruptions, but with any luck, they would arrive just after dawn.

"He's beautiful." Creslyn's soft voice carried on the wind, a whisper of awe. "What's his name?"

Drake swallowed and kept his gaze focused on the inky horizon. "Svartos."

"Svartos," she repeated, and his dragon's name rolled off her tongue, mimicking his accent almost perfectly.

His grip on the reins tightened.

She reached out, running the tips of her fingers along one of the beast's scales. "And where are you taking us, Svartos?"

"To Brackroth." Drake inhaled. It was a mistake.

Her scent filled him. She smelled of delicious citrus and fresh rainfall. His blood thrummed and his cock thickened. Drake rolled his eyes to the starlit heavens, cursing whatever god or goddess saw fit to seek his ruination.

He did not have time for distractions.

"Brackroth." Creslyn shifted, pressing into him, the curves of her body arousing him further. "Sounds lovely."

"Why are you not afraid?" he demanded, annoyed with himself, yet agitated with her serene countenance. "Why are you not screaming your pretty little head off and insisting I return you to Aeramere, where you *belong*?"

She shivered then, goosebumps raking across her smooth flesh. Though whether it was because of the harshness of his words or the chilly night air, he didn't know. Nor did he care.

"I knew you would come for me." Creslyn lifted one shoulder, then let it fall carelessly. "Ariesian told me that if you didn't marry Novalise, then I would be the next choice. So, here I am."

Damn that bastard fae lord.

She spoke with such nonchalance, such certainty, that his blood boiled.

Drake glared down at her, annoyed by the flower crown that blocked his view of her face. "I don't know what he told you, but whatever you're expecting—"

"I expect nothing," she interjected.

"And do you make it a habit of showing such blatant disrespect to a prince?"

"Only when I must."

He bent down, so his lips hovered above her pointed little

ear. When she trembled once more, he knew it was not because of the cold. "Might I suggest you keep your mouth shut? Otherwise, I may be forced to cut out your tongue."

She jerked, turning slightly to look up at him. There was no malice in her expression. No fear or anger. Instead, those berry-painted lips curved into a seductive smile. "Pity. I'm rather fond of using it."

"Fuck," he muttered.

"Come again?" she asked, her tone sugary yet sharp.

"Nothing."

Fuck. Fuck. *Fuck.*

Hours passed without another word between them. At one point Drake thought Creslyn might have fallen asleep, as her head had come to rest on his shoulder and she'd curled into him, her breathing even and deep. The dress she wore rippled in the breeze, gradually revealing swaths of her flawless skin, and every minute she was in his arms felt like an eternity he would never escape. But now she was awake and alert as finally, blessedly, the snow-topped mountains of Brackroth came into view as the sun vanished behind the ever-cloudy skies that languished across the city.

Despite the early hour, here was the one place the sun would never shine.

Brackroth was gloomy and cold, lacking warmth and light. Black spires rose from a mountain's ledge, the rooftop of Drake's palace piercing through the stretch of gray mist. Svartos swept down, through the dense cover of clouds, and landed in the clearing inside the towering palace walls.

Drake jumped down, but left Creslyn perched on the back of his dragon.

She could figure out how to get down on her own. Right now, he needed an ice-cold shower.

"Your Highness?" she called out.

He turned back, watching as she slid out of the seat on the

dragon's back, her dress rising almost all the way to her ass, revealing the sexiest pair of legs he'd ever seen.

This was it.

For living a life in the shadows, for being born of darkness and death, for being a monster walking among the realms, this was to be his punishment. He'd been given a faerie he wanted to fuck all day and night, a female to be used as a weapon against him, to deter him from his path of destruction.

Creslyn's heels clicked noisily as she walked around, staring in wonder at her new surroundings. Those sapphire eyes found him.

Drake bowed. Curt. "Welcome to Brackroth, *solysa*."

Then he walked away, already knowing he'd made the biggest mistake of his life.

ACKNOWLEDGMENTS

Sometimes I look back and I still can't believe I've made it this far. One fantasy romance series is done and now another one (or two) is underway. It will always leave me a little breathless and giddy when people tell me they love my books, because all I've ever wanted to do was tell stories.

I'd love to thank all of my beta readers who helped to make this book sparkle. You all know who you are and without you, Constellations wouldn't be able to shine. To my amazing editor, Emily Michel, for making my writing stronger and introducing me to the wet shirt trope. To Elayna, for her gorgeous map-making skills. I can't wait to watch you take on the world. And to my wonderful cover designer, Lexie, who took my random assortment of ideas and made one of the most beautiful covers I've ever seen.

Thank you to Chyanne, Lindsay, and Carrie for holding my hand and lifting me up, for letting me bounce ideas off of you, and for simply being there always. To Emilia, for reminding me to breathe when I got overwhelmed, and for always taking the time to help me when I needed it most. And a very special thank you to my discord darlings, for keeping me afloat when I was drowning. So many of you stepped up to help with graphics and forms, to just take some things off my plate when I was on the verge of burnout. You will forever have my heartfelt gratitude.

A huge thank you to my amazing PA, Margie. Without you, I would be forever lost. Thank you to my hype team for believing in me, cheering me on, and for always offering me the best kind of support.

To my girls, Lobug and Breezy, I love you both so much. I know it seems like I'm always working, and I will promise to be more present for you. To Nate, I love you always. Thank you for never telling me "no".

And lastly to my readers, for loving the worlds I create, and for sometimes even loving me. Without you, none of this would be possible. Defy the stars, now and always.

ABOUT THE AUTHOR

Hillary Raymer is a fantasy romance author. She's a wanderer, a storyteller, and the founder of BohoSoul Press.

Hillary has always been a dreamer, and lucky for her, she turned those dreams into stories. She has an unfinished Bachelor's Degree in English because she ran off and married a Marine halfway through college. She has an affinity toward plants, loves the mountains, and enjoys scoping out metaphysical markets for crystals. Wanderlust comes to her naturally, and she's doing her best to instill the same wild and free values in her daughters. When not writing, Hillary can be found attempting to do yoga, buying more makeup she doesn't need, or discovering small businesses on Etsy.

Join her Court here https://discord.gg/EfHVy93Gvz

For exclusive access to current projects, merch, and other sneak peeks, subscribe to her Ream here https://reamstories.com/hillaryraymer

ALSO BY HILLARY RAYMER

The Faeven Saga

Crown of Roses

Throne of Dreams

Realm of Nightmares

Void of Endings